Stephen Deas

HERALD OF THE BLACK MOON

BLACK MOON, BOOK III

ANGRY
ROBOT

ANGRY ROBOT
An imprint of Watkins Media Ltd

Unit 11, Shepperton House
89 Shepperton Road
London N1 3DF
UK

angryrobotbooks.com
twitter.com/angryrobotbooks
The Time Comes

An Angry Robot paperback original, 2023

Cover by Kieryn Tyler
Edited by Robin Triggs and Travis Tynan
Set in Meridien

ISBN 978 1 91520 265 9
Ebook ISBN 978 1 91520 260 4

Printed and bound in the United Kingdom by TJ Books Ltd.

9 8 7 6 5 4 3 2 1

MIX
Paper from
responsible sources
FSC
www.fsc.org   FSC® C013056

For Nigel, Matt, Sam, Ali, Pete, Tony & Michaela

Man with no shadow that nobody knows
Comes to harvest that which he sows
Great white tower made of stone that grows
Home to the makers of all of man's woes

The four old mages fall from the sky
Now the dead in peace may lie
Two born low and two born high
Touched by silver, three will die

Dragon-queen and dark lord's bane
Each will wax and then will wane
The Bloody Judge lifts his hand
All is razed to ash and sand

Black moon comes, round and round
Black moon comes, all fall down.

PROLOGUE
The One-Eyed God

The song rattled through Seth's head as he crashed through worlds. He shot over mountains and rivers and seas. Faces loomed, sudden and random. An angry god, a vengeful goddess. Once, he thought he saw Myla reaching for him, quickly lost in the storm. His head was a tornado, blistered by fever. And that song, over and over. He'd heard it in Deephaven. A group of children, holding hands, dancing in a circle, falling to the ground as it ended, laughing, and then doing it again.

Deephaven...

You did that. All you.

No! No, I didn't!

The Avenue of Emperors. The abandoned wagons. Animals, wounded and exhausted, trapped in harnesses, resigned, waiting to die. He'd felt the same. Having to stop. Catch his breath. His skin burning in salted wind. A glimpse of Myla, on the waterfront, on the back of a horse. She'd come too late or else the ship hadn't waited. Watching Deephaven float away while sailors heaved on giant oars, pushing the ship out to sea.

Myla on her horse fighting Dead Men as they poured across the dock. Wishing he could help; but he'd thought he was dead so what could he do? *She* was probably dead too by now. He was sorry about that. Hoped he was wrong; but he'd seen what was waiting for her. He'd seen the Wraith.

Prophet...

1

Why had it called him that?

People running. A flurry of lowering of boats. His head flopping and lolling. Sick, so very sick, his organs like fractured glass, grinding and tearing one another. Then Deephaven far behind, only the harbour towers and a pall of smoke where some part of it burned.

His face! A voice stricken with fear. *His face!*

His face?

An awful blackness. A void closing around him. The one-eyed God in his head, laughing and wagging a finger. *I told you so! You know what you are! You know* exactly *what you are!*

The walls between worlds crumbling and tumbling. The dead pouring from the dark heart of the underworld. Xibaiya, the One-Eyed God named it. The One-Eyed God who kept popping up in the maelstrom of his mind. The One-Eyed God who always laughed when Seth asked who he was.

I'm you. Don't you see?

A man on a black horse carrying something precious from a dying city. A giant in plated metal bringing two people together in a room of blank white stone. Each bowing to a sigil-emblazoned archway, and then gone. Ice and snow where three great towers impale the ground and rake the sky; a hole in the earth, a bright column of spirits spiralling into infinite depths; the Cathedral of Light in Torpreah, a thousand priests bowing before him. Seth the Autarch! The skin of his face melting into crawling ants and wasps and beetles and the world smells of fish and of salt water...

Fever dreams. Between them, an eternity of nothing except the One-Eyed God, telling him how it was all his fault. How what he'd done in the House of Cats and Gulls was the last crack in a dam waiting sixteen years to break.

All this ruin and more to come.

He baulked at the idea that the Silver Kings had appeared out of myth to murder an entire city simply because *he'd* happened to be there. A deranged notion. The sigil he'd seen reflected at the bottom of the well in the House of Cats and Gulls clearly had nothing to do with it. Nor the way it hadn't come back after he'd dropped a stone into the water, mostly to see whether it would. *Couldn't* have been *his* fault. What idiot wrote a warding sigil in water?

That smell again. Brine and fish. His thoughts kept snagging on it.

You'll find yourself in Valladrune, like it or not. The cracking of the seal. The return of That Which Came Before. The Black Moon rising into the sky. The end of one cycle and the start of the next. You've tripped it all into motion. You.

How about you fuck off? Fever dreams, or was he possessed?

The One-Eyed God told him then how he'd lose a hand to Myla's sword. *There's nothing you can do to stop it.*

Then, for another eternity, nothing.

Salt water and fish. A wall of planks swaying back and forth before his eyes. It took what felt like several years to work out why.

I'm on a ship.

The thought delighted him, mostly for how mundane it was.

He opened his eyes and looked about. Discovered he was in a nice cabin with a mirror on one wall – nice except for how the One-Eyed God with the Ruined Face was in the mirror staring back at him. Seth tried telling him to fuck off, which didn't work. After a few depressing experiments, Seth reckoned he understood why.

The face was his own. He *was* the One-Eyed God. Just as the annoying fucker kept telling him.

I've gone mad. Was he still feverish?

No. I'm what you become.

"No, thanks." Seth had seen the future once before, or what he'd supposed had been *meant* to be the future, some version of it. He'd been at the top of the Moonspire at the time, a place where visions were *supposed* to happen, unlike ship cabins. *That* future had looked a bit shit, frankly.

You can't change it. You can't run from what you've done.

Sure of that? Seth fumbled in his pockets until he found a stick of charcoal. He rolled back a sleeve and started to draw a sigil. *Because I rather think I can.* He grinned at his reflection in the mirror, fairly certain he was at least a little bit mad. *I can forget, you see.* Discovering that the One-Eyed God was in fact himself, a lot of things made sense, mostly concerning how irritating the smug fucker was.

Go murder some more priests. Set fire to villages. Drown some kittens, maybe? Whatever lights your fire. You can't stop it, so you might as well have some fun.

Seth looked at the almost-finished sigil inked into the crook of his arm. Strange things, memories. Some were anchors of identity: the white stone vault under the Circus of Dead Emperors in Varr and the dead rat in the temple kitchen the next morning; sitting on the steps of a temple as boy, another boy coming up and offering him a peach. Others were chains and tethers: Lightbringer Suaresh pissing in his face, and the day they'd thrown him down the temple steps. Memories could be beacons of hope or splinters that never healed, like what he'd done to the priest in Deephaven, like putting a candle in Myla's window so the men hunting her would know where to find her, and why did *that* one haunt him so?

I can forget.

The effort of moving was almost too much to bear. He couldn't remember the last time he'd felt so empty. He raised a hand and brought it to his face and stared. Half the skin was one great scab. He could barely move his fingers. Pain scorched his arm.

A last look in the mirror. The One-Eyed God with the Ruined Face. *His* face. It had *always* been his own face. His face. His words. His future. A future the One-Eyed God had shown him in his fever. No triumphant return to the faith that rejected him; instead, he was going to open a door, raise the Black Moon and bring the end of everything.

He was, was he? No. *Fuck* that.

He wished Myla was here. She'd tell him what to do; although what she *might* tell him was to dig a deep pit, climb inside, then pull the earth down on top of himself.

You used a sigil to make an old man walk into a temple and set himself on fire.

By fucking accident!

All he'd ever wanted was the truth. Hadn't meant for it to end the way it had.

Could say that about a lot of things.

You can't undo what you've done.

Except... when the monks had caught him in Varr, he'd used a sigil to make himself forget... Well... it had worked, so he didn't know what exactly it was that he couldn't remember. Something to do with how come Lightbringer Suaresh had shown up dead in Tombland in his night clothes, he reckoned, but never mind... Point was, the monks had asked their questions and Seth had told them he didn't remember. They hadn't liked that, but he wasn't lying – he really *didn't* know what he'd done – and so what could they do? He remembered making himself forget, so it obviously hadn't been nothing.

He couldn't undo what had happened in Deephaven. But he *could* forget. Almost everyone else in Deephaven was surely dead. If *every*one forgot something, wasn't that the same as if it had never happened at all?

Where to start?

The Moonspire and his vision of the future, the woman in red and black and white and gold whom he'd thought was the Princess-Regent? He'd seen her in the flesh once. At the Hanging Tree in the Circus of Dead Emperors, when Seth had been on his way to...

No. Don't think about that.

Back further? Back to Varr? Forget it all? Forget Myla? Forget Blackhand? Forget that he wasn't a priest?

Not that far.

No, and not the Moonspire either. In his vision, Myla had told him to use a sigil on her. Hadn't bothered saying *what* sigil, mind, which had left Seth thinking that if Gods wanted to drop hints to mortals, they could maybe try being a bit fucking clearer about things.

No, the Moonspire could stay. No one was going to murder him for having a vision *there*, crappy or otherwise. Was sort of the point of the place.

After he and Fings reached Deephaven, then? When he'd started looking for the warlock who'd once lived there, although *that* thought had been with him long before... Or when he'd first met the Taiytakei mage? The popinjay who'd known the warlock Saffran Kuy, who'd had taken Seth to the House of Cats and Gulls. Start there? Wipe the rest clean?

Careful...

What would he remember? That he'd gone to Deephaven, visited a Taiytakei sorcerer about an old warlock, then woken up, days later, on a ship, on the way to a city he didn't know without the first idea how he'd got there.

Dumb. He'd think the Taiytakei sorcerer had done something to him and then made him forget. The last thing he needed was future-Seth running around like a demented chicken, frantically asking questions, digging up the exact same shit he was trying to bury. No, he was going to have to let himself remember more. If he didn't, he'd never let it go.

You can't stop it.

I'm going to scrub you out. Every vestige of you. Every memory of the one-eyed fucker. Too late to avoid the ruined face but he still had both hands, thanks. No, he was *not* becoming that twisted vision of himself. Visions in the night? No different from dreams, really; and people forgot their dreams all the time. He wouldn't even know the memories were missing...

That was the trick to forgetting, learned the hard way in Varr. Had to make himself forget so he'd never even know that anything was gone.

He closed his eyes, sighed, then opened them again. There was a good chance he was going to bollocks this up. He'd been doing a lot of that, this last year.

You murdered a priest. Made the man set himself on fire.

That could go, too.

He wondered about erasing the night he'd betrayed Myla, the night he'd set the lighted candle in her window as a sign to the Spicers waiting outside. But no; she was gone, and maybe having that little splinter in his head would do him some good one day. She'd deserved better.

We both did, he thought, and finished the sigil.

PART ONE
Myla

Being handy with a sword is all very well, but there's always some awkward bugger who can do it better. Being handy at running away? Different story. All you have to worry about is not being the worst.
– Fings

I
The Coming of the Silver Kings

Act in haste, repent at leisure. One of Sword-Mistress Tasahre's irritating little sayings, and right now, on the back of a stolen horse, Myla was feeling it. It was all very well deciding that no, you *were* a sword-monk, and so you'd stay and defend the city you called home while your sensible friends and family all fucked off on a fast ship to... well, anywhere else, really. It was another discovering you were the only thing between a crowd of panicked civilians and a horde of homicidal dead things with a handful of half-god sorcerers telling them what to do.

The waterfront was fast becoming a massacre. The thin line of militia and Longcoats had dissolved at the onslaught. The Dead Men tore into the crowd; the crowd was trying to get away, except their only escape was into the sea. All alone, there wasn't much she could do about it. Even a hundred sword-monks, out in an open space like this, would have struggled to hold so many Dead Men at bay.

She sliced open a Dead Man, its trapped soul freed by the touch of her Sunsteel blade, and almost lost her sword. Another thing she was discovering the hard way was why soldiers on horseback carried long curved swords rather than short stabbing ones. Even as she recovered her balance, a dozen more Dead Men streamed past in pursuit of easier prey than a crazed monk on the back of an unruly horse. She *had* learned how to ride – was quite good it, really – but *not* how to fight at the same time. Sword-monks learned their fighting on their feet.

She swung at a Dead Man, missed, clipped another, ending it, then almost fell out of the saddle as her mare jerked and reared and skittered sideways. The animal was a clenched fist of tension and energy, clearly with strong views on the circumstances in which it found itself. She could hardly blame it.

The last ships were leaving the harbour, including the *Speedwell*, carrying – she hoped – her brother and her sister, and Orien if he had any sense, and probably Fings and Seth. Heading *into* the harbour were a dozen white ships like the ones she'd seen on the river a couple of nights back. From the Solar Temple up on the Peak, and from Deephaven and Four Winds Squares, came flashes of light. Silver moonlight and brilliant sunlight and orange fire. If sword-mistress Tasahre was still fighting, she wasn't alone.

The mare decided it had had enough of the idiot on its back and bolted, hooves skittering on the cobbles, leaving Myla to either cling on or else sprawl to the ground in the middle of a sea of Dead Men who'd immediately try to kill her. And there were thousands, and nothing she could do would stop the slaughter; so she settled for living, steering the mare's headlong charge towards the streets of The Maze that would lead her up the hill to The Peak where she might yet be useful. More Dead Men – some live ones too from the looks of them – poured from the Maze onto the Waterfront. The mare crashed through and they didn't try to stop her. In the distance, Myla caught a glimpse of a silver-armoured half-god – Wraiths, Tasahre called them. It, too, ignored her, its attention firmly on the carnage of the waterfront.

I'll be back for you, Myla thought, though she knew she probably wouldn't. She'd already fought one tonight, although *fought* was generous. Been a minor distraction while Tasahre did the hard work and killed it, and Myla had seen how the sword-mistress had struggled, how the creature had killed another monk more skilled than Myla, one who was tattooed against the creature's sorcery, tattoos Myla didn't have.

The mare raced between the giant shadow of warehouses, knocking down the occasional Dead Man coming the other way. Like the Wraiths, the Dead Men seemed drawn towards the waterfront, blind to everything else. At the end of an alley, faced with a blank brick wall straight ahead and dark narrow streets to either side, the mare skidded to a stop, breathing hard. Myla understood its fear. An entire city was being murdered, not with swords and blood and fire, but by sorcery, by creatures that were supposed to be myth and legend, demons from an age long relegated to stories.

What had Orien called them? Silver Kings? Which was another name for the half-god children of the Moon who were supposed to have disappeared centuries before the empire ever existed.

She coaxed the mare down a pitch-black street, trotting forward, trying as best she could to retrace her path to The Peak. On her way to the waterfront, she'd felt where parts of the Maze had been touched by these Silver Kings, cold and lifeless, streets scattered with the shattered remains of the ice-knives that had fallen from the sky. The ice hadn't fallen everywhere, only in certain places. She wondered vaguely why. How had the Wraiths chosen which parts of the city should die first?

She'd felt that hail. On Deephaven Square. Holding Sarwatta Hawat as a shield against its edges, then sheltering under Orien's fire, then Tasahre's shield. She touched a hand to her stomach. Her tunic was sticky again. Still leaking from where Sarwatta had pricked her.

The mare calmed a little. Myla nudged her on until the abandoned streets of The Maze spat her onto the Avenue of Emperors...

The carnage made the breath catch in her throat. A litter of abandoned carts, overturned wagons, and corpses. She was too young to remember the war that had put Khrozus the Usurper on the throne, but you couldn't go five minutes in Deephaven without hearing someone talk about the siege, when Talsin the Weak had tried for six months to batter and starve the city into submission. He'd failed because he'd never managed to blockade either the harbour or the river, and so the parade of wagons up and down the Avenue of Emperors had never stopped.

It was stopped now. The drivers were dead, the animals gone, as though after the ice had fallen someone had come through and cut them loose. Unlike her, they'd had the sense to flee.

She could almost hear her mare thinking: *Yeah. About that...*

The flashes of light subsided. She pressed on, beyond the statues of the dead emperors of Aria, towards Four Winds Square, then to Deephaven Square, where she couldn't help a look as she passed the House of Hawat.

Abandoned. Empty. Like all the others.

The dome of the Cathedral of Light was gone. She'd been there when it had fallen. The Sunherald's Spire, still standing when sword-mistress Tasahre had sent her away, was a tumbled ruin. The square was a carnage of lacerated corpses, the air rich with the tang of scorched dust and the stink of damp, burned flesh. She paused where she'd stood when the ice-knives had fallen. Her last memory of Sarwatta Hawat was of seeing him stagger away, still somehow alive. Most likely he was dead now; and if he wasn't, so what? If he'd survived, did she care? None of that mattered now.

She slowed as she reached the temple gates, awed by what she saw. A scaled tail poked through the smashed wall, as thick as a horse, half buried in rubble. She dismounted and climbed the broken stones, and there it was. She'd seen it in the sky, back when she'd climbed the roof of House Hawat. Now it lay sprawled across the temple yards. Claws like swords, one great wing furled across its back, the other flopped across shattered flagstones and colonnades. A dragon as big as a Black Ship.

She'd never seen anything like it, yet here it was. A monster, straight from the stories the Black Ships carried between worlds.

A *dead* dragon. Which meant something had killed it...

Another flash of silver moonlight from across the temple compound. They were still here, then. Still fighting...

Except they weren't. When she skirted the ruin of the Cathedral of Light, picking her way through fallen buildings and the scattered bodies of the dead, all she found were men and women dragging bodies and tossing them onto a pyre. No Dead Men. No Wraiths.

"Who goes there?" A pair of scared Sunguard spotted her. Their swords were drawn, though they looked more likely to turn and run than put up any kind of fight. Myla almost answered with a name that half of Deephaven probably knew, and for all the wrong reasons. The name that had been sentenced to die in the slave mines of the empire for gelding Sarwatta Hawat. She'd stabbed him several times more since then, which probably wasn't going to help.

That name was dead. Had died when the Wraith had come to Deephaven Square.

"Myla," Myla said. "A sword-monk. I'm here to help."

2
Fire and Needles

Tasahre, for some reason, wasn't pleased to see her. The sword-mistress muttered something about "more baggage" and sent Myla to help throw bodies on the pyre. Myla found a soldier, the two of them found a corpse, they carried it to the flames and tossed it in, then back for another... all through the night until her back and shoulders ached. She eyed the men and women around her while she worked. A couple of hundred, maybe. Mostly soldiers, a score of sword-monks keeping watch, Tasahre flitting among them, pacing the square, tense as a coiled spring. Now and then a shout of alarm: everyone stopped and braced for a horde of Dead Men or worse; but it always turned out to be more survivors, stragglers looking for sanctuary.

A knot of figures stood apart from the toiling soldiers. Silhouettes plucked from the darkness by the flames of the pyre. When the flames faltered, stifled by the volume of corpses, one silhouette raised her hands. Fire poured from her fingers, bathing the pyre until it raged. As the sorceress turned her back, Myla walked to stand in front of her.

"Lady Novashi." The last time they'd seen one another, Myla had been naked and clutching a candlestick, fresh from bludgeoning a demon that had walked through a mirror at an extremely inconvenient moment. The time before, they'd been on a bridge in Varr, and Myla had been handing back the Emperor's Moonsteel Crown.

The sorceress looked Myla up and down. "Oh. It's you."

"Is Orien here?"

He wasn't, which left Myla with nothing much to do but pile bodies. She hoped Orien had had the sense to get on the *Speedwell* with Fings and Seth, although she worried that maybe he hadn't. It helped, worrying about him. Stopped her from worrying about how long they had before a horde of Dead Men and Wraiths came storming up from the docks to murder them all.

Dawn broke. No Wraiths, no Dead Men. With the rising sun, the piling of bodies paused. It would need to be finished; but in daylight there wasn't much chance of them returning as Dead Men. Myla rocked on her heels, exhausted and ready to sleep, preferably having knocked back a bottle of something good beforehand... but no one was getting any rest today.

Sword-monks began hurrying everyone away, through the remains of the temple, out into Deephaven Square and to the Palace of the Overlord and his spoiled brat of a son. Around her, monks and priests talked of wards and watch rotas and patrols. She kept away from all that, stayed with the exhausted soldiers, all of them wishing they were somewhere else.

From behind, Tasahre caught her arm. "Oh no, sword-monk. You don't get to sleep. None of us get to sleep."

"I'm done," Myla said.

Tasahre ignored her. She led Myla up a winding stair to a room at the top of a small tower, looking out over the remains of Deephaven. She went to a balcony facing the rising sun and, for a moment, simply stood. Praying, Myla understood. After a moment more, Myla joined her.

"We have to keep burning the bodies to ensure they don't come back," said Tasahre at last.

"Mistress?" A good dose of daylight was as effective as Sunsteel and fire – or at least, that's what she'd always been taught.

"We put them down and they keep returning. I don't know why. Their souls are tethered. The Wraiths have done this. I'm not sure what will free them." She looked Myla in the eye, sizing her up as if they hadn't known each other for ten years. "You should have boarded that ship."

"I'm starting to wish I had."

Tasahre sniffed and then cocked her head. "Liar."

Myla shrugged.

"What did you see at the docks?"

Myla told her. When she finished, Tasahre guided her back inside. "Strip," she said, then rolled her eyes when Myla didn't. "I have something to give you. It'll hurt, but since you think you're a sword-monk now, you'll tolerate it without complaint."

Myla shrugged her tunic over her head, wincing as she pulled it free of the wound in her stomach. It was bleeding again.

"We'll start with that." Tasahre wrapped a strip of cloth around her, pulling it tight. "You lasted through the night so it can't be deep. Barely a scratch."

"Hmm." It had hurt like a bastard when she hadn't been too busy fighting or running for her life to notice.

"There were more than a hundred sword-monks in this city yesterday." Tasahre stepped back and circled behind Myla. "Now I have twenty-three, all more deserving of my time than you. Yet here I am. Like it or not, you'll be number twenty-four."

"Thank you."

"Thank me again when we're done." Myla felt the prick of a needle in her back. "If you must scream, do it quietly. I'm going to mark your skin with sigils. Like the rest of us, only for you it means getting them all at once. When I'm done, you might be useful. If I get any of them wrong, the next time you meet a Wraith, it'll kill you. Sit still."

Myla sat still, gritting her teeth. It wasn't the individual pricks that were hard to bear, more the sum of them, the growing sense of burning spreading steadily across her back.

"You know your legends?" Myla heard the concentration in Tasahre's voice.

"Yes."

"Then you know the Silver Kings were once the half-god

children of Fickle Lord Moon. You know the Hungry Goddess summoned the Black Moon to extinguish the sun. You know the Silver Kings sheltered and preserved our ancestors and bargained with the Hungry Goddess. You know the Shining Age ended with the cataclysm of the Splintering that brought down the Black Moon and broke the world. You know that the Silver Kings departed to the next life."

"Not all of them, apparently," said Myla, wincing as Tasahre continued pricking her.

"Some remained. Diminished and rejected, but a crippled half-god is still a half-god." She hissed. "Wraiths."

"Why are they here?"

"I don't know," Tasahre said, though it seemed to Myla that the needle-jabs came with a touch more venom. "Sixteen years ago, a warlock was driven from Deephaven."

The warlock Saffran Kuy, whom Tasahre had famously fought and failed to kill. Somewhat less famously, Tasahre had later very nearly been killed herself by an anonymous thief-taker with some connection to Kuy. "You think it's because of him?"

"I do. But I don't know how."

Sixteen years seemed a long time to Myla, but she kept that to herself. Best not provoke the sword-mistress while she was busy stabbing with her needle.

"There was another warlock in Deephaven these last few weeks. An acolyte perhaps, maybe an abandoned apprentice, someone Saffran Kuy left when he fled. Someone who has been very quiet all this time but who knew enough of their sigils to both kill a Lightbringer I called friend and to steal one of Kuy's relics. On the next day, the Wraiths came. I don't believe in coincidence, Shirish."

She worked in silence after that, while Myla sank into a trance of pain and fatigue.

"Get dressed," Tasahre said at last. "You're far from finished, but the whole work will take days we don't have. Until it's done, leave anything more than Dead Men to others."

Myla picked up her tunic and looked at it, at the large dark stain of crusted blood that covered its front. She didn't have anything else to wear.

"Mistress?"

"Shirish?"

"I'm Myla now. Shirish died in the square last night. At your suggestion, if you remember."

"I also suggested you board a ship and disappear. I'd assumed my suggestions aren't good enough for you."

"The Wraith in the temple. What would have happened if I hadn't been there?"

For the first time, Tasahre almost smiled. The start of a slight curl of the lip before she crushed it dead. The only answer Myla would ever get, most likely.

Left alone, she went in search of somewhere to sleep and instead ran straight into another sword-monk whose face she vaguely recognised but whose name she didn't know. One of the monks Tasahre had sent when the Longcoats had taken Myla in chains to their slave barge. He looked her over, tried not to stare at the bloodstain on her tunic, then nodded.

"There's someone looking for you," he said.

Myla's heart spiked, imagining Sarwatta. It would be so like him to survive the death of an entire city and still single-mindedly think of revenge.

"Scrawny fellow with a pointy beard. And an orange robe," said the monk.

Myla's heart spiked again, for entirely different reasons. "Where?" she squeaked.

The monk pointed. Myla forgot she was tired and ran. It took a bit of searching and a lot of asking, but a man in an orange robe wasn't exactly trying to hide, and it wasn't long before she found him.

"Orien!" she howled.

He was standing with a tall black-skinned Taiytakei, him in his stupid orange, the Taiytakei dressed up like some popinjay. Orien managed a brief startled look before Myla jumped on him and wrapped herself around him and hugged him, then stopped hugging and squealed away when he tried to hug her back.

"Ow, ow, ow!" she said. "Bad idea! Bad idea!"

"What?"

"I spent half the morning having needles jabbed into my back."

His gawping surprise switched to alarm as he spotted the blood on her tunic.

"Got slightly stabbed too. Only slightly. Don't touch my back." She hugged him again. "Or the stabbed bit. I thought you were dead!"

"I thought *you* were dead!"

"Did you get Soraya to the *Speedwell*?"

"Yes."

"Why didn't you go with her? Are you stupid or something?"

"Why didn't I...? Why didn't *you* go with her? She's *your* sister! *I* had something more important to do." Orien reached into a crate and pulled out a bottle of wine. "I brought this for you."

He clearly hadn't. The bottle had clearly just been sitting there, part of a collection of supplies someone was putting together. Didn't matter. Myla grabbed him by the face, gave him a huge wet kiss on the lips, and snatched it from his hands.

"This is why I fucking love you, you idiot," she said, and danced away. And yes, the wine did help dull the pain, but it wasn't why she fell asleep smiling.

3
A Tale of Two Mages

Finding time for each other was hard amid the constant rush of soldiers and sword-monks, amid the gathering and burning of corpses and the building of defences against the inevitable return of the Dead Mean. Myla and Orien managed, in the late afternoon, to snatch a few hours. They should have spent it sleeping but... well, it *was* the end of the world, or something very much like it.

"Something about you has changed," said Orien when they were both spent.

"I killed a Wraith," Myla said. "Or at least, I helped a little." When Orien didn't reply, she propped herself on one elbow and prodded him. "How did you end up here? And who's the Taiytakei?"

Orien told his story: how he'd taken Myla's sister to the *Speedwell*, headed back for the temple and been almost crushed by a stampede of people running in terror. How he'd been stupid enough not to take that as a hint and had shortly run into a handful of Dead Men, all flailing arms and incoherent howling, looking to chew pieces off anyone they could reach. How he'd set himself on fire, which had set *them* on fire when they tried to eat him, and it had all turned out rather well.

"It was easy," he said. "I thought that was why everyone was running. But then there was something else. A man, or something like one, in silver armour."

"A Wraith." Myla nuzzled hard up beside him. "One of your Silver Kings." Orien was lying flat on his back, staring up at...

well, not at anything at all. He was in his memories, watching it happen.

"Yes. I suppose. It looked at me from down the street and then pointed its silver sword at the ground between us like it was issuing a challenge. Massed behind it was a horde of Dead Men. Some live ones too, I think. I didn't wait to find out. I ran for the Guildhouse, but I must have turned myself around because I ended up in the fishing quarter, all nets and lines hung out to dry. The boats were all gone, of course. There weren't many people, and those that remained were leaving in haste. It was oddly quiet. And there I was. A mage sent by the throne to protect and shepherd this city, barely able to conjure enough fire to light a candle. I wondered what to tell them. That I was an apprentice? A beginner hopelessly out of my depth? That I'd conned and blathered at every step to become what I am? That I was a fraud?"

"You're not a fraud."

He didn't seem to hear. "I *did* go back to the docks. I *was* going to take a ship if I could. I got close enough to see them, and all the people trying to get aboard. I saw Dead Men, too. Now and then, another of the silver ones. They knew I was there. Even the ones that didn't turn and look, I felt the flicker of their consciousness wash over me, noticing my existence and then dismissing it. *They* knew what I was, that I was no threat. I could see how they were herding everyone towards the sea, to the open space of the docks where there was nowhere to hide. I knew I should go and fight, but I didn't. It was just me. What difference could I have made? There were too many."

Myla grunted, eyes closed. "Neither of us could have changed it."

"Half a year ago, I was nothing, a nobody. In the months since that night in the *Unruly Pig* when I came to you, I've realised almost every ambition I ever dreamed. I won the favour of the throne for my mistress, secured favour for myself in turn. I've met the Princess-Regent. It's possible she even knows my name. I've been my mistress's agent in this city, her voice – through her, the voice of the throne itself. I've fallen in love. And now these...

these *things*... these Wraiths, these Silver Kings... they walk out of legend and history, calm as you like and into our lives, destroying it all as surely as if I'd fallen to their swords or their knives or their raining blades of ice. And you! Almost certainly dead, and if you weren't, then you were gone, and pride and ambition had made me stay, and perhaps even a sense of duty, all of which were turning to ash."

He looked at her. "I've seen them close enough to look into their eyes and read their souls, obliterating hope as the sun destroys shadow. Nothing will stop them, Myla. We should steal horses and ride away before it's too late."

Myla murmured something about staying and fighting until they couldn't. Orien turned away.

"I don't know how I found myself at the old Moon temple. I thought it was abandoned but then I heard a crash of furniture. Someone was inside, someone who probably didn't know the city was under attack. I went to warn them. I could do *some*thing right, at least. That's where I found my new friend. Of course, I knew then that he obviously *did* know, and so my first thought was *what's he doing in an abandoned temple?* He was clutching a chair in one hand and a piece of cloth in the other. There was a lantern... And then I saw."

He turned back to Myla. "Beside the lantern, I saw the head of a Silver King, lying on the table. Dead. He'd cut it open. He knows things about them, Myla. More than you or I. He knows..."

But whatever Orien said next, Myla never heard. By then, she was asleep.

4
The Fall of Deephaven

The Palace of the Overlord, Myla slowly discovered, was being held by a couple of dozen sword-monks, a hundred soldiers, a handful of mages and, as it turned out, the Princess-Regent of the empire and a small entourage who, for some reason, had arrived in Deephaven in secret only days ago. Myla had seen the Regent two days earlier, in the House of Fire, disintegrating demons. To sword-mistress Tasahre, the Regent's presence in Deephaven was no coincidence; Myla was inclined to agree, but was also too busy to give it much thought.

Whatever the Regent's reasons, she left Tasahre to give the orders. At all hours through the day, nervous soldiers and sword-monks slipped into the streets, looking for survivors. The few hundred souls who'd reached the temple that first night grew to a thousand, then two. The Wraiths never ventured up to the Peak. Myla didn't understand why when a frontal assault would surely have brought them quick victory, yet instead, they whittled at the survivors through roaming bands of Dead Men. The battles were brief and gruesome: the Dead Men had nothing but their hands, while swords and spears were little use in stopping them. The soldiers learned quickly: Sunsteel, Moonsteel, fire; any of those and the Dead Men were stilled. If you had none, you ran.

The searchers, in turn, learned to avoid the harbour and the River Docks, Craftsmans' and the Market District, all of which were overrun. From elsewhere, in ones, twos, threes and dozens, survivors trickled in, until the fortified palace of the Overlord was bursting at the seams.

A few thousand from a city twenty times that number. Myla tried telling herself the rest had managed to flee; but she'd been there at the Sea Docks at the end, had seen how many ships had sailed. Even if half the people of Deephaven had escaped, which she doubted, that still left the other half; and now they were all out there, somewhere. Doing... well, there it was: no one knew. The Wraiths had come with some purpose against which the surviving monks and mages apparently didn't matter. Now and then, Myla wondered what that was; mostly, she put the thought aside and got on with what was in front of her. She was here, exhausted but alive. She was helping people survive. For now, that would have to do.

Looking for Orien one evening, she found herself outside a closed door, raised voices on the other side. Lady Novashi and the Princess-Regent. Eavesdropping on their conversation was probably treasonous, but Myla decided they were long past that and pressed her ear against the door.

"Not yet. Not until I know their purpose!"

"Highness! You pulled their dragon from the sky! You can kill them! They murdered your father! They killed my half-brother!"

"And they will pay."

"*When* will they pay?"

"At the City of Spires. The Moon Priestesses will help us."

"*Will* they? Are you sure?"

"Yes, I am."

The first Myla knew of the sword-mistress behind her was the touch of a hand to the back of her neck.

"Scurry away, half-monk."

Myla scurried away, back to her routine of sleeping through the afternoons, evenings with the sword-mistress for another hour of needles in her skin, then out all night, hunting packs of Dead Men and praying she didn't find a Wraith instead. Then the rising sun, exhaustion, dawn prayers, sleep again, out again with soldiers and handcarts, carrying bodies to the pyres. Until the morning the sword-mistress told them they were leaving.

"Gather what you can," she said. "Deephaven belongs to the dead now."

An hour later, Myla sat on her mare, watching grim-faced soldiers marshal men, women and children too stubborn to flee and too lucky to die. The River Plague had struck, these last few days, and would only get worse, all of them crowded together. Was that why Tasahre had decided to abandon her city?

She shifted to be next to Orien. They'd hardly seen each other but they were alive, which was what mattered. The mage was sitting awkwardly, uncomfortable on horseback, waiting next to the Taiytakei popinjay. Vanamere... something-or-other. She had an idea that Orien and the popinjay were spending a lot of time together. She couldn't be sure, but it triggered an unexpected spike of... was that jealousy?

Get a grip!

The Taiytakei's horse was loaded with so many bags and boxes that Myla was surprised it could move.

"Got everything?" she asked acidly.

"Don't be absurd. This is little more than my collected journals and a few of my most irreplaceable artefacts. Decades of work and this is all I can salvage! It's ridiculous! I hope these Silver King ghosts aren't prone to random outbursts of violence, arson and pillaging. I can't stand to imagine it all lost forever."

Before Myla could tell the popinjay what she thought of that, another rider drew alongside. He had an impressive black horse, a fashionably pointed beard, and eyes of angry iron. Orien bowed. Myla, who had no idea who he was, didn't.

"Monks escort the vanguard." Pointy-Beard nodded at Myla. "My soldiers will hold the flanks." A look flashed to Orien. "Mages at the rear. Understood?"

"I wouldn't worry," said the popinjay when Pointy-Beard rode away. "The Silver Kings don't want the city. Once they've finished killing everyone and summoning them back into their unholy army, they'll move on."

Myla glared. "This was my home."

"Mine too." The Taiytakei turned and smiled, an expression Myla found faintly disturbing. "I have found this city to be spiteful and full of prejudice, wanting in trust and brimming with ignorance. Yet for all the faults of your people, here I am, faintly humiliated and more than a little disappointed at how few of my kind have stepped up to defend her. That we have failed is regrettable, but it is the *manner* of our failure that piques my ire. I see men from far away cities armed with useless swords and arrows and yet willing to fight, and I am ashamed. On reaching Varr, I shall present myself to the Guild of Mages with the utmost haste. If our kind are to be the guides and mentors of this land, we must be its defenders too."

Guides and mentors? Myla wasn't sure about that. In particular, she wasn't sure whether *his kind* meant sorcerers, which he obviously was, or his equally obvious Taiytakei blood.

"I think that's his weird way of wishing us luck," Orien said, dismounting. He looked up at her. "If I try to do this from the back of a horse, I'm going to fall off, and none of us want that."

He opened his arms to her. Myla jumped to the ground and leapt into them and hugged him tight. "Gentle, gentle! Sore back!"

"We should both have boarded that ship," he said. "What a life we might have had."

"But we didn't." She kissed him then, long enough to draw hoots and whistles from the soldiers around them. When she let Orien go, she flipped them some rude gestures. "And you lot can all fuck off, too." She was smiling, though, and so were they.

At the front of the assembling column, Pointy-Beard was addressing the other sword-monks, apparently oblivious to their lack of interest. Myla fell in with them and waited as the Spoiled Brat, draped in silk and steel and gold, took his place at the column's head. He turned to the soldiers arrayed behind him, raised his sword in salute and cried out:

"For the Emperor! For Aria. For the Moon and the Sun!"

It roused a bit of a cheer, although Myla supposed it would have roused a bigger one if the Princess-Regent had done it. For all the Regent was trying to pretend she wasn't here, rumour abounded that she'd sorceried seven shades of shit out of a pair of Wraiths and then brought down their dragon on that first night. How much help she'd had from Lady Novashi, Myla wasn't sure, but she'd seen the Regent in Orien's Guildhouse on the day the mirror-demons had come. One snap of her fingers had turned three at once to dust.

She's not what she seems. Tasahre's dark whisper.

The column pushed into Deephaven Square, past the wreckage of the solar temple with its dead dragon, now somehow turned to stone. Myla rode with the monks, the newest and least of them. For some reason, the Dead Men had taken a liking to the fallen temple, which annoyed the monks immensely. A group split off, running into cloisters and chapels and other buildings that still stood. She heard their cries and whoops of triumph but felt no urge to join them. An anxious hand slipped down to pat her saddlebags, feeling the lumps that were the six bottles of wine she'd liberated from the cellars before they'd gone out last night, and which constituted the entirety of her worldly possessions.

Gather what you need. And so she had. Six bottles of wine and the two Sunsteel swords on her back.

And then Tasahre was beside her, grabbing her reins and forcing her to a stop as the head of the column reached the Avenue of the Sun, striking towards Four Winds Square, as the monks returned from scouring the temple grounds.

"You and I have an errand to run," the sword-mistress said.

They sat, Myla uncomfortable, Tasahre as serene as moonlit water. It felt like hours passed before the tail of the column finally rode out. Eight riders: two brutes in heavy black armour that covered them from head to foot; the Princess-Regent in Moonsteel mail, smaller and shorter and with the Sunsteel Crown glinting on her brow; Lady Novashi, the Red Witch in her luscious orange robes, rich like cream and velvet. Spread around them, four other riders, none wearing any formal colours.

"Watch those four," murmured Tasahre. "The Regent's Hawks. If she needs something done with a light touch, chances are it'll be one of those she sends."

The Regent spared Myla a look as she passed, not exactly hostile but a long way from friendly.

"She's at the heart of this somehow. I don't trust her and nor should you."

"I don't," said Myla, "but nor will *she* trust *us*."

Tasahre spat.

"You *do* know she grew up believing that a band of rogue sword-monks ambushed and murdered her mother on the road from Deephaven to Varr? Lady Novashi's mother too, I believe."

Tasahre didn't answer. Maybe the sword-mistress hadn't heard this version of the Sad Empress's death?

"That's what they say in Varr, at least." Then, when the Regent and her entourage had vanished into the Avenue of the Sun and the sword-mistress still hadn't moved: "Something about an errand?"

"Yes. The other warlock who came to Deephaven. We're going to hunt him down."

5

The Memories of Saffran Kuy

Something happened in Deephaven. The thought buzzed through Seth's head like an angry bee.

No shit.

Saying *something* had happened felt like a bit of an understatement, when what had *actually* happened was that Deephaven had fallen, in the space of a single night, to an army of Dead Men and half-gods – oh, and also maybe a dragon – all of whom were supposed to be entirely mythical, not that they seemed to have let that bother them.

He knew all that because he'd been there. Sure as shit wouldn't have believed it otherwise.

Fine. Something else *happened in Deephaven.*

Yes. Clearly, a lot of things *had* happened in Deephaven, but what he had in mind was a something in particular. Or, rather, he *didn't* have it in mind because he'd obviously made himself forget it and had then been too fucking stupid to properly fill the hole left behind.

Fuck you, past me.

He knew the feeling of a void where a memory used to be. He'd done it before. Pitiful, that first time, a naïve plan full of more holes than Fings' pockets. He might have forgotten what he'd actually *done* back in Varr, but he still remembered writing the sigil and why, and it wasn't long before he'd had a shrewd idea of what *had* happened to Lightbringer Suaresh...

Still... it had done its job. Another thing he remembered:

how it had felt, deceiving those sword-monks. So, *so* smug...

Dumb luck that he'd got away with it. Fings had broken him out and they'd run. Now, apparently, he'd done it to himself again, only instead of forgetting a couple of hours, he'd erased an entire day. He'd done a better job insofar as he didn't remember writing the sigil, or anything about *why* he'd done it... But he *had* done it. He could feel the hole.

What the fuck did I do this *time?*

Leave it be.

Given everything he *did* remember, it must have been something quite special. If ever he was quizzed by a witch-breaker or a monk, his guilt was going to light up like a heretic's pyre.

You made yourself forget for a reason. Leave it be!

Great advice. *How*, exactly? *Mental note: next time you fuck with your own head, do a proper job of it!*

What he *did* remember was already enough to damn him. Running to Deephaven with Fings because a pair of sword-monks had caught him talking to corpses and making Dead Men, all those unhealthy warlock things they liked to use as an excuse to set people on fire. He remembered the Taiytakei popinjay, their deeply unpleasant visit to the House of Cats and Gulls, and what the popinjay had said after. He remembered the Wraith and what *it* had said, too. If he could remember all *that*, surely it didn't matter what *else* he'd done.

Something worse, apparently.

He wasn't sure what *worse* could look like, but that didn't stop his imagination from having a spirited go. Was he somehow responsible for *every*thing? Surely not. The notion that he'd somehow summoned an army of mythical and murderous half-gods and Dead Men? Absurd!

Although... a part of him *did* quite like the idea...

He shook the thought away. *I will never, ever, do this to myself again.*

Fings was on deck, so Seth got up and riffled though Fings' stuff in case there were any clues. Nothing.

What did you expect? A note? Things Not To Mention To Seth? The idiot can barely write his own name.

He'd woken in his underclothes. Presumably, he hadn't been half-naked when Fings had found him on the Avenue of Emperors. Maybe he'd had something in one of his pockets? Some clue?

A note in case I made myself forget something and then wished I hadn't? Diaries of my guilty secrets? I'm not that stupid!

Really? Seems like there's a fair pile of evidence to the contrary.

It occurred to Seth then that maybe this wasn't a healthy conversation to be having with himself. He brushed *that* thought aside too. They'd probably burned his clothes or thrown them overboard, him having the plague and all, but not before Fings had gone through all the pockets. *That* was as inevitable as sunrise, Fings being who he was.

But he'd gone through Fings' stuff and come up empty-handed. Which left...

Lucius's chest.

Lucius, who wasn't around to ask...

What if you do find out what you forgot? Presumably past-you had his reasons.

At the very least, I can do a better job of forgetting it again!

The chest wasn't locked. Seth opened it, and there was his satchel. Full of stuff. The obvious oddity was a glass globe about the size of his cupped hands. Saffran Kuy's Orb of Memory – he remembered that much, although he had no idea where he'd found it. He lifted it out and held it. He was going to find out what he'd done and then never, ever, *ever* do this again.

Heavy bastard...

A gentle explosion detonated inside him. The memories in the globe, rushing to fill the hole in his head. He sucked them up, feeling them slot into place, one by one. Not *his* memories, more like they were taking up lodgings, but...

...And he was holding the globe as though it were his lover's heart, and looking into it and seeing memories and...

Oh. Oh fuck, fuck! Stop!

He dropped the globe. It landed with a heavy *thunk* and rolled across the floor.

He *did* remember now. Sort of. No... *He* wasn't remembering! *It* remembered *him*! He was in a room in Deephaven. He could smell the sea, and hear it, the noises of ships out in the harbour. The murmur of the waves. A conversation walking past his window. Calls and shouts out in the night...

Are these my *memories or his?*

...A dark night and he was feverish with excitement. He was going back to the House of Cats and Gulls. There was something buried there...

That was me, wasn't it? Or was it?

A Silver King, pointing its sword at him... *Prophet!*

Okay, that was definitely mine. One he wouldn't forget in a hurry. *But that came after...*

The rush subsided. Seth glared at the globe. Thing was, he remembered having it and what it was, but he didn't remember finding it. Didn't remember using it either, although he must have done; otherwise how did he already know what was inside it?

Past-Seth was, he decided, a bit of a dick, one who deserved a slapping, if only for being too fucking incompetent to do a proper job of things.

Still you *you're talking about here...*

Still fuck off. He reached inside the globe again, more cautious this time, digging, searching for a beginning...

The first basic principle of knowledge is to understand that the animating force that brings life to all creatures differs from the higher spirit... He was in a small wooden room, looking down on Saffran Kuy. The way the room swayed was somehow familiar. Kuy, like Seth, was on a ship. On his way to Deephaven from... somewhere. Seth found himself wondering where that somewhere had been, why the warlock was fleeing, what he'd done... But then, judging from his own life these last few months, that was how it was for a warlock. Everyone wanted to murder you and so you were always running. Fleeing from murderous lunatics with Sunsteel swords.

And Wraiths...

The image of the cabin flickered and fell apart, scattered into fragments too fleeting to forge into sense. Seth frowned and then smiled as he understood: the globe was trying to give him answers, but his thoughts were flitting from one question to the next too quickly for it to follow. He tried again.

The higher spirit grants compassion, nobility and all the goodly morals that separate us from animals. The animating force is concerned with lusts: food, water, dominance, copulation, control. All creatures have it. Death is simply a severing of this force from the flesh that carried it. Such a force severed from its body we call a remnant. Such remnants are everywhere. See, now, how you can feel them.

A new presence in his head. A tickle in the back of his mind, as though something was quietly being rearranged.

In time, they fade. While they exist, those who practice sorcery may coerce them to act upon the world. Other mages do not recognise the nature of the well from which they draw, but we *do. This makes necromancy the purest, the easiest and, ultimately, the most powerful of the arts, for it acts directly upon, and acknowledges, the true source of all power.*

A dead warlock wanted to teach him necromancy? Bound to end well, that...

Seth heard a noise. A door opening and closing. He snapped out of the globe. The change left him dizzy and confused; in one moment, he was Kuy's apprentice, in the next, he was Seth, sitting in Lucius's cabin, one good eye, one blind, bandages wrapped across his face.

The noise came again. A door closing. Voices. Lucius and Fings. Seth hid the globe under his blanket and pretended to be asleep as the door opened. Fings poked his head inside. "Seth? You awake?"

Seth stayed very still. A moment later, he heard the door close again. Fings outside.

"Still asleep. Best let him rest, eh?"

From under his blanket, Seth tried reaching out with his thoughts, tried to feel the animating forces that supposedly surrounded him the way Kuy had shown his apprentice...

Shown *him*...

And shuddered with fear and surprise when it worked... when it actually *worked!* He could feel presences around him as though he was floating in water, filled by swarms of blind fish whose scales brushed against him as they swam aimlessly back and forth. Fascinated, he closed his one good eye and let the sensation grow, reaching further. Somewhere nearby, he felt a change. A sense of order, of organisation... Fings! He was feeling Fings!

His eye snapped open. He could sense *people.*

I can do sorcery!

The understanding hit him like a velvet fist. No sigils, no papers, no books. Just him. He, Seth, could sense people out in the world around him without having to see them. A balancing of the scales for the loss of one eye? Dumb luck, more likely; but did it matter? He was a *sorcerer!* He had power! Who knew where that might end?

You know the answer: somewhere bad.

He delved into the globe once more.

Even mundane applications have great power. A remnant can be driven into a corpse to create a mindless servant. This can happen spontaneously, and frequently does, although such remnants rarely have the vigour to persist for more than a few hours. With application, remnants can be questioned. They are barely intelligent, aware only of their immediate vicinity, little more than raw animal force. But they are ubiquitous. Nowhere save the deepest, darkest corners of the earth is devoid of them; for wherever there is death, there you will find them. With skill and practice, remnants may be coerced to possess, displace, or feed from a weaker soul. They can be called upon to assist with almost any task if the caller has the wit to properly instruct them. A whirl of remnants may lift their caller into the air. A blast of them can rot, wither, corrode, inflict disease, age, or even sever the ties between another animating force and its vessel of flesh and bone. Their energy can be given to heal, restore, regenerate, even from the brink of death. Their power, if harnessed correctly, has no limits...

No limits...

He'd had this same bright feeling of the world at his feet once before, offering itself for conquest if only he worked hard enough. Like a coy lover, beckoning him closer, he'd felt it on the day he'd walked into the temple of the Sun in Spice Market Square to become a novice. Chosen by destiny for something beyond ordinary, or so it had seemed. Here it was again; only this time, the power was offering itself, not like a coy lover but as a hungry siren, begging to be taken. Something for nothing. No need for years of study, for hard work. Just a few bits of paper, a dose of the pox, and here he was, a mage.

This? This *is what I made myself forget?* Why the fuck had his past self tried to hide *this?* Irritatingly, what Past-Seth *had* done right was leave no clue as to why he'd stripped his memories in the first place.

He looked in wonder at the globe. *Where did I find you...?*

Probably in the House of Cats and Gulls, he supposed.

You did this to yourself for a reason! Let it be!

He wasn't sure he could do that. Why make himself forget something like this? He couldn't see it. It didn't make sense.

But you did *do it. So you* did *have a reason.*

Maybe it wasn't a very good one?

Sure. Because you're the sort of person who likes to fuck about with his own head just to keep his future-self amused, right? Have you ever considered a new life as a farmer or fisherman? Something a bit less complicated than being... you?

Piss off!

Maybe Past-Seth wasn't such a dick after all. Maybe *that* was the message. Past-Seth had to have known he'd get this far again. Maybe this was where to stop? *Let it be. Don't go further.* Was that what he'd meant?

No. Because he wouldn't stop. And he'd have known that. He knew himself *that* well, at least.

Take this gift and don't ask how you got it, or why, or what it cost you? Let it be lost in the cataclysm that followed? Was *that* it?

I could at least have left myself a note!

He'd gone to Deephaven to unravel the lie at the heart of the Path. To strip their illusions and expose their falsehoods. He'd gone hoping to learn the secrets of a warlock. Not to *be* one.

Yeah, tell yourself that if it makes you feel better. Nothing to do with not wanting to be burned as a heretic by a pack of angry monks in Varr, eh?

Will you ever *go away?*

I'm you, *you moron, not some fucking ghost. So no, I won't.*

Knowledge was power, power was knowledge. Neither was inherently virtuous, neither was inherently wicked. The Path itself taught that. The measure of a man wasn't what he knew or the power he held. It was what he chose to do with those things.

He stopped and listened and, for once, didn't hear a little voice in his head telling him he was being a dick and an idiot. Just... silence. He poked again at the orb, trying to get a sense of who the warlock Saffran Kuy had really been. What he'd wanted. His purpose. He wasn't expecting an answer, but the orb turned out to have one all ready and waiting.

You are on the path of the abyss. No Sun to light your way. No Moon or Stars to guide you. No Earth to comfort you. Only the nothingness of the between places. You have hung between life and death and so, for a moment, the void has touched you. You belong to the dead. To the Nothing. To the Lord of Endings. Our path is simple and pure. To unfetter That Which Came Before. To unmake this sham of creation. To begin again.

Seth considered this. Sounded a bit... extreme.

Sounds like the rantings of a deranged fucking lunatic. Unmake creation? How exactly is that supposed to work? Also, you realise you're a part of said creation, right?

It was nice, he thought, to able to agree with himself for once. And then the globe said his name, and he dropped it as though it had stung him.

6
The House of Cats and Gulls

After the noise and dust of the column, Godsway was quiet, the corpses that once littered it either burned or having quietly risen and removed themselves, Dead Men lurking somewhere out of the sun. Moon Street was messier, scattered with abandoned handcarts discarded as people tried to flee, with half-eaten carcasses of animals killed in the rain of ice-knives. The air stank. Gulls, feasting on carrion, eyed Myla with hostility, squawking resentment at being disturbed.

At the waterfront, Tasahre slowed. The river docks were where it had started, where Dead Men had come swarming from the water, hauling themselves ashore to wreak havoc and slaughter among crowds trying to flee the plague. This was where the Wraith of Deephaven had first shown himself.

"Where are we going?"

Tasahre guided her horse between crates and barrels and boxes and split-open sacks and bags, the remnants of a thousand lives scattered across the stones. She stopped outside an abandoned warehouse where the door hung open. Gulls lined the roof and strutted among the jetties, all staring at Myla as if calculating the best way to murder her. Myla saw cats too, dozens, lean scrawny feral things watching from every shadow.

"Mistress?"

Tasahre dismounted and drew her swords. For a moment, Myla thought she caught a sense of... was that fear? Anxiety, at least.

"This is where it started, Shirish. The House of Cats and Gulls."

The inside of the warehouse was a ruin, burned out more than a decade ago and looking as though it hadn't been touched since.

"I hadn't been in Deephaven long." Sunlight streamed through holes that had once been boarded-up windows, though the boards had long ago been torn away. Shutters hung broken and limp.

"Mistress?"

"This place never truly shed its taint." Tasahre picked her way deeper into the ruin as though she knew exactly where she was going, into rooms illuminated only by the feeble light making its way from the door and by the pale glow of her Sunsteel blades. Everything was wrecked, burned and black with soot and ash. Myla saw black rings of scorched powder, now and then, encircling the remains of some long-dead fire.

"Salt and iron?" she asked.

Tasahre nodded. "We burned everything that would burn."

The story of Tasahre and the warlock of Deephaven was the story of Tasahre and the thief-taker's apprentice, of the scar on her neck where the thief-taker had almost killed her. Myla had a sense that it was the story of other things too, secret things the sword-mistress never shared. "Was the thief-taker's boy your lover?" Myla asked, because that was the rumour.

Tasahre snorted. "No; although he certainly hoped to be. Why? Is that what people say behind my back?"

Myla shrugged. "Why are we here?"

They stopped at a narrow opening into a lightless passage. A foul smell wafted out, rank with putrefaction. The stink made Myla think of the river mudflats at low tide on a hot summer day. "I drove both swords right through him and it wasn't enough." Tasahre took a long breath. "Everything that wouldn't burn, we carried to the temple. Sixteen years. I'd almost forgotten. And then, the night before the Wraiths came, someone took something. Something we missed." She started down the passage. "I don't know what to expect here, Shirish. Nothing good."

"My name is Myla now, sword-mistress. Shirish died in Four Winds Square when the ice knives fell."

"Why Myla?"

"My childhood nickname. My Lady. Myla."

Tasahre stopped. The passage ended at a set of narrow steps leading down. "This is where he kept it."

"Kept what?"

"I don't know, but I *do* know he left something behind. He never came back for it. Years later, I received word that he was dead. Killed by..." Tasahre started on the steps. "More years passed. I started to doubt. And then *you* came, and in your wake, someone set about finishing what Saffran Kuy started, all those years ago."

The passage was almost black, the only light from Tasahre's swords as they descended, slow and careful and silent. At the bottom, Tasahre cocked her head, straining to hear. A second passed and then she started to–

A shape shot out of the darkness, barrelling into the sword-mistress, knocking her sideways. Myla jumped the last half of the stair, landing in a crouch, swords drawn, looking this way and that. Her blades gave a dim light. She saw Tasahre stagger to her feet, holding one blade. The other lay in the dirt a few feet away. The place stank of rot thick enough make her gag. The floor was sticky mud and...

Corpses. Dozens. All shredded by large and powerful claws.

Around her, the cellar disappeared into darkness. There was no sign of whatever had attacked the sword-mistress.

"Are you–" Again, the shape hurtled from the gloom, charging on all fours like a dog, except too powerful and too big. Again, it launched itself at Tasahre, taloned arms lashing at her. The sword-mistress pirouetted away. Her Sunsteel flashed. The creature bounded back into the darkness. Myla saw blood. Three deep slashes across Tasahre's ribs.

"It touched you!"

Tasahre spat. "I touched it back."

Myla heard a slither, whirled to face it but saw nothing. "What is it?"

"I don't know. Something more than a Dead Man."

Another skitter. Myla whirled again, swords raised.

"Back to back, Shirish."

"Can you still fight?"

"For now."

Myla glimpsed a shape lurking at the edge of the light. More like a wild pig than a dog. It stared at her, then slunk into the gloom and vanished. "You think *I* had something to do with all of this?"

"You weren't the only one to come from Varr. Others followed."

"*Fings?*" Myla couldn't suppress a snort of laughter. The idea of Fings having anything to do with something that wasn't petty larceny... And then she stopped laughing, because Fings *had* stolen the Moonsteel Crown a few months back, because Sulfane had put him up to it, and Sulfane's cause had been something darker. *Fings did this?*

"Why is the Imperial Regent in Deephaven? Why did she come in secret? Why do the Wraiths–"

The creature burst from the darkness, charging at them. Tasahre jumped away. Myla did the same, letting the thing pass between them. The creature swung a wild taloned hand. Myla slashed and severed its wrist. Tasahre skewered it in the side, deep enough to have her sword ripped out of her hand. The creature's legs buckled. It skidded across the mud; and then Myla was on its back, driving both swords in deep. It heaved once, shaking her off, then shuddered and lay still.

Tasahre retrieved her fallen sword and gave the dead thing a poke. "The night before the Wraiths came, a priest went missing – one of the priests who came here after the warlock fled. He returned later that same night carrying some of what we took from here, all those years ago. He sat in the middle of the Equinox yard and set himself on fire. You saw the aftermath, that morning you refused me, preferring to chase that Hawat fool."

Myla crouched beside the dead thing and peered at its face. "I've seen one these before."

"The warlock who followed you from Varr took something from us, and then, when he had it, he came here."

"This is like the creatures that attacked the House of Fire!" Myla shivered, remembering the talons and the teeth as the *thing*, whatever it was, had forced its way through the mirror in Orien's room, through silvered glass as though through stubborn flesh. She'd rammed a candlestick into its eye socket and then clubbed it round the head while Orien set it on fire. It had done the trick at the time.

Tasahre pulled her second sword free and then crouched beside Myla, inspecting the creature's head.

"Look!"

By the light of Tasahre's sword, Myla saw. The creature had a mark between its eyes.

"A warlock's sigil. Someone killed this thing and then brought it back and set it to guard this place. The warlock was here when the Dead Men came from the river." She rose, then swayed a little, one hand moving to her side and then flinching away.

"You're hurt."

"I'm aware."

"We should get out of here."

"Kuy left something behind. Something I never found. Something this other warlock was looking for."

Myla steadied the sword-mistress; but when she tried to guide Tasahre back to the stair, Tasahre wasn't having it. "Mistress, if there *was* something here, he found it and used it. The result is what we see around us, and why Deephaven has fallen to ruin. It's too late!"

"It had better not be."

"But it is!"

Tasahre grabbed Myla, one hand on each shoulder. "When you stand outside, do you see the sun in the sky?"

"Of course!"

"Then it is not too late!" The sword-mistress had a wildness in her eyes, one Myla had never seen until now. Easy to put it down to the wound Tasahre had taken, but also wrong.

"Mistress?"

"I taught you of the Angry Goddess and the Black Moon, of the Shining Age and the War of Splinters that ended it. How the greatest of the half-gods bound the Angry Goddess, the two of them forever entwined. Well. The warlocks have stories too. In *their* stories, the last half-gods made a key to unlock that binding before their power was taken. That is what Saffran Kuy sought. The key that would free the Angry Goddess from her chains and raise the Black Moon into the sky once more. You will know, monk, when it is too late, for there will be no doubting it!"

Myla took a step back. "But... wouldn't that be the end of everything? Everyone... Everyone would die. *Every*one, even warlocks. You'd have to be..." She couldn't find the right word. *Stupid* was barely the start of it.

"You'd have to be insane."

If I can't have it, no one can. Words she'd heard in the *Unruly Pig*; but such thoughts would have to wait until she and Tasahre weren't wounded in a dark cellar in a hostile city, possibly with another demonic dead-but-not monstrosity lurking in the gloom.

"Let's get out of here," she said.

"Not yet. Stake one of your swords in the ground at the foot of the stair so we know which way to run, should running become necessary."

Myla did as asked. When she returned, Tasahre was crawling in the mud, peering at it. Footprints, Myla realised, after a moment of thinking the sword-mistress had lost her mind.

"The Dead Men came from there." Tasahre pointed into the gloom. "They went for the stair. They knew the way out." She walked to the stair and dropped back on her hands and knees.

"What are you looking for?"

"Footprints that go somewhere else." Tasahre was breathing hard, the pain of her wound cracking her composure. "The Regent and her little brother, our new Emperor, should have wintered in Tarantor with the rest of the court. *He* did, but *she* didn't. As best I can tell, no one knows where she was for three months before Midwinter. No one knows where she was when Emperor Ashahn was killed, yet suddenly she's in Varr to receive her coronation? She drags half the court back from Tarantor, has her brother crowned in Varr, not in the cathedral in Torpreah..." She stopped, bringing the light of her sword closer to the ground. "Here!"

Myla looked. Sure enough, a set of footprints led away from the churned mass where the Dead Men had come through. "Likely as not, the Torpreahns would have murdered both her and our new Emperor, Sun bless him, and then crowned one of their own."

"Then she comes here in secret." Tasahre growled, though whether in frustration or pain, Myla couldn't tell. They were both on their hands and knees now, crawling through slime and dirt, fetid with the stench of rot, of the river, of the corpses of so many Dead Men.

"I heard her talking," Myla said. "They mean to head for the City of Spires. There's something there they need. I think... I think they were *expecting* this."

They followed the footprints, Tasahre still on her hands and knees, Myla keeping watch on the darkness. The cellar had the stillness of a mausoleum.

"Here!"

By a wall of mouldering brickwork was a hole in the earth, a recent one. Beside the hole, carelessly abandoned, was an iron box pitted with rust. Myla touched it. Her fingers came away smeared with dirt.

"Someone dug this up," she said. "Only days ago."

Tasahre bared her teeth. "Open it!"

Inside was a sheet of fine leather with a single symbol, not a sigil but a piece of heraldry. A winged serpent rampant wearing a solar halo wrapped around a sword. Myla frowned, trying to place it. Tasahre snatched it away.

"Valladrune," she hissed.

Myla had no idea. "Who?"

"Not a person. A place. Let's go." Tasahre winced as she rose. She was panting for breath. "There was poison on those claws. I may need your help, Shirish."

"My name is Myla now." Myla helped Tasahre to the stair, retrieved her other sword, then watched Tasahre struggle her way up into the warehouse. Outside, back in blessed daylight among the hostile gulls and scattered detritus of the river docks, she saw the creature's claws had cut Tasahre deep. Tasahre was soaked in her own blood. A wound like that...

The thought that Tasahre might die was too horrible. She pushed it away, darted across the docks and came back pushing a handcart.

"What are you doing?" growled Tasahre.

Myla braced herself. This was about to get difficult. "You can't ride like that. It'll kill you. So, you're going to get in this, and I'll get you back to the column, to someone who can help." Tasahre cocked her head; Myla, reckoning the Sword-Mistress was about to say something that had more to do with pride than common sense, got in first. "And before you let your ego contradict me, take a moment. You're little use in a fight right now, and I'm only a half-monk."

Tasahre glowered, on the cusp of something angry, and then started to shake and laugh and then winced and staggered in pain. "Fuck you, Shirish."

"Myla!"

"Myla. Whatever." Tasahre let Myla help her into the cart, then caught her hand. "If a Wraith comes, leave me and run. You can't face one on your own."

"I'll not–"

"Before you came to Deephaven, you did the Regent a service." Tasahre gripped Myla tight. "Use that. Get close to her. She knows more. Maybe the truth about Valladrune. The real truth. Dig it out. If this wound kills me, you have to get there before the warlock. You have to stop him."

Myla pulled her hand free. "I will. But you're not going to die, so shut up and let me run."

Tasahre growled. Myla gripped the shafts of the handcart and ran for the River Gate as fast as she could, shooing the horses ahead of them. It was sunny, the middle of the day, so there were no Dead Men or Wraiths on the docks; even from here, she could see the line of the old city wall as it ran to the river and kissed the water where the River Gates stood. As she ran, she thought about what Tasahre had said about the old warlock of Deephaven, how ridiculous it was, because what sort of idiot would bring about the end of everything if it included themselves? You'd have to be a very special kind of stupid…

You'd have to be insane…

And as she thought, another possibility sidled up, insidious and corrosive. Maybe you *didn't* have to be stupid or mad. What if you were very clever but also very angry? What if you were angry and bitter and determined to prove something to the world, no matter the cost?

7
The Warlock

There *were* advantages to almost dying of the plague, Seth supposed. Not many, but some. Convincing Fings, for example, that it was perfectly normal to have no memory of anything after they'd gone to the temple in Deephaven on the evening before the Wraiths came. Pretending to spend most of his time asleep when what he was *actually* doing was studying Saffran Kuy's memories. Small perks, hardly enough to make up for losing an eye and having a face that looked like someone had set it on fire; but hey, you took what you could, and all of *that* was, in turn, a small price for what he was learning from the orb.

Wherever he'd found it...

Stop thinking about that! Except of course, he *did*. All the time.

He'd gone with Fings to the Solar Cathedral for Twilight Prayer. He remembered that. Fings had seen a Wraith and reckoned someone ought to know. Seth had reckoned he'd had a point. They'd listened to the Sunherald of Deephaven blather about white ships on the river, about a coming darkness, a corruption, about how Khrozus the Usurper had made a pact with a warlock to bring down the righteous emperor Talsin, the blasphemy of a sorceress on the throne, all leading to an exhortation that those who were strong and righteous must stay and fight the coming evil. It had been, Seth remembered, all jolly exciting, listening to the Sunherald as good as declare holy war on the Sapphire Throne right there in front of him. He certainly hadn't expected it.

If Twilight Prayers were always like that, I'd have gone more often...

He wondered, briefly, if that was why the Wraiths had come. Maybe the Princess-Regent had heard the Sunherald going on about how she was a threat to all that was good and holy. Maybe she hadn't liked that and had decided to do something about it.

Naughty, naughty priests, saying such things. My friends here would like a word regarding your attitude...

He stifled a giggle. That one time he'd seen the Princess-Regent, she hadn't *looked* dangerous. A slip of a girl. He'd wished her luck from afar, reckoned she'd need it, reckoned she'd need a lot more than luck to see out the year, and then gone on his merry way, off to...

Off to betray his friends to the Spicers and the Deephaven mercenaries hunting Myla. Now *there* was a memory he wouldn't mind losing.

You deserved what happened to you. Every bit of it.

Hard to argue.

Myla was gone. Left in Deephaven and likely dead. It surprised him how deeply he felt that. Didn't even like her, not really. But still, there it was.

She was everything you wished you could be.

Bollocks! He'd never wanted to be good at slicing people up. Hadn't been all that interested in having a drinking problem, either.

She had faith and courage. She was honest. She knew who and what she was and accepted it.

He wasn't entirely sure that Myla would recognise that version of herself. And anyway, so what? Rediscovering his own faith didn't seem likely, but courage and honesty? He could work on those, couldn't he? As for what he *was*...

What did I do in Deephaven?

Back to Fings and their visit to the temple. Twilight Prayer. He remembered talking to a novice, spinning an unexpectedly prophetic story about Dead Men rising from the river. The novice returning with the sword-monk who'd once been Myla's teacher. He'd slipped away, not much wanting to be near a walking, talking, lie-detecting warlock killer. He remembered the cold shock of understanding as he'd realised Fings and the sword-monk somehow knew each other, that this wasn't the first time they'd spoken...

Leaving the Hall of Light. Mayhem in the temple yards outside. All of that, clear as anything, and then... And *then* a full day had passed, and he was coming out of the House of Cats and Gulls being chased by Dead Men. Right there was the hole in his memory. Right between leaving Fings in the temple and it suddenly being the end of the world.

And he'd had Saffran Kuy's orb.

Was that where I found it? The House of Cats and Gulls?

Made sense. He remembered his first visit well enough, with the mad Taiytakei mage. He shuddered, glad to be away from *that* lunatic...

He remembered the fall of the city. Feverish with plague, running through the streets this way and that, feeling like he was at death's door. Dead Men and crazy people, head full of obsessive fevered thoughts that made no sense. He had to go... well, somewhere. Some place that was important that he couldn't now remember. He had to find Myla. He had to tell her... something. He wasn't sure what *that* had been, either. He remembered knives of ice falling from the sky, standing face to face with Fings' Wraith, what it had said and...

Whatever you did, you made yourself forget for a reason!

Had that all been the same night?

He sighed and went back to Kuy's orb. As he did, he caught sight of himself in Lucius's mirror again. His new face bothered him, not because it was ruined but because it was somehow familiar. Yes, still *his* face, the unscarred half clearly recognisable. But he reckoned he'd seen this new face once before, a long time ago, back before Midwinter in Varr, before the whole business with Sulfane and the Path and fleeing to Deephaven had kicked off. He'd had visions for a while, back then. He'd thought they were sendings.

That face, *his* face, the one he saw every day in Lucius's mirror. Had it been there with him? Something about two gods throwing lightning at each other over a world covered in ice?

But those visions had stopped months ago, shortly after Midwinter. Hadn't had one since. *That*, at least, was a relief. It rarely ended well, in Seth's opinion, when a God decided they had something special in mind for you.

8
A Hill on which to Die

Four monks waited at the River Gate. One took the horses, the others Tasahre in her cart. Myla followed as they ran with the sword-mistress, taking it in turns to pull her through the sprawl beyond the old city wall, the maze of slums built around and eventually on top of Emperor Talsin's doomed attempt to carve a channel from the river to the sea. It had come as no surprise to anyone that he'd failed; it *had* come as a surprise to quite a few when it started a war. *If* that was what had started it.

They caught the rear of the column as the edge of the city sprawl gave way to trees and muddy fields. The monks hustled Tasahre into the back of a larger cart and fussed, shooing Myla away, because what could she do? Myla had the impression she was supposed to go ahead, to the vanguard, but Orien was with the rear of the column with his mistress and the Princess-Regent, still pretending she wasn't here. Once it was obvious that Tasahre wasn't imminently about to die, Myla drifted away, waiting for Orien to find an excuse to join her.

"Still no Dead Men," she said, when he did. "Or Wraiths."

"Perhaps they've moved on."

"Moved on where?" Myla rather preferred the idea of putting them behind her.

"I saw you with the sword-mistress. Where did you go?"

She told him, not seeing much reason to keep it secret, although skipping Tasahre's suspicions about the Princess-Regent. She and

Orien were lovers, yes, but lovers didn't have to share *everything*, and Orien was besotted with the empire's new ruler while Myla rather saw Tasahre's point. She didn't want them to end up arguing.

"I saw Tasahre at the Guildhouse, you know," he said when she finished. "The Princess-Regent spoke with her. I think your mistress knows more about all this than she deems fit to share."

Yours too, Myla thought, but didn't say it. Tasahre and the Regent, eh? A sword-monk and a Moon-Witch. Truth was, they probably *both* knew more than they were saying.

"Why not bring your mistress here? Her Highness may be able to help. Vanamere almost certainly could. He is a healer, of a sort."

"I don't think Tasahre would appreciate being treated by a mage."

Outside the city, the land around the road was swampy forest punctured by clearings. In the distance, when Myla could see between the trees, the land away from the river turned into fields on gentle hills, streams and hedgerows. She sighed. It all looked so peaceful.

Get close to her. She likely knows the truth about Valladrune...

Soldiers from the vanguard came riding back, exchanged words with the Regent's guard, then rode off again. The words were passed to the Regent in her Moonsteel mail, tiny beside the men around her yet somehow the centre of everything. Her and Orien's orange-robed mistress, riding beside her.

What do you know that you're not telling us?

Myla knew she should return to the head of the column to be with the other sword-monks. But it was nice here with Orien. The sun was high and warm, the air fresh with forest smells, a distinct improvement over the stink of Deephaven; and yes, the column ahead meant the road was a mess of mud and shit, but that was her horse's problem, not hers. She wondered when they'd reach the river fort where she'd been taken as a slave. Around nightfall, perhaps? It was a good defensible position, so they'd probably stop. She wondered how she felt about that and found she felt nothing. *That* had been Shirish, and Shirish was dead. She was Myla now. Myla the sword-monk.

The road wound round the base of a grass-covered hill. On a whim, Myla cantered up and stopped there, looking down over the column snaking along the road ahead. Its size surprised her. She'd seen the soldiers and refugees at the Overlord's palace, but not spread out in a line like this, more than a mile long. She saw mounted soldiers ride beside the endless line of carts and mules and people like a cloud of flies around a plodding ox. Had it grown? Hangers on picked up as they'd moved throughout the day, perhaps? People who'd managed to hide and knew a last chance to escape when they saw one?

"Have you ever heard of a place called Valladrune?" she asked when Orien came to join her. She wasn't sure what answer she expected: either ignorance or else he *had* heard of it and, in an effort to impress, would wring every drop of knowledge, speculation, and rumour he could muster and shower it on her like summer rain.

Not silence, though. Or that when she turned to look, Orien would be staring back at her with an expression of mild horror.

"What?" she asked.

"Valladrune doesn't exist," he said.

"I'm reasonably sure it does."

His neck muscles tightened as though his lower jaw was making a spirited attempt to reach his nose. "No," he said again. "Valladrune doesn't exist. It never did, and if you speak that name in front of anyone at court..." He trailed off. Given what they'd been through over the last days, whatever warning he was about to give would have to be quite something to make an impression.

"Well, now I really *am* interested."

"Will the sword-mistress survive?" he asked.

Myla glared, partly because she didn't want to contemplate the alternative, mostly at the obvious attempt to change the subject.

"Yes," she said. "Back to Valladrune, fire-mage."

Orien looked a little sick; and then his face went wild with horror. "Oh! Crap!"

A swarm of Dead Men was rushing from the treeline on the

side of the hill away from the road, straight towards her and Orien. Hundreds! More! Thousands?

Shit!

Myla turned abruptly, towards the column, waving her hands, shouting: "Dead Men! Dead Men!" Orien's horse spooked; Orien pitched forward, slid sideways, clutched a handful of mane, slid some more, wrapped both arms around his mare's neck, half on, half off, the whole horde of Dead Men still coming right at them. At *them*, now. Her and Orien.

Shit, shit, shit! A distant part of Myla reckoned she was right: must be pushing a thousand of the buggers. "Orien! Bad fucking time to forget how to ride a fucking horse!"

Orien's horse bucked, trying to rid itself of the annoying encumbrance around its neck. Myla caught it, grabbed Orien, and heaved him upright, turned away from the onrushing Dead Men and kicked to a canter, heading for the road. At the bottom of the hill, she saw the Regent and her guard had stopped, Orien's mistress tossing fire from hand to hand.

Oh...

As the Dead Men crested the hill behind her and Orien, Lady Novashi let fly. The air bloomed with fire, arrowing darts zipping and fizzing, hundreds at once, like the rain of ice-knives back in Deephaven, only with flames.

Shit...

Yeah, the horses did *not* like that. She had to let go of Orien's mare, her own in such complete panic that it was all she could do to stay on its back as it launched into a mad gallop sideways across the hillside, away, away from the fire, away from the screaming howling horde...

Orien!

She risked a glance over her shoulder. The hillside was a carpet of Dead Men, hundreds, thousands, rushing on, catching fire, some falling, some not. Lady Novashi – the Red Witch, the soldiers called her – flinging fire like sailors threw curses, no sign of stopping.

This was what a mage could do? No surprise Tasahre bristled at the thought of them. And Orien wanted to be like this...?

Orien! He was on the ground in the middle of it all, picking himself up, stumbling blindly. She had no idea where his horse had gone. Far away if it had any sense.

A silver rider streaked over the hill, mounted on an equally silver warhorse, scattering Lady Novashi's fire like leaves in a storm, racing through the horde of the howling dead. A Wraith. The first she'd seen since the night they'd come.

Oh, fuck! Really?

Was she ready? Didn't matter. She was who she was. She screamed and pulled on the reins, trying to make her mare stop and turn. The mare bucked and shied. No, it absolutely was *not* going back, thanks.

I am so going to regret this. Myla jumped, landed hard, rolled to her feet. Drew her swords. The Dead Men rushed on, halfway down the hill now, dropping like flies and still coming; Myla ran towards Orien, knowing she'd never get to him before the Wraith...

The Wraith crashed through the ranks of Dead Men, rode straight at Orien and then right past him. It charged the Red Witch at a full gallop. The Red Witch hurled a tornado of fire. The Wraith brushed it away. At the last, it raised its silver sword...

As the sword came down, it vanished into glittering dust. The Wraith crashed past the Red Witch, between the two black-armoured knights. The knights swung, slow and futile, like boughs of a tree trying to swipe a bolt of lightning. The Wraith shot between them, never slowing. A blink and it was through, disappearing into the trees beyond the roadside, and the black-armoured soldiers he'd struck were...

Were still on their horses. She hadn't expected that...

Orien!

Orien was running for the road, stumbling and nowhere near fast enough to outrun the onrushing Dead Men. They'd nearly caught him.

Idiot!

Another flash of silver at the top of the hill. A second Wraith, mounted on a silver-clad horse. Then a third, and a fourth. Standing on the hilltop, watching their Dead Men pour down the hill.

Fucking fuck!

Another firestorm filled the air. The Dead Men closing on Orien dropped like wheat under a scythe, but there were so *many*. Orien slowed, lit a feeble fire of his own...

No! Idiot! Keep running! She raced on towards him. A glance to the road: Lady Novashi, a mask of concentration; the Regent beside now her but with her back to the onrush of Dead Men as though they didn't matter, eyes firmly towards the trees where the first Wraith had vanished...

It would be what it would be. Myla ran into the havoc of flying fire and screaming corpses, slashing and cutting at anything that came near, a Sunsteel sword in each hand, steadfastly ignoring the voice in her head telling her how stupid this was, a voice which sounded annoyingly like mistress Tasahre, never slowing until she was at Orien's side. She flashed her teeth at him.

"Run, you stupid fuck!" *Fight until you can't* was the sword-monks' creed, but not today!

Orien's face was a rictus of fear. Dead Men swarmed at them, Myla slicing and ducking blows and barging Orien out of the way and trying to keep them both alive; there were far, far too many for even a dozen sword-monks to hold at bay, and the only reason she and Orien were still alive was the constant rain of fire and the odd way the Dead Men behaved, as though they weren't interested in *her* at all and only wanted to get past...

As she fought, she thought perhaps she understood. These weren't like the Dead Men she knew, the mindless things that stalked the streets of Varr and Deephaven. *These* Dead Men had purpose, given by the Wraiths, and that purpose was to kill Orien's mistress, the Red Witch. And maybe Orien too, because he *was* still a mage, even if he was a bit shit.

A glance to the hilltop. One Wraith on his knees, plunging his sword into the ground. The earth cracked and groaned. Down on the road, dark coils exploded from the soil, wrapping the legs of men and horses alike, dragging them down. The horses screamed and so did the men; and then the shadow-coils glittered like moonlight and were gone; and then a Dead Man was about to rip off her face, and she was back to fighting for her life...

A cold blade of ice flew past her cheek. She felt a piercing despair as if her soul was being ripped from its foundations. Tasahre's tattoos on her back were suddenly burning hot. The feeling faded, became far away, still present but as though it was happening to someone else.

Orien!

He'd fallen to his knees, weeping. A Dead Man grabbed at him. He didn't seem to notice, nor when Myla's Sunsteel sliced through the Dead Man and the thing collapsed on top of him. Thoughts entered her that weren't her own. She saw herself hanging by the neck from a lonely tree, pecked by crows. Bleeding to death from a knife in the guts, lying in a muddy hollow. An overwhelming sense of loneliness and failure...

The tattoos on her back blazed hot again. The visions remained distant. Not *her* thoughts...

Orien howled, a cry of anguish; suddenly, he was on his feet, running blindly, as fast as he could, oblivious to everything, and Myla was running after him, shouting his name, trying to keep the pursuing Dead Men from killing him.

9
A Flare in The Darkness

She caught Orien deep among the trees beyond the road. Exhausted, breathless, arms aching and burning. She tried shouting his name; when that didn't work, she settled for jogging alongside him. She supposed she *could* tackle him and bring him down, hold him until his panic subsided or else yell in his face until he did what he was told, whichever worked. On the other hand, given what was behind them, running *did* make sense. And it *was* what she'd told him to do...

She flicked a glance over her shoulder. No Dead Men.

Thank fuck. Yes, she could handle Dead Men, but not when they came mob handed and she was already close to the end of her rope.

Orien had raced down the hill and crossed the road barely a dozen yards from the Regent and the Red Witch. *That's* where the Dead Men would be. She and Orien, when it came down to it, didn't really matter...

Good.

No. Not *good. You saw a Wraith ride into these trees, remember?*

That wasn't a happy thought.

Orien was stumbling through a fog of fatigue. Myla looked around. No Wraiths that she could see. A part of her screamed to go back, to fight until she couldn't, because that was what sword-monks were for. Another part, quite a *large* part if she was honest, was discovering itself quite grateful to Orien for giving her an

57

excuse *not* to do that. She wasn't sure she liked this other part, but there it was.

She spotted Orien's horse ahead, ambling down some narrow woodland trail as though it had largely forgotten about being caught in an apocalypse of fire and the living dead only a handful of minutes ago. A relief, because now they could both climb on its back and run away some more if they had to. Always better to be on horseback when it came to Dead Men...

And Wraiths.

The horse gave her a sceptical look and trotted away, keeping its distance.

Fucking horses. Fucking Wraiths.

She hadn't seen what happened to the Wraith that had charged the Red Witch. Nearby, somewhere, in these trees, or had it gone? The others, though... Standing on the hilltop like they were waiting to see what happened? Why? A sword-monk attacked as a last resort but then attacked with everything, nothing held back. The only reason to do otherwise was when you knew an enemy was too strong to face head-on. A calculated feint, looking for weaknesses in an enemy's defence...

Was *that* what this was? The Wraiths had thought they couldn't win? But why would they think *that*? Yes, the Red Witch could likely slaughter her way through an entire continent of Dead Men judging from what Myla had now seen, but the Wraith had shrugged off her fire as though it was nothing. The one in Deephaven had done the same.

So why hold back?

Orien's horse stopped to chew on something. There was no sign of her own mare. Myla wished it well. She hoped, vaguely, that it would have the sense to keep going until it reached the open pastures around the Mirror Lakes, live a long and quiet and happy horse-life, never troubled again by Dead Men and mages and fallen half-gods. It *would* have quite a story for the other horses, she thought, so they'd probably take it in.

Orien sagged to a stop, heaving for air, propped against the trunk of a tree. His horse looked at him, then at Myla, then took a few anxious steps back. Myla could almost see what it was thinking: that they were both mad and that it wanted nothing to do with them.

"I think it's saying it doesn't want to go anywhere near that hill again," Myla said. "And that it doesn't quite trust you to be of the same mind."

"Myla!" Orien blinked as though he hadn't had the first idea what she was talking about.

"Yes. That's–" She'd been planning something vaguely caustic, but he cut her off by launching himself at her, wrapping himself around her and holding her in a crushing hug.

Ow! OW! The stab-wound in her stomach burned, the slashes on her side from the mirror-demon, the red raw skin of her freshly needled back. She weathered the pain as Orien shuddered in her arms. Fuck, was he sobbing?

"Hey! Safe now." Possibly a bit optimistic, but it was what he needed to hear.

Orien broke away, shook his head. He wouldn't look at her. "They're all dead, aren't they?" He squatted with his back to the tree, head held in his hands.

"No." She had no idea, but again it was what he needed to hear. She coaxed his horse closer, settled into loosening its girth and reins and tutting to herself. Whoever had saddled it hadn't really known what they were doing. Orien, probably.

"You should take him and go," Orien said, bitter and humourless.

"She's a mare, not a he-horse," Myla told him, thinking even Orien should have been able to spot *that*.

The horse, apparently unphased, went back to chewing on some undergrowth.

"We're going to die."

"And when we do, our souls will return to the Sun to be forged anew and be reborn," agreed Myla. "But not today."

"We'll be devoured by the Hungry Goddess and the... the..." He gasped and shuddered and groaned, as though the words were choking him. Myla let out a long sigh, trying not to lose her patience. *Still could be a Wraith nearby.* A good part of her wanted to pick Orien up and shake him. Flopping about having existential crises could wait until they were safe.

"Does your horse have a name?" she asked instead.

Orien didn't answer.

"Orien, look at me!"

It took him a few moments. When he managed, his eyes were full of despair.

"You should give her one," she said,

"Surrender. Hopelessness. Failure."

"Fuck's sake! Look, yes, it *was* a bit touch and go, I'll give you that." *Yeah, and might be touch and go here, too, any minute now if we don't get moving.* "You want to have a breakdown, have it later. You and I can both deal with Dead Men, and there can't be *that* many of them."

Well, there could, and there had been, but never mind. She squatted beside him and held his hand.

"As for those idiots in silver who seem to think this is some sort of game, Tasahre and I took one of them down in the temple in Deephaven. Rumour persists that the Regent killed one as well. If another happens along, I'll be here to protect you, and you'll be here to help me fight it." A more accurate truth was that she and Tasahre had killed the Wraith of Deephaven only after it had single-handedly destroyed the temple and murdered about a hundred priests, that at least one other monk had died, that Myla had been little more than a minor distraction, that if another Wraith came along right now, well, they'd both be dead, and yes, she'd seen at least four of the bastards while Orien had been running away, one of whom had vanished into these same trees. But he definitely didn't need to hear any of that right now.

"I'm guessing, knowing you, your horse is called Horse," she said. "Probably Mister Horse, since you apparently don't know boy-horses from girl-horses. If you came from the south, you'd probably name her Celeriac, or some other root vegetable. I think that's the fashion these days. But we're the Regent's servants, for better or for worse, and your mistress is Lady Novashi of Neja, the Red Witch, so I'm thinking we should follow a northern style, where a horse's name declares its master's demeanour to the world."

Orien got up. He didn't look like he had any idea of where he was going or what he was going to do, but hey, any movement was progress.

"It doesn't matter," he said. "The totality of their victory will obscure our utter failure. Our puny smoke will be lost in the greater conflagration."

"That's your horse's name? Bit of a mouthful, don't you think?" She sighed and held him by the shoulders and forced him to look at her again. "Do you know what I saw up there? A fuck of a lot of Dead Men on fire and a fallen half-god discovering that slicing up your mistress wasn't as easy as he'd hoped."

Orien pushed her away. "What *I* saw was men dying all around me. Soldiers, swords in hand, falling, blood streaming from their eyes. The Silver Kings moving among them, unseeing, uncaring. Where they walked, the dead rose, for the month of Storms has made way for the month of Rebirth, and all that has perished under the ice shall be reborn..." Orien put a hand to his eyes. When he drew it away, he gasped and flinched and then stared in horror as though his fingers were stained with blood. He whirled about, looking ready to bolt again. Myla grabbed him before he had the chance and held him tight.

"Hush. None of that was real."

"Everything had gone. Everyone was dead." He started sobbing again. "*You* were dead. I was the last. And all around me, they moved with eyes of vermilion sorrow. They came to me with mournful whispers in the air. *We did not wish for this*, they said. And then they killed me and moved on."

"Well, I'm not dead yet, and nor are you. But yes, I did see something like that as well." Myla pulled him closer, scanning the woods as she did. His words set her on edge. All this pseudo-poetic doom-prophetic bollocks wasn't the Orien she knew. "I saw myself hanged from a tree and pecked by crows. I saw myself bleeding out and dying in the mud somewhere. Always alone. That was the strongest feeling, that loneliness. But it wasn't *real*, Orien, none of it. Those thoughts came from the Wraiths. They were losing." A guess, but it seemed like a helpful sort of thing to say. Besides, if she was wrong and the Wraiths *had* won in the end then, well, they were all fucked, in which case she didn't want to know.

He relaxed a little. She let him go, and they walked side-by-side through the trees, leading Orien's unnamed horse. The wood was quiet, the air warm. If she tried hard enough, she could almost pretend this was nothing more than two young lovers going for a stroll. The fantasy pleased her, until Orien opened his mouth and wrecked it.

"You saw how useless I was," he said.

"We did our part." She touched his shoulder. Tempting to ride off and never look back. By now, one way or another, either everyone was dead, in which case no one would care, or else they'd won, in which case, well, Orien was right, the two of them really *hadn't* done much to help and so probably wouldn't be missed. The truth they both knew but never said was that Lady Novashi seemed to regard her erstwhile apprentice in much the same way you might regard someone else's puppy: fine for the occasional game of fetch but otherwise beneath notice. If she was honest, Myla was quietly getting quite cross about that.

Probably not the best time to be bringing that up.

"Walk with me a while," she said. "Let's give your horse a name. Then we'll see."

"Six months ago, I was a nothing in the Guild of Mages. Then I might have called him Flame In The Darkness."

"I like that. But... still a she-horse."

This earned a frown. Then Orien grinned. "Fire Ascendant!"

"Kelm's Teeth! Please, no!"

"Why not?"

"Because only a pretentious egomaniac would call their horse something like that! How about Lucky Bastard."

"I don't feel very lucky."

Myla pouted. "Take a moment to see who's standing next to you and consider whether you want to rethink that."

Orien had the sense to keep his mouth shut. After a bit, he said: "Lucky Bastard is a name for a sheep or one of those toy dogs that became fashionable a few winters back. How about *Inferno*?"

Still awful, she thought, but let him have it. Better than *Fire Ascendant*.

Behind them, the horse that might now be *Inferno* snorted.

"Oh, now everyone has an opinion, do they? Little Puff of Smoke? Seems apt since my sorcery is so feeble that Silver Kings bathe in my flames as though they're nothing."

"They bathed in your mistress's flames as though they were nothing too," Myla said. "In case that helps."

They found a stream, stopped to drink, then walked in silence. The day grew older, the sun rose higher. Under the canopy of leaves, their shadows grew smaller.

"Lost in the Woods?" suggested Myla. "Because we will be, if we're not careful."

Orien turned to her, his face all serious. "You may laugh at this, and I don't blame you. But here's an oath for you, under sky and sun and all these trees. When I next turn my fire on a fallen half-god, they *will* feel it."

"As I drive my swords through whatever is under that silvered armour." Myla grinned, and then Orien grinned too, and now, at last, she had him back. "I suppose we should return and see how it ended." She didn't much want to. The woods were peaceful, and when had she last had any of that? Days? Weeks? Months? Almost a year since her stupidity with Sarwatta Hawat. And it *had* been stupid. No sense pretending otherwise. A year of running and fighting and then running some more.

Then again, if she hadn't fled to Deephaven and fallen in with Fings and Seth and the rest of the Unrulys, she wouldn't be here now, with Orien. They would never have met.

"I suppose," Orien sniffed.

"Well… We *could* wander the wilderness for a few years, you unravelling the secrets of your inner fire, me honing my sword forms." She wrapped an arm around him. "Return to Varr, wild and threadbare, to find it besieged by Dead Men, the Empire on the brink of collapse. You'll conjure a firestorm to make even Lady Novashi applaud while I take the heads of your Silver Kings one by one?"

And gold would fall from the sky into magic pots that followed at their feet, and the Regent would honour them with titles and a see-you-later wink. It made her smile. A girl could dream, couldn't she? And there had to be *some*thing, something other than the bleak and inevitable despair of the Wraiths.

"And then what?"

"A house in the country, somewhere warm and sunny? Some little Mylas and Oriens running about the place?"

"I'm not sure about that. The idea of small children who excel at both stabbing things *and* throwing fire somehow fills me with trepidation."

She laughed at that. "Fair, I suppose." None of it would ever happen, of course, but they were both smiling, and that was what mattered.

"Not Flame," said Orien. "Flare. I'm going to call him Flare in the Darkness."

"Still a she-horse!" Myla said and kissed him on the cheek. "You *do* know how to tell the difference right?"

10
The Popinjay

The road, when they returned, was a hellscape. Charred corpses, the stench of burned cloth, hair and skin, enough to make Myla gag. No dead Wraith, no dead soldiers. No evidence to say which way it had gone: either the Red Witch had burned all the Dead Men and someone, somehow, had dealt with the Wraiths, or else they hadn't, in which case the horde was presumably tearing its way further up the road, carving slaughter through the Deephaven refugees. She stopped and listened and didn't hear distant screams. Didn't hear much of anything except a lot of delighted crows, agitating for her to go away so they could get on with things.

They found the Regent and her black-armoured guard back at the rear of the column, riding as though nothing had happened. She had fewer soldiers with her – possibly because they were dead, possibly because they were further up the column, spreading the news of her victory. It *was* possible, Myla supposed, that they were looking for her and Orien; but from the way Lady Novashi didn't seem to notice Orien's return, Myla reckoned probably not.

"We won, then," she tried.

This earned a nod from one of the Regent's hawks. They were grim and haunted-looking and clearly wanted her to go away.

"We killed the Wraiths?" Myla persisted. Sword-monks were never good at taking hints. "Are they dead? If so, how?"

Stony silence. Victory was victory, wasn't it?

Oh well. I had a nice walk in the woods, I suppose.

The raw fury of the Red Witch had been fearsome, yet Myla couldn't shake the feeling that Lady Novashi wasn't the real power here. She remembered how the Wraith's sword had turned to dust in the moment he'd been about to take the sorceress's head. How, when demons had come through mirrors back in Deephaven, the Regent had turned three into ash with a single flash of moonlight.

"Our Moon-Witch is equal to them, then?" she tried.

The Hawks ignored her. She considered asking the Regent herself, then thought better of it.

Since no one was in the mood to offer answers, and since her horse had decided to bugger off to live its best life somewhere quiet rather than get caught up in a war of mages, she was left to trot along on foot. She reached the vanguard tired and covered in dust, smelling of manure and in a bad mood. The sword-monks there paid her as much attention as Lady Novashi gave Orien, a reminder of where she stood; still, she made a nuisance of herself until she found the sword-mistress in a cart, a little way behind the head of the column, a monk sitting beside her. The Taiytakei popinjay was riding alongside, the monk in the cart regarding him with such a glare that Myla reckoned a careless person might cut themselves on it.

She climbed into the cart. Tasahre was so still and pale that she might have been dead except for the slight rise and fall of her chest. Her skin shone with sweat.

"I keep telling this one: that wound is poisoned," called the popinjay. "She'll die if you don't do something."

"No one asked you," snapped the monk. He shot Myla a look. "When we reach the City of Spires, the Moon Priestesses will do their work."

The City of Spires was probably three weeks away, at the speed the column was making. Myla shook her head. "One way or another, she won't need them by the time we get there."

"No," said the popinjay. "Because she'll be dead. You have a day at best."

"Go away!" The monk gave Myla a baleful look. "You, too."

"I was with her when she took that, you know." Tasahre was a mess. Someone had cleaned the blood, but the creature's talons had ripped her deep, worse than Myla had thought. The wound was covered with moss and honey; but no one walked easily away from an injury like this, poison or no.

"You're Orien's roll in the hay, aren't you?" called the popinjay. Myla scowled.

"I hear you faced a Wraith. Why aren't you dead?"

It was a pity she didn't have an answer; she would have enjoyed not telling him.

It started to rain. The popinjay sighed and bowed his head. "As I've been telling your friend here, I *could* help her."

The sword-monk beside Tasahre shook his head.

"As your better half may have observed to you, I am, among other things, a healer."

Myla blinked. "You want some holes put in you so you can get in some practice?" Better half? Roll in the hay? He could go bugger himself with *that* nonsense.

"Oh! Feisty!"

"You will not touch our sword-mistress, mage," said the monk beside her.

The popinjay sighed, theatrically sorrowful. "The restoration of something broken requires more skill than smashing it to bits with a hammer and is thus inevitably more satisfying, but I can go either way if I have to. I'm good at what I do. It's such a pity you're all idiots." He rode away.

"I can't be the only one who wants to stab him," Myla said.

"There's a queue," agreed the monk.

The rain turned to a steady downpour. That was Deephaven for you. It would come hard for an hour and then stop, like it did almost every afternoon through the months of Rebirth and Floods. Myla helped the monk raise an awning over the back of the wagon, then settled to wait. She wondered what the column would do as the sun set. Push on or hunker down? Either way, that was when the Dead Men would come again, if they came at all. Tasahre would have known what to do, but it looked more and more like the sword-mistress was preparing to make her peace with the Sun instead. She twitched and moaned until Myla had to look away. Tasahre had taught Myla to fight – not only with her swords but with everything – had taught her to keep her head when others panicked, taught her to look calmly at wherever she found herself, confront the biggest threat and dare it to do its worst. She'd taught Myla that a sword-monk fought until she couldn't, that death didn't matter because the Sun would take her into its forge of souls. She'd taught Myla to show whatever mercy she could because that was the way of the sword-monk. Fearless compassion. Once mastered, Tasahre said, the world would sit and beg for you like a hopeful puppy.

Now Tasahre was dying, and there were threats everywhere. And yes, Myla could fight a dozen Dead Men and win, but if she tried to face a Wraith, she'd lose; and so, right now, the biggest threat of all was that Tasahre would leave them.

They needed her. They all did.

Myla needed her, at any rate.

And so, as the light began to fail, as the column halted for the night and Tasahre slipped steadily away, Myla stole into the darkness, thinking to find Orien and take what comfort she could, and that she was a coward for not staying to the end. She found the mage among the rear-guard, sitting by a fire with the popinjay, the two of them alone; and that was when Myla understood she hadn't come looking for Orien at all, but the Taiytakei popinjay.

"In other days, perhaps," the popinjay was saying, "but this is no time for charity. You have the talent to learn but the raw power is missing."

Myla paused, lurking in the gloom. There was something off about this mage. She'd felt it from the moment she'd seen him. Something she didn't like that was more than his irritating manner.

If I don't do this, Tasahre will die.

"We all have our limits." The popinjay clapped Orien on the shoulder and sighed. "Even you, sword-monk. Yes, I feel you lurking in the darkness. I know why you're here, so you might as well come out and ask."

Myla came and sat at the fire beside Orien, leaning into him. They could both do with that, she thought. "Well?"

The popinjay raised an eyebrow. "Our mighty sorceresses have raised a barrier against the Dead Men and their half-god masters." He bared his teeth. "If they fail, I dare say we'll be dead by dawn." He gave Myla a sharp look. "You *do* understand that we're at the end of something here, not the beginning?"

Myla glared, not understanding at all. "No, I don't. Perhaps you could explain?"

The popinjay shook his head. "You'd need a warlock to do *that* justice. Which I'm not, in case you were wondering."

"What *are* you, then?"

The popinjay considered this, then abruptly rose and took a step closer, by which time Myla was on her feet as well, revisiting some earlier stabbing-related thoughts. The popinjay offered his hand and smiled. Myla gave it a look as though it was a snake. After a second, he withdrew and sat down again. Wary, Myla did the same.

"I *am* a healer, among other things," he said. "I had quite a name for it once. A different name from the one I wear now. It was a *long* time ago." He gave Myla a little glance then, a flash of something old and angry. "Ask what you came to ask, sword-monk."

Myla kept watching his eyes. "What's a Taiytakei doing living in Deephaven?"

"Is that what I am?"

"Clearly."

In a blink, the popinjay transformed, the darkness draining from his night-black skin until he was as pale as moonlight. "And what about now?"

Myla wanted to tell him that *now* he looked like a white-skinned idiot instead of a black-skinned idiot, or maybe that he looked like a ghost; but the words stuck in her throat. *Tasahre is dying!*

The popinjay's skin returned to its usual midnight black. "My people don't have mages. You are either an Artificer or an Enchantress or else an anathema, and thus prey for the Elemental Men."

"For the *what*?" asked Orien.

"Sorcery broke the world," said the popinjay. "The half-gods did it, not us, but the Elemental Men aren't bothered by the difference. Their purpose is to ensure it never happens again." He smiled a nasty toothy grin. "I can tell you this: they're going to get *absurdly* over-excited when they learn what's happened here. A sorceress who can face down a Wraith? Bring down a dragon? They'll shit themselves! Yes, we'll have some *very* interesting times when *that* happens. When it does, my advice is to be far away. But for now... well, they live in another world, and it will take time for the news to reach them." He set his eyes on Myla. "Ask what you came to ask."

"*Can* you heal Tasahre?"

"Yes."

"And what will it cost me?"

"Nothing." He glanced at Orien. "Might cost *him* something, though."

"What?"

The popinjay sniffed. "A patron. The Guild, the throne, some enlightened nobleman. North or South, Sun or Moon, I do not care, simply that I be left in peace. However, I think I might aim high on this occasion. What I require in exchange for your sword-mistress's life is an audience with Her Highness."

Myla laughed. "And you think Orien can do that?"

"Hey!"

The popinjay bared his teeth again. "I think *together* you might. The sword-mistress's right arm and the Red Witch's apprentice? Yes, I think you might. I have information, you see, about the enemy."

Myla snorted. "I'm a long way from being Tasahre's right arm."

"You fought while others fled." The popinjay poked a finger at her. "You'd do well to remember that. Courage, loyalty, integrity, these will matter in the days to come. Besides, you *did* kill a Wraith. And you..." The popinjay fixed Orien with a look so penetrating that it froze Orien as thoroughly as if two hands had gripped to his shoulders. "I've shown you what I took from Deephaven. You *know* she'll want to know about *that*. I'm almost doing you a favour!"

"And what *did* you take from Deephaven?" asked Myla, quite enjoying the idea that maybe the popinjay was secretly an assassin trying to get close to the Regent to indulge in a bit of murdering. It didn't seem likely, but it *would* mean that no one would mind her sticking a sword though him. He was starting to remind her of Sulfane.

"That's between me and your witch-queen," said the popinjay. He looked at them both. "Yes, or no?"

Orien nodded. After a moment, so did Myla. *Find the biggest threat. Face it and dare it to do its worst.* Well, the world offered a rich selection of threats right now; and while she couldn't shake the thought that the popinjay was one of them, he certainly wasn't the biggest. So yes, she'd go along with this. Not that Tasahre would thank her, if she ever found out.

The same sword-monk was standing watch as they reached Tasahre's wagon. Myla sighed. She *could* try feminine wiles followed by a quick kick in the balls, she supposed, but he probably wouldn't fall for it. Same problem with punching him out: he was a monk, so it might not work, and then she'd have to fight him, which would be noisy and messy and need a lot of explaining even if she won, which she might not. She *could* try simply telling him the truth, she supposed, but monks *really* didn't like mages, and the popinjay hadn't exactly endeared himself to anyone.

She sighed. Sword-monks, frankly, could be a bit of a pain in the arse.

The monk's eyes drooped with fatigue. Myla sighed and went to sit beside him.

"Tasahre was my teacher," she said. "I'm going to sit a vigil here through the night whether you like it or not, so you might as well go and get some sleep. Fuck knows we could all do with some."

She was a bit surprised when that worked. A few moments later, Orien and the popinjay sidled out of the darkness.

"You might want to be somewhere else while I do this," the popinjay said.

"Leave you alone with her? Over my dead body."

"I *could* arrange that."

"I'd like to see you try."

"You really wouldn't."

They glared at one another. Eventually, the popinjay sighed and put his hands to Tasahre's skin.

"I *could* bring her right back," he said. "Fix everything and have her wake up right as rain. Or I could be subtle. Do enough to be sure but leave her body to do the bulk of the work. Her recovery will be slower that way and will take weeks, but she'll never know. Will she approve of my... intervention?"

There *was* a lot to be said to having Tasahre back on her feet, yelling and shouting and generally giving everyone a hard time and getting things done.

"No," Myla said. "If she ever knows about this, she'll take my head. And then yours too, probably."

"Well... *I* can always grow a new one. I don't suppose you can, though."

Myla closed her eyes and sighed. *Fine.* "Better she doesn't know." She hated to be doing this. It was, in more ways than one, a betrayal.

The popinjay lifted his hands away. "Right. That's that, then."

"That's *it*?"

"What were you hoping for? Fireworks?" He bared his teeth in that grin he seemed to think was a smile and climbed out of the cart. "We have a pact, yes? You and I and your better half?"

Myla gritted her teeth. *Don't stab him! He's not worth it!*

After the popinjay was gone, Myla settled beside Tasahre. She'd meant what she'd said about keeping vigil.

"I'm sorry," she whispered, "but I can't let you go, not yet."

Given a choice, Tasahre would never accept help from a mage. Myla tried, half-heartedly, telling her conscience to get lost; but that rarely worked even at the best of times, and certainly wasn't going to work now.

A rumble of thunder echoed through the night. Before long, rain ran in rivers from the awning. Myla huddled inside, a hundred questions full of caution and warning buzzing in her head. She'd do what she could to honour her pact with the popinjay. It seemed a small price, somehow. When he got his audience, she'd make sure she was there to sniff out any lies; but until that time, her place was at her sword-mistress's side, to see for herself that the popinjay's sorcery had been honest; and so that was where she stayed as the column moved on, as the days stretched into one another, becoming a week and then a twelvenight. No matter how the other monks glared and did everything short of drawing a blade to let her know she wasn't welcome, she didn't move. Tasahre's fever broke. A few days and the sword-mistress was eating again; a few more and she was trying to get about, snapping at anyone who tried to help, generally being as irritable as fuck, all of which Myla took as a sure sign of recovery. By the end of the second week, she was sparring again, though it broke Myla's heart how quickly the sword-mistress tired. And, of course, since Myla wouldn't go away, *she* was the one who bore the brunt of Tasahre's frustration.

She took it. Didn't mind, as long she had an hour or two with Orien each night to vent some spleen. The popinjay, it seemed, *had* done honest work. Maybe she was wrong about him?

"We will have our audience," Orien told her, two weeks after they'd left Deephaven. "When we reach the City of Spires."

She was with him again a few nights later when the word reached them. No crack of lightning to herald the moment, only the two of them bedded down for the night in yet another abandoned village, taking comfort in one another. Or, as the popinjay liked to put it – and yes, she mostly still wanted to stab him – fucking like rabbits. Call it what you like, that was what they were doing when the whisper drifted down the column and rather spoiled the mood.

The City of Spires is gone.

INTERLUDE
Repent at Leisure

On the night the Wraiths came to Deephaven, the popinjay had gone for a little jaunt to the temple. He was quite sure the city was doomed, on account of the enemy consisting of the city's own dead citizens, inconveniently lively, supplemented by a horde of relentless homicidal maniacs with no apparent sense of self-preservation – he had no idea where *they'd* come from – guided by a handful of interestingly dangerous half-gods and, startlingly, an actual dragon. Knowing himself no match for either a dragon or a half-god, he was leaving the fighting to others and, unusually for him, being inconspicuous.

It had turned out worthwhile, that jaunt to the temple. He'd seen the Wraith bring down the dome, had been rather surprised at two sword-monks managing to get the better of it, and then very surprised indeed when they simply left its decapitated body in the rubble.

They don't know?

Everyone was rather busy after that, what with a dragon and hordes of Dead Men making a mess everywhere; and then someone, somehow, brought the dragon crashing down and killed it, collapsing several large buildings and a particularly tall tower in the process. If the temple falling hadn't caused enough of a distraction, *that* certainly did the trick.

Their loss, my gain. In the chaos, he helped himself to the dead Wraith, torso and head both. A sword-monk had challenged him, demanded an explanation – duly given, something about running errands for mages – and then let him go, having more important things to worry about, and so he slipped away back to his lair, alone in the old temple to the Moon where he treated Deephaven's terminally ill as a way to keep attention from his... other activities.

Time was clearly short, so he made the most of it. Fortunately, he always had his journals close to hand.

Sunday, fifth week in the month of Rebirth (following Equinox festival). Subject appears encased in metallic armour.

The chance of a lifetime: to study a half-god. Although, in retrospect, it perhaps *had* been a mistake leading that warlock-wannabe into the House of Cats and Gulls. The obliteration of the city he'd called home for half a century hadn't been the outcome he'd had in mind.

Cause of death... Well, not having a head, thanks to a pair of monks with their sigil-etched skin and their Sunsteel swords. Wraith-killers, even if they barely remembered that was what they were for.

There was something *else* in Deephaven, though. Something strong enough to knock a dragon out of the sky which made it a something he *really* didn't want to think about; but he'd have to, sooner or later. Half-gods were bad enough; but if the Elemental Men ever caught whisper of a sorcerer who could take on a dragon... well, he *really* didn't want to think about the consequences, other than to ensure he was far away when they came...

The armour is segmented and reminiscent of certain insects. Skin below the neck all covered. Predominantly silver in colour. No apparent clasps or fastenings. Blades, curved, attached to the outside of the forearm. Forged of the same metal as the armour. No indication of welds, seams, or other evidence of construction. Armour gives every indication of growing naturally from the skin of the wearer. Carapace? Etched with markings, numerous, significance unknown.

Unknown but akin to the tattoos worn by the monks who'd killed it.

He put down his pen and tapped the silvery skin of the body, ran his fingernails and then his fingertips over its surfaces, then picked up a fine surgical knife, stained blue from his earlier dissection of whatever had hauled itself out of a mirror that afternoon, apparently with some misguided intention of eating him.

He began tracing the etchings in the armour with his finger; when the etching began to glow, he quickly stopped. A soft light, so dim that if he hadn't been in such a gloomy room, he might not have seen it.

The distant screams were subsiding. It was almost over. Ah well. Deephaven wouldn't be the first city he'd been forced to flee.

He picked up the severed head and ran his fingers through the dead half-god's hair, noting its lustre. *Appearance suggestive of an albino. Hair white but full and has the texture of youth. Muscular development requires internal examination. Facial features show little subcutaneous fat. Suggestive of Torpreah, or (more likely) Anvor. Average height. Teeth all present, no sign of deterioration. Eyes reddish-black, supporting the supposition that the subject is albino.*

The bodies of the dead mostly left him unmoved; all he wanted was to open them up and understand what had made them fail. But not here. Here, he felt as though he was staring at perfection.

Ah well. Even perfection didn't last.

He opened his roll of surgical tools and tried various implements on the armour. None made a scratch. He noted this down, then picked up a saw and stared at the skull. The solar monk who'd stopped him as he'd carted the body from the fallen temple hadn't said anything about not cutting it up. Most likely, it hadn't occurred to her that anyone would want to.

He peeled back the scalp and put it carefully to one side. Wigmakers paid well for a good quality scalp. *Size and shape normal. No evidence of abnormalities.* Sawing open a skull without damaging the organ inside was always a challenge. *Thickness normal. No immediate evidence of injury.* He remembered thinking he should really stop, not stopping even as he thought it...

But then he *did* stop, because there it was. The thing he'd hoped for, nestled between the two lobes of the brain, buried deep, almost out of sight. Something he'd never seen before, glowing with a bright moonlight silver.

He stared at it for a bit, then hurriedly started packing.

Three weeks and several hundred miles later, he still thought about that night, that moment. He wasn't sure it was wise to reveal the secret he'd found, but it was a little late for doubt. An impulsive request, but he *would* need somewhere quiet where he could continue his work in peace once this was all over.

He'd had a good chat with the dead Wraith on the road from Deephaven. He knew why they'd come and what they were after. Turned out it really *had* been a mistake, leading that warlock-wannabe into the House of Cats and Gulls. The obliteration of a city? Oh, they had bigger plans than that.

Ah well. So yes, he *would* share what he knew, because these poor souls *did* need to know what they were up against.

Tasahre, too, was thinking about that night, about what she knew and what she didn't. In the monasteries of Torpreah, they told stories of how the four gods of the Sun, the Moon, the Stars and the Earth had sprung from the Void. How men were children of the Sun, how the long-departed ephemeral spirits were children of the ethereal Infinite Mistress, how the Wraith she'd fought in the Temple of Deephaven had once been a child of the Moon.

In those stories from Torpreah, back when Deephaven had been nothing but a distant name on a map, the Earth Goddess had raised the Black Moon into the sky to blot out the sun. The half-gods in their citadels of sorcery had found a way to bring it down, then departed when the power they unleashed had shattered the world. Amid the strife that followed, the Paths of the Sun and the Moon were born.

In Deephaven, in the possessions of the warlock Saffran Kuy, she'd found different stories. Lies and falsehoods, but she nonetheless read them, thinking they might help her better understand her enemy. In these heresies, she found no consistency. The Silver Kings were sometimes noble allies, other times monsters and enslavers. The Hungry Goddess had been killed, bound, bargained with, or had simply relented.

There *had* been a war, they all agreed on that. A Silver King *had* mastered a power to bind the Hungry Goddess. Different names in different places: Seturakah; Black Moon; Splinterer of Worlds, saviour or destroyer, but he was always there. Some called him The Silver King, gleefully conflating all the half-gods with the single one who'd bound a goddess and in doing so had broken the world.

Lies and heresies, but she'd come to understand the warlock's belief in the years after he'd gone, that the Splinterer of Worlds had found something beyond the Gods and mastered it, that the shattering of the world had been the last gasp of a desperate Goddess, taking him deep inside her, the only way to keep in check whatever he'd unleashed.

Saffran Kuy. Sixteen years and still he haunted her. She'd been naïve, young, not fully inked, far from the peak of her skill. Going after him alone had been a mistake. She'd put both swords right through him; good enough, as it had turned out, to kill a Wraith, yet not enough for Kuy. She'd caught him a second time, as he was about to flee. His thief-taker had surprised her. She'd very nearly died. Kuy had escaped.

A second mistake. There wouldn't be a third.

Years later, sword-mistress of Deephaven and with the power to send spies across the sea, she learned that Saffran Kuy had been killed by the thief-taker's apprentice. The boy was a mercenary king now, raising merry chaos in some far-away corner of another world. The Bloody Judge, they called him. A killer with a hatred for warlocks, they said, and she took comfort from that. Still kept a spy watching him, though she wasn't sure why it mattered.

Was Kuy dead? Someone had gone into the House of Cats and Gulls on the night the Wraiths made Deephaven into a necropolis.

Someone had left that demon to stand guard. Someone had taken whatever Kuy had hidden all those years ago and had left a single symbol, the sign of what had once been the Twelfth House of the Empire, extinguished from history by the usurper-emperor Khrozus and his general, the Levanya; and yes, Khrozus was long gone, but the Levanya was very much alive, lurking in the shadows behind this sorceress, this Princess-Regent, his great-niece, who somehow also happened to be in Deephaven when the Wraiths came. Hard, too, not to remember that the year Tasahre had driven Kuy from Deephaven had been the year the Sad Empress had given birth to this Moon-Witch. On the first morning of the new year, they said, a day of bright portents and powerful omens; but whispers she'd heard since said otherwise, that the birth had been in the night, after the sun had set forever on that year, when Fickle Lord Moon reigned unchecked, and all omens were reversed. Tasahre rarely put stock in such things, but still...

Someone *had* come to Deephaven these last few weeks, kindling old ashes back into flames.

Two mistakes. There wouldn't be a third.

PART TWO
Seth

If Gods can read minds then the trick to betraying them is never having the first inkling you're about to do it.
– Seth

II
Audience

Myla sat in the back of the cart with Tasahre as they passed the place where the City of Spires should have been. Tasahre was back to inking Myla's skin as she had in Deephaven, which at least gave the sword-mistress something to do that wasn't shouting at people. Where towers and temples and the five great spires had once stood, now sat a lake of almost supernaturally still water. The column trudged on, but Myla felt it falter. The City of Spires had been a promise of sanctuary. Now, people had started to leave, a trickle that would soon be a flood. Setting their own paths.

"No surprise they're abandoning us," said Tasahre, and Myla had to agree. Two thousand refugees squashed along the imperial road to Varr, no idea where they were going, only what they were running from. Their supplies were exhausted. Everyone was foraging. There wasn't enough food. People were hungry. *She* was hungry.

And where was the danger? Since the hill outside Deephaven, no one had seen a single Dead Man. People *had* died, yes, but from injury, sickness, accidents, fights. She knew of at least three murders. Things being as they were, now was a good time for settling scores.

"We could have done better," Myla said, "with how we shared what we had. I could have helped with that." As the daughter of a merchant, she probably knew more about logistics than all the other sword-monks put together.

"Then that's what you should have done instead of gluing yourself to my side like a lovesick puppy."

Myla ignored that. "Dozens slip away every day. I've watched them go. We'll lose them by the hundred soon." Did they know where they were headed, or were they simply sick of following a bunch of sword-monks who frankly didn't know any better than anyone else what they were doing?

"We will now." Tasahre paused briefly from her work and tipped her head at the empty lake.

"Most people think we're lost. I wish they were right. How can a whole city simply disappear?"

Tasahre grunted something which could have meant almost anything, but in this case, Myla suspected, meant the sword-mistress didn't have a clue. "I imagine the Moon Priestesses saw what happened to Deephaven and didn't fancy being next."

"Oh, and cities do that, do they? Take a look at what's coming, think to themselves, 'nuh uh, buggered if I'm having a piece of *that'*, and up and vanish? So... what? During Khrozus' Revolt, Varr and Deephaven were both having a bit of a snooze and got caught off guard?"

"They can vanish when they have five Moonspires," said Tasahre softly.

She stopped stabbing needles into Myla's skin. Up ahead, a dozen riders were forcing their way against the flow of the column. A pair of soldiers led them, but the rest were in blue. Blue robes. Myla remembered what *that* meant.

"Mages."

"Apparently so."

"Fuck."

"Quite."

Myla blew out a long breath. "I have something to tell you."

"And I you, but both must wait." With that, Tasahre clambered off the cart and heaved herself onto a horse, heading for the mages, probably to threaten them for the sake of appearances before letting them through. The sword-mistress wasn't her old self, not yet, but she was on the mend. By the time they reached Varr, she'd be back to making Myla look like a novice again.

Which made Myla smile, because that was as it should be.

She kept smiling as she watched Tasahre with the mages, imagining their conversation, then stopped, thinking of the conversation she ought to be having with Orien. When Tasahre didn't immediately return, Myla went to look for him, found him, and somehow still didn't have it. Which was awkward, because there was something he needed to hear, and it was bothering her, but she didn't quite know how to tell him.

Lady Novashi summoned them that evening. They found the sorceress by a fire at the lakeside in the darkness, clustered with six mages in blue Guild robes around her, the mages from earlier in the afternoon. Irritatingly, the popinjay was there too. Another few minutes and so was Tasahre, along with three more sword-monks.

"This is a first," muttered Orien. "Monks and mages working together."

"Well. Not really." Myla leaned into him, enjoying his warmth, still vexed because she hadn't told him the thing he needed to hear.

"Could be we're just going to have a big fight. You know, to see who gets to boss the other around."

"There's something I need to tell you." The second time today she's said that to someone.

"What?"

"Not now. But remind me later."

The popinjay plonked down beside Orien, touching him on the shoulder and wiggling his fingers. "A little something to perk you up? A touch of the old enchantments. Same thing I've been doing on the horses to keep them going?"

"Oh, so now he's a horse, is he?" Myla raised an eyebrow. "What's going on and why are *you* a part of it?" She vaguely hoped the popinjay wouldn't have a good answer and would slink away into the night. Instead, he beamed.

"Ah, my stabby friend! Your better half has honoured our pact. Took his time about it, but here we are. The only mages to act in Deephaven's defence!"

"Really? And what, exactly, did *you* do?"

The popinjay ignored her. "And the two monks who faced a half-god and not only survived but killed it. The only one, as far as I know, unless the rumours of our glorious Moon-Witch's exploits in Deephaven are true."

Myla frowned, thinking of the hill outside Deephaven. *Those got away, then?*

Yes, said a voice in her head; and for a moment, the world popped right out of focus, and then popped back again. Myla yelped and jumped and looked around, but there was no one there.

I didn't have the chance to properly end him.

"Who are you? Where…?"

The popinjay clapped Orien on the shoulder and said something he obviously thought amusing, both apparently oblivious.

You know exactly who I am, said the voice in her head.

She *did* know, too. There was timbre she recognised. From that night…

On the bridge in Varr.

Yes.

When you returned my brother's crown.

Just a few words exchanged between them. "You said a storm was coming from the sea. Is this what you meant?"

And you replied that your teacher would say that it is we *who must be the storm. I liked that.*

Yes. She remembered that.

And there she is, and Myla knew they were both looking at Tasahre. *And here are you, and you* do *know who I am, and we* will *be the storm.*

"Your Majesty?" Myla's thoughts stumbled over one another. It was hard to keep them in order. Hard not to be angry, too, at being intruded into like this. "Why do I only hear you in my head?"

I am not the emperor. Your Highness is appropriate. Shall we continue as we are, or shall I come into the light and speak openly so that everyone may hear what we have to say? What is your choice?

"I imagine you'll do as you wish, Your Highness."

How very considerate. Yes, thank you, I will. And there is no need for you to speak. I will know what you wish to say.

Suddenly, Myla was back in Deephaven. She saw herself arrive, the fight by the docks, conversations with Tasahre, the white ship on the river in the dead of night, saving her sister from Sarwatta Hawat, knives of ice falling from the sky, Dead Men everywhere, the battle in the temple between Tasahre and the half-god...

She was in Varr, at night, on a bridge. Showing the Moonsteel Crown to Orien...

...Fighting through narrow alleys. Putting Dead Men down with Sunsteel...

...The column leaving. Slipping away to the House of Cats and Gulls. What they'd found there, what Tasahre had said...

She tried to fight that last bit, what Tasahre had said about the Regent not being what she seemed, knowing more than she was saying, telling Myla to get close if she could. Futile. Stopping the memories was like trying to stop a river armed only with a bucket of sand.

"I really don't appreciate you doing this!" It was about the best she could manage.

...Riding from the city. The battle on the hilltop. The distant sense of dreadful futility and despair that had sent Orien howling, running for the woods...

...Going after him...

Lift your eyes to mine.

Myla did as she was told, unsure whether she was doing it because she wanted to or because she didn't have a choice. There might have been a hundred other people around her or none; all she could see was the brilliance of the sapphire throne, a small dark-skinned figure sitting in it, dressed in white, surrounded by blue, two emerald eyes boring into her own, dissolving everything into cascades of joyous chords, while far away, a voice of many melodies spoke in the celestial rhymes of creation...

A throne? We're by a fucking lake! Get out of my head! Get OUT!

Abruptly, Myla found herself back on the lakeshore, staring at the Princess-Regent, exactly as they'd been on that bridge in Varr. The only thing that hadn't been an illusion were those eyes...

"You'll do," said the Regent.

"Do for what?" *She's shorter than me,* Myla thought, and then: *what would happen if I punched her in the face?* Because she *did* quite want to, all things considered.

I'd probably stop time and stab you a few times and then set you on fire. Something like that. The Regent's eyes never flinched; Myla had no idea whether that had been intended as a joke or as a real threat, but she *was* a sword-monk, and so she was buggered if she was going to lose a staring contest with a mage.

Behind her, Tasahre cleared her throat.

People tend to think of mages as old men. I prefer sorceress.

How about Moon-Witch?

Tasahre cleared her throat again. Forcefully enough for Myla to wonder briefly whether there was something wrong with her.

There'd better not be. Especially given that secret you haven't quite got around to sharing with her.

Get out of my head!

I see your fear. The Taiytakei did as he promised. No more, no less.

GET! OUT!

Tasahre cleared her throat so loudly that Myla swore she felt the air shake. She blinked.

"I heard music," said the popinjay, his eyes full of wonder. "Did anyone else hear music? What was it? It was beautiful!"

He wasn't alone. The mages looked dazed; and it dawned on Myla that whatever the Regent had done, she'd done it to *all* of them, all at once, all in their own private little worlds, except perhaps Tasahre, who merely looked irritated, and Lady Novashi, who looked like she'd seen all this before and found it all slightly embarrassing.

If it helps, you pushed back harder than most. I even felt it.

There was a devil inside Myla sometimes, one which tended to come out at unfortunate moments; now, apparently, was one of them. She stood up and faced the Princess-Regent – someone to whom she should be kowtowing with her face planted in the dirt – and scowled. "If you do that again, I will slap you as I would slap an unruly child!"

The silence was quite something. She could almost hear Orien willing himself to cease existing, right there beside her. Even Tasahre, who'd known Myla most her life and really shouldn't have been surprised, froze for a moment with her mouth hanging open.

The Regent waggled her head, clucked her tongue, and nodded to Tasahre. "I'll keep this one. She can spy for you, as you asked, and pass on all the secrets you think I'm hiding." She crossed the circle of firelight then, finally giving Myla a chance to get a good look at her. A calf-length coat of black Moonsteel mail, half-hidden under skirts of vermillion and gold that hung from her waist. The black armour had a way of merging with the night, making her look at first glance like a disembodied head floating above a pillar of dull surly fire. Myla wondered whether the effect was an accident, or whether it had been designed that way.

The Regent settled with her back to them all, facing the water. "And now we wait," she said.

They waited. After a few minutes of nothing, a quiet murmur of conversation resumed between the blue-robed guild mages and Lady Novashi, Orien straining to hear but not daring to move closer, Tasahre and her monks sitting still, eyes closed, doubtless picking out every word. Sorcerer-talk and politics. From what reached Myla, the Lords of the South were refusing to swear allegiance to the new Regency, preferring to raise an army and march on Varr. Apparently, Deephaven being attacked by half-gods and Dead Men had struck someone as a fine time to start a civil war.

Fucking idiots.

And then the moon rose, and the murmurs fell silent, and all watched as five great towers shimmered into view beneath the still waters of the lake, then temples and streets and squares and people. The City of Spires. Or its reflection, at least.

How? How did they do that? A hundred questions hung in the air.

"Traitors," muttered one of the mages.

I was born here. Thoughts inside her head again. Then, abruptly, the Regent rose. "Show everyone what you wanted me to see," she said. She didn't turn away from the lake as she said it.

The popinjay reached into a sack and pulled out a large glass jar. He held it up. Inside was a silvery serpent, about the length of a handspan and glowing with bright silver light.

Moonlight...

"Best we have no secrets," said the Regent. "Don't you think?"

From someone who'd come rummaging uninvited inside her head, that seemed a bit rich, frankly. Myla bit her tongue so as not to say so out loud, then realised that not saying it out loud probably didn't make any difference. *Fuck's sake!*

The popinjay looked sheepish, so it wasn't *all* bad. "Yes. Of course. I, ah... Found this inside a dead half-god's head. Well..." he frowned.

"A dead half-god's head?" asked Tasahre.

"Er... yes."

"And where, exactly, did you get one of those?"

"Er... To get to the point... those Soulsilver knights are merely shells. Or perhaps, *vessel* would be a better word." He gave the jar a bit of a shake. "*This* is an actual half-god. Which is why, if you ever kill another, you need to kill *this* bit. Otherwise... well, otherwise they just pull it out and put it inside someone else and there you go, a new knight of Soulsilver and you're right back where you started. Even a Dead Man will do, and it's not as if there's a shortage of those after–"

"We get the idea," said Tasahre.

The Regent turned to her mages. "You will find a place in the Kaveneth for this man to work. You will learn from each other. You will find a way to stop them. Spill your secrets tonight. All of you. Don't let them fester, for they will do you no good." For a moment, as the Regent faltered, Myla thought she saw her for what she was: young and scared. A flicker, and then it was gone. "At dawn, those of you here will leave this column and come with me. We will make for Varr at speed. From Varr, we will march to war, and be it the Autarch and his Torpreahn puppets, be it an army of the ones we once loved returned as Dead Men, be it the half-gods themselves, if you face your enemy with honesty, and face the comrades who fight beside you with the same, you will always be strong."

With those words, the Regent walked away, following the water's edge until she vanished into the night, leaving Myla to wonder what the fuck all that had been about, and whose side was she supposed to be on anyway, if the Autarch and his Sunguard were marching side by side with the Overlord of Torpreah to reclaim the throne for the old dynasty.

Whatever side doesn't murder entire cities and turn them into Dead Men.

The bit about facing your comrades with honesty still felt a bit fucking rich, although mostly she was thinking that because she still hadn't told Orien the thing he needed to know. She managed to keep on not telling him by going to Tasahre instead, as the sword-mistress left her place by the fire.

"I have a confession," she said. And then, when Tasahre didn't seem inclined to send the other monks away. "Alone?"

Tasahre cocked her head, then gestured for the others to walk ahead.

"After Deephaven. Your wound. You were... you were dying."

Tasahre cocked her head a little more.

"You *were* dying, sword-mistress. The Taiytakei mage said he could heal you. So I brought him to you."

Tasahre stood very still. For a long time, she said nothing.

"You were dying and–"

Tasahre slapped her. "You let a mage touch me? You *brought* a mage to me, and let him touch me with sorcery?"

"We needed you alive, sword-mistress. We still do."

"*We* needed, or *you* needed?"

"Both."

"Well," said Tasahre. "Then you'll both have to manage without. I'm leaving."

"Mistress! You can't! We–"

"If it had been my time to die, I would have gone to the Sun and been forged anew." She shook her head. "Be with your mage. Defend your Moon-Witch monarch. Do what you will, but do it without me."

"Where... are you going?" Myla's words felt small.

"Have you forgotten? I have a warlock to kill."

12
The City of Blinding Light

Day after day after day, the *Speedwell* followed the coast. For a lot of that time, they were in sight of land, which Fings reckoned was just as well. Not being able to see something solid made him queasy. Add to that all the things that suddenly became unlucky as soon as you were on a ship, and he felt he was walking on eggshells. He could *sort* of understand why the sailors considered having a plague victim aboard to be a bad omen, even when Fings had offered them scented masks and explained how a tasselled hat would see them right. And yes, never set sail on an Abyssday, he could certainly get behind *that* one. But the rest? What was wrong with people who had red hair, for Kelm's sake? And whistling? He *liked* whistling! Never mind the looks he got when he forgot to step out on deck right foot first and swing a salute to the wind.

Right now, though, he felt cheery. Three weeks and a thousand miles between him and Deephaven, the wind in his hair and the end in sight across the water. The sailors didn't like the Deephaven refugees being on deck but, overwhelmed by sheer numbers, they were contenting themselves with sullen glares. Below deck was hot, noisy, and smelly; and frankly, after the last couple of days in Deephaven, Fings preferred to be outside with plenty of open space around him.

He had to shield his eyes against the dazzle of the sun off the white stone of Helhex, its wharves and warehouses and temples and palaces and temples and... well, more temples. He'd heard it called the City of Light or the White City, the latter of which made sense on account of it being largely white. Lots of temples didn't sound like a place he was going to enjoy; but on the bright side, lots of temples meant lots of priests and monks, the sort of people with definite views about hordes of Dead Men and silver-armoured Wraiths and all the other bollocks they'd left in Deephaven. Yeah, right now, Fings reckoned he was happy to be around people who could take care of shit like that.

There were probably *some* buildings that weren't temples, he reminded himself, on account of people needing places to live and the like, and markets and so forth.

A crow landed on the ship's rail a few feet away. It stretched its wings and gave him a look like it was wondering whether he still needed both his eyeballs. Fings flapped a hand. The crow hopped a couple of steps, stretched its wings, and went back to looking at him. Fings went back to looking at the city in the distance. Solid ground. All the money he'd had, all those sacks of silver stolen from the emperor's barge last year, all that was gone. But they were alive, and being alive and skint, he reckoned, was a whole lot better than being an undead slave to a bunch of Faerie-Kings.

A city full of temples probably wasn't the best place for Seth either, given how he'd left Varr. Still, all Fings had to do was keep his hands in his own pockets and out of other peoples', which surely couldn't be *that* difficult, while all *Seth* had to do was keep his mouth shut and not fuck about with heretical warlock shit.

"Arse!" cawed the crow and flew away.

"Yeah," agreed Fings, and went back inside.

The others were in Seth's cabin. The cabin was supposed to be Soraya's, Myla's sister. It had become Seth's because it was the only cabin they had, and because Seth had had the plague and so had to be carefully kept out of sight of the ship's crew, who would likely have chucked him overboard had they known. This hadn't sat well with the heavily pregnant Soraya; it had sat even less well when the baby had decided, two days out from Deephaven, to make its entrance. Soraya, not having much choice in the matter, had been left to get on with it on deck in front of a crowd of onlookers. Or so Fings had heard; he'd given the whole farrago a miss and had largely tried to avoid Soraya ever since.

Soraya, he reckoned, would have helped the crew throw Seth into the sea, given half a chance, not because he had the River Plague but because she wanted her cabin back. Fortunately, Fings had helped Lucius – Soraya and Myla's brother – rescue Myla from Deephaven slavers, so Lucius had intervened, and now Soraya was permanently cross with him.

Families, eh? He shook his head.

"The last Empress, sun bless her, died of the great pox," Lucius was saying. Seth was giving Fings a look. With his face swathed in bandages so only one eye peeked out, the other having fallen to the pox, Fings couldn't tell what sort of look it was.

"She was murdered," Soraya snapped. She was holding the baby, which was about the only way to shut it up. Fings suspected she was contemplating lobbing *that* into the sea, too, and that a growing number of sleep-deprived refugees and crew wouldn't have batted an eyelid if she did. "By a gang of assassins pretending to be sword-monks who waylaid her coach party."

"That was the one before," said Lucius. "The Sad Empress."

"Yeah!" Fings grinned, because for once he knew something. "I remember the one that died of the pox. Whole city draped in grey for days."

"Died of the pox is what they *said*, yes." Seth was giving him a look again. Fings still wasn't sure what it meant but decided not to say what he'd been about to, something along the lines of how an empress dying of the pox showed it could happen to anyone, how things could be a lot worse than having half your face reduced to a mass of scars and losing an eye.

Yeah, okay. Could be a lot better, too...

He scuttled back topside and settled down to watch the city on the shore grow as the *Speedwell* sailed closer. Yes, a city of priests and monks wasn't going to be fun, but it wasn't as if they were planning to stay. Lucius and Soraya meant to continue inland to Torpreah, the old capital, and Torpreah sounded *much* more like Fings' sort of place. He reckoned he'd stick with them a while, then head back north to Varr, maybe have a pile of adventures on the way, although preferably not like the ones he'd had in Deephaven. He'd get home to Ma Fings and all his sisters before the Sulk set in, pockets empty and with a hatful of wild stories. North to Varr meant crossing something called The Fracture, apparently, and then a desert and all sorts, so some of his stories might even end up being true.

He'd make up something about his brother, Levvi. How Levvi was captain of his own ship, not some sail-slave bound to the Taiytakei and, for reasons Fings knew he'd never understand, happy to stay that way.

"It's not coming back."

Fings almost jumped out of his skin, his thoughts that far away. Seth had crept beside him, his one good eye screwed up against the glare of the sun. Seth hadn't been himself since Deephaven. You had to expect that, Fings supposed, what with almost dying of plague on top of everything else.

"What?"

"I remember the two of us going to Twilight Prayer in the temple. After that, nothing. Tell me again."

"You buggered off. I went looking for Levvi." They'd been through all this more times than Fings could remember. "Next I saw you was the following night." Which wasn't true, but the one *other* time, Seth had had a dead demon-thing in his room, and Fings reckoned Seth was better off not remembering that. Reckoned *he'd* be better off not remembering it too.

They'd rolled it up in a carpet and stuffed it in a handcart. Seth had wandered off to get rid of it.

Seth was giving him that unfathomable look again. "And you found me half dead up the top of the Avenue of Emperors with the city being overrun by Dead Men and Silver Kings, carried me back and across the docks and onto the *Speedwell*."

"Right."

"It all just sounds a bit... unlikely."

Fings shrugged.

"How'd you find me?"

"Luck." Fings knew perfectly well that a shrewd man made his own luck. If Seth didn't see that too, after all these years, well...

"What were you doing there?"

"Could ask you the same."

"I'd tell you if I could remember!"

"Was looking for Myla," said Fings, a little sulky. "That fire-mage of hers said she was at the temple. Thought she ought to know the ships weren't waiting. You'd have done the same if it was me." So Fings liked to think. *Myla* would have done the same, for sure.

"And that's it?"

Fings bit his lip. He *was* skipping a few things, and Seth probably knew it. Then again, he'd been here before with the whole *don't look inside the box* malarkey, and he *had* looked inside the box, and had eventually rather wished he hadn't. Same rules applied, he reckoned. "Yeah, but... Look, I don't know half of what you were up to in Deephaven but... whatever it was... probably as well you *don't* remember."

"What the fuck's *that* supposed to mean?"

Fings sat on the rail and swayed from side to side. "It was them mages, right? Being around them. That Taki one was up to some right dodgy shit. And that fire-witch, too. Would turn anyone's head in on itself, she would. Don't know how Myla deals with it all. She's a sword-monk, so I suppose she's used to it, but we're just ordinary. Like I said, a blessing."

Seth pointed at his bandaged face. "This? You call this a fucking *blessing*?"

"Course not. Just... It is what it is. Done and behind us, right? Best let it go. You and me now, like it used to be."

That's what happened with mages. They messed you up. Messed *everything* up. You only had to look at Deephaven. Mages up to their eyes in whatever all *that* had been. Seth had gotten caught up in it, that was all. Had to be. Anything else, well... would be like saying Seth was a mage himself, which was nonsense.

Even as he thought it, he could hear Myla in his head as though she was right beside him. *He knew exactly what he was doing.*

Seth levered himself away. His one good eye glared from under wrappings of cloth. "Right."

"Listen. Don't know much about it and I don't want to, neither, but you were messing with sorcery and warlock shit. Next thing that happens, you get the pox. Doesn't that seem a bit strange?"

"You... think this is divine punishment?" Seth gave a hacking laugh. "It's not. Not that the Gods wouldn't do that sort of thing, but I'm beneath their notice. *That* was made very clear, right before the Sunguard kicked me down the temple steps in Varr."

He limped off. Fings watched him go. Couldn't help a sinking feeling that one day he'd have to choose between sticking with Seth through something truly bad or letting him go. Didn't much fancy either, if he was honest. A quiet life, that's what he wanted. For a bit, at least.

Helhex harbour was full of boats and ships, a makeshift armada ferrying survivors of Deephaven to safety. The *Speedwell* dropped its sails, tossed a couple of anchors, and invited its unwanted passengers to kindly fuck off. Fings scampered down a net thrown over the side while Seth was lowered on a hoist. A quick flurry of oars to the shore and he was in a heaving mass of people crowding a wooden pier. Seth followed, carried by two cratered sailors from the *Speedwell* who seemed to expect Fings to slip them a few bits every time they did anything. Fings pushed through the milling throng and the sailors followed. He had no idea what to do in a place that wasn't swarming with Dead Men trying to kill them, but first things first: he found some space, wiped the sweat from his brow, knelt, quietly kissed the earth, and whispered a prayer of thanks to any god who happened to be listening.

City of Light? City of Overpowering Heat felt more like it. Because yeah, the air here was hot and heavy.

The Sweaty City...

The crater-faced sailors helped Seth into a handcart. Half a dozen old greybeards dressed in ill-fitting uniforms were yelling at the refugees, huffing like they were somehow important or possibly because they were about to collapse from heat exhaustion. Meanwhile, Lucius and Soraya were talking to two men in expensive clothes. All smiles, touching and hugging in that curious way southerners did, intimate yet formal. Money changed hands. Two other men showed up carrying a weird contraption like a tiny carriage with a chair inside, supported by two long poles. Soraya climbed in with the baby, the men hefted it onto their shoulders, and off they went, Lucius leading the way up long steep streets, empty under the sweltering sun, on and on, Fings with little choice but to push Seth in his handcart and follow as best he could.

Away from the waterfront, Fings reckoned he saw more feral cats than people, although the cats were mostly curled up in shady nooks, sleeping. The sun being the way it was, he reckoned the people of Helhex were all doing the same if they had any sense. Eventually, Lucius stopped; the men carrying Soraya set her down, Lucius gave them money, they swapped a couple of jokes, and were gone. Fings, gasping from the effort of pushing Seth, wasn't sure the smug bastards had even broken a sweat.

Another well-dressed man came out from one of the houses. He talked to Lucius, more money changed hands, and suddenly the two might have been brothers. They went inside, Lucius and Soraya and the man from the house laughing together at some shared joke. Fings followed, hefting Seth out of his cart and over a shoulder, plonking him into a chair as soon as they were across the threshold. Fings slumped into another and sighed a happy sigh as a woman brought pitchers of cool water followed by slabs of bread and dripping. After three weeks at sea, the bread tasted divine.

The house was mostly empty, the man was saying, trying to keep smiling as he finally noticed Seth. No one else here on account of the war.

Oh. There's a war now, is there. Fings sighed.

The man had lots to say about that, but Fings didn't listen. He sat back with a full belly, enjoying the pleasant afterglow of all that sun on his skin, quietly sipping water, until his eyes grew heavy and his head began to nod.

Yeah. Bit of peace and quiet...

13
A Force for Good

On the chair next to Fings, Seth slumped, eyes closed, pretending to be asleep. The scorch of the midday sun had mellowed to a balmy evening. A fresh breeze fluttered through open doors and windows. After Varr's freezing winter and Deephaven's constant rain, he reckoned he could get used to this.

"So, we're going to show up on father's doorstep penniless, are we?" While Fings snored, Lucius and Soraya were talking.

"I brought as much as I could."

"Not enough."

"Are you going to blame *that* on Shirish, too?"

"I blame her for enough other things. I don't need to add our poverty to the pile."

You don't know what poverty is, thought Seth. *You have no idea.*

"And Sarwatta's bastard? Am I supposed to show up on their doorstep with *her*, as well? Mother will never forgive me."

"You did what you did to keep us safe."

"And now I'm ruined."

You don't know what that *is, either.*

They walked away. Seth stayed. He was comfortable and didn't want to move, flopped in his chair, limbs dangling akimbo. He'd grown up sleeping on a hard floor with a threadbare blanket. *This* was luxury, not poverty.

"Seth? You awake?"

Fings. He didn't stir. Didn't need to open his eyes to know where

Fings was. Just… thought about it, the way Kuy's memories in the orb had shown him. Since working with the orb, he was sensing more and more, every day. Posture and emotion. Right now, Fings was squatting beside Seth's chair, thinking how sometimes a thing needed to be said, preferably when the person you were saying it to wasn't actually going to hear it.

Seth stayed still. *Am I going to like this?*

"You and me, we been running the Spice Market since we were nippers," Fings' voice was a whisper. "Everyone else comes and goes, but not us. I'm your friend, the best you got. And so you got to listen, right? I don't know much of what you were up to in Deephaven, but you were heading somewhere dark. You were always the clever one, but… I'm afraid for you, brother. I know Myla came over all Do-As-I-Say-Or-Be-Damned, but if she'd been on that ship, she'd have been putting a mask over her face and wrapping cloth round her hands to take care of you, pox and all, even while she was giving you lip for being a dick. She'd put you straight. But she's not here, and so all you got is me, and I don't know what to do. This path you been taking, it's wrong. I'd blame it on the Murdering Bastard, but we both know you were heading this way long before. We got a chance at something new here, brother. Let's take it, eh?"

Seth felt Fings looking at him, half hoping Seth would open his one eye and say something sarcastic. But no. Tempting as it was, Seth reckoned it was better for them both if he didn't.

A chance at something new? Couldn't say Fings was wrong.

So maybe you should listen, eh?

Maybe I should. Nice to agree with himself for once.

He was slowly coming to understand how the warlock Saffran Kuy had worked his evocations. He could even see why the Path of the Sun got as pissy as they did about warlocks, but that was more about what warlocks *believed* than what they *did*. Yes, warlocks used sigils, but what *was* a sigil? Nothing more or less than a precise set of instructions for the ubiquitous remnants that were the true source of every mage's power. How other mages conjured them... he didn't know. Shouted at them in their heads? Danced in circles? Tapped patterns with their fingers? Did it matter? They were all ways of getting the same message to the same destination. As for the source of power itself? No more inherently good or bad than a knife. You could kill a man with a knife or cut a rope and set him free.

Going to be a good little warlock then? A necromancer-healer?

Would that be so bad?

Would the Path see the difference? To them, a warlock is a warlock.

He'd call himself something else, then. An incanter? An evoker?

You can call yourself a jiggling hierophant if it makes you happy, but no sword-monk will see the difference. Warlocks use sigils. You use sigils. Schnick-schnick. That's the end.

Sad, but probably true. *I'll just have to be careful, then.*

Like you were in Varr?

He'd started by passing messages from dead loved ones to their grieving relatives. He'd ended as a convenient alternative to torture for a cabal of murderers.

No. Not like Varr. I'll be discreet.

Quietly drawing no attention? Taking no credit? You have *changed.*

Maybe that was what he needed. *Like Fings said, a chance at something new.*

It'll catch up with you. Whatever you did in Deephaven. Whatever you made yourself forget.

Deephaven was gone. Anyone who hadn't fled was surely dead. So maybe it wouldn't.

He was about to open his eye and get up and say something to Fings along the lines of yes, things would be different; but now Lucius had returned, and with bright mischief in his thoughts. Seth felt a glance given his way, the acceptance that he was asleep, that maybe it didn't matter.

"You're a burglar, right?" said Lucius.

"Er..." Right now, Seth knew Fings would be covertly checking his exits.

"Look, whatever you've done in the past, I don't care. Thing is,

I lost almost everything running from Deephaven the way we did. We *all* lost everything."

Some of us didn't have much to start with.

"I have just enough left to start something in Torpreah. But I'll need materials, and I don't have enough for both. I *could* go to a moneylender. But there's an alternative if you're interested. Help me out and I'll cut you in. You and your brother. In Torpreah, we'll be partners."

Seth listened as Lucius outlined what he wanted Fings to do.

Chance of something new, eh? A chance to be different? So much for that.

Ah well. Maybe it wouldn't be so bad. Lucius was no Blackhand. Besides, *he* could still be different, couldn't he?

14
The Cloth Merchant

Fings scampered and leapt across the roof of the city. Helhex by night was a different world. Air rich with the scent of the sea. Big flat rooftops, narrow streets, crumbling stone full of footholds, stars brighter than he'd ever seen. When the breeze came off the water, he wondered why the people here didn't simply sleep through the day and only come out at night.

In Varr, the city Longcoats generally gave a beating to anyone they caught after dark who didn't look like they had money. Helhex was different. People carried carved wooden tokens with writing to show who they were. Would be as easy as anything for Seth to forge once he was back on his feet, Fings reckoned. Not that Fings needed one, on account of how ridiculously easy it was to get about without, on account of the Helhex Longcoats mostly sitting around the various barricades they'd erected, apparently with the absurd idea that their Longcoat Roads were the only way to get about. Most of the regulars, it seemed, had gone off to fight in the war everyone was banging on about; the ones left behind were the old, the slow, or else those with a highly developed sense of not poking their noses into other people's business in case said business poked back. Sometimes Fings had to stop himself from singing under his breath, it was so easy; the only hard part about what Lucius wanted was knowing where to look.

Almost a pity they'd be leaving.

Then why not stay? It was one thing to want a roof over your head, but it didn't have to be an *expensive* one. Place like this, Fings reckoned he'd settle for a bit of sacking propped over a stick, and that mostly for some shade.

He climbed onto the roof of where they were staying – the *Elegant Gentleman* – and dropped to the balcony outside Lucius's window. Lucius and Soraya were arguing. They'd been arguing a lot since coming off the *Speedwell*.

"I'll stand by your side until they throw us both into debtors' jail if that's where you want to go. But I need something to work with when we get to Torpreah! I've sold everything I can spare. We've got a dozen emperors. That's all there is, but it's enough for us to start again. *We* can start again."

Whatever Soraya said, Fings didn't hear, too busy thinking what he could do with a dozen gold emperors. *Could live off that for years...*

"Come here." Lucius shifted to soft reassurance. "You did what you had to do."

The baby was whimpering again, building a head of steam towards what, in Fings' experience, would soon be full-on screaming. He sighed. The rooftops were so peaceful...

"Soraya, Shirish is almost certainly dead."

Fings had been trying not to think about that. He'd seen a woman on horseback with a pair of Sunsteel swords glowing in the night as the *Speedwell*'s sails filled. He'd seen her swords rise and fall as the horde of Dead Men swept across the waterfront. He'd seen the Faerie-Kings in silver looking on. Then he'd looked away; and when he'd looked back, the woman with the swords was gone. Hadn't realised it was most likely Myla. *That* had come later.

Sometimes, when he closed his eyes, he heard the screams, wafting out across the water...

"I hated her." Soraya was sobbing. "I hated her *so* much."

Fings tapped on the shutters. The voices stopped, even the baby's mewling. Lucius let Fings inside.

"Well?"

"Yeah. It can be done."

"You'll come with me tomorrow, then?"

It never hurt to case a target in daylight, so Fings nodded, then showed Lucius the contents of his bag. Tomorrow morning, some rich young clerk was going to wonder where he'd put his clothes. The thing with rich young clerks, though, was they could always afford a new set.

"And the other thing?" Lucius asked.

The *other thing* was more troubling. "Yeah," Fings sighed. "I found a place. The rest you'll have to deal with yourself."

"Tomorrow morning." Lucius patted him on the shoulder. "Bright and early."

In the room they shared, Fings found Seth sitting on the edge of his bed, staring into space. The scars from Seth's fight with the plague were healing, but there were other scars, Fings knew. Ones he couldn't see.

"How you doing?" he asked.

Seth shrugged. "I've lost an eye, my good looks, and a day of my life. Could be worse."

Fings didn't say anything. He'd known Seth since they were boys, knew Seth's tells like he knew his own. Seth wasn't lying. Whatever he'd done in Deephaven, he really couldn't remember.

This is what happens when you mess with mages.

Best to let it go.

Next door, the baby's whimpers were building to screams. He heard Soraya trying to soothe it, the desperation as her gentle words broke into sobs. He winced.

"Last night we'll be having to put up with any of that," Fings said.

Seth raised an eyebrow.

"They're going to leave it."

He was a bit surprised to see Seth frown, like of all the things they'd talked about, *this* was what mattered. "*Leave* it? And you're okay with that?"

"Don't matter what I think."

"You don't abandon a child. Who does that?"

"People who are desperate, I reckon." Fings gave Seth a look. Hadn't expected this to strike such a chord. "Anyway, I found a place where priests take children who ain't got nowhere. It ain't great but it ain't nothing."

Seth sighed and shook his head. When he didn't say anything, Fings curled up and went to sleep. He'd had a busy evening.

He woke to find Lucius already up; so off they went, walking the city streets, Fings soaking up the feel of the morning while Lucius chattered away. Torpreah, apparently, was a couple of hundred miles inland, beyond a range of mountains, set in a beautiful fertile valley where two rivers, the Vidra and the Li, flowed together between the Thimble Hills. The Torpreahn armies were marching against the Sapphire Throne in the cause of Light, stripping men from the cities in the south. Fings didn't have much of an opinion on this except to be glad it was happening somewhere else, but he could sense, now that the soldiers were gone, how lost the city around him felt without them. He felt its fear, paranoia spreading under the relentless, sweltering heat, exposing itself in makeshift barricades blocking the roads, in the Longcoat militias, in the way that priests and witch-breakers and sword-monks passed with a wave and a nod, while anyone else needed a token to show they had permission to move outside their quarter.

Tokens. It had taken Fings about five minutes to steal a pair. So, across the city they went, a merchant and his man, Fings dressed up all smart and gaudy like a clown, until they were among the warehouses of the docks. Fings pointed out the cloth merchant; they went inside, and Lucius was soon talking to the traders as though they were old friends. In Helhex, Fings was beginning to understand, this could mean they really *were* old friends, or could just as easily mean they'd never set eyes on one another until five minutes ago. Southerners were strange.

He took his time eyeing the place. The warehouse was a quad of three-storey stone buildings around an open yard. A gang of men were loading barrels into an unharnessed cart while a second stood empty. Windows overlooked the inner yard, but none faced the streets outside. An arched tunnel ended at a pair of heavy gates splitting the western side of the quadrant. Right now, the gates were open. At night they were closed and barred.

Some agreement reached, one of the traders led Lucius through a door and up a flight of steps, extolling the virtues of his wares and how fine they were – how, despite these trying times, they remained extraordinarily affordable. Lucius asked to see his Taiytakei silks. The trader obliged, bragging of its exceptional quality. The two batted numbers back and forth, all with lots of smiling and patting each other and the like, behaviour that would get you a quick punch in the face if you tried it in Varr. They agreed a price for a shipment of Taiytakei silks meant for Deephaven, suddenly available on account of Deephaven being overrun by Dead Men and worse. Fings reckoned the coin was enough to buy several kingdoms, which Lucius didn't have, but that didn't matter. What mattered was that Fings knew where the merchant kept his silks.

After they were done, the trader offered sweet tea and cakes. He and Lucius talked for what felt like hours, exchanging family histories and gossip as the sun crept higher. Lucius spun a story of how he'd escaped Deephaven with his fortune intact, how he planned to continue selling Taiytakei silks into the northern Empire, transporting them overland instead of by sea and then up the great river. They talked about twist count and weave depth and a whole bunch of other things Fings didn't understand. As they did, Lucius dropped a couple of names the trader recognised. Lucius knew his stuff, Fings supposed, stifling his yawns.

After Deephaven, the talk moved to the war, how the Torpreah Road was thick with soldiers and priests and sword-monks heading north, how the priests who hadn't marched with the army were responsible for the barricades on the roads, how no one could go anywhere without permission, how the city was now all but run by the temple Witch-Breakers, which was all very well, but Deephaven was a thousand miles away, and no one had seen a Dead Man in Helhex for years.

It was pushing midday by the time Fings and Lucius left, walking empty, heat-scoured streets full of sweating air and dust. Fings found himself imagining the city as the bleaching bones of a long-dead behemoth baking in the desert, as though life had marched away leaving nothing but a husk.

The thought led him to the corpse he'd seen in Deephaven, flayed of its skin, the Taiytakei popinjay hunched over it, eagerly taking notes. He shivered.

Back in the *Elegant Gentleman*, Fings brushed himself down, exhausted, filthy, sticky with his own clammy sweat. He looked in on Seth, but Seth was asleep. This struck Fings as entirely sensible, so he settled on the floor to doze away the day. He had a busy night coming, after all.

He barely heard Lucius and Soraya leave again, later that afternoon. Not his business, nor when they came back, hours later, Soraya quietly sobbing. It was only in the middle of the night, as he was getting ready to go out again, that he realised he hadn't heard the baby's cries.

Ah well. That was that, then.

15
The Gift of Forgetting

That morning, while Fings was with Lucius, Seth trudged the empty streets of Helhex, coming to one dead end after another. Helhex being a holy place, he'd learned about it during his time as a novice. He knew it was oldest city in the empire, founded by the first ships from Anvor. He knew it lay at the mouth of the Vidra, where the Vidra Gorge cut through the Barrier Plateau from Torpreah, over rapids and waterfalls to empty into the sea. He knew it was home to the Order of Witch-Breakers, the arcane priests who dabbled in sorcery to hunt warlocks, as well as at least one order of sword-monks, who preferred simply stabbing them. He knew there were more temples in Helhex than in Varr, despite Varr's much greater size, and almost as many as in Torpreah. He knew that he didn't want to be here, that Helhex was dangerous for someone like him.

They'd be leaving soon. Good. Whatever had happened in Deephaven, whatever he'd made himself forget, the more distance he put behind him, the better.

Let it be.

Yeah, but how was that supposed to work when the last thing he remembered before the hole in his head was slipping out of a temple, a sword-monk giving him a nasty look? And then POP! A whole day later, bolting out of the House of Cats and Gulls, the place overrun by Dead Men and Wraiths, sick with the River Plague and running for his life.

What did I do?

And then on a ship, half dead, a week gone this time, blind in one eye, half his face and a good chunk of the rest of him a ruin of scars.

What the fuck did I do?

He considered disappearing. Leaving Helhex and Fings behind. Might be for the best, but the thought was an idle one: he didn't have money to hire a boat to take him through the gorge or the strength to travel by land. In normal times, he might have begged a ride on one of the frequent caravans for Torpreah. But times *weren't* normal. There was a war. The soldiers were gone, most of the wagons and horses too. The caravans had all but stopped, and Torpreah was more than a hundred miles inland, and Seth could barely walk a hundred yards before he needed to rest.

And all the while, the summer sun beat down, and the air lay still and humid over the city.

What did I do?

He dozed. When he stirred, later in the afternoon, Fings was back and asleep. Seth reckoned best to let him be.

Another walk, then? The least he could do was recover his strength. They had no money, which meant it wouldn't be long before someone did something desperate and stupid, fucked it up, and then they'd have to run again. The thought wasn't bitter, simply an acknowledgement of the truth of their lives.

Be nice if we could change that, eh?

Not that he knew how.

After a while, he smelled smoke. Blown by the wind from somewhere where something was on fire. He heard distant shouts and felt a familiar anxious shiver. He'd seen fires in Varr now and then, in the summer heat when everything was as dry as old bones. Whole buildings turned to flames, a wall of heat and then the wind would start, until there was a column of flame to touch the sky. He knew how it went. In Varr, they let the fires burn when they got bad, relying on the city's canals to stop the spread.

Helhex didn't have canals.

He went a different way. After a time, the shouts dwindled.

Either the wind had taken the fire in another direction, or it was doused. A few hours of excitement and everyone would be back to snoozing. Seth, exhausted by now, reckoned on doing the same. He returned to the *Elegant Gentleman* and climbed into his cot. When sleep proved elusive, he lay still, reaching out with his thoughts, picking up the people around him. Saffran Kuy's little trick.

The globe was where he'd left it, buried at the bottom of his satchel. He wondered whether he ought to smash it. Whatever he'd done in Deephaven, maybe it *was* best to let it go. Maybe what he needed was to let *every*thing go. All the old dreams. Was it time to find some new ones?

If it was the orb you wanted to forget, you wouldn't have left it lying around where you'd find it again!

He felt Lucius and Soraya come back at sunset, two metaphysical lights, beacons swollen with emotion. One was bereft, filled with guilt. Sorrow and anger and bitterness too, but guilt was strongest. That would be Soraya. Lucius was the usual mix of apprehension and determination, but he carried anxiety today, and a streak of helpless hopeless fear.

Something's happened. What?

It took a moment before he understood what he *wasn't* seeing. The baby. A small presence full of need and want. Where it should have been... nothing.

What have you done?

He wondered if they'd killed it. The idea fitted their emotions. But no. Wanted or not, all life was sacred. Soraya and Lucius were too pious for infanticide.

Fings' priests, he supposed.

He must have fallen asleep then, because suddenly it was the middle of the night, and Fings was slipping out through the window, and Lucius was heading out as well, both filled with bright thoughts of anticipation. Seth waited until they were gone, then padded to Soraya's door. He knew she was awake. Awake and drowning and alone.

Her thoughts were all sharp edges. *Guilt, guilt, guilt...*

Yes. Well. I know what that's like.

He didn't bother knocking. If he had, she'd either have ignored him or else told him to go away. So no, he simply walked on in. She sat in the middle of the floor, wearing a shift, holding a tiny knife. The knife, he knew at once, wasn't for him. She meant it for herself. At least, she was thinking about it.

"Don't," he said.

"Go away!" she hissed.

"No." He sat, keeping his distance, and looked at her. Sometimes, when the light caught Soraya just so, she looked like Myla. Myla, who'd gone all the way back to Deephaven to save this woman in front of him, who'd been prepared to be hanged if that was what it took. He didn't know much of the story, only bits and pieces, snatches overheard from Fings and Lucius. Seemed a waste, all that effort only for Soraya to open her wrists.

I'm doing this for Myla, then?

No. He was doing this because someone was in pain, a pain he could understand and had the power to take away. And so, he would. Or at least, he'd offer.

Necromancer-healer, remember? It sounded so ridiculous, yet here it was.

"I know guilt," he said. "I know what it's like to do something that makes you so ashamed you think it can never go away."

The knife didn't waver. Soraya glared at him, hostile and angry. "What do *you* know about guilt?"

A lot more than you care to hear.

"I was going to be a priest. I was good. Clever. But I asked a lot of questions. Wrong questions. I thought the Path was hiding something, you see. I thought they had some great dark secret. Well, fact is they do, but it wasn't the secret I thought. I did some… questionable things." A generous way to put it, but this was supposed to set Soraya at ease, not send her screaming for a witch-breaker. "I learned a few tricks. Not the sort of tricks a novice should know. I'm not certain, but I was probably responsible for the death of a Lightbringer."

Lightbringer Suaresh. His first attempt at making himself forget. Driven by survival, the need to be able to lie to a sword-monk. Not driven by guilt. *That* belonged somewhere else.

Soraya regarded him, scornful. "Am I supposed to ask what happened?"

"Even if you did, I wouldn't have an answer because I don't know. I... made sure of that. I can make people forget things. That's the trick I learned. That's what got me kicked out."

Liar!

Yeah, but best not to mention those other *tricks, eh?*

He'd caught her attention. "Forget?"

"Is there something *you'd* like to forget?"

Soraya snorted. "I'd like to forget my sister ever existed."

"Myla."

Soraya made a sour face. "Changing her name, pretending it never happened. What do you want from me, failed priest? A confession?"

"Only if you want to give it. You might listen to mine, though. It's about your sister."

"Isn't everything?"

"You know the name Jeffa Hawat? You know who he is. Was."

Soraya laughed. "Are you serious?"

"I'm sorry. I barely know you." Seth shrugged. "Myla never talked about her past. At least, not to me. All I knew was that she was running from something. If I'm honest, for the half a year I knew her, she was kinder to me than most. She never did me any wrong, but I still betrayed her to Jeffa Hawat. I told him where and when. He set a trap. People were killed, people I might have called friends, if I was feeling generous. Not Myla, though. She got away; and then, the very next time I saw her, she stood for me against a pair of sword-monks, a fight she knew she couldn't win. If she hadn't, they would have killed me; as it was, I escaped. She didn't know what I'd done, and I never told her. I look at what she did for me, what I did to her, and I'm ashamed. I like to think that that shame will help me never be that person again."

He was a bit surprised, if he was honest, hearing those words coming out of him the way they did. Hadn't expected them. Certainly hadn't expected to discover he meant them.

Well, well, well. Look at you, eh?

"Thing is, I think she would have stood for me against those sword-monks even if she *had* known."

"She slept with my fiancée," said Soraya. "When he tossed me aside, she stabbed him, ran away, and left me carrying his bastard. After she was gone, when my… when my *condition* was obvious, Sarwatta gave me a choice – bear his child or he'd take his revenge on Lucius. And yes, my sister came back, and yes, she saved me from him, and yes, she wasn't wrong; he *was* a shit-stain, a worthless, soulless, pus-bag. But you know what? I still hate her." The last words came out as sobs. "She destroyed me." She dropped the knife. "She ruined everything!"

"Where's the child, Soraya? What did you do with it?"

Soraya shook her head.

"I was born into nothing, unwanted in a place that was shit. You could have left it somewhere to die. You could have thrown it overboard on the ship. You didn't do either of those things. What *did* you do with it?"

"The priests." She was struggling to make words. "Your brother found a place. They take orphans. To serve the Path."

"Then perhaps she will be raised by good men and women who will love her and give her purpose. Did she have a name?"

Soraya shook her head, a sharp, quick gesture. "Couldn't…"

"I don't know how many people died in Deephaven. Whoever she becomes, you saved her that. You gave her a chance at a life."

Another shake of the head. "Shirish. She did that."

"No." Seth reached out a hand to touch Soraya's shoulder. He expected her to flinch away, but she didn't. "*You* did. You brought her here, despite everything. You loved her the only way you could."

"No!" Soraya shook him off. "I didn't! I didn't love her at all! I wanted her gone! That was all. That was all it ever was! I wanted it gone! I want *all* of it gone. Shirish, Sarwatta, everything!"

Seth smiled. "Well..." He paused a moment. "I can do that. If that's really what you want."

Soraya looked at him hard.

"It is a priest trick."

Liar!

"It is meant only for Sunheralds and Dawncallers to know. They use it only rarely. It's for those who've done something truly heinous, yet whose desire for repentance and service to the path is greater still."

Liar! Liar! Liar!

"I'm not supposed to know it, but I do. You can forget everything."

Silence.

"But... Soraya... There is a price. Your sister has been a part of your life for a very long time. To forget her means to forget everything around her. Every part of your life she touched will be gone. You were close once, I think?"

A slow nod.

"Before... this thing she did?"

Another nod.

"I could make you forget what she did and everything that came after. It would be... about nine months, I suppose? It can all go away, every trace of it. You would remember being in love with your fiancée, and with your sister too, and everything that happened this last year will vanish into mist. You can wake up tomorrow morning and have no memory of any of it. But here's the price: you won't remember how you got here. You won't remember what your sister did to hurt you, or that she came back to save you. It will all be gone."

He sighed. "The first thing you'll do is wonder where you are, then how, then what happened. You'll be confused. You'll talk to your brother. You'll discover that months have gone by, and that you have no memory of them. Understanding what you've lost will come slowly, a creeping bewilderment that turns to dread. You'll think yourself mad, or worse. You'll start trying to fill the hole. It will become an obsession. Trust me that I know. Our Dawncallers use their power only rarely with good reason. To simply forget... Alone, it's not the answer."

"Then why are you here?"

Seth got to his feet and stood by the door, ready to leave. "Because there *is* a way. Write it all down. Everything as you *want* to remember it. A letter to yourself to fill the hole where memories used to live. One to explain why you took them away. When you've done that, come to me. If you still want to forget, so be it. When it's done, I'll give you your letter, written in your own hand. You must explain to your future self what she has lost and why. Think of it like drawing a splinter from a wound. The splinter goes, allowing the wound to heal, but wound is still there, at least for a while. This wound is in your soul, so you *really* need a reason not to pick at it."

Yes, he'd had some time to think about that, these last couple of weeks. What he *should* have done, instead of leaving a hole in his own head with nothing to fill it.

16
SILKS

Fings would be the first to admit that the world was full of stuff that didn't make sense, and that most of that stuff was, in fact, people. The Sun rising and crossing the sky? Well, the Sun was the source of all motion, the spark of life, the creator, bringing warmth and light to his people, so that made sense. When the Sun set, the Moon took over. The Moon was the Fickle God, the Trickster, the lord of Thought and Memory. Fings came up with all his best ideas at night, so *that* made sense too. In fact, most things that had nothing to do with people made sense. What *didn't* make sense was Myla not staying with her sister all the way back to the *Speedwell*, or even going to Deephaven in the first place. What *didn't* make sense was Seth getting stricken by plague and almost dying. What *certainly* didn't make sense was Levvi, choosing to stay where he was, a slave-sailor for the Taiytakei.

He could really do, he decided, with being around people who made sensible decisions for a while. Which was why he was on the roof of a warehouse in the dead of night; because Lucius had made the eminently sensible decision to steal a cartload of Taiytakei silk, set up shop in Torpreah as a tailor, and cut Fings in on the profits. The traders in Helhex clearly had plenty to spare, and while the Longcoat militias *did* have a penchant for searching everything and taking a healthy fraction of whatever they found – *someone* had to keep the city safe from spies and saboteurs from the North, after all – Seth was obviously still recovering from the

Deephaven River Plague, and no one in their right mind was going to manhandle a plague victim to see whether the soiled blanket underneath just happened to be hiding a few dozen bolts of precious silk.

You had to admire how Lucius had thought it through. So here Fings was, squatting on the edge of a roof, looking down over the yard where he and Lucius had stood that morning, finally doing something he understood.

The gates would be shut and barred, locked, and chained. The merchants here seemed mostly concerned at stopping large gangs of ruffians from breaking in, overwhelming their *own* gang of ruffians, piling everything on a few carts and riding off. It left Fings curious to know what would happen if, say, a fire broke out. If the keys to that gate were far away then everything would burn, so maybe the keys *weren't* that far away...

He tutted and rolled his eyes at himself. *Stick to the plan.* That was how you kept the Fickle Lord sweet. Stick to the plan, don't push your luck, don't get greedy.

He counted the watchmen again. Three in the yard, clustered around a brazier beside the wagon they'd loaded that morning. Four inside the warehouse buildings, wandering about with lamps, which meant Fings could follow their progress through the windows. Of course, he was counting lamps, not people, so there could be more.

The windows were shuttered but the lamplight filtering through the cracks betrayed how poorly made those shutters were. He fixed a line of rope to the rooftop and let it dangle over the edge. It was a simple matter of climbing down, slipping a blade through the gap between the shutters, lifting the latch, sliding in, then closing them behind him. The sort of thing he'd done a hundred times, the work of thirty heartbeats. What he needed, though, was for those three men in the yard to not look up while he did it; if they *did* look up, well, with the moon as it was, they'd likely see him. And yes, you *could* take your chances, cross your fingers, hope to get lucky, but Fings was a firm believer in making his own luck. So he rubbed the charm around his neck and the other charm in his pocket, muttered prayers to the Moon and to the Goblin King; but he also hefted a small stone at the far corner of the yard, where, five minutes ago, he'd dropped a pair of half-eaten rats.

The stone clicked on the warehouse wall, loud enough for Fings to hear but apparently not loud enough for the men at the brazier. He threw another. This time, their conversation stopped. He saw them turn. One went to look, sunk into a crouch, then called the others. He heard their voices: *will you look at that* and *what could have done it* and so forth.

Heard them, but wasn't looking at them anymore, because he was sliding down his rope. He'd made his thirty heartbeats.

The shutters were such a poor fit that he might have slid his hand between them to lift the latch, never mind a blade. He slipped inside.

The next bit was easy. He'd spotted a couple of watchmen on the floor below, where the silks were kept, but none up here. He crept his way until he found a ladder masquerading as a stair, a block and tackle hanging from the roof above for shifting goods between floors. He waited, lying in the darkness until the gloom below lit up with lamplight and the watchman came past. Two watchmen, as it turned out, not that it mattered. He let them pass, then dropped down, silent as a shadow, and followed.

They were talking, one banging on about someone who was his sister or cousin or some relative or other and who had two suitors, one of whom was a jerk with money, the other of whom was also a jerk but penniless, and so had gone off to fight in the war in the hope of making his fortune. A long story, lots of courtship and back and forth, that sort of thing. By the time the watchmen turned to go back the other way, Fings was rooting for the one who'd gone off to fight. Showed commitment, he thought.

The watchmen waved their lamp haphazardly about, peering at whatever it illuminated. Hiding was as simple as staying crouched behind boxes. After they passed, Fings went back to following, creeping through the shadows in their wake, as much because he wanted to hear the end of the story as anything else. When they reached the silks, Fings let their light show him what he was looking for. He watched to see if they paid attention to what was lining the shelves around them; but no, they barely noticed, which meant they probably wouldn't notice when some of it wasn't there. He silently thanked them for their help, let them move on, then slid two dozen bolts of silk off the shelves, tied them in a bundle and slung them over his shoulder. About as much as he could carry. About as much as they could hide in a handcart under a blanket with a pox victim sprawled on top.

The watchmen circled back. Fings hid and let them pass again. The other one was talking now. Something about bandits in a gorge and a posse of witch-breakers heading to deal with them. Once they'd moved on, he made his way back, to the ladder, to the shuttered window overlooking the yard, and peeked between the cracks.

The three watchmen in the yard were around their brazier again. Fings had heard about little darts you could buy in the Glass Market off the Circus of Dead Emperors in Varr. Put them in a long glass tube, blow hard and they'd fly as far as a man could throw a stone. The alchemists mostly tried to sell darts to put men to sleep or kill them, but Fings had seen others too. Right now, he was thinking of the little pouches of powder they dropped into fires, the ones that exploded with a loud bang and a shower of sparks. No harm done, no one hurt, everyone very surprised and bit dazzled. Would have been perfect right now.

He didn't have any pouches like that. Even if he did, it was a long way to that brazier, and what happened if you missed? He settled for the tried and tested, the thing he knew that always worked, which was patience. He'd squat in the shadows for as long as it took. Could be they'd head inside to brew some tea. Maybe they'd settle to a game of cards or dice. Could be they'd stay out there all night; but the moon was only half full and waning. It would set long before sunrise. Dark enough for Fings to take his chances if some handy cloud didn't come by first.

Sure enough, after an hour or so, the watchmen went inside. Fings had no idea why and didn't wait to find out. He opened the shutter, slipped out, closed it behind him, climbed to the roof, unfastened his rope, scampered to the edge of the warehouse overlooking a reassuringly dark and narrow alley, lowered the bundle of silks to the ground, climbed down after it, and vanished into the night.

Tea, he decided. They'd probably gone inside to brew a nice pot of tea.

17
The Sapphire Throne and Khrozus' Chair

Someone gave Myla a new horse. She rode with Orien. When he fell behind, she rode with the other monks. When even *they* couldn't keep the Regent's pace, she simply rode, wishing it would all be over. She ate the food put in front of her, collapsed into whatever bed or hay-pile was available, woke in a sea of aches and pains and then did it all again, day after day after day. She wondered, sometimes, what would become of the refugees; but that wasn't her problem now. The Deephaven soldiers and most of the sword-monks had stayed behind. This mad ride to Varr was her and a few other monks, Orien and the Red Witch, and the Regent and the posse of hawks and black-armoured bodyguards who never seemed to leave her side.

They reached the capital under a full moon, rode past the Kaveneth, across Khrozus' bridge over the Thort, past the tower of Talsin's Folly. A boy took her horse. A servant led her to the most luxurious bed Myla had ever met and offered her a decanter of wine. Myla vaguely considered proposing marriage, knocked back the wine, shed some clothes, sprawled inelegantly, face down, and went to sleep for what she hoped would be several years.

She woke with a thread of drool hanging from the corner of her mouth. She didn't dare move. Move, and everything was going to hurt.

She wasn't alone.

Orien?

She was carrying his child. The secret she hadn't told him because she wasn't sure how he was going to react.

She shifted, looking; and yes, everything *did* hurt. The bedroom was larger than most houses. Elegant drapes lined the walls, the glass in the window so clear you could almost imagine it wasn't there. There was a bath made of what looked like silver. She might have been interested in finding out, if it wasn't for the couch embroidered in gold which had the Taiytakei popinjay sprawled across it, leering at her. For the life of her, she couldn't remember whether he'd been with them all along.

"Oh for... Couldn't get a room of your own?"

Fleetingly, the world popped out of focus, then popped back again. The popinjay beamed. "Oh now, *I've* been up for some time. We have an audience with the emperor. Chop, chop!"

"Good for us." Myla slumped back into the bed. It was warm and comfortable. "But no. I'm going back to sleep."

"Your presence is required, Shirish."

"Don't call me that. Also, fuck off!" When Orien caught up, they were going to have to have a lengthy chat about his new friend, starting with the popinjay's attitude to privacy. In the meantime, *fuck off* had apparently been too subtle, because the popinjay stayed exactly where he was while Myla threw on the same stinky sweat-stained clothes she'd worn all the way from Deephaven.

And won't that be fun for whoever has to stand anywhere near me.

She slid her swords into place across her back and threw the popinjay a nasty look. *His* shirt, she noted, was fresh and clean.

In the hall outside, a man in immaculate scarlet gestured them to follow; when they did, two soldiers in Moonsteel mail fell in behind. Everywhere she looked, Myla saw gold, silver, marble columns, wooden carvings, silk hangings, fortune after fortune on every wall, in every hall. She couldn't help imagining Fings' face if he'd been here to see it.

Maybe, if we meet again one day, you can help put this wealth to better use.

They crossed a hall decorated with every possible size and

colour of crystal, then another, one side hung with maps, the other with portraits of the Imperial Family and of the emperors before them.

"Did you see that?" asked the popinjay.

"See what?" asked Myla, momentarily forgetting that she was ignoring him.

"The picture of Khrozus has an arrow sticking out of it."

A hall covered in gold leaf, then a chamber filled with glass and liquid silver; and then, quite suddenly, Myla was staring at the dazzling brilliance of the Sapphire Throne, *the* Sapphire Throne, and it was only as she took another step that she realised she'd walked right into the Imperial Throne room, swords still on her back, and no one had stopped her.

Her, the popinjay, and the man in scarlet. The soldiers in Moonsteel had stayed outside.

"What are we doing here?" she asked. To the left of the Sapphire Throne stood the chair Khrozus had supposedly carved with his own hands after wresting the empire from the indolent excesses of Talsin the Inept. Roughly cut from simple wood by a man for whom words were nothing and actions everything. Or, if you preferred a different story, carved from the bones of his enemies after their crucified corpses had been picked clean by crows. There were other stories, worse, although that was probably all they were, stories; but this *was* his throne, nonetheless. The legacy, spirit and blood of the Usurper, the Butcher, the Liberator, the Bastard, the man who'd ripped the Empire in two and forged it anew, for better or for worse.

"Before His Majesty enters the room," started the man in scarlet, "you will kneel and place your hands on the floor in... *Excuse* me! *What* are you doing?"

Myla had climbed the three steps to Khrozus' chair and was having a good long look. Wood, not bone, so at least *that* story was a lie. She wondered what the scarlet man would do if she sat on it. Or spat on it. Both were tempting. It looked uncomfortable though, so she did neither and walked back. "Carry on."

The scarlet man gave her a glare like he was trying to cut pieces of her soul to keep as trophies. Myla, who'd twice faced Wraiths and survived, smiled back at him. One thing she knew, though: she didn't belong in a place like this. She rather wished she hadn't drunk all the wine last night and had saved some for this morning.

"As I was *saying*. Kneel and place your hands on the floor, then lower your heads to your hands. You will look at nothing but the floor an inch away from your face until you are told otherwise. You will be silent unless you are spoken to. His Majesty may or may not choose to speak. Her Highness *will* speak, but prefers to converse privately; however, you may refuse and speak openly if you wish." The way he spoke made abundantly clear his opinions on doing things the way the Regent wanted.

A trio of men walked in then, mid-conversation, took one look at Myla and the popinjay and stopped. They seemed, Myla thought, more her parents' generation than her own. At first glance they were the typically arrogant, entitled men who grew up in places like this, used to getting their own way. A second glance suggested they were also men who'd seen a fair bit of trouble and weren't afraid to see some more.

They all looked each other over. Belatedly, Myla recognised one of them from the road from Deephaven. One of the Regent's Hawks. She cocked her head and gave him a nod. Anyone who stood their ground in the face of a Wraith deserved respect.

The man squinted at her, nodded back, then nudged his friends. "That's the monk I was telling you about. The one who ran into the middle of a horde of Wraiths and Dead Men." He gave her a wary look. "You're a brave idiot, I'll give you that."

"How kind, although I'm not sure why I might not say the same of you. How did it end? I didn't see."

"They left. So did we."

"They let you go?"

Another door opened and spat out a cluster of blue robes led by a haunted-looking man with streaks of grey in his beard, both of which made him look older than he probably was. The popinjay bowed. Myla stayed as she was. She didn't entirely understand the antipathy between mages and sword-monks, but she was buggered if she was going to bow to anyone who hadn't shown they deserved it. Besides, her last encounter with a Guild mage hadn't left the best impression, and she was slowly getting annoyed at apparently being the only one here who didn't have a clue who anyone was. She would have asked, but the door behind the mages had barely closed before a loud knocking reverberated through the hall.

"The emperor!" hissed the man in scarlet. "Abase yourselves! Avert your eyes!"

The popinjay dropped to his knees and pressed his face to the floor. As did the mages and the other men. After a moment, Myla copied them. Tasahre might have stayed on her feet, but defiance wasn't *always* the best course, and maybe the bit about only bowing to people who'd shown they were worthy could have an exception when it came to actual emperors.

Footsteps. Four... five sets of them. A silence...

"You may rise," said a very young voice.

On the Sapphire Throne sat the boy-emperor, ten years old. To his right, on Khrozus' throne, sat the Regent. Both with their crowns: Sunsteel for the designated heir successor. Moonsteel for the Emperor himself. The crown Myla had briefly held, before she and Orien had given it back.

Nice to see it where it belongs, I suppose.

They were resplendent, the emperor in black and red and gold, the Regent in more of the same but trimmed with white. Behind her, Lady Novashi stood in flaming orange threaded with silver beside a woman in red and white silks and carrying a sword. The only sword in the room apart from Myla's own.

No one had asked her to surrender them. Wasn't that a bit... odd?

To the right of the Sapphire Throne, at the child-Emperor's left hand, stood Lord Kyra Levanya, Overlord of Varr and general of the Imperial armies. An old man now, but in younger days he'd been... Well, the Levanya had been a lot of things. The Butcher of Deephaven, for a start. The man who'd nailed Emperor Talsin's grandson alive to the city gates. The most wicked man to ever live, Tasahre would have said, and Myla's family would have agreed, along with half the people of Deephaven, even if most of them hadn't been alive when it happened.

Her fingers twitched. Seeing the Levanya had her thinking about her swords. *Why am I here?*

The world popped in and out of focus. Myla started in surprise. *Because I have a place for you.*

She closed her eyes, forced herself to be still, then carefully pictured walking up to the Sapphire Throne and punching the Regent in the face. She felt the Regent, inside her head, watching her imagining doing it, too. *Good.*

Good?

"Stop it!" Myla said, and it was only then she realised that no one else had said a word, saw the startled looks on the faces around her, and understood what was happening. The Regent was inside them all, all at once, talking to them. Exactly as she'd done by the shore of the lake where the City of Spires had once stood.

Yes.

Her Highness prefers to converse privately. That's what the scarlet man had said. In hindsight, Myla thought he might have been a bit clearer about what that meant.

I suppose he might.

"Why can't you..." She stopped, almost switched to finishing the thought in her head instead, then decided fuck it, she wasn't having this. "If you have nothing to hide, speak openly."

The Regent's face tightened a little. Her eyes locked to Myla. "The Lords of Torpreah in the south have raised their banners against us." *Of course I have things to hide!* "In the north, Lord Yelchis has done the same." *Half these people here, this is all they can understand.* "We will raise banners of our own." *What would you have me tell them? That the half-gods have returned?* "We will face them in the field and deal with them as they deserve." *That they have taken Deephaven, slaughtered its inhabitants, brought them back as an army of Dead Men and are heading for Varr?* "What else is there to say?" *The ones who need to know, know. To everyone else? They are Half-Gods! What fool would stand in their path?*

Myla looked around the audience hall. *The fools in front of you, I suppose.*

For the briefest instant, the Regent slipped; Myla caught a vision of the Levanya, the Butcher of Deephaven, standing at the emperor's shoulder, and of the Regent's father, the late Emperor Ashahn, and of his father in turn, Khrozus the Usurper. A sense that all had known the Wraiths would one day come...

The moment came and went. Myla found herself remembering a conversation with Seth. *Khrozus came to Varr in the middle of summer. That first night, the rivers froze, and he just rode right on in, straight past Talsin's defences. How did he do that, do you suppose?*

The Regent saw the memory too, of course. Myla snarled. "Get out!"

Do you think my steward standing beside you knows of any of this? The soldiers outside? The palace servants? What would happen if they did? How long before the whole city knew? How long would we last? Do you think it a coincidence that–

What do you want?

Are all sword-monks as rude as you? There was a twang of petulance in the Regent's thoughts. Myla supposed she wasn't used to having people interrupt her.

Indeed.

If you want civility, fuck off out of my head. I don't recall inviting you.

To Myla's surprise, the Regent did exactly that. The sensation was like having a thick warm blanket suddenly pulled away on a very cold winter's night. The next surprise was that she and the Regent were alone. Even the emperor had gone. Myla blinked a few times. A moment ago, they'd all been here. "Where–"

"We finished without you," snapped the Regent. "You stood quietly and behaved yourself."

"I did... *what?*"

"You were becoming vexing. I stilled you while I dealt with the others."

"You did... *what*?"

"Yes, I can do that. I do try not to, but *some*times, when people *insist* on being *crushingly difficult...* Why do you think you're here, monk?"

"I suppose because sword-mistress Tasahre and I killed a Wraith."

"That's doesn't make you as unique as you think."

"Then what?"

"Work it out."

The Regent snapped her fingers and suddenly wasn't there, and Myla didn't know whether she'd simply vanished into the air, or whether she'd slipped inside Myla's head and put her to sleep for a minute while she walked leisurely away.

Well, fuck you, Myla hoped the Regent was still listening. *Next time you do that, I'm going think about having sex with Orien until you stop.*

And then: *And I'm supposed to* spy *on her?* She shook her head, because surely Tasahre asked the impossible.

18
The Vidra Gorge

Fings, Lucius, and Soraya left Helhex before dawn with two handcarts, one carrying Lucius's chest, the other with Seth lying on a ratty blanket hiding two dozen bolts of Taiytakei silk. In the vague hope that it might save them from questions and robbers, Lucius had had them dress in the coarse-weave robes of beggar-pilgrims. Fings saw the sense, but the robes were scratchy and made his skin itch.

The road from Helhex to Torpreah climbed to the rim of a gorge, wider and deeper with every hour. The Vidra purred below, between trees and rocks; ahead loomed the black silhouettes of mountains, the sky behind bright with the coming day. For the first half-day, the land around the road was lush and green; on the far side of the mountains, Lucius said, was a desert. No water, little shelter from sun or wind, lots of dust. Fings wasn't sure how he felt about that. A part him was excited because he'd never been to a desert before, or any mountains, so it was all new and interesting. On the other hand, it sounded like hard work and not much fun.

The air grew warm and then hot. Around midday, they stopped to doze in the shade of some trees beside a stream, drank water and stretched their legs. Fings found a comfy-looking tree trunk and settled for a catnap, but sleep evaded him. Too many thoughts, most of them about Seth. Fings had bought some bad-smelling ointment for Seth's scars, had even *paid* for it, although best not ask in whose pocket the money had been shortly before.

The apothecary had seemed to think that people who didn't die of the Deephaven River Plague weren't dangerous once they started getting better. Fings wasn't so sure about that, so he'd bought a funny-shaped piece of iron on a string which was supposed to ward away all manner of illnesses. He was wearing it now, along with his tasselled hat and the scented mask he'd had in Deephaven, all of which made him feel better about things.

He didn't mind pushing Seth along the road – they were brothers, after all – but the whole business reminded him of some half-remembered story of a One-Eyed God, pushed around in a cart by a fool. The pair travelled from place to place. Wherever they stopped, ruin followed. The One-Eyed God had known exactly what he was doing but the fool had never understood. Was that what he was? Seth's fool?

Admittedly, he *also* remembered stories about giants, and people turning into stars, and men made of trees, or possibly it was trees made of men, and someone who was supposed to die twice and then be born again and save the world, none of which made much sense. Seth wasn't a god, but neither was he the Seth who'd left Varr. Truth be told, Fings wasn't sure *who* Seth was these days. Wasn't sure Seth knew, either.

Something had happened in Deephaven.

Yeah. Well...

Yeah. But something *else* besides Dead Men and Faerie-Kings.

They walked late into the night. The sky was clear, the stars countless and brilliant, like nothing Fings had ever seen. The air turned cold, forcing the three of them to huddle together. He expected Soraya to complain about that – she seemed to like complaining about things – but she didn't. If anything, she was oddly quiet. Kept throwing looks at Seth like she was trying to figure him out.

Good luck with that.

Then off again before dawn, cold and stiff and sore. One day gone. According to Lucius, the trip to Torpreah took a little over a twelvenight if you set a steady pace.

Yeah. If you're not pushing two lumping great handcarts…

The road rose higher. The air became dry, the land turning brown and bare except the occasional slash of green that marked a stream. At each, Fings and Lucius and Soraya stopped, climbed down from the road to drink and fill their jugs and bathe their feet, catch their breath, maybe exchange a few words. In these shady glades of life, the world seemed better. Then back to the sun and the heat.

The mountains rose around them. They passed few travellers coming the other way. Three men on horseback who trotted by without a word. A pair of pilgrims who stopped and talked for a while. Fings learned of a town ahead, Narvel's Pass. From there, the road wound through the mountains for another day, then dropped to follow the rim of the Vidra Gorge across a waterless arid plateau.

The gorge was already deep, and steep and narrow. The Vidra, far below, flowed loud and restless, all frothing rapids and cascading waterfalls, scattered trees, boulders the size of houses lying smashed in the river's midst.

The climb twisted between pillars of rock. In the shade of these, they sheltered from the midday heat. Then on into a valley of thorny bushes and spiky grass. They reached Narvel's Pass after dark, a crooked gate in a half-arsed barricade around a few dozen shacks, the last outpost of civilisation before the long road to Torpreah. Their arrival sparked a brief flare of excitement, damped to despondent gloom at the sight of four beggar-pilgrims, one of whom was clearly sick. To Fings, the town felt like a trapped animal. After talking to a few people, he understood: Narvel's Pass lived on the back-and-forth of trade between Helhex and Torpreah. With the coming of the war, the wagons had stopped, and so had everything else. Half the townsfolk had already quietly upped and left.

"We'll stay a couple of days before pushing on," Lucius said, and Fings was fine with that. Food, water, shelter, a place to rest. Frankly, that was all he cared about.

He was less fine with it when a party of Witch-Breakers and a dozen Sunguard rode through on the next morning. Although, thankfully, they didn't stop. Later, a company of armed men came in from the plateau. They claimed to be militia, called themselves the Homeland Defenders, but Fings didn't buy it. He knew how men looked when they were sizing up a place, reckoning among themselves whether a job could be done. The look these men had was exactly that, a hunger for whatever they could take.

They didn't stay. When they headed out, it was towards Helhex, not towards the plateau. Still felt like a bad omen.

"We should go," he told Lucius. "Before that lot come back." Not that he wanted to, because everything still hurt.

They didn't, of course, because nothing was going to get Soraya back on the road so quickly. A day later, the men *did* come back, and this time they stayed. They drank, were loud and violent and helped themselves to whatever they wanted. Fings kept his head down and stayed out of sight. Everyone else did the same; come morning, the men had left again. Hadn't come to much, insofar as no one was dead and nothing was on fire; still, Fings didn't like it, not one bit, knowing those men were on the road ahead.

"I think we should turn back," he said, but no one wanted to know.

They gave themselves another day and then made the climb to the pass. Seth was walking now, a few hours each morning, which made for an easier time of it, although the climb quickly knocked the stuffing out of him. Lucius too, the load in his cart doubled by the keg of water that was going to keep them alive across the plateau.

"It's all downhill from here," he said, gasping but bright-eyed, which made Fings smile.

The pass descended into barren stone and sand. Boulders lay scattered among tangles of thorns. Distant monoliths of crumbling rock poked at the sky. The sun beat down. The only living things Fings saw were snakes, spiders the size of his hand, and skinny rat-like things that scurried off at the first sign of their approach.

Sure, they had food and water, blankets to keep them warm at night. But to Fings, a city boy, born and bred, all this emptiness felt alien. They could die out here and no one would know. No one would ever find them. They'd be lost forever.

Yeah. He'd seen enough of mountains and deserts now, he reckoned. Enough to know they weren't for him.

"We'll get there," Seth said, out of nothing. Fings hadn't even realised he was awake.

"Sure. And then we'll have to get somewhere else, and on it goes."

"Yeah. I know."

Fings huffed a bit as he pushed Seth's cart, wrestling with words until he finally forced them out. "Can I ask you something?"

"What?"

"I keep seeing you staring at that glass ball thing when everyone else is sleeping. What is it?"

Seth gave him a long one-eyed look before answering. "Someone else's memories."

"Memories?" Fings scrunched up his face. "Whose?"

"I don't know, exactly. It passes the time when I can't sleep."

Fings wasn't a sword-monk and so he couldn't smell lies. But he *had* known Seth for a very long time, had had a lot of practice at knowing when Seth was feeding him bullshit. "Right," he said, fists clenching a little. "So... Where'd you get it?"

Seth gave him a baleful look. "I don't know. I don't remember. That's partly why I keep looking. I'm trying to work it out."

"First that crypt thing under the temple in the Square. Then stealing that book for you." Fings shook his head. "Then that place in the Undercity. They kicked you out for that, but you didn't stop, did you? I never asked what got you locked up, when I got you out of that cell in Varr. Starting to think maybe I should."

Seth shook his head. "You don't want to know."

"Going to Deephaven. That wasn't about helping Myla. Not for you."

"It was about not being burned alive by sword-monks."

"Yeah… But it was *also* about that warlock she told you about. Or are you going to tell me I'm wrong about that?"

"Bit of both."

"I talked to her, you know."

"Who, Myla?"

"Myla's teacher. The one who fought that warlock all them years back and drove him away. I saw you go to where he lived. You and that Taiytakei popinjay. That place on the waterfront by the river."

"I wasn't myself."

"Right. Well. So, who were you, then?"

Seth rearranged the scars on his face into something like a crooked smile. "I don't remember most of what I did in Deephaven. Maybe it's best that way?"

"A shadow may last an hour, but the sun is eternal." One of Myla's sayings. Fings wasn't much for religion, not in a go-to-temple, pray-to-the-rising-sun sort of way. But he knew what was right and what was wrong.

"The Sun is eternal, the source of all life," Seth growled, finishing the quote. "Except it isn't, and even the Path acknowledges that. As for the Sun shining with the same brilliance upon all his children? Look at me!" His fingers scratched at his scarred face. "The Sun is eternal? No. He sets and darkness comes. The Sun is never failing? The Sun is ever constant?" The scabs on Seth's face oozed blood where he'd torn them open.

Fings stared. He still saw the old Seth now and then, the boy he'd met all those years ago on the temple steps, the one he'd grown up with, the one he'd watched take his novice robes. As much a brother as Levvi in Deephaven. But something had changed, something more than the pits and craters on the ruined half of Seth's face. There was another Seth in there now, sitting alongside the first. As though Seth's scars ran right through him.

"I came from nothing," Seth said. "Just like you. The worst of the worst, thieves and pickpockets and beggars. Me and you and Levvi and all the rest. When the Path took me, I probably looked like I was brimming with faith, but what you saw was gratitude, Fings, nothing more. The life they offered was so far beyond anything I'd had. And then they threw me out, back where I'd come from."

He sat back. "I'm not sure how much I ever *believed*. But they showed me a world, Fings, a life I couldn't have dreamed without them. And then they told me no, you can't have it, back to the gutter with you." A shudder wracked his face. "And then all those months with Blackhand. I was so pathetically fucking grateful for every scrap he gave me."

"Yeah. Well." Fings' voice was flat. "Blackhand's dead now." He shivered at the memory. "What's done is done. Not much point hating a ghost, if you ask me."

"I never abandoned the Path. *They* abandoned *me*."

"If Myla was here, she'd tell you you're an idiot."

A flicker of a smile crept across Seth's lips. "Perhaps. But she's *not* here, is she? She's gone, like everyone else. Besides, who's *she* to lecture *me*? *I* just talked to the dead a bit. I didn't make them that way in the first place."

Fings looked away, biting his lip. He reckoned he'd never forget that last sight of Myla, alone on the back of a horse between the panicked crowd at the docks and the onrush of Dead Men, sword aloft in the night.

"Might not be dead," he said, although he didn't believe it.

"She went to Deephaven to atone. To prostrate herself before the Sun, to ask for penance and forgiveness. Look what it got her. There's no forgiveness, Fings. The world is harsh and cruel and will never let you go. Punishment is arbitrary. Now leave me alone."

Seth's eyes had turned watery. Kelm's Teeth, was he weeping? They looked away from one another, each lost in their own private misery. Times like this, Fings would usually have left Seth to be alone; but Seth was in a handcart, and the cart was hardly going to push itself.

"Crap," said Seth softly.

"What?"

"I miss her. Honestly, I hardly fucking knew her, but I miss her. She was so sure about everything. I wish I had that certainty. But I suppose this is how it goes, isn't it?" He nodded towards Lucius and Soraya, walking ahead along the road. "They'll be rid of us in Torpreah. Like fucking lightning, you mark my words. You'll walk away too, one day. Everyone does. In the end, I'll be truly alone. The way I was when you found me." Seth began to shake. He turned away.

Fings stopped pushing the cart. He squatted, reached into the cart and put a hand on Seth's shoulder.

"Oh, go away, will you? Go on, just fuck off! Get it over with."

"Ain't going to do that."

Seth clutched Fings' hand, squeezing hard enough to hurt. "Why? Why not? What am I to you but a burden?"

"You're my brother. Way I see it, if we ain't got each other, we ain't got nothing."

They stayed that way for a while, silent, Seth hunched in the cart, Fings crouched beside him, holding hands like they'd be torn apart and thrown to the corners of the world if either let go. It was Fings, in the end, who slackened his grip. By then, Lucius and Soraya were almost out of sight.

There was no shelter from the sun after the mountains. When the midday heat came, they strung Seth's blanket between the two carts and sprawled beneath it, dozing as best they could. In the evenings, they walked in silence, too drained for conversation. As the cold night came and they settled again to sleep, Fings asked Lucius about Torpreah. Reckoned he'd be hanging around a while, at least a month or two, before cashing in his slice of whatever Lucius had going and heading back to Varr, him and Seth, so it gave them something to talk about. Lucius reckoned on selling fashionable clothes to the rich, which meant having the right look, the right voice, the right words to attract the right custom. It meant knowing cloth, which he did, knowing the fashions of the city, which he could learn, and moving in the right circles, which he'd work out when he got there. It meant getting into their houses, which had Fings imagining himself standing in the background, quietly sizing wherever they went up for a bit of robbery. Would hardly hurt, would it, heading back home, pockets stuffed with Torpreahn silver?

Lucius started on about permits, about the papers they'd need, the letters he'd have to write. How important it was to write orders and receipts in the most elegant hand. His wild idea of hundreds of personal invitations, hand-delivered to the doors of the rich middle-classes and even the nobility, inviting them to indulge in his premium services at a steep discount. How he'd have to hire a scribe, how expensive such people were in Torpreah because they were in such demand. Fings couldn't help but grin when he heard that. It might be dark, the sun might be out of the sky, but sometimes you felt its warmth, nonetheless.

He didn't say anything about Seth being one of the best forgers in Varr, not yet. But as he settled to sleep, he felt Seth touch his arm.

"Thank you, brother," Seth said.

"You're welcome, brother." Fings smiled again, because sometimes you just got a good feeling that everything was going to go right.

Four days after crossing the mountains, the men from Narvel's Pass fell upon them in a swirl of noise and dust, and everything didn't go right at all.

19
Snake Juice

Myla's days in Varr turned to weeks. The Month of Floods gave way to the Month of Lightning. Far to the South, Torpreahn armies crossed The Fracture unopposed. In the west, the Wraiths and their Dead Men reached the lake where the City of Spires once stood. Whispers spoke of the Wraiths gathering, a ritual days long to summon the city back, ending in failure. The City of Spires, it seemed, remained stubbornly not where it was supposed to be.

Meanwhile, Varr filled with soldiers while the Regent's council debated which enemy they should face first. All of this Myla *heard*, but what she *saw* was largely confined to the palace, where she gawped at the opulence; to the training grounds, where she and the Regent's four Hawks spent hours each day, sparring and talking and gradually becoming friends; and to the House of Fire, the blackened shell of a once-grand manor where Orien spent most of his time. The house belonged to Lady Novashi's uncle. Orien had met him once, an encounter he'd still be talking about on his deathbed, Myla thought: a thundercloud disguised as a man, with a frown to wilt trees and crumble stone. He'd returned to Neja, so Myla never got to see for herself, but the ghost of his presence haunted the place.

As for Lady Novashi, she and Myla reached a silent accommodation, a mutual acceptance that if they simply ignored each other, maybe it was possible for a mage and sword-monk to coexist. When the Red Witch came to the House of Fire, Orien and the Guild mages would listen and try to learn; if Myla was there, she usually ended up listening too, not having anything else to do. The mages would nod sagely and spend the rest of the afternoon setting things on fire until it got dark. Occasionally Orien mastered something new. Those were the good days, always a joy seeing his delight in whatever new trick he'd discovered. Most days he didn't. *Those* days, more and more, left him in a dark mood.

There's a storm coming from the sea. Can you feel it? The Regent's words, back on the bridge in Varr, Midwinter, the night Myla had returned the Moonsteel Crown. Orien would be explaining how he'd unravelled a new mystery and Myla would find herself remembering the Sapphire Throne. He'd conjure fire and she'd hear the Regent in her head. Now and then, she was summoned to the palace to stand at the Regent's side, the menace of a near-drawn sword. Sometimes the audience was with only a handful. Other times, hundreds. Either way, all anyone saw was the brilliance of the throne, its figurehead child-emperor, and a small figure in black and red and gold and white in the chair beside him, emerald eyes dissolving their worlds into a cascade of joyous chords while a faraway voice of many melodies spoke into their thoughts in the celestial rhymes of creation and told them what to do. Anyone who stood before the Regent, she climbed inside their head and made them fall in love. The most dangerous of mages, hidden in plain sight, and how old was she? Sometimes she looked her age, but inside her... inside was something ancient. As though nothing could surprise her. As though she'd seen it all before.

The threat of a near-drawn sword? No. Myla was simply the Regent showing off her pet sword-monk. They both knew it; and here Myla was, trying to be Tasahre's spy, and they both knew *that*, too, which made the task obviously impossible.

There's a storm coming from the sea. Can you feel it?

She lay awake in the middle of the night, Orien beside her, snuffling into the blankets. He'd been in a dark mood again, another day of failure. She'd managed to talk him out of it, as she did most days, but it was getting harder, and she still hadn't told him she was carrying his child. She played the conversation over in her head and it never ended well, but she wouldn't be able to hide it forever. Orien, admittedly, would probably need her to paint a big sign on herself before he worked it out, but Tanysha, the Regent's Hawk with whom Myla talked the most, already suspected.

The Regent knew, of course. The Regent knew everything. The Regent had known what was coming to Deephaven. Even back on that Midwinter bridge.

She wondered, sometimes, if she should leave. Pack her things and quietly walk away. All this inactivity rankled. What she *should* be doing was... but there it was: *what* should she be doing? Not *this*, not sitting around, but what? Run off and put down a few Dead Men? Try and find a Wraith to fight? A way to a quick death was all *that* was. Even Tasahre had needed help, and Myla was a long way from being Tasahre's equal.

A knock on the door startled her out of her reverie. When it came again, she shrugged herself into a tunic and went to see who was bothering her in the middle of the night. The Guild mages were quartered in the Kaveneth, so the House of Fire was largely empty after dark.

"Get dressed," Tanysha said. She moved past Myla, dropped something on Orien, then gave him a good hard poke. "You, too, mage. Up!"

Orien grunted and pulled the blankets tighter. Tanysha prodded him again. Myla lit a lamp.

"Excuse me? Middle of the night here?" She liked Tanysha, but still...

"Come on, mage!" Tanysha yanked the blankets away, then grabbed the bundle of cloth she'd dropped on Orien and shook it out. A brilliant orange robe, trimmed with intertwined threads of vermilion and gold. "Up, up!"

"Enough!" Myla grabbed her arm. To Myla's surprise, Tanysha snatched at Myla's wrist, half-caught it and twisted; Myla wriggled free and then, for no apparent reason, they were fighting, a fast exchange of grapples and attempted holds until Myla had Tanysha pinned to the floor. "What the *fuck*?"

"One day, monk. One day." Tanysha squirmed in Myla's grasp.

By now, Orien had rolled out of bed. He shrugged on his new robe and looked himself up and down, but mostly he was looking at Myla and Tanysha.

"Um... Do you two want to be left alone for a bit?"

"Piss off," said Myla. She let Tanysha go. As she did, she caught a look between Tanysha and Orien. The kind that spoke of shared secrets. She wasn't sure she liked that look.

Orien brushed his hands down his robe. "These are..."

"Fit to cock and strut in front of the court," said Tanysha. "Present from your Mistress. Come on! Robe up, sword-monk! We're summoned. Middle of the night? No one cares!"

"Summoned where and by whom?" snapped Myla.

"You'll-see-when-you-get-there and by who-do-you-think?" Tanysha gave Myla an arch look. "You can stay if you want. It was *him* I was sent for. But no one said anything about stopping you if you want to tag along." She grinned. "And we both know you're bored witless."

Myla grunted, stewing on the look she'd caught between the two of them. Tanysha was right, though. She *was* bored.

She dressed, picked up her swords and then, seeing Tanysha frown and shake her head, reluctantly put them down again.

They followed Taysha. A boat from the Emperor's Docks took them across the Thort. On the far side, they climbed the winding path to the Kaveneth, gates open, presumably because no one in their right mind went uninvited into a den of mages. They crossed the outer yard, through more gates and another courtyard, to a narrow door into an even narrower passage lit by... Myla wasn't sure, because there weren't any lamps or torches, more like the air itself was aglow. Down a narrow stair, then another, past more narrow doors.

Why is everything so fucking narrow? "Is it all like this?" Myla asked. She'd never been into the Kaveneth, had quietly assumed it would be like the palace, spacious and airy and full of light. This? *This* felt like a prison.

Yet this is where the Regent's mages make their nest? Why?

Another dizzying set of steps ending in a gloomy room full of barred doors into tiny empty cells.

It is *a prison, then. Or was... Oh.*

The room had been cleared apart from a single table in the centre. On the table lay a dead Wraith, stripped of its armour, which was piled neatly on the floor nearby. Naked, the body looked almost human. But it *was* a Wraith or, at least, had been one when it had been alive. The angular face. The long silver-white hair. And those vermillion eyes, she knew, if she were to look closer...

Not the Wraith we killed in Deephaven.

No, because this one still had a head. Which meant...

Which means someone else has found a way to kill them.

Another sword-monk? No.

Why not?

Because... well, because it still had a head.

Tiny flames lined three of the walls. The fourth remained in shadow. No candles, only flames, the same trick Orien had used on the night they'd met. When she looked closer, she saw a pile of partially dismantled machines in a corner, including a chair that looked like Khrozus's chair but with a metal spike pointing up from the seat. A Pear of Torment. She recognised it because that had been Tasahre's favourite story about Saint Kelm.

Around it, a discarded collection of chains and manacles.

They tortured people here.

She almost missed the Taiytakei popinjay, rootling around under the table, until he popped his head out.

"Orien! My friend!"

The popinjay, but no one else. Which was odd, because Tanysha served the Regent. Maybe Lady Novashi at a pinch, but not the popinjay. Her skin prickled.

"Just the four of us?"

The popinjay bounced to his feet. "Just us." Myla sniffed the air but didn't smell a lie. Tanysha, though, gave a slight shake of her head, although Myla wasn't sure whether that meant *no, we're not alone* or *if you ask, I won't answer.* Either of which, she supposed with a sigh, came down to the same thing.

"That's not the Wraith we killed in Deephaven," she said.

"Indeed not." The popinjay shook his head. "This one's new. We have two, in fact."

"How?"

"You're more likely to know about that than I. *I* barely get to leave this room!" The popinjay beamed as he went to Orien and gripped his shoulders. "But you! Friend! How *are* you? I have so much to thank you for. Thanks to you, I find myself an advisor of sorts to Her Majesty. Or perhaps that's too far... Still, nevertheless... An inquisitor of the secrets of the world!"

"Her Highness," said Myla, almost without thinking. "We have an emperor, who sits on the throne. His sister's title is Regent, not Queen."

"Forgive me, forgive me! My people have... different customs. But yes, yes. We spoke at length about what I did for your mistress. The mending of flesh. The repair of damaged muscle, bone, and sinew. The ejection and disruption of necrotic matter and malign miasmas. Long discourse on how the same forces can rend as well as mend, which of course they can; whether flesh and bone can be induced to deviate from its natural form in some manner, which it also can; and if so, whether such a change can be permanent, of which I am... less sure; and whether, if so, it can be detected, and..." He frowned. "Come to think of it, I suspect this may have been her fiercest interest of all."

"So... You're going to change that into something that isn't a Wraith?"

The popinjay ignored her, his focus entirely on Orien. "No matter! I shall apply my most avid attentions and shall soon have the question resolved. But you, my friend! What of you? You've been in her presence too. I see it in you. I had heard whispers that it was dangerous to look her in her eye. Now I see how true they were! Beautiful and powerful and sat upon the Sapphire Throne!"

"The *emperor* sits on the Sapphire Throne," growled Myla. "Not the Regent."

The popinjay bared his teeth and carried on as though she wasn't there. "Are you one of the besotted? Do you, too, have a head full of smouldering Moongrass? Did the hand of the divine reach out and touch you?"

Well, it's certainly touched you, Myla thought, without much sympathy. She wished she'd brought her swords.

"Of course not," Orien said, which smelled to Myla like a lie. She sighed. Somehow, in some way or other, the Regent was watching, because why had else it been Tanysha who came for Orien and not some other lackey. The popinjay, apparently, hadn't worked that out.

Not as smart as you like to think you are.

"Enjoying all this flattery?" she asked the empty air.

"Have a care, friend." The popinjay was still talking to Orien as he took an empty jar from behind the dead half-god's corpse. He tested the lid, found it tight, then dropped to his hands and crawled across the floor. Myla sidled up next to Tanysha and whispered in her ear.

"I know you're here," she said.

From under the table, the popinjay swore. "Bloody thing's escaped again. They sent me a mage. Master Rubens of the Guild. A man afflicted with the same passion for knowledge as I. I think they sent him here to get him out of the way. Their loss, but ever since he's been coming to assist, we keep losing Sparkler."

"Sparkler?" asked Orien.

"The glowing snake thing the Wraiths have in their heads that makes them... well, that makes them half-gods. You remember! That one from Deephaven I showed you outside the City of... well where the City of Spires was *supposed* to be. Rubens and I gave them names!"

"They murdered an entire city, and you gave them *names*?" asked Myla in disbelief. "What are they to you? Pets?"

"Them?" asked Orien, which was possibly more relevant.

"Well... two out of two. Haven't cut this one open yet. Call it a careful guess, if you like. And best *be* careful, too. If it gets you, it *will* try to burrow into your skin and make you into one of them." He scrabbled for something under the table. "All the half-gods we've seen have been covered in Soulsilver, yet those seen last year by her Highness and the Lady Novashi were apparently... Oh."

"*Last* year?" Myla reached to grab the popinjay, planning on giving him a good shake until some answers fell out, but Tanysha caught her arm.

"They made themselves known before Deephaven," Tanysha murmured, and Myla wasn't sure whether this was Tanysha speaking or whether the words came from the Regent.

The popinjay jumped back to his feet with a yelp of triumph. "Got you!" He held out his hand for Orien to see. He was wearing a thick leather glove like a blacksmith might wear against the heat of the forge. Hanging from it by a pair of fangs was a silver serpent, a handspan long, glowing with moonlight. The popinjay dangled it in front of Orien, then picked up a pair of tongs and carefully removed both serpent and glove into a small iron chest under the table, closed the lid, locked it, and slipped the key in his pocket.

The chest, Myla saw, was chained to the floor. She cocked her head as the popinjay caught her eye. "You think someone's going to steal... *that*?"

"Oh yes! And you're here to see why." He beamed and bared his teeth and beckoned them into another room, smaller, occupied by a large writing desk covered in papers and volumes of what looked like a journal, all careful tidy writing and annotated drawings. The popinjay picked up the top volume and riffled its pages. "We spent our time on the armour at first. Fascinating. Like a new skin. I assume there's a clever way for putting it on and taking it off, but for the time being I'm forced to compel the dead body to expel it. Taxing, and very vexing. There are souls trapped inside, too, same as you'd get in a Soul Jewel except without the jewel. That's why we took to calling it Soulsilver..."

"A *what* jewel?" asked Myla.

The popinjay gave her a sickly grin. "Something I, ah... once came across in my travels."

"You're telling me, a sword-monk, that there are souls trapped in that pile of metal back there?"

"I... suppose I am." The connection clearly hadn't occurred to the popinjay. Now he was weighing up the consequences of what he'd said and not much liking where they went.

"They need to be set free." If she'd had her swords, she'd have done it right there and then. Taken Sunsteel and rammed it through every piece of the popinjay's cursed armour until there was nothing left, because she'd seen how Tasahre's swords had gone straight through the stuff as though it was smoke.

"It is almost impervious to sorcery," the popinjay was saying, back to ignoring her and talking at Orien. "Poor old Rubens has been doing most of the work on that since... Ah, yes, here we are. Month of Lightning, Abyssday, week two. Full moon. Yes, yes, that was the day; was it only a twelvenight ago? How time flies. Yes, but that's not why I brought you here." The popinjay pulled a vial out of his pocket, half full of a liquid that shone with silver light. "Pure divine essence! This is what makes them into what they are! One drop and you're a god for a day. Well... A bit less than that. An hour, maybe. Still. The secret of their power. To a sorcerer, more precious than gold! This is the Wraith from Deephaven, the one your sword-monk helped to kill–"

Fuck's sake. "I'm right here, you know." Myla took a step closer. "Mage, what are you–"

"–which makes poor Sparkler over there the only one I have left. Any mage would trade an arm or leg to get hold of him, and so into the chest he goes." The popinjay swatted Myla away, almost a push, and it came as such a surprise that he got away with it. "Look at the Sapphire Throne! Look around you! Everywhere dripping with wealth, yet the crowns the Emperor and his Regent wear are plain. No diamonds, no emeralds, no rubies, nothing. Why are those crowns so precious?"

Myla glared, about ready to rearrange the popinjay's teeth for him, but Tanysha had a hand on her arm again. *Let it go.*

The popinjay held up the vial. "The circlets came from Anvor, and before then, who knows? They weren't made for kings, they were made to *make* kings. You've felt her presence. But it's not *her*. It's this!" He opened the vial and held the stopper in front of Orien's face, a drop of glowing liquid hanging from its tip. "One touch and you'll be burning cities to the ground! If you've ever taken a lungful of Soaring Cloud, you'll have an idea how it feels."

Orien took a step back. "A lungful of... what?"

The popinjay coughed. "They crush it into powder and put it into little bags. You blow into the bag and then... never mind. The pursuit of knowledge, you understand." He moved suddenly, a quick dart of the hand, touching the glowing droplet to Orien's lips. Myla lunged, but too late. Orien staggered back, blinking as the glow spread across his face.

"Hey!" he said, and then: "Oh. Oh!"

He held up his hand. It was on fire.

"I don't... what?"

"Oh dear." The popinjay looked suddenly shifty. "Oh no! My papers!" He gave Orien a hefty shove towards the door. "Out! Out, out!"

The flames were spreading up Orien's arm. He flailed. "I can't... I don't... Um... Help?"

Myla grabbed Orien's other hand, the one that *wasn't* on fire, and pulled him away. She flashed the popinjay a glare. "Fucking idiot!"

To the river, she was thinking, but she only got Orien as far as the dead Wraith before he exploded in light and searing heat, and someone had their arms around her, pulling her away, and Orien was right there in there front of her, a white-hot inferno of flame, eyes wide, paralysed and terrified. She tried to struggle free.

"Don't," said Tanysha. Although, of course, *not* Tanysha, because Tanysha was presumably only fireproof when she had a Moon-Witch riding in her head.

I wish you wouldn't call me that.

"What have you done?"

I'm going to let go now. Stay close. Even I have limits.

The hands fell away. Myla spun round. Tanysha was right there but her eyes had gone green. Bright, emerald green.

"What have you done to him?"

Look at him! The strength! It's astounding!

Orien appeared to be getting himself under control. He raised a flaming hand; but when he spoke, his voice somehow wasn't his own.

"I remember you," he said.

"Orien?"

"What have you *done*?" Orien's flame dimmed a little. His eyes changed as though he was suddenly aware of where he was, and what was happening, and who was standing in front of him. When he spoke, he sounded like Orien again. "I... Myla? Highness! I..." He dropped to the floor and kowtowed.

"He sees through you," said Myla.

Apparently so.

The Regent, still looking like Tanysha, went to Orien and touched his head, apparently not bothered by him being a blazing inferno. "Your mistress awaits outside. Go to her. Become what you seek."

Without another word, Orien got to his feet and walked away. When Myla started after him, the Regent caught her arm.

"Let him go."

"Fuck off." Except, as soon as she was free of Tanysha's touch, she felt the fire again, the heat blazing from Orien that meant she couldn't get close, never mind touch him. A few steps and she gave up.

I did warn you.

"Do you have any idea how annoying you are?"

Your resentment laces your every thought.

"And yet still you do it. One day, someone's going to stab you."

And you'll stop them.

"I rather think I'll be cheering them on." *And now I'm going to think about having sex with Orien until you go away.* And she did, and it was quite gratifying, really. She could almost feel the Regent flush with embarrassment.

Since he's on your mind...

Sex, sex, sex, sex!

If you're going to…

Sex, sex, SEX!

"Oh enough! Fine!" Tanysha glared. "What I was *going* to say is that if you ever plan on sharing your little secret, do it sooner rather than later. He'll be going to Neja. You'll be staying with me. If things go badly, you'll not have another chance."

"Go away!"

"This is how we win! I brought you to see this so you could tell your sword-mistress. Better you know it through your own eyes. She'll be pleased with her spy, don't you think?"

"What *are* you?"

"He'll take it better than you fear, by the way." And then Tanysha was walking away, and Myla was alone with the popinjay, in a room that stank of burned meat, neither of which was pleasant company.

Well, fuck this and fuck you.

She found Orien outside. He and the Red Witch faced one another, each a pillar of flame, locked in some pyromantic dance, each throwing darts of fire that the other would catch and throw back, or else shoot out a dart of their own to collide with the first in a shower of sparks. She stopped to watch, anxious and awed and with a touch of regret. This *was* what Orien wanted, no doubt. And she'd let him have it too, if it could be his, because who was she to put a cage around another's dreams… yet it was hard to see herself by his side if this was his path.

Except… All this power he had now, throwing fire as easily as breathing? The popinjay said it wouldn't last, so what happened when it was gone? It was a cruelty to give him a taste of what he most wanted but could never be. When it faded, she wasn't sure what he'd do.

She trotted away, took a boat across the river back to the House of Fire and collected her swords. By the time she returned to the Kaveneth, Orien and the Red Witch had gone; since she couldn't see any pillars of fire rising anywhere from the city, she supposed the lesson was done for the night.

Ah, well. She had a lesson of her own. She rather wished the popinjay was still around to watch as she destroyed his pieces of half-god armour and set free the souls trapped inside. He'd be angry about that, she supposed.

Good. *She* was angry too.

Back at the House of Fire, close to dawn, she found Orien sitting in the darkness; and whatever had taken him in the Kaveneth, whatever the popinjay's potion had done, all that was over. He was back where she'd found him earlier that evening, moping and brooding.

"I'm so fucking furious–" she started, but stopped as Orien looked up at her, one finger raised. He'd been drinking, she realised. The general scorched odour of the house hid the smell, but he wasn't quite steady. She sighed. All in all, getting drunk *did* seem like a fine idea right now.

"You know what that was?" he asked.

"A demonstration." You didn't have to be a genius to work *that* one out.

"Do you know why they picked me?"

Myla reckoned she did, but she wasn't going to say.

"Because I am the weakest, which made the demonstration more poignant. Because I'm so feeble that if it can do that for someone like *me*, imagine what it can do for a *real* mage."

"Someone said that, did they?"

"They didn't need to."

And what could Myla offer against something so crushing? That being a feeble mage was a lot more than being no mage at all? That sooner or later, he was going to have to accept what he was, and what he wasn't.

He was in no place to hear that, though. Not now.

So... maybe don't say anything at all?

Maybe that was best. She sat beside him, tight and close, lifted his arm around her shoulders, grabbed the bottle he'd been swigging and necked a long slug of what turned out to be something like liquid fire. "When Tasahre and I fought the Wraith in Deephaven, I was lucky. Had I been alone, I wouldn't even have bothered it;

it would have killed me without a pause. But it would have killed Tasahre, too, if I hadn't fought alongside her. I'll never equal her; but in that moment, I made the difference. I was enough to turn the fight. One day, you will do the same."

She took another long drink, and then another.

"There's something else, though. Something new we're going to have to learn to do. Both of us together. And in this, I think you will excel. Something that no one else can do better."

She wasn't sure why *now* was the right time to tell him he was going to be a father, only that it was. He took it better than she'd feared. Almost like he was pleased. Neither of them said much after that. Just sat together and watched the sunrise.

"You should probably drink less," he said, after a bit.

"Yeah," Myla snorted. "They're going to send you to Neja to fight half-gods and the Dead Men. Did they tell you that?"

"Yes."

"I'm going with the Regent. South, I think."

"I know." He squeezed her hand. "She's not what she seems, you know."

"What do you mean?"

"In the Kaveneth... At first it was overwhelming. A feeling of sheer power. Then it was something more. I felt I wasn't alone. Like there was an echo of something else inside me, ancient and brimming with power. Overwhelming. And I couldn't... And then it faded, just a touch, and you were there, and Her Highness too, although she looked wrong, and for a moment, it was like the echo knew her. But not as *her*. As something else."

Myla rested her head on his shoulder. "I don't suppose you have the slightest idea what that means?"

"Not really." And then: "Thank you."

"For what?"

"For being you." And then: "Daddy Orien. Well. Didn't see *that* one coming."

20
DEFENDERS OF THE FAITH

Seth lay in his cart, hidden from the sun by a sailcloth. His scabs were healing, turning to scars. He spent as much time walking now as being pushed; but the heat of the sun was still too much, so bad he could hardly breathe. He let Fings do the work then, let the rocking of the uneven ground lull him to sleep. At night, he lay awake while the others snored, stared at the stars, and tried to think. He spent more and more time inside Saffran Kuy's memories. He knew, now, what the warlock was and what he'd wanted.

In Narvel's Pass, while Fings and Lucius had been buying supplies – in Fings' case, using the word "buying" very loosely – Soraya had come to him.

"I've written it all down," she'd said. "The way I want to remember it."

"I can help you forget," he'd told her. "Filling the hole with whatever story you've written: that's up to you."

Eventually, when he decided she'd understood, he'd asked one last time: "Are you sure?" She'd nodded, and so he'd done it. Afterwards, he'd given Soraya the story she'd written. She'd read it and asked him questions, trying to fill in pieces she hadn't written down, not that Seth had any answers. The important thing was that she understood what he'd done, right from the start, and why she'd asked for it. *That* memory, he'd left carefully untouched; and even then, it had been a rough ride, her acceptance of what he'd done for her.

Oddly, the story she'd created to fit where her memories had once been looked to Seth exactly like the story she was trying to forget.

"It's the feelings," she'd told him, before he'd taken her memories. "I don't want to forget what happened. I don't want that at all. What I want to forget is how it felt."

On reflection, he could relate to that.

A lesson for next time, eh? He still poked at the hole that was his last day in Deephaven. Not that there would *be* a next time, not for him, and probably not for anyone else, either. Soraya seemed happier now, true, but it *had* been quite a night, putting her back together from the story she'd written. Touch and go, at times. He liked to think he'd done something good; but it gnawed at him, knowing she knew his secret. He couldn't be sharing it around, how he could sigil memories out of people, not if a sword-monk might one day hear of it.

You could always make her forget.

He drifted in and out of sleep thinking yes, he probably should. The more he considered what he'd done for her, the more he saw how what she'd wanted hadn't been to *forget*, exactly, but to blunt their jagged edges. He was still pondering the difference when the cart stopped and he heard unfamiliar voices, loud and angry. Then Soraya, then a shout, some swearing, some sort of fight…

"Put that down!"

"Lucius! Don't!"

"Get on the ground. All of you!"

Everything went quiet.

He reached out his thoughts. Six new minds. Men. Six… other things. The men tasted predatory. Poised on the edge of violence. He felt for Fings and Lucius and Soraya and found them, all afraid. Soraya in particular. The six… things… They were… animals?

A squeal and some laughter. The sound of a horse pissing in the dirt. Horses, then. Six horses.

Now you know what horse-thoughts look like. If you live long enough, that might even be useful.

"Krick! Put that down!"

Any moment now, someone was going to tear the sailcloth away. When that happened, Seth reckoned the best he could do was pretend to be dead.

"Etan! Get one of *them* to push it. Kelm's Teeth!"

The cart began moving again. Turning back the way they'd come. Seth breathed a sigh of relief. While they were moving, he was probably safe.

And what happens when they stop?

The urge to peek was stupid but irresistible. He didn't dare raise the sailcloth more than an inch, so all he saw was a single horseman, riding nearby. Enough to recognise one of the militiamen who'd ridden through Narvel's Pass. And yes, the world was full of crooked Longcoats who'd dish out beatings for fun or coin, who'd look away if silver crossed their palm... but this was different. *This* was rape and murder. He could feel the shape of it in their minds. These men were killers.

When they stopped, they were going to look in the carts, hoping to find something of value. Instead, they were going to discover a half-dead beggar. They wouldn't have to lift a finger to murder him. All they had to do was toss him out and leave him for the sun.

And how ironic would that *be, to be killed by the Sun?*

He had a half-empty skin of water in the cart, some stale bread and a blunt paring knife that might even be able to hurt someone if they stood still long enough. There was Kuy's globe, which might be handy for bashing someone over the head, but he doubted he'd get the chance.

Well, then, warlock. Get me out of this one.

Kuy's memories didn't have anything useful to say about escaping bands of murderous bandits. Hadn't been the sort of problem the master warlock had ever faced.

There must be something, right?

There is. Sigil them and turn them into Dead Men.

Yeah. Do you think they'll form an orderly queue?

Still, better than nothing. He rummaged and found a quill. No ink but there was always blood. No paper but there was sailcloth. He grabbed the globe and dived inside. Sigils...

It is the nature of remnants to diminish and dissipate so they may join the essence of the universe and return renewed. This is not choice but instinct. Through use of sigils, the artist offers this end. To the remnants, a sigil is both map and guide, a means to diminish. For the artist, it sculpts the energies released. Thus, sigils must be precise. Whether drawn by pen and ink or inscribed by a finger in the air is of no import, but accuracy is vital. To progress far, the student must undergo apprenticeship as a scribe and must excel.

Yes, yes, yes. Blah, blah. Seth glared at the globe. The Path had been the same. Hours of tedious lectures on history and philosophy and mysticism, five minutes of anything useful. Although the bit about drawing sigils in the air was good to know. It would never have occurred to him on his own.

How to get rid of murderous bandits? He doubted he'd get the chance to slap a sigil on each in turn while their friends stood conveniently still and didn't get all stabby. In a city, at night, he might slip out, turn one into a Dead Man, or steal his will, then turn it on the others. Out here in broad daylight, no cover anywhere... Probably not.

What did that leave? The usual choice was beg, bargain, bribe or threaten. Circumstances being what they were, he couldn't see what he could offer by way of a bribe or a bargain. He *was* quite good at begging, mind. Well-practiced...

No!

Oh, so what then? Threaten them? Woo-woo, smoke and scary noises, fear the terrible sorcerer who can barely stand up before he faints from exhaustion?

Maybe the globe had a way to scare them?

The animating force within us sees any aroused remnant as a threat, a hungry ghost, a potential usurper eager to taste life once more. This we feel as fear. Intent is unimportant. You may heal an injured man by directing the energy of remnants into his ailing flesh. Yet watching relatives will

*feel fear, even as they see the wounds heal, and may thus turn against the
artist irrespective of outcome…*

The cart began to move faster. Seth's heart raced. Sigils made
remnants do stuff. Remnants doing stuff frightened people. He
could work with that, couldn't he? He remembered the first time
he'd used one, down in a dark alley in Varr, and yes, he *had* been
scared, although mostly of Myla.

He needed something stronger…

He skimmed Kuy's memories, searching. The globe was full
of sermons and explanations, short on demonstrations. There
were sigils for pushing remnants away, for drawing them closer,
for giving energy and taking it and a hundred and one other
things. Sigils for speaking with the dead, for manipulating them,
yet Kuy's memories never held the *designs* for his sigils, only
what they did and how they worked. Which made it all very
interesting, but also very useless. Every time, when Kuy drew
a sign, it was hidden. Behind his apprentice, behind a screen,
behind a book. Every single one. He was, Seth came to realise,
doing it deliberately. Taunting Seth from beyond death.

Another hour passed. The cart stopped and Seth still hadn't
discovered something to drive away a band of angry bandits. He
heard more voices, like maybe the angry bandits had returned to
their camp and were saying hello to some more angry bandits.

How delightful.

He gripped the paring knife. For all he'd learned from Kuy's
memories, he still only knew the same six sigils he'd learned in
Varr from the papers Fings had stolen. Right now, that felt like a
lifetime ago.

*I can make them forget things. I can kill them. I can bring them back
as Dead Men. I can make them do what I say.*

Which *was* all very useful, but only if he could slink among
them in the dark and take them one at a time, in which case a
good sharp knife worked just as well.

*If slinking about in the dark and taking them one by one is the way it
must be, that's the way it must be…*

The sailcloth drew back. A man looked down at him, blinking in surprise. A part of Seth was terrified. To his surprise, another part felt icy calm, as though it had already seen the future and was simply waiting to act its part.

"There's another! This one's sick."

Seth drew a sigil in the air. "Let me keep the knife," he said, praying that the whole bit about drawing sigils in the air wasn't bollocks. As he spoke, he palmed the paring knife.

The man hauled Seth out of the cart, took him to where Fings and Lucius and Soraya lay sprawled on the ground, and tied him up. He gave Seth a quick pat-down, found the knife tucked up Seth's sleeve, said nothing and left it there. Seth took a moment to catch his breath – apparently, he'd been holding it – and looked around. Sheets of canvas strung between poles to make shade, although obviously not for *him*. A litter of junk and blankets. He counted eight horses that he could see, who were presumably loving it out here in the relentless heat. He reached out his thoughts to count the men. Twelve.

Twelve men against a cripple with a fruit knife.

No. Twelve men against a mage with a fruit knife and some sigils.

He'd prayed as he'd drawn his sigil in the air. Prayed to the Sun, and how stupid was that? The Sun had no time for him, while the warlock Kuy was clear that sigils drew their power from something entirely separate from Gods.

Fings was groaning, flat on his face. Lucius might have been dead. Soraya was shaking, head turned away. Seth couldn't see her face. He watched the bandits search the handcarts, emptying them and scattering what they found. They were happy enough with Lucius's stash of gold Emperors and his bolts of silk, and with the half-full cask of water, too. Nothing else held their interest. Seth winced as one picked up Saffran Kuy's globe and then tossed it aside.

'Let me keep the knife'? That was the best you could do? What was wrong with 'set us all free in the middle of the night after everyone falls asleep', or 'please quietly murder all your friends while they're snoozing

*in the sun until you're the only one left', or maybe 'please drop a handy
sword nearby,' or, I don't know, almost anything more useful than a
fucking paring knife?*

I'm alive. And they don't know what I am. Hindsight, Seth thought,
could piss off.

He baked in the sun. Towards evening, four of the men rode off.
The eight that remained loitered listlessly about, eating, drinking,
playing dice and bones, keeping a vague half-an-eye on Fings and
Lucius. Now and then, one came and poked at them with a toe.
From the way they talked, Seth reckoned they hadn't expected
captives and didn't quite know what to do with them. As the sun set,
Seth wriggled his fingers, slipping the paring knife into his hand, and
set to sawing at the rope around his wrists.

"Fings!" he hissed when no one was close. "I got a knife. After
dark. You and me. We slip away."

Fings grunted. It was hard to tell what sort of grunt it had been.
Yes? No? I can't?

You callous, cowardly fuck.

Yeah, because what he'd been thinking was that he and Fings
might slip away while these fuckers had their fun with Lucius
and Soraya. Except... Well, that wasn't going to work, was it?
Because where would they go, out in the desert with no food or
water? These men, whoever they were, had horses. They'd notice
they were down two captives soon enough. If they could be
bothered, they'd ride him down, and then what? Quite possibly
they *wouldn't* be bothered and would simply let him die of heat
and thirst.

If Myla was here, she wouldn't leave anyone behind...

*If Myla was here, none of this would have happened in the first place.
Also, if she knew about that orb, she'd likely stab me.*

No. But she *would* have smashed it.

Would that be so bad?

Yes!

Come on then, warlock. Prove it. Think of something.

He reached out his thoughts again. Lucius had taken a beating and was in a bad way. Soraya would put up a fight. Give her the knife and she might stab one before the others wrestled her down. Fings? Fings' skill was not getting into fights in the first place. His special talent was to not be around by the time anything kicked off.

Darkness came quickly. The moon was a sliver of silver, high in the sky, the stars the brightest he'd ever seen. Two of the men came for Lucius, still barely conscious. Soraya bucked and screamed at them. That, Seth reckoned, was his cue to do something.

He didn't move. Too scared.

You're a fucking sorcerer!

I'll be a dead sorcerer.

Get up! Do something!

If Myla was here–

But she's not! She abandoned us in Deephaven! She stayed behind! She didn't get on the fucking ship!

Boo fucking hoo!

She's dead!

Which means it's up to you.

FUCK'S SAKE! "Fings!" he hissed. "Knife." *He* wasn't going to need it, after all. He staggered up, tossing the paring knife at Fings as he did. Looked around. Six men were looking back at him with a curious interest, like they were wondering what he was about to do, and getting ready to laugh when he made a spectacle of himself.

Two more off in the darkness, dragging Lucius. Fings had his back to Seth. Soraya was staring after Lucius. Only the soldiers were looking at him.

Fuck you all. He made a sigil in the air and threw it at the nearest. "You!" he said. "Kill all your friends and then yourself."

The soldier blinked, looked a bit nonplussed, then whipped out a knife and stabbed the man next to him. For a second, no one else moved, too stunned. Even Seth.

Don't gawp, you festering cluster of stupidity!

He made a different sigil and pointed at another soldier. "Die!"

Nothing happened. *Well. Fuck.*

"He's a fucking mage!" It finally seemed to be sinking in, what Seth was doing. For another wasted second, they all stared at each other, and Seth even had a moment to hope they might all simply run away, but no. Two grabbed at the man who suddenly wanted to stab everyone, the other two ran at Seth, knives drawn.

Seth threw another sigil. "Flee!"

Which worked on one, but not the other.

Fuck!

He just about remembered how to move in time to duck a swing that probably would have taken his head clean off, and then the last man crashed into him, sprawling them both to the ground; and that, Seth knew, was about to be that. He'd failed, and it was really fucking annoying that he'd failed, because if he hadn't frozen for a second after the first sigil then he could have thrown one more, and one more sigil would have been exactly enough to make the difference.

But oh no, you had to stand like an idiot, marvelling at how clever you were.

He fought back, of course, but he was weak and pathetic and sick; even at his best, he was never going to win. A few desperate seconds rolling around in the dirt and then Seth was sprawled on his back, helpless, a man with a knife straddling him, punching him in the face until all Seth saw were stars and lights, and then a knife, about to come down.

A stupid pointless death at the end of a stupid pointless life.

The knife never came. Instead, something warm and wet and tasting of iron poured all over his face. He couldn't see, even as he felt the weight of the soldier go limp and slide off him.

"Seth!"

Fings?

"Seth! Get up!"

Getting up was far too difficult. He heard voices nearby, shouting. Two, was it? Three? He crawled on his belly, no idea what he was doing or where he was going, fumbling at his face and his one good eye, wiping away the blood. He made out three blurry shapes, saw one stagger, clutching himself, a second crumple and lie still. The third...

Who was it? He didn't know.

Lucius? Soraya?

His head pounded.

"Seth!"

Fings!

The third shape ran away, vanishing into the dark. The inside of his head was roaring water...

Water?

...And he was lying on his back, staring at the stars, and Fings was crouched over him, shaking him, and Seth had no idea what had just happened.

"Seth!"

He clasped his hands to his ears. *You fainted? How fucking useless are you?*

The two men who'd taken Lucius were coming. He heard the scrape of steel.

Move!

Fings, backing away. About to bolt. Doing what Fings always did.

MOVE!

Seth sat up and made a sigil in the air. "Go away," he said, and threw it at them. "Both of you! Just fuck off and disappear!"

The two men stumbled to a halt. They stood for a moment, mouths working to find words and not doing much of a job of it. If the big one frowned any harder, Seth thought, he'd twist his face right off his skull.

And then they trotted away. Together into the night. Just like that.

Two at once. There's a thing.

Would have been even more of a thing if you'd done it five minutes ago.

Yeah. Well.

Didn't matter. He'd done it. *He'd* done it. Him. Seth. Useless, pathetic Seth, and he'd saved them all.

Everything hurt, but not inside. Inside, everything was bright. He looked around. Had anyone seen what he'd done? He couldn't see either Lucius or Soraya. Fings, though…

"How…" Fings was gulping air like a fish. "What just happened?"

Seth tried standing and discovered his body was firmly set on staying where it was. He shrugged. "You tell me."

"They just… Well… they just sort of… turned on each other."

"Yeah." Seth bit his tongue. "Did you see what started it?"

Fings didn't reply.

"They were drinking," Seth said. *Do I have to sigil you? Do I have to make you forget?* One got into some sort of argument with two of the others. It turned into a fight. A stabby one. I had that knife. I thought it was the best chance we'd get." Let that be the story. Best Fings didn't know the truth. *I really don't want to sigil you.*

Fings blinked, a bit uncertain. "Really?"

"Yeah, really."

"Wow. Lucky for us, I guess. What about them last two? What was that thing you did?"

"Priest sign. I guess they recognised it. That or they didn't fancy taking you on."

Fings didn't say anything. Just looked at the bloody knife in his hand.

"Go find Lucius and Soraya. Make sure they're all right."

"Right."

He scampered off. Seth stayed right where he was, mostly because he didn't seem to have much choice in the matter. His face was going to be even more messed-up, but he couldn't quite bring himself to care.

I did this. Me!

He drifted for a minute or so and found himself wandering into the visions he'd had all those months ago back in Varr. They fluttered through his head, an indistinct murmur. After a bit, Fings came back, and Soraya, Lucius propped between them. Since they clearly weren't going anywhere in a hurry, Fings set to rummaging through the camp, pilfering as much as he could carry, coming by now and then to show Seth what he'd found, which was probably more about checking to make sure Seth hadn't died than anything else.

Much later, when the others were asleep, Seth got up. The soldiers who'd ridden off *probably* weren't coming back tonight, but maybe they were, in which case he'd better be ready for them.

He found the four bodies of the men who'd died and stopped beside each. He found the soldier who'd almost killed him, neck hacked open by a paring knife. Fings. As far as Seth knew, Fings had never killed a man, although he wasn't *entirely* sure. There *had* been that business in Locusteater Yard, the night the Spicers had come.

Fings had saved him, then. Nothing new about *that*. But for once, it was Seth who'd done the heavy lifting.

His hand moved to his face, wondering what it would look like when the scars finally healed. He was a mess, yet felt a strength he didn't remember, could feel himself healing, inside and out. It seemed fitting, somehow. The plague had transformed him. He'd shed his skin like a snake. Maybe Past-Seth hadn't been such a dick after all, wiping away whatever had happened in Deephaven.

He carved a pair of sigils into each corpse. While the others slept, he talked to them. Not about anything that mattered, simply to know who they were, what they'd wanted, why they'd done what they'd done, what they'd hoped to become. When he finished, he wondered why he'd bothered. By and large, all he'd learned was that they were what they seemed: a bunch of murderous arseholes.

He told them to lie still and carry on as they were, acting like they were dead, then told them what else to do when their friends came back, which was nothing pleasant.

At dawn, Fings and Soraya piled everything back into their carts, took all the water they could find, and lifted Lucius into Seth's cart, leaving Seth to walk. It would be hard, they'd be slow and need lots of rest, it would take days longer than Lucius had planned, but they'd survive. They had food and water. In time,

Lucius would be walking again. Seth was getting stronger, and so it would all get steadily easier, and out here in the south, all roads eventually led to Torpreah.

It would be quicker if you simply told the Dead Men you made to get up and carry everything.

He tried to imagine explaining his Dead Men to Fings. Or Lucius or Soraya. Couldn't see it going well. None of them were ready. Not yet. Besides, Dead Men never lasted long, out in the sun.

He clutched his globe and kept on smiling.

Interlude
The Road Less Travelled

Seven of Torben's deserters were in the clearing, the other four further out, keeping an eye on things just in case, which only went to show what a bunch of incompetents he'd chosen as pickets when a sword-monk sauntered out of the shadows, casual as anything, having slipped by his watchers as though they weren't there. She walked right into the middle of them, stopped and had a good look at what she'd found.

Everyone froze. A few of the more stupid of Torben's deserters started for the nearest weapon, be it a sword or an axe or simply a big stick; Torben stopped them with a furious glare sprayed across the clearing, then watched the monk watching his men. He took in her robe and the Sunsteel swords across her back. He took in the scar across her throat. He was too old for this. Grizzled, with white in his bristles, Torben's band joked behind his back that he'd fought in the *last* civil war, too. They could have joked to his face and he wouldn't have minded. Nothing wrong being old. Being old said you knew how to stay alive.

He hadn't fought in the last civil war – he wasn't *that* old – but he did remember it. He got up and planted himself in front of the monk.

"What school?" he asked.

The monk looked him up and down. She sniffed. "Are you deserters from the army I passed a few days back?"

Torben sighed. "We're scouts." Which was true enough, because

167

he knew better than to lie to a sword-monk, but it was also true that they *were* deserters, and that sometimes what happened to deserters was that monks hunted them down and killed them.

The monk screwed up her face. "Scouts usually run *ahead* of the main force, not behind. Are you deserters, yes or no?"

Torben looked around at his men. Outnumbered ten to one and this monk had beaten them without even drawing a blade. She obviously knew the answer to her own question, so why hadn't she started killing them?

"*I'm* a deserter," he said, and then spoke up, loud, so all his men could hear, because this was for them. "As for these men, you'll have to ask them one by one. If they've got any sense, they'll scatter the moment you draw a sword. They'll run, as fast as they can, in different directions, without stopping or looking back, for at least a day."

The monk gave this some thought, then favoured him with a little nod, as if she recognised that loyalty deserved at least a little acknowledgement before she ran him through.

Her swords stayed on her back.

"What do you want?" Torben asked.

"Directions," she said. "To Valladrune." She kept her gaze on him; and yes, he had enough years in him to remember back to when Valladrune had been a city full of people and not some ghost haunting the fringes of history.

"Don't know it," he said after a bit.

The monk sniffed. "Liar. Where is it?"

"Don't know it," he said again.

"Can we pretend for a moment that it doesn't not exist? Or would you prefer the sword?"

Torben grunted. "Fine. Valley of the White Winds. Right on the edge of the Thimble Hills. North and West. Not many people living that way. Don't suppose I need to tell you why." He shrugged. "You want to find it, you could use a guide who knows the land."

"And you could do that, could you?"

"Not if I'm dead."

The monk drew one of her swords. "I don't need the rest of them."

Torben surprised himself by jumping forward rather than running away; but this monk, whoever she was, wasn't hunting deserters, which very possibly made her a deserter herself. "These are my scouts," he said. "We stay on our feet, we move quickly, we sleep light. Most of all, where one goes, we all go."

"Including death?"

"Including death." Torben reckoned he might have to have a few quiet talks with himself about this sudden streak of stubborn pride. But, well... the words were out now. Could hardly take them back.

The monk seemed to give this some consideration. "Where are you heading?" she asked.

"You have a name?" asked Torben.

"Oh yes," said the monk. "Several. I asked you a question."

"The Valley of the White Winds, I'm guessing," Torben said. "Which will be as far as we go. The last couple of days... well. Ghosts and demons and Dead Men are all very fine for the likes of you. Not so fine for the rest of us."

"And five minutes ago? Before you saw me? Where were you heading then?"

Torben shrugged. "Somewhere else. Hardly matters now, does it?"

"Not really," Tasahre agreed.

PART THREE
Fings

Kindness is not always the easy choice, but it is always the right one.
– Myla

21

The City of Gold

From the top of a cliff, Seth stared down at distant Torpreah, bathed in the glowing evening light, framed by a ring of six mountains, like six giant fingers poking from the earth. Six mountains and six mountain-top monasteries for those six elemental dragons the Path cared to venerate. The water dragon of the East, where monks learned to pour arrows like rain. The air dragon of the North where, Seth guessed, Myla's sword-mistress had been raised. The earth dragon of the West, where the witch-breakers were trained before taking their duties in Helhex. The dragons of metal, fire, and light, arrayed to the south. Between the mountains, the twin rivers intertwined and splayed across the landscape like a sunbeam emanating from the source of all light.

Torpreah. The City of Gold.

Seth noted the empty places, the two gaps in the ring of mountains where the dragons of ice and of darkness stood watch. The priests in Varr rarely talked about those, but Seth had heard of offering places, secret and forbidden, destroyed now and then by the witch-breakers only to quietly return.

A lake formed the northern edge of the city. The Shroud, they called it. The Shroud of the Sun because of the way the waters caught the light at sunset. Close to the shore rose an island covered in golden domes.

"The Autarch's palace," said Lucius. "The heart of Torpreah. The Isle of Light."

It had taken most of another twelvenight to finish crossing the plateau along the edge of the Vidra Gorge. Slow and hard and painful, especially the first days. The others had fretted about the surviving soldiers chasing after them. Not Seth, though he couldn't tell them why, not without admitting he'd left a posse of Dead Men with instructions to murder the fuck out of their former comrades, should the chance arise. He reckoned Soraya would have been okay with that. Not Lucius, though. Certainly not Fings.

He'd watched them carefully in the days after. Hard to say whether any of them had seen what he'd done. Not Lucius, and the wondering looks he occasionally saw from Soraya *could* have been for what he'd done for her in Narvel's Pass. Fings, though... Fings, who'd been closest, had been oddly quiet since that night. Could be because Fings had killed a man. *Could* be...

The clifftop path passed under the Dusk Gate, an ornate stone arch marking the boundary between the lush valleys below and the arid plateau from which they'd come. Beyond, the road wound steeply down. Another hard day, that slow descent, but Seth felt a lightness. The end of their journey. They were here, alive, ready to start anew. Even the air itself seemed to quicken with life.

On the outskirts of the city, Lucius found a boarding house like the *Elegant Gentleman* in Helhex, a place for Fings and Seth to stay while he and Soraya sought out what was left of their family.

"Just don't start any trouble," he said, before he left. He'd been looking at Fings.

He needn't have worried. Those first few days in Torpreah, Fings did little more than stare, eyes wide, mouth open like some ignorant country peasant. In Varr, they had Archer's Way, a street twenty yards long where the stones were set in silver; here they had the Avenue of the Morning, running from the Dawn Gate to the Citadel of Light, straight as an arrow, forty men wide, lined by ancient trees and, once it passed through the gates of the citadel itself, paved with raw gold. Sprawled in front of the citadel, an expanse of white marble big enough to host an army and edged with gilded pavilions around the pillar of rock that was Torpreah's heart: the Pillar of Light. A stunted echo of the Thimble

Hill mountains, the Pillar was a column of raw weathered stone, shrouded in draping green, rising to the height of a hundred men. A gold staircase, the Stairway of the Sun, spiraled around it. Every few dozen yards, caves or hollows held shrines and altars. After everything he'd heard in Varr, Seth would have made the climb on his hands and knees if that was what it took. Fortunately, Fings offering a shoulder to lean against was enough.

Atop the Pillar of Light was a plaza paved in gold-veined marble, large enough for a castle, with a cleft from the eastern edge to the middle, much like a round of wood cut from a tree might split as it dried. Men in robes and fine cloth gathered in knots, and so did men in rags, rich and poor mingling in a way Seth had never seen in Varr. Shrines and altars and prayer stones ringed the cliff edge. He shuffled to the northern edge, vaguely aware of Fings following, and stood in thrall, Torpreah spread below him around the southern shores of the Shroud. He felt dizzy, nothing but a few hundred feet of sheer rock and empty space between him and waters below, then lifted his eyes to where the Isle of Light rose from the lake, its clusters of golden domes, its manicured gardens, its carefully curated avenues, its quietly magnificent palaces of white stone, its temples and shrines. The Palace of the Autarch and The Sanctuary of the Ever-Radiant Sun. The home and heart of the Path he'd spent so many years yearning to serve.

Lightbringer Otti, back in Varr, had often told the story of the first servants of the Sunking crossing the sea. They'd put ashore at Helhex, followed the Vidra gorge inland, and found a valley of paradise where two rivers flowed together, twisting in and out of each other between hills that rose like the fingers of a titan from the soil. Exhausted, they'd camped for a week by a lake with an island overlooked by a monolith. A Dawncaller had swum the narrow stretch of water and, on the shores of the Isle of Light, been granted a vision of an empire ruled from a throne of light that would cast the Sunking himself into shadow; then, as the vision passed, dark clouds had gathered in the heavens. From their midst, a ray of sunlight had struck the Pillar of Light and cracked it. Enraptured, the Dawncaller had climbed the sundered cliff and built a shrine, and that was how the king of all cities had begun.

Torpreah.

Fanciful, Seth thought, because since when did sunbeams split mountains? But still, standing in that place, it was hard not to feel a shiver of awe.

On the far shore of the lake rose another pillar, the Pillar of Dusk. The priests had found shattered towers there, crumbling walls, spikes of white stone hidden within the forest, all long overgrown with trees and grass. When Seth looked across the Shroud, there it was, where the Vidra and the Li came together.

White stone, he mused. *Like the City of Spires? Like the vaults under Varr?* No way to know without going to see.

He surveyed the city, marvelling at how easily those classroom memories returned. The eastern quarter where the three Gates of Dawn stood guard. The southern quarter and the Zenith Gate...

A breeze brushed across the plaza. He looked for Fings so he could point at how beautiful this was, tell someone how his heart ached; but Fings had slipped away to lurk around a group of rich-looking women. Thieving, probably – which was what Fings did, and it had never bothered Seth before; but here and now it felt wrong.

"Fings! We need to go."

They descended the Stairway of the Sun together, followed the Avenue of Morning, crossed one of the magnificent bridges that spanned the Vidra and walked into the flesh of the city, the beating stinking heart on the southern shores of the Shroud.

"What were you doing up there?" Fings asked.

"Looking at the past," said Seth. "And maybe the future." Which earned him an odd look, like maybe Fings thought he was suffering from a touch of the sun. Which maybe he *was*, only not in the way Fings was thinking.

After two days, Lucius returned full of news. He and Soraya had negotiated a lease on a shop and hired some seamstresses and were now clothiers. Seth and Fings packed their bags; the rooms above the shop were free, and so Fings and Seth could have them for as long as they wanted. Which, Fings pointed out, wasn't going to be long because they'd be going back to Varr before summer's end; the two of them, back to the Spice Market and the *Unruly Pig*, to Dox and Arjay and Brick and Topher, and Ma Fings and all Fings' sisters; and yes, the summer was still young, but it *was* a long journey, and they really didn't want to be getting to Varr as the Sulk was setting in.

Seth made some agreeable grunts. When the time came, Fings would return alone. He didn't know it yet because Seth hadn't told him, and Fings was too... naïve, perhaps? Whatever the word, it would never occur to him that Seth couldn't simply walk back into his old life in the Spice Market, selling pastries outside the temple. In Fings' world, you did shit that got you in trouble, you kept your head down until it blew over, then got on with things as though it never happened. Seth's world wasn't like that. Not anymore.

Would he have wanted to go back to that even if he could? Not really.

Lucius needed a scribe to write some nice-looking letters. Seth offered himself. They bought quills and inks and argued over whether the letters should be written on paper or parchment or vellum. With coin in his pocket, Seth bought books. Religious books. Books of the Path. He read them when he wasn't writing letters for Lucius. Carefully, word by word, even though he already knew half of what they said. For a while, that became his life: writing for Lucius, and in time for others too, every spare hour in between dedicated to studying the Path and the teachings of the warlock Saffran Kuy, letting both sides of something fill his head, searching for what he was sure must be there, if only he could find it.

The common origins. The point of divergence. The loose thread in the philosophy of the Path.

When he found that thread, he thought, he'd tug on it, and see what happened.

22
Purchasing by Other Means

I'm doing this for family, Fings told himself, as if saying it enough would make it true. What *was* true was that he'd been with Lucius to the houses of four different rich men and hadn't stolen *any*thing. He wasn't sure why Lucius kept bringing him, unless Seth was right, and it was to make sure nothing went missing from the shop. Which was silly, because Fings slept in the room over Lucius's shop, the nicest room Fings had ever not paid for, and Lucius was promising a cut of the profits, and why, for love of the Sun, would he ruin all *that*? It was the most basic rule of life: don't piss where you sleep.

Yeah, he thought ruefully. *Not always been the best at that, though, have you.*

"You can't be showing up at a man's house in the day and then stealing from it at night, either. People are going to work it out," Seth told him, which seemed a grossly unfair thing to say, even if it had been exactly what Fings had been thinking. He let it pass, knowing better than to argue when Seth went off on one. Stand and smile and nod and sing a little song in his head until it was all over; that was the way.

"We're foreigners here," said Seth, rather pointedly. "We stand out. Remember what happened to Torpreah Jis?"

Torpreah Jis had been found one morning hanging from a rope suspended across Buttonmakers' Row with his belly slit and his insides hanging out, not because he was foreign but because Torpreah Jis had stabbed three men dead and cut up two women, all of them having brothers or sisters or husbands or wives among the Seamstresses' District Longcoats. Although maybe it *was* because Torpreah Jis had been foreign; otherwise he'd have known what you could expect, doing what he'd done. Come to think of it, being foreign was about the *only* reason Fings could imagine for supposing you could mess with the Longcoats of Seamstresses' District and get away with it. Even Blackhand and the Murdering Bastard had known better.

Maybe Seth had a point. *May*be.

Anyway, here he was, standing with Lucius outside some rich-looking townhouse, dressed like a fool, which was apparently how Torpreahn menservants liked to be, and it was the fifth time Lucius had taken him on a house call and, like all four times before, Fings hadn't stolen *any*thing. Myla, if she'd been here, would have been proud.

He sighed and tried not to think about that. Myla was receding, the memories of her fading from Fings' head. In a way, that was the worst of it. Hadn't noticed it until she'd left for Deephaven, but having her around had been... nice. She'd been good for Seth, too; Fings had no idea *what* was going on with Seth these days, but he was pretty sure Myla being here would have helped. Was like having a big sister. Well... *another* big sister, except one who was useful.

The door to the house opened, followed by the usual rigmarole of being led to a room somewhere at the back and then waiting for some fat-fingered rich man to show up and start lording it about. Lucius got out his measuring line and chatted about whatever today's fat-fingered rich man seemed to find interesting – usually the war – while Fings stood quietly out of the way, stepping forward when Lucius asked for samples of cloth or thread to show, eyeing up whatever room they were in, assessing its worth and how many things he could slip into his pockets without anyone noticing, then forcing himself to leave everything exactly as he found it. It was a sort of torture, really.

He paid attention when people talked about the war. There rarely seemed to be much real news. The lords of Torpreah had marched off with an army that might have been a few thousand or might have been a hundred times that, depending on who was making up the number. The army had apparently reached the southern edge of some place called the Raven Hills, not that this meant anything to Fings. He listened because he reckoned he'd have to go much the same way as the army to get home, preferably without actually running into it, so where it went was worth remembering. Today's fat-fingered merchant seemed to think the army would reach Varr around the Solstice of Flames, and that was when the fighting would start.

Fings reckoned on hanging around Torpreah until all that nonsense was over and done with. True, he *did* want to get back before the Sulk settled in, but it would be unfortunate to show up and find the whole place under siege and crawling with soldiers.

The Solstice of Flames rang a distant bell of memory. Hadn't the Solstice of Flames been when old Khrozus the Usurper had fallen on Varr back in the civil war? Ma Fings, old enough to remember how inconvenient it had all been, never shirked from telling him and his sisters whenever they complained about anything.

Lucius finished up. From the genial smiles, it had gone well. Back outside, Lucius made notes in the little book he always carried, while Fings, who couldn't read or write, did the same in his head; only *his* notes were about the houses to either side, how many windows they had, where they faced, whether their shutters looked in good repair, how easy it would be to get to the rooftops, that sort of thing. Couldn't help himself, really.

One caught his eye, further up the street, bigger than the others. It had a turret on one corner. Hard to miss on account of the way its gold paint caught the sun. *Some rich bugger.*

Plenty of those in Torpreah.

At the shop, Lucius busied himself sketching designs. Fings sat in the back with the seamstresses, something he did a lot these days. A strange gang, they were. Ma Hiva was the boss, older even than Ma Fings. She sat in her chair and didn't say much, but when she did, the others always listened. Then came her daughter, missing half a leg, who'd once been a sailor. She probably had a real name, but everyone called her Peg. She was the talker, free-wheeling stories of her time at sea which the others always declared preposterous, but still they listened. So did Fings. He liked Peg's stories.

The other three were the same sort of age as Fings and Seth or even younger. Yrma seemed to have taken a shine to him, which Fings found vaguely unsettling and had no idea what he was supposed to do with. When Peg wasn't telling one of her stories, they gossiped constantly. Right now, they were talking about some trouble or other that had kicked off overnight down by the lake. A pair of monks from the island had gotten into a disagreement with someone called Wretched Morrow, apparently some gang boss a bit like Blackhand had been in Varr. Thinking how someone like that could be useful to know when it came time to leave, Fings quietly remembered the name. Reckoned he might be needing someone to shift a few things.

A couple of minutes later, he quietly forgot it again. Wretched Morrow had apparently decided to make a fight of things and gotten herself skewered.

"I heard," said Ma Hiva, immediately the centre of attention, "that they were looking for some warlock. Tale I heard was that some bunch of no-goods roaming the pass picked the wrong travellers to rob. Killed them all on the spot, he did, and brought them back as Dead Men."

Fings stayed very still. If he wished hard enough, maybe he could disappear, and they wouldn't notice?

"Throwing lightning from his hands and talking to ghosts and everything."

Fings relaxed a bit.

"Good for him," sniffed Peg without looking up. "Nothing but thugs and thieves up there these days."

This started something of a debate on the relative merits of rapacious murdering thieves on the one hand and demon-summoning masters of dark forces on the other. Fings reckoned he saw his chance to escape, but as he got up, Yrma caught his arm.

"Fings! You came across the pass." She leaned a little towards him from her chair, eyes all big and wide. "Did *you* have to fight any bandits?"

"Er…" He didn't know what to say, so settled for the comfort of lying. "Er, no. No, didn't see anyone at all."

Ma Hiva gave him a sharp look. "I'm sure I overheard Master Lucius saying how you'd been set upon. Heard him say you escaped when the robbers got drunk and started fighting among themselves."

Which *was* the story as Seth had told it, and neither Lucius nor Soraya had ever said otherwise. Fings, though… Fings had seen enough to know there was a bit more to it than that.

He gave a nervous laugh. "Well… You know…Always good to have some stories to impress the customers, right?"

Ma Hiva held his eye a bit longer than was comfortable, until Yrma asked who Lucius had visited today. Fings, sensing safer ground, gratefully settled to telling them where he and Lucius had gone, what everyone had said about the war, what the house was like, that sort of thing. They always asked, and Fings always told them.

"You see a house with a turret on one corner, painted gold?" That was Peg, who usually pretended not to pay attention.

Fings nodded. "Yeah."

"Rancid Ibsios." She made a face.

"Who's Rancid Ibsios?" asked almost everyone at once, all of them sensing another of Peg's stories.

"Rancid Ibsios. Well…!" Peg launched into a lengthy stream of cursing and invective that Fings, from his weeks on the *Speedwell*, understood to be sailor talk. The other women stared in shock, all except Ma Hiva, who simply rolled her eyes. Scattered though the swearing was enough for Fings to work out that Rancid Ibsios, as well as being a liar, a swindler, a cheat, a murderer, and several other things that were worse, had once owned a ship that Peg had sailed and had fucked over the entire crew, leaving them penniless. Mostly what seemed to stick in Peg's craw was that he'd taken a spyglass, gifted to her in a distant port from a man who'd wanted to marry her. She even had a tear in her eye by the time she was done, which was enough for her story to end in silence. Hard as iron, most of the time, was Peg.

Later, after Lucius shut the shop for the evening and the women had all gone home, Fings went for a bit a wander. It was good to get out, he told himself. Get his bearings, familiarise himself with the local streets, that sort of thing. For some reason, the streets he decided to familiarise himself with were the streets from that morning, right up to the street outside the house with the golden turret. He wasn't quite sure why, but Peg's story of the spyglass stuck with him. He wondered if Rancid Ibsios was at home, and whether he knew that he was called Rancid by people who remembered him less than fondly. While he was wondering, he was also counting windows and checking shutters and looking at the roof and all the usual malarkey. It would be tough to get inside, dangerous too, not knowing anything about what was waiting for him. But of course, none of that mattered, because he wasn't going to *do* anything. He was just thinking, that was all. Scratching the old itch.

Don't piss where you sleep, remember?

He still wasn't going to actually *do* anything three hours later when, in the dark of night and with a feather between his teeth, he made his way unseen up onto the roof. Although it wasn't *really* pissing where he slept, was it? Since it wasn't *this* house that he and Lucius had visited?

Still, bit of a stupid idea, right? I mean, you should probably just go home.

He was still thinking how yes, he probably should, even as he hung off the side of the turret, quietly levering open the shutters of the top window. He could see lights behind some of the other windows, coming and going. The dead of night and people were up and moving about, all of which made this a bad idea.

He paused, stroking the lucky charms in his pocket and around his neck, whispering quick prayers to Fickle Lord Moon and to the Goblin King.

Still a bad idea, even as he slipped through the open shutter, except, as luck would have it, he landed in what looked like a library. Moonlight streaming through the window. A simple staircase spiralling down from the middle of a round room, walls lined with shelves of books, maps, scrolls, stacks of paper, although Fings had no way to know which of them might be worth something.

Three windows looked out north, east and west, two shuttered, one open because Fings had just opened it. In front of the south wall was the wheel from a ship, mounted on a solid-looking stand. Fings wondered if it had been Peg's ship. There was a brass name plate, but he couldn't read, and she'd never said a name.

Distant sounds wafted from the stair. People moving. A conversation somewhere, loud but far away. No one had any idea he was here.

He should *probably* leave, he decided. Slip back out the way he'd come.

Yeah.

He sighed and gave the wheel a little spin, mostly to make his presence in the room feel a bit more real. It didn't move. Not that it was fixed in place, more that there was something…

He tugged harder. This time it *did* move; as it did, one of the shelves shifted and the wall behind it cracked open.

Well, well, well…

Fings listened hard. The sounds from the house hadn't changed. On tiptoe, he crept to the crack in the wall. It wasn't much, but one set of shelves had started to turn. He went back to the wheel and turned it some more, because, well, how could you not? He was a bit disappointed there wasn't some whole secret maze on the other side, or at the very least a mysterious passage, but then he *was* at the top of a tower.

The shelf turned fully, revealing a different set of shelves on the opposite side, now facing into the room. A few books that looked to Fings a bit like they might be ledgers, although he couldn't be sure. A nice-looking dagger, more ceremonial than functional and probably worth an Emperor or two. A stack of letters. A spyglass.

He peered over the edge of the stair. Found only darkness and silence, so he crept down into what turned out to be an empty bedroom. He felt his way around. The bedsheets felt like silk. A door led into the rest of the house, outlined by a dim light filtering around the edges. He listened. The sounds of the house stayed distant. He opened the door a crack.

This is stupid.

Thing was, he already knew what he was going to do. He was going to take Peg's spyglass and give it back because that was right. And, since he hadn't much liked Peg's story of Rancid Ibsios, and since Rancid Ibsios didn't sound like the sort of man who'd take kindly to being burgled and very much *did* sound like the sort of man to hold a grudge, he was going to cover his tracks.

The door opened onto a balcony around an inner yard. The yard was empty. The voices were coming from a room on the far side, a floor down. They were loud and merry, like someone was having a feast.

Candles mounted behind glass shrouds on each wall gave a little light. Fings wriggled one free and then went back to the library, helped himself to the dagger and the spyglass and the ledgers, then scattered the papers and some of the scrolls at the foot of the shelves. As an afterthought, he turned the wheel back the other way, setting the secret shelf as he'd found it. When he was done, he set the candle carefully on the floor among the scattered papers, climbed out the window, back onto the roof, shinned down on the other side of the house, and scarpered.

A day later and the shop was buzzing with the news of how the house of Richma Ran Ibsios, second cousin to one of the Lords of Torpreah, had caught fire in the night and half burned down. Rumour had it that the Autarch himself had been there, although no one quite believed that. It occurred to Fings, as he listened, that perhaps he wouldn't mention this to Seth. Seth would have opinions, and Fings was fairly sure he didn't want to have to listen to them.

Peg never said anything about the brass spyglass she found sitting on her chair a couple of mornings later. Fings *did* find out, eventually, that the one she'd lost all those years ago had been dented and broken, that the whole story about it being a gift from a lover was bollocks. Truth was, she'd won it in a game of dice. Had probably cheated, too.

All of which made him smile.

23
THE FOREST

The Month of Lightning gave way to the Month of Flames. The Imperial armies marched from Varr's South Gate, trumpets and horns echoing along streets and canals. Myla and Orien rode ahead with Lady Novashi and two dozen blue-robe mages to the city's edge and beyond, beneath the walls, past the fringe of the Imperial Forest, towards far hills that signed the road to Torpreah. A mile outside the gates, riders emerged from the trees to greet them. Three more mages in blue and the Taiytakei popinjay. Myla let out a long sigh. Did he *have* to show up *every*where?

"Lady Novashi. Well met." The mage with the salt-and-pepper beard who looked older than he was. The Sorcerer-Royal, she now knew. Master of the Guild.

"Astrin." A flash of something between them. Shared secrets born of a shared comradeship, Myla thought, which was a bit of a surprise.

"The half-gods have been continuing along the river. Slowly, driving panic before them."

"Calling us out." Lady Novashi snapped her fingers. "I know what they—"

"Until yesterday," interrupted Astrin. It took no small courage, Myla thought, to interrupt the Red Witch. "Yesterday, they turned for Neja. Your kinsmen have doubled back to defend their homeland. The half-gods offer a dilemma: defend Neja and leave Varr open to the South or else fight the Torpreahns while Neja

187

falls and their army of the dead grows stronger. Either battle we would be pressed to win. Or we *could* attempt both fights at once and lose twice, which I am disheartened to see is what we appear to be doing." Astrin's lip curled. "Perhaps you might have some insight into Katleina's thinking that you'd care to share? There *are* some who might question the strategic abilities of a sixteen year-old girl. But of course, it doesn't come from *her*, does it."

Astrin seemed barely aware of the other mages around him. Interesting, Myla thought, that he called the Regent by her birth-name rather than her title. Interesting that he'd say what he did. It was a bit close to treason, wasn't it? Especially in front of so many witnesses.

The Regent knows something she isn't sharing. He *knows it too. As does the Red Witch...*

She studied the mage. Palace gossip claimed the Sorcerer-Royal had disappeared for some months at the end of the previous summer, at much the same time as the Regent, and that he'd returned with her shortly before midwinter much changed. And as she looked, there it was. A haunted expression when he thought no one was looking. The same face she saw on Orien, now and then, ever since the fight on the hill outside Deephaven. The face of someone who'd met a Wraith and survived.

He's terrified.

"As it happens, the Levanya agrees with you," said Lady Novashi. "Her Highness does not. I have no insight to offer as to why, so ask her yourself. If you get an answer, please do share. It's *my* homeland the half-gods now threaten." She nudged her horse into leafy darkness, forcing Astrin to turn and follow. Myla and Orien exchanged a glance.

"I've no idea," said Orien when Myla cocked her head. "I don't know why either of us are even here."

"I know why *you're* here. But this is mage business, not monk business."

Orien glowered. "*Competent* mage business, however."

"Probably there's some competent monk business going on

somewhere else," Myla said. "Which is why I'm here." Tasahre must be at the ruins of Valladrune by now, hunting a warlock. *That* was sword-monk business, not this.

Orien snorted. "I doubt anyone would dare question *your* competence."

"Apparently, I have a bad attitude." Astrin and Lady Novashi were deep in conversation, riding side by side. It was probably very interesting, possibly something she should be listening to, but there didn't seem much chance of that. Tasahre had made a bit of a mistake, she thought, choosing her spy.

Or else she was simply trying to be rid of me.

They rode to the top of a rocky outcrop, reined in their horses, and waited. Eventually, the cacophony of horns and trumpets drew close, the rumbling pounding of a thousand hooves and ten thousand boots as the earth shuddered to the beat of drums. First came the emperor's cavalry, brilliant white and gold over black Moonsteel. In their midst, the child-emperor and the Levanya, Overlord of Varr, Commander of the Imperial Legions. Following in vibrant blues and a scatter of orange, the two guilds of mages, nearly a hundred sorcerers. Then more cavalry: the red, white and black of the City of Spires, the blue and black of the Levanya, a token squadron in the silver and gold of Neja. Standards waved, spears gleamed, horses pranced and shimmered, men shouted, dust and the smell of horses clogged the air. Then the footmen. Hour after hour, the heart of the Empire's strength marched past while Myla and Orien and the Red Witch and the Sorcerer Royal and all their mages sat and did nothing but watch.

"Well," Myla said, when it was finally over. "That was a morning I'll never get back." She ached from neck to arse, sitting still for so long. How did people get used to this, day after day? She wrinkled her nose at the road, littered with manure, dust hanging thick enough to choke, the smell of horseshit gently growing stronger.

"Really?" said Orien. "I thought it was quite impressive."

"Strongly in contention for the most tedious five hours of my life."

"You probably really do have a list, don't you?" Orien huffed and turned away. With a small shiver of horror, Myla understood he really *had* been impressed.

"Wait until you try motherhood," said Lady Novashi as she passed. Myla stared after her, aghast, partly shocked that Lady Novashi had overheard, more that the Red Witch had spoken to her, most of all that somewhere out there might be some little Red Witch children.

If there are, she keeps it very quiet. Why?

The mages had a camp in the woods. Myla led her horse, taking her time, then slipped away for a piss. This whole misguided affair was stupid. The real enemy was to the west, not the south. *Her* enemy, anyway. She should be riding for Neja, not Torpreah. They all should...

She stopped. Voices in the trees ahead. Quiet and quick.

"...and her bodyguard will join us here. We make our own route South, free from spies and assassins, of which there have been far too many of late."

Lady Novashi. Intrigued, Myla crept closer.

"Like fugitives, while a great army marches not more than a league behind us?" Astrin's words dripped disdain. "An army laden with tents and pillows and other softness which we will doubtless sorely miss."

"Has a familiar ring, does it not?"

The voices drifted back towards the camp. Myla considered following but settled for letting nature have its way instead. When she was done, she lingered. Orien would be with his mage friends and the odious popinjay, conversations that veered wildly between boring and incomprehensible. She wandered further into the trees, found a stream, took off her boots and cooled her feet. What she wanted was to wash off the sweat and the persistent smell of horse. And maybe to be alone for a bit, to think. To decide what she should do.

Further from the camp, the stream widened into a pool.

Why not?

She picked up her boots, waded through the water until she was knee deep, took off her swords and robe and...

"Clearing your mind for the days to come?"

She almost jumped out of her skin. Ten feet away, the Regent was watching her, dressed for all the world as though she'd come into the forest for an afternoon of sport. Myla couldn't imagine how she'd got so close without making a noise.

"You *do* remember you're supposed to kowtow. That sort of thing?"

Myla considered this. She was standing half-naked, knee deep in running water, holding her robe in one hand, her swords in the other.

"Bugger that," she said.

A movement behind the Regent. Tanysha. Which was fine, unless Tanysha felt duty-bound to try and kill her for not showing the proper respect... which would be awkward, because Myla rather liked Tanysha, and Tanysha was annoyingly competent for someone who wasn't a sword-monk.

"Come on in. The water's lovely."

"I'd have to undress." The Regent put on that false smile she was so fond of. "Imagine if one of my mages strayed from camp to answer a call of nature. He'd never get over it."

"You'd know if someone was coming long before that mattered."

"True enough." The smile stayed. The Regent didn't move.

"Not going to just jump inside my head this time?"

"Oh, I have no wish to further explore your nightly exploits." She scowled. "Quite an effective defence. I'm surprised no one else has thought of it."

"What are you?"

That stopped her. "I beg your pardon."

"You heard."

"*What* am I? Why? What am I supposed to be?"

"A naïve young princess."

"Ah. Far too young and inexperienced to be leading the Empire against a threat such as the Wraiths. Something like that?"

"Something like that, yes. But that's not what you are. So, what are you?"

"Are you trying to catch me in a lie, sword-monk?"

"I'm trying to catch you in a truth. Do you mind if I dress?" Myla didn't wait for an answer, which was presumably why the Regent didn't bother to offer one.

"I suppose, like everyone else, you're wondering why we head south and not west. The... Silver Kings? Is that what you call them?"

"I prefer Wraiths."

"Wraiths, then." The Regent made a sour face. "They're the greater threat. That's what you think, isn't it? So why not face them first? The Torpreahns may take Varr behind us, or they may not, but if we were to be victorious against the Wraiths, we would surely rout them on our return. But then, I suspect you don't much care either way on that count."

Myla wrinkled her nose. "Not really. But the reasoning behind your choice is obvious. I'm surprised your mages don't see it."

A shadow passed across the Regent's face. "Is that so?"

"Your army can't fight Dead Men. They don't have the will and they don't have the weapons. After any battle, win or lose, the Wraiths will simply bring back those who fell and grow stronger. We both saw it in Deephaven. And if you *did* somehow arm your soldiers with fire and Sunsteel, if you somehow made them a threat, the Wraiths would dance away. *Their* army needs neither food nor water. How far can the one you unleashed today travel before it begins to starve? As you struggle to force an engagement, the Torpreahns seize Varr and strangle your supplies until you're forced to face them anyway. The longer you delay, the more you are disadvantaged. So, yes. You turn south. They've forced you to that."

"Perceptive little sword-monk, aren't you?"

"I was a merchant's daughter. I understand logistics. What I *don't* understand is why you don't send *me* to Neja. One monk will make no difference against the Torpreahns. More so against Dead Men."

The Regent pursed her lips. "The Dead Men don't matter. Only the half-gods. And *you* can't fight them. Only I can do that."

"But I *have* fought them."

"Your sword-mistress killed that one, and it *was* only one."

"And your sorcerers? Against an army of Dead Men, Lady Novashi is worth legions. We've both seen that. Do you mean to turn her on the living? Because if you do, you should send me to Neja first. I will not sit idly by and watch you burn men like a farmer burns his stubble."

"Sit."

Such was the command in the Regent's voice that Myla was halfway to the ground before she realised what was happening. She stopped herself. "I'll ask one more time. What are you?"

"Have you worked out why I chose to keep you?"

"Because I speak my mind?"

The Regent smiled, apparently genuinely amused. "*Everyone* speaks their mind to me, whether they wish it or not. You already know that. No." She tapped the Sunsteel Crown. "Because you had my brother's crown in your hands, and you gave it back." She sighed. "Well, *I'm* going to sit down." She settled on a tree root. "There will be no great battle with the South. This army marches to distract the eye, no more. I will confront the Torpreahns at Knife Hand Pass, south of the Raven Falls, before their armies leave the hills and spread across the plains. Either the lords of Torpreah will kneel and pledge their allegiance to my brother, or Novi and I will leave them in such disarray that even a band of vagabonds could hold the walls of Varr against them. They will learn the hard way what I am." The venom in the Regent's voice almost made Myla flinch.

"And what *is* that?"

The Regent ignored her. "And *you* will come with me, sword-monk, and do something for me that only a sword-monk can do."

"I will, will I?"

"Yes, you will, and willingly, too." The Regent shivered. "My grandfather was the Emperor Khrozus. He died before I was born, so

I never met him. I hear he was a monster, but he was no sorcerer. My father tried to become one, but he never amounted to much. Your young fire-mage could have matched him." She gave a chuckle. "You might tell him that before he destroys himself trying to be more than he is. But if there are no mages in my bloodline, where did all *this* come from?" She held up her hands and snapped her fingers, jumping sparks into the air.

"And the answer is?"

"Grandfather Khrozus spent a year of his life in Valladrune shortly before the war. A very odd place for him to be, given that Valladrune might as well have been in Emperor Talsin's back pocket. You *do* know what happened in Valladrune?"

Myla raised an eyebrow. "I've heard the Butcher of Deephaven razed it to the ground, killed every man, woman and child and then salted the earth for three days' ride in all directions. When he was done, Emperor Khrozus declared it had never happened because Valladrune had never existed." Their eyes met in a hard and unyielding place. "The same Butcher of Deephaven who now leads your armies."

"You propose an alternative?"

"If pushing the Lords of Torpreah into a last-man-standing, no-mercy, no-quarter-given war to the very bitterest of bitter ends is what you want, he's perfect. If you have in mind a more peaceful resolution, I'd suggest… almost anyone else."

"Someone once told me that sword-monks don't have friends. I begin to see why. How does your fire-mage manage?"

"Turns out that his arrogance and my self-righteousness cancel out. Both of us being arseholes helps us see past one another's flaws." The line was Orien's, whispered under the sheets in the dead of night. It seemed apt.

The Regent smiled. An honest smile, for once. She got up and began to pace. "I think the coming of the Wraiths has to do with what my grandfather was doing in Valladrune before the war. I want you to find out. I assume you know how he took Varr? The story of the river freezing in the middle of summer?"

"Story?"

"Oh, it *did* happen. My grandfather had a sorcerer. Maybe more than one. But a sorcerer like that... Well, hard to find and comes at a price. I want to know who it was and what promises were made. As for your story of Valladrune... *That* story is wrong. You're going to find the truth for me. That's what sword-monks do, isn't it?" And, with that, the Regent walked away.

Myla took a deep breath and let it out, long and slow. She sat for a while, thinking about what she'd heard and wondering what to do with it. Finding Tasahre and telling her everything seemed a good start. As for the rest? Unravel a pact made in secret some forty years ago in a place that had since been burned to the ground by people who were almost certainly long dead? She didn't even know where Valladrune was. Hadn't ever heard of it until Midwinter.

From Fings, of all people.

She bathed, which was what she'd come here to do, after all, and thank fuck for finally not smelling of horse. Going south would take her to Tasahre and, most likely, to Torpreah, where Lucius and Soraya should be. It cheered her, thinking of seeing her brother again. All the trouble he'd doubtless found for himself.

In a way, that settled it.

Fine. In case you're secretly eavesdropping, I'll do it. And also, if you are, fuck you sideways with a shovel for being in my head again.

Then, since this was probably the last night they'd have together for a while and possibly ever, Myla went looking for Orien.

24
The Fork in the Road

In Torpreah, too, the Month of Lightning gave way to the Month of Flames. Almost daily, Fings badgered Seth with plans for how they'd return to Varr once they had news of how the fighting had gone. Each time, Seth waited it out, quietly wishing Fings would go away. Quietly wishing, if he was honest, that *everything* would go away. He felt the crisis coming with remorseless inevitability, no matter how he wished it wouldn't. Fings' life was in Varr. Family, friends, everything he knew; sooner or later, Fings was going to leave. A part of Seth wanted desperately to go with him. It was just... well, the whole bit about not wanting to be murdered to death by angry stabby sword-monks. Not for what he'd done in Deephaven, because whatever *that* was, it had surely died with the rest of the city. But Varr...

He wasn't the man he'd been back then. *That* Seth had done something terrible to Lightbringer Suaresh and then made himself forget. *That* Seth had taken money to summon the dead back to life for quick interrogations by highly questionable people. *That* Seth had been caught by a pair of sword-monks, escaped, and fled to Deephaven. *That* Seth had been searching for the secret rot at the heart of the Path of the Sun, certain it was there, determined to find it, no matter cost or consequence.

That Seth was gone, not that the sword-monks he'd escaped would care. All *this* Seth wanted was time and space and quiet. To be left alone to study. To walk the long, slow path to knowledge.

To unpick the secrets of the sigils, which he'd have to do on his own. The memories of Saffran Kuy were a map; but to reach a destination, even with a map, a man still had to walk the path.

Maybe the rot he'd been looking for was real, maybe not. He didn't know. All that certainty – and he remembered *that* much at least – had gone. One truth remained: whatever he'd done in Deephaven might be forgotten, but not what he'd done in Varr. He could never go back.

All the while, he dug deeper into the memories of the warlock Saffran Kuy, buried in the orb he didn't remember finding. The further he went, the more the not remembering niggled him, like someone had gone out of their way to put Kuy's story in his path, knowing he wouldn't be able to resist unravelling it. And unravel it he did: fractured memories from long ago of a place that wasn't Deephaven, a city that wasn't Torpreah but whose architecture was the same and was surrounded by the same hills. Visits in dark places from three men who called themselves mages, one of whom just might have been the old mage of Tombland, decades younger than when Seth had known him as the dread king of Varr's underworld. Memories of standing among ruins of white stone, the Pillar of Dusk at his back, looking across the Shroud at the Pillar of Light in the distance. Turning to the Wraith beside him.

Yes. A Wraith.

Of walking through overgrown ruins. Descending golden steps into a room of black marble. Of wind blowing through windows, the three mages again, Kuy with a book in his hands, drawing sigils from it.

The Book of Endings. The book Seth had been looking for in Deephaven.

A sense, after that, of a long time having passed. Another room of black marble, not the same as the first. The Wraith and the warlock exchanging whispers. The warlock dissolving into shadows. A flood of sword-monks, blades drawn, faces grim. The Wraith a fury of silver blades and violent moonbeams, killing and killing until the monks took it down. The warlock perfectly still, an invisible shadow, watching, quietly signing a sigil as the monks set the dead Wraith ablaze.

And then, for years, nothing.

The Festival of Fire came, and the blood-moon night of the summer solstice. Seth hadn't had any visions for a while, but he wasn't surprised to get one tonight. He *was* a bit surprised to see an old man at the head of a rag-tag band of armed men camped in a field near Torpreah's north gate.

Haven't seen you before. He went to the old man and kicked him hard in the shin, because, well, fuck having visions, what good had they ever done? It seemed to do the trick because the world dissolved, turned upside-down, and he was suddenly in a steep-sided valley at the dead of night at the top of a waterfall watching Myla murder a half-god. *That* was new, too. Then the same tedious shit he remembered from Varr, high over a city on three hills, ice and mountains and sigils written in the sky, storms and lightning, the moon tinged with blood, fire and ice splitting the night. It was all very apocalyptic.

Bored! Bored, bored, bored.

The dream, vision, whatever it was, shifted again. Four figures, two either side of a pair of archways, one a grey path to an uncertain future, one a black road to oblivion. The first figure wore harsh black armour and carried two swords, like the swords of a Wraith, or maybe a sword-monk. The second was a woman in regal robes, the third was the same woman again, tousle-haired and flushed, clutching a silk sheet against around her skin. The last figure wore a great white battle helm of carved ice, fingertips crackling with lightning.

Still bored. He'd seen all this in Sivingathm's *Heresies.* The faces there had been blank, but the symbology was the same: The Warrior, the Empress, the Lover, the Sorceress.

He recognised the face of the Empress and the Lover here. The Empire's Princess-Regent. When he'd seen her in the Circus of Dead Emperors, he'd given her a week before someone stuck a knife in her back. Turned out he'd been wrong about that.

In *Heresies*, each archway had a guardian, barring the way. When Seth looked, they shimmered into light. The guardian of the uncertain future was Myla. He supposed that shouldn't surprise him, not with what he'd seen at the top of the Moonspire and with another blood moon in the sky.

The guardian to oblivion had one blind eye and a ruined face. *His* face.

Fuck off! Fuck right *off!* Seth signed a killing sigil in the air and then suddenly he was awake, thrashing and shouting. He struggled out of bed, opened the shutters, let the dawn light flood in. Scattered around the floor were a dozen books. He picked one, opened it at random and began to read. Anything. Anything at all, but the words wouldn't stick in his head. The air seemed to stir. *You are mine*, it said. *Foolish to resist. Follow your destiny! In Deephaven you were so close.*

No. Whatever he'd done there, that wasn't who he was.

It is exactly *who you are.*

No! No, no, no, no! He ran out of his room. The day was barely born. Everyone was still asleep. He needed to talk. Someone. *Any*one. Someone who could help him.

Fings? But Fings could never understand. Nor could Lucius.

Soraya? She knew what he was. From the looks she gave him now and then, he'd come to wonder if she'd seen some of what he'd done in the desert and had simply chosen not to say anything.

No. Not Soraya. A priest.

He stumbled downstairs to the workshop, quiet and dark, then to the dawn brightness of the street outside. The daybreak sunlight cleared his head, the visions less real out in the light. He hurried through the streets, hiding his face from idle eyes. Hiding the scars of the pox until he rounded a corner to the temple of the Sun a few streets from Lucius's shop. He could have found his way there blind by now.

He hurried inside. Sunlight filled the domed hall. Dawn Prayer had started. He scuttled past the scattering of yawning faithful, past a Lightbringer with a face still full of sleep, into the rooms behind the dome. The cells of contemplation. Every temple had them, usually several, where Lightbringers and Sunbrights collected their thoughts before each ritual. No one could look at him here. No one could stare at his ruined face and then look away, pity and revulsion in their eyes.

But I want *the light. Don't I?*

He knelt and prayed. Not that any God would hear him.

Daylight flooded in through the open door. Seth squinted at the figure looming over him. The Lightbringer he'd passed.

"It's already over?" Seth asked.

"The Dawn prayer? Yes." The Lightbringer's voice was carefully neutral. Not quite accusing, yet not the peaceful, reassuring voice of his ritual. "What are you doing here?"

"I…" He was a novice caught in a place he shouldn't be by a temple Lightbringer. "I did something wrong. I need to find my way."

"I know you," said the Lightbringer. "You come with Lucius. You work in his shop." The priest's voice softened. "You should be out in the light."

"I… I don't know how." Seth's voice was a whisper.

"Is that why you came?"

"Yes. But I don't know where to start."

"A rite of purification? We could do that together."

What could he say? That he knew the rite, performed it on himself twice every day without fail and without effect? That what troubled him wasn't some petty crime or indiscretion but that he'd raised the dead, had almost certainly committed murder, had maybe brought ruin on an entire city, and all because… because…

Because of pride. Fucking pride. Because he'd been so sure he that he was right and that everyone else was wrong.

"I've fallen a long way," he said, the words halting. "Further than you can imagine. I need to find my way back. I want to, but… I don't know how. I don't think… I don't think I can." He shook his head and pushed past the priest. He wanted to shout aloud: *there's nothing you can do! Nothing. There never was.*

And there was Myla in his head, offering her hand.

Do better, she seemed to say.

"*Fuck* you!" *I don't know how!* "Leave me alone! You're dead!"

The priest recoiled. Seth span in helpless confusion. "Not you. I..."

Seth sank to his knees, head in his hands. "Yes. Help me. Anything."

25
A Touch of Silver

Fings sat in the boat, whistling quietly to himself, trying not to fidget in excitement. Lucius sat beside him, the pair dressed as exactly what they were: a prosperous up-and-coming clothier and his manservant. The island of the Autarch drew ever closer.

I'm doing this for family, he told himself, same as always, as if saying it enough would make it true. What *was* true was that he'd been with Lucius to the houses of more than a dozen rich men now and hadn't stolen from *any* of them. Seth simply didn't believe him, yet here he was, the very model of restraint.

Well...*Almost* anything. Nothing while he'd been there with Lucius, anyway, pretending to be his manservant.

Well... Fine, yes, a weird-looking glass-and-feather beaded necklace thing, but *that* had been lying around like it was about to be thrown away, and was obviously a lucky charm of some sort, even if Fings couldn't work out quite what. And, alright, yes, a silver lamp-lighter, but that had been *outside* the house and so it didn't count. Point was, he hadn't done anything like what he *could* have done.

And yes, the business with the spyglass. He tried not to think about that. The fire at the house of Richma Ran Ibsios had been big news among the men Lucius was courting. Rancid Ibsios, it turned out, was positively rolling in gold from selling war supplies to his second cousin. The most popular rumour was of a shady arrangement between Ibsios, a group of merchants from Helhex, and a spy for the Sapphire Throne posing as an agent of Varr's Sunherald, and that any day now, Ibsios was going to find himself carted off to the Citadel of the Sun to answer a lot of awkward questions, which was why he'd fled Torpreah after the fire and was holed up in his country estate surrounded by a hundred armed men.

Fings listened to all this and tried very hard not to look like he found it interesting. He'd gotten away clean; he was sure of that, so it wouldn't have bothered him... but then there was the spyglass. He was getting looks from Peg now and then. It was all a bit uncomfortable.

Ah well. He'd be leaving Torpreah soon. Just... maybe a bit sooner that he'd planned.

The old oarsman pulled slowly back and forth. Water lapped at the planks beneath his feet. Lucius was watching him. Lucius had taken to watching him quite a lot of late, right after two more houses got burgled that quite coincidentally happened to be near houses that Lucius and Fings had visited. Fings couldn't see the problem: these things happened all the time, surely? Rich men got rich while poor men worked; every now and then, rich men got robbed. Way of the world, that was; yet here was Lucius, looking at him like a hawk eyeing a mouse, simply *assuming* Fings had something to do with it without even a shred of evidence, and Fings *knew* Lucius didn't have any evidence because he knew how careful he'd been, how well he'd hidden his stash so no one would find it.

He'd stopped after the third. Mostly, if he was honest, because Myla would murder him if anything happened to her brother. *If* she was still alive. He still liked to imagine she was, even though he knew she almost certainly wasn't. If she wasn't, he was a bit nervous that she might come and haunt him.

Doing this for Ma Fings. Ma Fings, his sisters back in Varr, and a big sack of silver.

Would be a shame, leaving. Life in Torpreah was good. He had a roof over his head and a warm bed, all of it an arm and a leg better than he'd had from Blackhand in the *Unruly Pig*. Working as Lucius's assistant was steady money. Not much, but it got him into the houses of rich people. Lucius had been good to his word, cutting Fings a share of the profits in payment for the silks Fings had stolen in Helhex.

Varr. The silver he'd left behind was enough to keep his sisters and Ma Fings comfortable for years; but still, he had... responsibilities. So yeah, however good he had it here, he'd be leaving. Had it all worked out, too, a proper plan and everything: a quick spate of burglaries, half a dozen houses turned in a single night, and he'd be gone. Him and Seth and two of the seamstresses, which was a development he hadn't seen coming. He wasn't quite sure what to make of Crlya and Yrma except they seemed keen to leave Torpreah and had good dose of the sneaky between them. Debts, probably, because that's what it usually was. Didn't matter. He wasn't going to pry.

Lucius was eyeing him again, this time because the old man was pulling in the oars. A few dozen yards ahead, fingers of wood reached into the water. Another old man stood on them, ready to throw a rope. No, not a man, a sword-monk. A very, very *old* sword-monk, but a sword-monk, nonetheless. Fings felt a prick of apprehension. He'd had some idea of adding the Palace of the Autarch as a grand finale to his Night of Larceny, an idea he'd had as he'd told Yrma about breaking into the Temple of the Sun in Deephaven. It occurred to him now, as the oarsman and the old monk worked together to tie up the boat, to maybe consider how that particular escapade had ended.

Lucius was counting bits into the oarsman's palm. The old monk paid no attention. Boats came into the Palace of the Sun all the time.

"There are nine domes," Lucius said. "The big one in the middle is the Sanctuary of the Ever-Radiant Sun. They use that for the most important ceremonies, but most of the time it's empty. The other eight are for the eight elemental dragons." Lucius rambled off into details Fings would never remember even if he'd been interested. The Autarch's palace was around the Fire Dome at the southern end of the island, which was all that mattered. He knew that because Seth had told him, eventually, after a lot of badgering.

So he followed along wide gravel paths through manicured gardens, not listening, looking at the occasional statues, mostly of men but sometimes of symbols or objects, or simply shapes. Each had a lengthy inscription, which Fings supposed would all be deep and significant, if he could read them. From the top of the Pillar of Light, the domes on the island were spectacular; walking among them, they were hidden away, carefully obstructed by trees and high hedges, all except the gleaming bulk of the Autarch's white marble palace sprawling over the eastern end of the island. Which, Fings reckoned, was where all the best treasures would be.

No one seemed interested in who they were or why or where they were going. Fings couldn't stop grinning about that at first. A bit later, the grinning *did* stop. That was when he worked out that the old sword-monk on the waterfront hadn't been an aberration. The island was full of them. Crotchety old men and women who could smell a lie at a hundred paces and who, no doubt, could still chop him up even while being so stooped they practically lived their lives staring at their toes.

Maybe he... *shouldn't* try and rob the Autarch of the Sun?

He thought about that as Lucius met with the Dawncaller who'd invited them to the island, as they went through the usual ritual of measuring the man up. Fings reckoned Lucius must be doing well for himself, being invited to fit a Dawncaller for a new robe.

Yeah. Probably best to not *rob the Autarch.*

They were heading back towards the boats when a pair of sword-monks came round a corner ahead, walking towards them. Fings had seen plenty by now, was mostly thinking about how he probably maybe really shouldn't rob any priests or temples at all, which was why it took a moment to realise that one of these two sword-monks was familiar...

Oh, shit!

Myla's sword-mistress. The one who'd been waiting for him that night he'd crept into the temple to rescue Myla. The one who'd told him where Myla would be.

Shit! Shit, bollocks, shit! Right, well, that was that, then. *Definitely* no robbing any temples.

She looked at him like she was trying to place him. He forced himself to keep going like this was nothing unusual, like he had no idea who she was. He wasn't sure why. They'd spoken, back in Deephaven, and Fings had done what she'd asked, and it had suited them both just fine. No reason for any hard feelings, right?

Yeah... Still... Sword-monks and thieves. Not a happy mix.

Worked alright with Myla, didn't it?

Yeah. But Myla was Myla. Different.

The sword-mistress looked away, so maybe she didn't remember, which was probably for the best. Stayed with him, though, the knowledge that she was in Torpreah. Couldn't help wondering why she wasn't up north fighting the hordes of Dead Men. Couldn't help wondering quite a lot of things, really. Like...

Well, like whether she knew if Myla was alive. Like... whether, maybe, just maybe, Myla was in Torpreah too?

He could, he supposed, simply go and ask? He wasn't sure about that, but the thought kept bothering at him, which was why, long after dark, he swam back to the island, found a hiding place, stripped, unwrapped an oilcloth packed carefully in his satchel, and changed into the knock-off sword-monk robe Yrma had hastily made that afternoon.

Fings! What are you doing?

He had to know. That was the thing. Had to know if Myla had somehow survived. Had to know it without the sword-mistress ever knowing he was here. He had no idea how he was going to manage that, but sure as shit it wasn't going to be by sitting on his arse all night, picking his nose.

His fake robes were damp, cheap and wouldn't fool anyone who got close enough for a proper look in good light; but from a distance, he reckoned they'd do. He touched the charms in his pocket and around his neck. He didn't know where to start looking, so luck would have to guide him; luck always did. And so off he went, slinking among the maze of trees and hedges, glimpses of the nine domes looming between them like judgemental shadows.

He wasn't quite sure why he was doing this. If Myla *was* alive, she'd be looking for her family, wouldn't she? She'd find Lucius's shop. All he had to do was sit and wait, wasn't it? So why...?

At what he reckoned must be the Fire Dome, on account of it being decorated like a vast column of flame, he stopped for a bit. The doors were open, a yellow light spilling out, illuminating a procession of priests and monks. Fings settled to watch but didn't see either Tasahre or Myla. As the last monk left, the doors closed and the gardens sank back into darkness. Wherever the procession was heading seemed as reasonable a place as any to look, so Fings followed, muttering at himself to keep his eyes on the job. It was hard, with so many wonders strewn casually about the place.

The procession filed through a golden arch into a circular plaza, which Fings reckoned to be the size of a small town, while in the centre rose a white stone dome capped with gleaming gold and glass as clear as water and about as big as a castle. His heart skipped. The Sanctuary of the Ever-Radiant Sun. Had to be.

He spared a thought for Seth, who in better days would have given his back teeth to see this. But mostly what he was thinking was how much gold was on display.

The sword-mistress! Myla! No stealing!

Yeah, finding either of them while carrying loot from the most holy place in the Empire probably wasn't clever.

Seth... *That* was really why he was here. If Myla was alive, he had to find her before Myla found Seth. Because of what Seth had done in the desert, which Fings had seen and then very quietly kept to himself...

The procession filed inside. Fings, hit by a moment of madness, clamped a feather between his teeth, hurried out from the shadows and joined in at the back, head bowed, face hidden by his cowl. The Sunguard at the doors watched with bored curiosity but didn't stop him. What they *did* do was close the doors behind him.

Shit. Maybe stay outside next time, eh?

On the other hand, what was the worst that could happen? They'd discover he was an imposter; he'd tell them he was looking for the sword-mistress of Deephaven, they'd take him to see her, she'd remember him, he'd ask about Myla, that would be the end of it. Put that way, it almost made sense to simply throw back his hood and ask to be arrested.

Yeah… Maybe later, eh?

Until then, he didn't have much choice but to keep following the monks ahead, which was difficult because he almost had to close his eyes to stop himself gawping at what was surely enough gold and silver to fill an imperial treasury. The procession filed past it all and headed to the altar. The monks and priests fanned into a semi-circle and began a chant. Fings joined in as best he could, head still bowed, desperately trying to look like he was supposed to be there, albeit with a feather between his teeth. Everyone knew that holding a feather between your teeth made people not notice you, although he wasn't sure how well that worked on sword-monks. He'd tried it on Myla a couple of times to see what happened; mostly, what had happened was her telling him that he looked like an idiot.

He risked a prayer to the Moon, the Fickle Lord, the giver and taker of fortune. Wasn't sure how well *that* would work either, not in a place like this.

The monks stopped chanting. A priest went to the altar and said something that was probably deep and spiritual and important, but Fings was too busy scanning the hall for ways out and to see whether any of the monks was Myla.

Hold your nerve! Half the skill of burgling was patience, the other half was never drawing any attention.

As the priest finished, the semi-circle broke apart, separating into ones and twos and threes, each knot of people heading their own way. Fings had no idea what he was supposed to do, so settled for going to the altar for what he hoped would look like some very extra-devout praying. He didn't know how praying to the Sun *worked*, exactly, but he knew how it *looked*. He'd seen Seth do it enough times.

A hand rested on his shoulder. Fings almost jumped out of his skin.

"May the blessing of the Light always be with you," said the priest who'd led the prayer.

Fings grunted.

"I'll leave a few of the candles to light your way. Snuff them as you leave, if you would."

Fings nodded. The priest turned and left. Another few minutes and Fings was alone, the doors open, even if they still had a few bored Sunguard standing beside them. He slumped, let out a long sigh, then picked himself up and offered a prayer to the Sun, something he almost never did but which seemed appropriate, under the circumstances. He was about ready to slink away and go back to looking for Myla or the sword-mistress, figuring Lord Luck had given about as obvious a warning as he was going to get, when he realised what was behind the altar where he knelt.

The bones of Saint Kelm. Saint Kelm's *actual* bones.

His skull. His teeth.

Now, Fings didn't know much about who Saint Kelm had been or what he'd done. What he *did* know, though, was what everyone else knew, which was that Saint Kelm had been very lucky, and that it had something to do with his teeth, so much so that they were all most people remembered of him. Except Seth, of course, who'd once casually settled an argument Fings had been having with Wil by telling them there was nothing mystical whatsoever about Kelm or his teeth. He'd then started on at length about who Saint Kelm had really been and what he'd really done and all that, which *had* settled the argument, mostly by making both Fings and Wil discover they had other things they should be doing.

Right now, Fings rather wished he'd stayed to listen. What even *he* knew was the bit about how Saint Kelm's Teeth were on display for all to see in the middle of the high temple in Torpreah. And here they were. The most concentrated embodiment of good fortune he could imagine, right in front of him, still stuck in what was presumably Saint Kelm's jawbone, attached to what was presumably Saint Kelm's skull, spine, and all his other bits and pieces, only no one ever swore by any of *those* so presumably they weren't anything special.

One tooth. Just one.

No!

Except... Well, it was fate, wasn't it? Had to be! Him being a tooth-puller back in Varr when he wasn't being a burglar. And here was a tooth, asking to be pulled.

No! Don't you even think about it!

He felt his hand reaching of its own accord. He looked around. He really was alone in here. *One tooth. Just one.*

His heart was racing. His palms sweating...

No, no, no, he absolutely was *not* going to steal a piece of what was possibly the most holy relic in existence from the heart of the most holy place in the Empire while surrounded by hundreds and hundreds of sword-monks. He was not, *not*, NOT going to...

Bollocks!

Apparently, he already had. A tooth was in his hand. A molar, taken from the back where he hoped it wouldn't be too obvious

Maybe no one will notice?

They bloody well *would* notice. First thing in the morning. Dawn prayer. The Autarch himself probably. Bowing down to face the rising sun, calling out its blessing for the new day, and then hang on a minute, didn't old Saint Kelm used to have a full set of teeth? I'm sure they were all there last night...

Yeah. Sounded about right.

Put it back, you idiot!

But now it was in his pocket, and he was working out how far he could get before dawn, which would be plenty far enough if he could get off the island without raising the alarm.

Slip back to the room over Lucius's shop. No one will ever know.

He giggled a bit. Yeah, Seth would certainly have a thing or two to say about this little escapade.

Best not tell him, eh? Not until we're well on our way to Varr...

He slipped out into the shadows that surrounded the Sanctuary, then a quick dash across the open space of the plaza and into the trees.

You were supposed to be looking for the sword-mistress, remember? To find out about Myla!

Yeah, well. Not with one of Kelm's teeth in his pocket.

Another procession of a dozen sword-monks entered the plaza, heading his way, all carrying flaming torches. Fings swore under his breath – buggers were everywhere! He darted towards a chapel hidden in the trees. The doors were open but there was no light from inside.

Good enough.

He slipped in, reckoning on waiting for the monks to pass.

Crap!

A column of moonlight shone from the top of the dome, pale and silver, picking out a slab of stone in the centre of the floor, where a body lay under a shroud. Something near the body's heart was tenting the cloth, like whoever was under there still had a large knife, or maybe a short sword, stuck through them. Fings could have lived with that, but more troubling were the four sword-monks at work around the corpse, lifting it, sliding poles and planks of wood underneath, apparently set on moving it.

They hadn't seen him. Too intent on their work. He reached into a pocket, looking for a lucky charm. His fingers found the stolen tooth.

Not that! Not here!

He felt a sudden urge to follow the body, to sneak a look and see who it was.

Yeah. Maybe not, eh? He slunk further inside and hunkered down in the darkness. The sword-monks lifted the body and hoisted it on their shoulders. The procession with the torches was waiting by the door. It formed up around the stretcher bearers. Since following them was about the most stupid idea imaginable, Fings waited until they were gone, then slipped out alone, skulking through the moonlight shadows. He could see the procession a little way ahead, wafting in silence through the ornamental gardens, the paths and hedges and hidden nooks and crannies, the statues and miniature manicured trees. He still felt the urge to follow, to see where they were going and what they were up to...

Nope. No, no, no!

He was about to slip away when he spotted a lone sword-monk heading towards him along one of the paths. He had just enough time to scurry behind some bushes.

The sword-monk stopped and looked right at him. Fings looked back. The sword-mistress. Of course – and yes, he *had* come looking for her, but did he have to find her right *now*? Like *this*?

That was the trouble with luck, fickle sod that it was. Liked nothing better than taking the piss.

Fings stayed very, very still. What he *wanted* to do was run like buggery, but she'd see him the moment he moved and then he'd be screwed. As he was, crouched in darkness with a feather between his teeth, she likely *hadn't* seen him, and it was just that irritating sixth sense sword-monks had.

She turned away. Fings stayed exactly where he was. Eventually, when he was sure she wasn't coming back, he slunk off, slow and careful and quiet until he'd put some good distance between him and whatever those monks had been up to. By now, he had no idea where on the island he was and didn't much care. All that mattered was getting away.

He touched a few of his charms, whispered a prayer to the Goblin King, crept through palaces and temples and their gardens, until he found himself back where he'd started. He retrieved his hidden bag and took a deep breath. All things considered, a soaking wet monk hauling himself out of the water and traipsing through the streets at the dead of night would get a lot more attention than a soaking wet drunk in his underclothes, so he emptied his pockets into the bag, swam into the lake, stripped off his false robe, and left it to float away.

It was almost dawn when he got back to Lucius's shop. Exhausted and exhilarated, he fell into bed. There'd be some right old trouble on the island in the morning, he reckoned, but they'd have no idea who'd done it or where to look, and that left an entire city to search, and so he reckoned he was safe.

He took the tooth from its pouch. Just an ordinary-looking tooth.

Really, what *were* the chances that Myla's sword-mistress had recognised him earlier that day? And even if she had, she obviously hadn't seen him tonight, otherwise she would have come after him. And if she *had* recognised him and *had* seen him, well, Torpreah was even bigger than Varr, so how was she ever going to find him?

As for finding out about Myla... Well, the obvious thing, what he probably should have done in the first place, was to tell Lucius about the sword-mistress, and let *him* do the asking. Couldn't really do that *now*, though, could he...

Worry about it in the morning.

He smiled, pleased with himself, and went to sleep.

26
†HOU SHALL ΠOT SUFFER A WARLOCK †O LIVE

The knock came in the middle of the afternoon. Seth was in the shop with Lucius, going through the ledgers for the previous month, with Lucius pretending to watch but mostly dozing. The girls were in the back, drinking lemon water, fanning themselves against the heat and gossiping as they sewed. Fings was upstairs, probably asleep given he'd been out all night. Burgling, most likely, and Seth wished he wouldn't; but then again, Fings would need money to get back to Varr, and it was hard to begrudge him that.

The knock came again. When Lucius didn't move, Seth sighed, closed the ledger, and went to the door.

"Sarcassian personal tailoring and…" He trailed off with a squeak, finding himself staring at a sword-monk.

Fuck!

Not one of the sword-monks from Varr, thank Kelm, but still somehow familiar…

Fuck, fuck, fuck!

From Deephaven! The last memory before everything went blank! Him and Fings in the temple. Fings talking to a…

Myla's teacher! The one who skewered Kuy! Oh, you're so, so dead.

Shut up!

The monk studied him. "Do I know you?" she asked.

"I…" *Don't lie, don't lie, don't lie!*

Hard not to freeze in terror.

"Well… I don't think we've ever been introduced," he stammered, which was true enough.

Don't draw attention to yourself! Don't say anything!

The sword-monk peered as if trying to place him, then pushed past. Seth had to bite his tongue not to ask what she wanted. Probably not new robes, because life was never that kind.

Run while you can!

"Lucius Sarcassian?"

And how, exactly, is that supposed to work? I'd be pressed to out-run a dead cripple!

Lucius stared for a moment as he gathered his wits, then got up. "Yes?"

Get rid of her!

How, exactly? Sigils? Oh, wait, we tried that one in Varr. Didn't end well. They don't work on sword-monks, remember?

"You were on the island yesterday." *See! Nothing to do with us!*

"Yes." Lucius frowned. "Is something wrong?"

If she knew who we are, we'd have a pair of swords sticking out of us by now! Just stay calm.

Oh, right, like that was going to be easy.

And why am I talking to myself like there's more than one of me? Shit!

"The man who was with you. His name is Fings. Where is he?"

Fings? Fuck, Fings! What did you do?

"Who are you?" asked Lucius.

"Tasahre. Former sword-mistress of Deephaven. I taught your sister."

"My sister? Shirish?" Lucius was suddenly staring. Which was just as well because it meant that neither of them were looking at Seth. *Deephaven! Fuck! Fuck! What did you do?*

"Her name is Myla now–"

"Did she…"

Does she remember me? What if we spoke?

"She lives, if that's what you're asking."

"Is she…"

What the fuck did I make myself forget…? No, wait, that was clever!

If she asks questions, I can say I don't know, and it won't be a lie!

"She serves the Princess-Regent now." Seth heard Tasahre's curl of disdain.

Was that why I made myself forget? So I could lie to a sword-monk again?

"Fings. Where is he?"

Yeah, but lie about what? What did I do?

"He's–"

"Shall I ask the girls to make some tea?" asked Seth. *Shut up, you idiot! Don't speak! Don't make her notice you!*

"No." Tasahre shot him a hard look.

"I haven't seen him yet today," said Lucius.

Tasahre's eyes stayed on Seth. "Do *you* know where I can find him?"

Fuck! See what you've done! Seth shrugged. "I haven't seen him today either," he said, choosing his words carefully. He was fairly sure Fings was upstairs in bed, but he hadn't actually looked.

"That's not what I asked. Do you know where he is?"

Seth considered pretending he'd been struck suddenly dumb, or maybe collapsing theatrically to the floor like he was having some sort of fit. "What do you want with him?" he asked.

"That's not your concern."

"Has he done something wrong?" asked Lucius.

"Answer my questions here or you can both spend the next few days answering them on the island. Where is he?"

"In Deephaven, you helped Myla escape the Overlord's judgement," said Lucius. "Do your superiors know about that?"

"Is that supposed to be a threat, Sarcassian?" Seth found himself wondering the same, and how, given that his own sister was a sword-monk, Lucius could possibly imagine that threatening one was ever a good idea. Although… well, you had to be impressed at the audacity, right?

Lucius bowed his head. "No. Of course not."

"Your sister was a good fighter and I liked her, but she was a poor monk. I see now where she got her flaws."

The door to the back room opened and there stood Ma Hiva. "Begging your pardons, but I couldn't help overhearing. If you're looking for Mister Fings, I believe he's upstairs in bed."

"Show me!" ordered Tasahre. She pointed fingers at Lucius and Seth. "You two stay right here." She followed Ma Hiva. Seth heard them go up the stairs. And the sensible thing, he knew, would be to run, far away and never look back... but run to where? Maybe none of this had anything to do with him? Maybe *Fings* had done something in Deephaven, maybe *that* was what Seth had made himself forget. Maybe Fings had done something *here*... well, there wasn't really a *maybe* about it. Could never keep his hands to himself, that was Fings' problem.

He sighed, picked up the ledger, tore a couple of pages loose, and drew a sigil on each.

And exactly what are you going to do with those?

He wasn't quite sure, but he followed Tasahre up the stairs anyway, quiet as he could. *Get my brother out of whatever shit he's in. That's what I'm going to do.*

27
Raven Falls

Myla was in a bad mood. They'd risen early to leave ahead of the army, then pissed away half the day watching it all march past, boring as fuck, and now they were charging along backroads and tracks and sometimes across the countryside, all that martial might far behind them. Throughout the day, Tanysha and Myla rode ahead, making sure the Regent didn't accidentally run into any Torpreahn advanced scouts. In the evening, the Princess-Regent, the Sorcerer Royal and the Red Witch chattered like old friends out for a country jaunt, leaving Myla and Tanysha to twiddle their thumbs.

Just the five of them. Orien and the other mages had gone west for Neja and the approaching Silver Kings. With little else to do, Myla's thoughts kept snagging on him. She put on a brave face when she talked to Tanysha, but she and Orien were both riding into danger, in their different ways. She was afraid they'd never see each other again.

On the bright side, the popinjay had left for Neja as well.

They rode hard. After two days, they emerged into a sweeping plain, dotted with villages and full of tall yellowing grass rippling in the wind. Hills rimmed the horizon. A bright summer sun shone in a deep blue sky. They were well ahead of the main body of the army now, yet the Regent moved from horse to horse and whispered in their ears, laid a hand on each of them, and soon they were racing at a gallop, headlong, leaping hedges and streams, scattering cattle and farmers, until the hills grew from distant shapes to dips and swellings to crags and bluffs. As the enchantment faded, the horses slowed, parched and ravenous, until they reached a small river where the Regent called a halt. Myla, once her belly was full, kicked off her boots and waded in, letting the cold water soothe her feet. After a minute or two, Tanysha and then the Regent did the same. Myla thought about this for a moment, then splashed water at Tanysha – and it was completely by accident and not at all planned that some of it happened to hit the Regent as well. For a moment, as the Regent blinked in shock, Myla wondered if she'd misjudged; but then the Regent put on a fierce frown and threw water back at her, and then all three of them were splashing and kicking water at each other, squealing like girls while Astrin and the Red Witch tried very hard to pretend they weren't seeing what they were seeing.

Afterwards, as they sat drying out in the sun, they could have been anyone. Three young women out by the river, nothing special about any of them, simply having fun; but then, since leaving the army behind, the Regent had acted like a normal person, no more of this wandering into their heads and having a dozen silent conversations with a dozen different people all at once. Myla wondered why but she wasn't going to ask. Out of respect? Because she had no secrets in this company?

Maybe she just wants to be ordinary.

"Some of the time, yes," said the Regent.

Myla shot her a glare. The Regent shrugged.

"I am what I am."

Myla might have had things to say about that, but before she could order her thoughts, Lady Novashi asked the Regent what she'd done to their horses to keep them fresh. It was a well-judged intervention, Myla had to accept, after a flash of annoyance.

"I learned it from Vanamere," said the Regent.

"Did you learn anything else?"

"Oh yes. We'll keep that one close."

They followed the river through a wide green valley, shallow slopes covered in a thick carpet of trees, sparkling emerald greens where the light caught the leaves, glowering black where they fell into shadow. As the sun sank lower, they reached the Ravenwater and turned to follow it upstream. The trail grew steep and craggy, threading between tangles of rocks and thorns in among the trees, hither and yon, ever upward until Myla lost any sense of where they were. Long after nightfall, a distant rushing suffused the air, growing louder until it became a roaring thunder of white water falling from the sky.

"Raven Falls." Tanysha led the way up a steep winding path – Tanysha, who'd seen the barren ice-and-granite spires of Gods Home in the east and the Dragons Teeth in the north, where every peak lay hidden under a sheath of snow and cloud, eagles soaring high overhead the only sign of life. Myla idly wondered what it would be like to live in such an elemental place, among stone giants surrounded by air and water, high above the woes of the world.

Cold, she thought. And probably lonely and boring. But mostly cold.

An hour later, they were wading in moonlight through shallow water rushing over a bed of stones at the top of the falls, stopping to pitch camp at a tangle of boulders and the broken branches that had lodged between them. Myla settled by the edge of the falls, letting herself drift into their roar. Behind her, the steep sides of the Raven valley cast everything into shadow. Somewhere out there, two armies each the size of a city were on the march. Here, though… Here was peaceful.

Lady Novashi conjured a fire. Astrin paced as though expecting something. The top of the falls – devoid of firewood, wet, noisy and with no flat ground that wasn't boulders – seemed a terrible place to pass the night. Yet here they were, and so Myla pinched herself awake and set to keeping watch from the top of the waterfall, with a good view over the valley below. She and Tanysha *were* supposed to be the Regent's bodyguards, after all, never mind that the Regent clearly didn't need them.

She wasn't particularly surprised when a second party of riders came up the valley an hour later, a slender ribbon of fire wafting through the air in front of them, lighting their way. Lady Novashi's handiwork, no doubt. They disappeared and reappeared as the path zigged and zagged upward. When they emerged near the top of the falls, Myla saw six men, strong and determined and full of muscle, lightly armoured and carrying tall shields; but what held her eye were their swords, Sunsteel like her own, and tinged with gold. They passed her, an easy stone's throw away, and headed on, the Red Witch leading them. Myla watched, tired and yawning, mildly interested but...

The Red Witch faltered, sank to her knees, and pitched forward. Her fire died.

"Archer!" The shout came from Tanysha.

Myla stayed very still, scanning the darkness. "Where?"

One of the men with the Sunsteel swords staggered and stumbled. The others dropped to crouch behind their shields. And then, somehow, it seemed as though the moon grew brighter. Brighter and brighter, until Myla knew she wasn't imagining it; and on the ridge above her she saw a figure. A man with a bow, taking careful aim; and then she was running, across the water and up the scree, leaping from stone to stone in the darkness as though she had eyes in the soles of her feet, quiet and swift, although she was never going to get close enough for swords before he heard. Sure enough, she was barely halfway when his head whipped round, and he saw her.

"Here! Up here!" she drew her swords so that everyone would see their glow. The archer stared at her. For a moment, she thought...

Sulfane? But no. She couldn't see his face, but he was too short, his posture all wrong...

The archer aimed and fired; it seemed to Myla that she saw the arrow leave the bow and slice the air towards her exactly as instinct made her jink sideways. She felt the wind of it where her face had been a moment before. She ran on, bounding up the slope. The archer reached for another arrow. He'd have time to fire, too, before she reached him, and suddenly this didn't seem like such a clever idea... but then the archer changed his mind and loped away higher up the valley, between thickets of brush and fallen boulders. She gave chase, and...

And another figure was standing ahead of her where no figure had been only a moment before. Blocking her way in armoured silver.

A Wraith.

Oh. Shit.

Myla skidded to a stop. Fear hit like steel spikes, rooting her feet to the ground. Silent screams hammered her skull as the blood-red eyes of the Silver King filled her soul.

Oh no you don't!

The marks inked into her skin flared hot. This was what the Wraiths had done to Orien, sending him howling in terror and dread. But not her. *Not* her. She bared her teeth and raised her swords in guard.

"Do better," she hissed.

The Wraith levelled his own swords. He didn't move, only turned his head, slowly and deliberately, to look up the slope.

A second Wraith, swords drawn, looking right back at her.

Oh, she thought. And then: *fuck*.

28
Ask No Questions, Hear No Lies

There were, in Fings' view, better ways to wake up on the morning after lifting a holy relic from a sacred temple than finding yourself being prodded by a sword-monk. He opened his eyes. Towering over him was the sword-mistress of Deephaven, looking all angry – not, in Fings' experience, that sword-monks ever looked anything else.

Well, apart from Myla.

He stared back. There was no making sense of it. She *couldn't* have seen him in the darkness last night, just couldn't, and even if she *had*, there was no way she could have found him, and yet here she was. For a bit, he tried to convince himself it wasn't real, that maybe he was dreaming; when that didn't work, he started feverishly trying to figure how he was getting out of this.

"Well?"

What was her name? Tasahre! That was it. And here he was, lying in bed, and she was between him and both the door and the window.

"Er...?" he tried.

He *did* have one of Saint Kelm's teeth hidden in his satchel, and Kelm's Teeth *were* notoriously lucky... but under the circumstances, he wasn't sure that praying to a saint of the Sun was going to get him anywhere.

"Remember me?" asked Tasahre.

"Um." Fings nodded. Running for it wasn't going to be easy. He'd have to barge past her. Most likely she'd grab a handful of

him, and he wouldn't be able to tear free. Even if he did, both the
door and the window shutters were closed.

Bollocks! Sword-monks were quick buggers. Running for it
likely wasn't going to work.

Yeah, but what other choice did he have?

"In Deephaven, you came to me after Twilight Prayer with
your story of a Wraith on the road to Varr. You came with a young
Lightbringer. You spoke of someone with an unhealthy interest in
the House of Cats and Gulls. Do you remember that? You had...
concerns."

"Yeah..." Fings narrowed his eyes. He *had* talked a bit about
something like that, but why was she asking about Seth? *Seth*
hadn't stolen any holy relics recently. Had he?

"Where is he?"

"Er... *Right* now?" *What does she want?* Something to do with
that orb full of warlock memories Seth kept messing with,
probably. The one he brought out when he thought Fings wasn't
looking. Yeah... and would it be such a bad thing if someone gave
Seth a bit of a slap and took it away?

*Not that. You saw what he did in the desert. That wiggly-finger bollocks
that made them soldiers turn on each other...*

"Yes," said Tasahre. "Right now."

"So... this is about... Deephaven is it, then? Not–" Fings bit his
tongue. *You're such an idiot.*

"Not what?"

"Er... what you want with him, anyway?"

"Not *what*?"

Crap. Well, thanks, mouth. Now he was going to have to tell
her something, something that wasn't about Kelm's tooth in his
satchel, but also wasn't a lie. *Think, Fings!*

"Er... Nothing?"

Tasahre glared.

"Well... It's just... when we left Deephaven, Myla never made
it to the ship. As we were leaving, there was someone on the
waterfront, on the back of a horse, waving around a pair of them

swords you lot carry, which I could tell on account of it getting dark and I could see them glowing, and then all them Dead Men came, and the faerie kings were all there, and I didn't see what happened, but the sword person was gone. Afterwards I got to thinking... maybe it was Myla." He gasped for breath. "She's dead, right? She didn't get out." Maybe that would do. All true, after all.

Tasahre stared at him.

"So... I was thinking maybe that was why you were here. Because... Because Myla didn't get out of Deephaven. You came to tell her brother and sister that she was dead."

Tasahre frowned. "No. That's not what you were thinking."

Bollocks! Stupid mouth! But he had it now. A way out. Maybe. He reached carefully for his satchel and pulled loose the ledgers he'd stolen from Rancid Ibsios. "Well... There *was* this rich bloke who ripped off a friend. So... I robbed him. I stole these. Didn't know who he was at the time but..."

He stopped, because Tasahre suddenly wasn't paying attention. She sniffed the air and then stood very still.

"They say he was..." *Well, all right. Never mind, then.* Fings eyed the window. A sudden dash while she was distracted? *Might* work...

The door to Fings' room was closed when Seth reached the top of the stairs. Ma Hiva stood with an ear pressed against it. She flinched as she saw him, guilt flashing across her face.

"You shouldn't be–" she started, then stopped as Seth touched one of his sigils to her skin.

"Be quiet, be still, do as I say," said Seth as the sigil burned into her. "Shouldn't be up here because the big bad sword-monk said so; was that what you were going to say? Well, *you* shouldn't be eavesdropping on other people's conversations. So, what you're going to do now is leave. You're going to leave this house and leave Torpreah and never come back. You're going to start a new life somewhere you've never heard of before. There, you're going to dedicate your life to helping others. Go now. Shoo, shoo."

Ma Hiva stared at him, blinking fast, uncomprehending, then bowed her head. "Yes," she said; but as Seth moved to let her pass, the door to Fings' room flew open and there stood Tasahre. She grabbed Ma Hiva by the arm, and there really wasn't any way she could miss the sigil etched into the old woman's skin. The sigil that hadn't been there only a minute ago.

"Bollocks," said Seth.

Tasahre looked him up and down. "*There* you are," she hissed.

Seth slapped the second sigil onto her hand. "Be still, be quiet, do as I say." Not that he expected it to work. It hadn't worked on the monks in Varr. Truth be told, he wasn't sure *what* he'd been planning, coming up here.

Tasahre spat, grabbed him, and threw him to the floor. "You! Old woman! Stay here!"

Ma Hiva looked stricken. "I... I can't. I... I have to go." She headed on down the stairs.

"Warlock! What did you do to her?"

"I just sent her away!" squealed Seth.

In a movement too fast for Seth to understand, Tasahre had a sword at his throat. "What's in Valladrune, warlock?"

Fings, already at the window and opening the shutters, froze. In the blink of an eye, the world had gone mad. There was Seth, on the floor outside his door, a sword-monk astride him, one of those vicious swords at his throat, saying he was a warlock, which surely meant she knew what Seth had done in the desert, but *how*? How could she know?

Not that. Whatever it was he did in Deephaven...

He had no idea what to do.

"I..." Seth gulped for air.

"The House of Cats and Gulls. You were there."

"Yes but..." The House of Cats and Gulls? What the fuck did that have to do with Valladrune?

"What did you do?"

"I don't remember!" *What the fuck did you make yourself forget?*

"You're Kuy's apprentice."

"No! I'm not!" Valladrune? Valladrune was gone, long ago...

Tasahre's eyes narrowed. A moment of uncertainty. He was telling the truth, and she knew it.

Oh. Shit. Staring him right in the face all this time. Valladrune. *That* was the city he'd seen in Kuy's memories. All the answers he'd been looking for, and now he knew where to find them. And wasn't it just fucking great, having such an epiphany with a sword at his throat?

Tasahre's face hardened. "Does Shirish know? Does she know what you are?"

Hard to shake his head with a sword at his neck. He closed his eyes. Strip everything away and there it was. The thing that shamed him most of all. The one person apart from Fings who'd treated him with any kindness, and he'd betrayed her, not once, but over and over and over.

"No," he said. He might have said more. Might have said how he'd wanted to tell Myla everything but had never found the courage. How pathetic he was, how much of a coward. But he didn't.

Tasahre spat in his face. "The one thing we learn above all else: thou shall not suffer a warlock to live." She shifted her weight and drew back her sword, ready to drive it through him, both hands, to pin him to the floor as he died; and that was when Fings hit her round the head with a chamber pot.

In Fings' imagination, what was *supposed* to happen next was that the sword-mistress crumpled sideways, her sword fell out of her hand, she lay all still and quiet for a bit, long enough for Fings and Seth to run like buggery until they were somewhere safe, and then she'd get up and walk away, a lump on her head and in a bit of a bad mood, no real harm done.

The crumpling and sword-dropping bits happened well enough, and then it all went horribly wrong. Tasahre howled and clutched the back of her head, very much *not* still and quiet, and also with a lot more blood than Fings had expected, which, in truth, had been no blood at all, and now all three of them were covered in piss, too, and he could see she didn't quite know where she was right now – also that she was really, *really* angry.

Crap! "Run, you daft bugger!" You had to be mad as a bag of bats to have a go at a sword-monk, Fings knew this, but what he *also* knew was that Seth was family, and about as good at running away as a horse with no legs. So Fings didn't run, which he knew he should; instead, he jumped on Tasahre, knocking her down as she tried to get to her feet. Didn't see he had much choice.

Seth scrambled up. Tasahre's eyes were glazed like she didn't quite know where she was. She threw Fings off and tried again to get up, and so Fings jumped on top of her for the second time.

"I'm sorry," he said. "I'm sorry. I just can't–"

A blinding pain stopped whatever he'd been about to say because suddenly he couldn't breathe. He rolled sideways, chest heaving as he tried to suck air. He staggered up, grabbing Tasahre's sword, waving it haphazardly in her general direction. It crossed his mind that now would be a good time to say something clever.

And then his legs stopped working and he fell over.

29
SCARS

Myla glimpsed flames from below, the knights behind their shields, Sunsteel swords drawn. The Wraith on the slope above flared with light and hurled a moonbeam. She caught it on her swords, felt smug for an instant, and then a bolt from the second Wraith smacked into her. The sigils on her skin flared and pain lanced pain through her. She crashed across the scree and slid and tumbled down the slope, and the best she could do was curl up tight and tuck everything in and hope that nothing broke.

She slid to a stop, a mangled mess of bruises; she lay for a moment, and then another bolt of moonlight hit her, another flare of agony as she slid further. She got as far as her hands and knees this time, before yet another bolt hit her, this time from below. She screamed.

"This. Really. Fucking. *Hurts*!"

She got one sword raised, enough to block the next blast from above. She staggered to her feet. Something was wrong with her left arm, something that made it hurt to move and sapped the strength from her fingers so she could barely hold her sword. She saw a third Wraith near the falls, saw him gesture at her, blocked the bolt he threw, then blocked another from above, reeling with each.

"Really? It takes *three* of you?"

Below, in the shallows of the river, steels clashed. The moon had dimmed to its usual radiance. She heard Tanysha call out but couldn't see her.

The next moonbeam slipped through her guard. The sigils inked to her skin flared, pain sending her to her knees. She screamed again, a snarling howl of defiance. Open and exposed on a steep slope made of loose stone, there really wasn't much else to do except stand and take whatever they threw.

"Fuck you! Try harder!" Because there *was* something she could do. One step after the next, she could climb that slope, because for as long as she had their attention, that was three half-gods everyone else didn't have to worry about, and if it took three Wraiths to stop one sword-monk then maybe these Wraiths weren't everything their legends said.

The air sparked with pent-up power. A dazzling white fire erupted from the river behind her. A sunbeam seared the air, shooting up the slope, punching through the Wraith who'd first stopped Myla as though he was paper. He crumpled. An invisible hand plucked the other from the earth and hurled him over the hills, wreathed in flame. Myla turned to see the one by the waterfall slice the air with his sword and a hole open as though he'd ripped into the weave of the world. He stepped through, the tear closing behind him, and appeared again by the body of the first Wraith and took its head. There wasn't much Myla could do except watch as he cut the air again and disappeared.

And then it was done, and only a single Wraith remained, down in the river, its face a frozen mask of pain, the Regent standing behind it, fingers pressed to its temples.

"Myla!"

The soldiers still on their feet stood huddled together, Sunsteel at the ready, walled behind their shields.

"A bit of haste, monk! This isn't easy!"

Myla scrambled down the slope, battered and struggling to stay on her feet. When she reached the Regent, she almost laughed. The Wraith was a full head taller. Stood behind it as she was, the Regent was almost on tiptoes to keep her fingers pressed into its skin. She was breathing hard and sweating, although not as hard as the half-god.

"I'll ask you again," said Myla. "What *are* you?"

"What I am right now is quite preoccupied!" hissed the Regent. "Kill it!"

"Me?"

"It has to be you!"

Myla blinked, bewildered. "Why?" The Regent had somehow snared a half-god. And yes, she'd seen what they'd done in Deephaven, and thus had no doubt the half-god would have run her through if their positions were reversed, and yet...

"Should we not talk to it?" she said.

"I already *know* what it would *say*."

Unbidden memories flashed through Myla. Deephaven. Cowering under Tasahre's shield as knives of ice flew from the sky. The Wraith in Deephaven Square, surrounded by a thousand Dead Men. The sword-monks falling, people she'd once called friends. The crowds huddled in the temple yards, bloodied and terrified...

The fall of the temple. The sword-monk as his face turned to dust. The priests, butchered and made into Dead Men...

The hilltop...

Orien's terror...

The Regent hissed and then abruptly let the half-god go. "Kill it."

The Wraith lurched a step forward. Without thought, Myla lashed with her one good arm. Her Sunsteel took the half-god in the neck, cutting through its silver armour as though it was silk, severing its spine. The Wraith's head toppled one way, its body the other. Myla stared at it as it fell, then levelled her sword at the Regent's face.

"You!" she growled. "What did you just do to me?"

Tanysha took two quick steps closer, sword drawn.

"See," said the Regent. "They die."

"I already know they die!" Myla sheathed her sword, closed the distance between them and grabbed the Regent by the collar, pressing her face in close. "Why did you make me kill it?"

The Regent held her ground. Quivering, but it was fury, not

fear. She had a clawed hand raised, held close to Myla's face, Moonlight flickering around her fingers.

"Let. Go."

"No."

You know I could turn you to dust with a thought. Right here, right now.

"Then either do that or get the fuck out of my head!"

The moment stretched, and then the Regent gently lowered her hand and bared her teeth and forced the expression into a smile and, very much to Myla's surprised, pulled Myla into an embrace. As she did, she hissed into Myla's ear.

"These are men of the south. They had to see the half-gods for what they are. They had to see one die, and it had to be you. *You* are a sword-monk, while *I* am a sorceress. *You* are a devout follower of the Sun, *I* am not. *You* are holy, *I* am an abomination. They will return now with what they've seen, and they will take with them an offer of peace. I will pledge myself to the first son of Torpreah. The emperor will pledge to the first daughter. Our houses will be united. That is how this war ends. You have made all this possible."

"You *used* me."

"All *I* did was remind you what they are. *Your* memories, not mine. I left you a choice. I didn't have to. You struck of your own free will. Now let go."

"You still used me."

"That is what rulers do. Now let. Me. Go!"

Myla let go. As she and the Regent stepped apart, the Regent gave a tiny bow. "Thank you, sword-monk."

"Did you know the half-gods would find us here?" Myla asked.

I made sure of it.

"And the archer? Who was that?"

I don't know.

Myla said nothing. All of this? Right from the beginning? Was that all she'd ever been, a useful tool? A pet monk to show off to the lords of the south, who believed that monks were something holy?

No. But I sit upon a throne, and you are but one of millions of souls in my care. Rulers have few friends.

Myla turned her back and walked away. *Rulers have few friends...* was that regret she'd sensed? Sadness? And at the same time, the idea that *she* was something holy? You had to laugh. None of them had any idea who she was.

Except no, that wasn't true. The Regent knew *exactly* who she was. Probably knew better than she did, which was why the Regent had done what she'd done and said what she'd said, knowing all along that Myla would let her get away with it, because in the end, there *was* a sense to it. The Regent's words hadn't carried any taint of deceit. Which, now Myla thought about it, was probably the only reason she'd spoken them aloud.

Fuck you. We're done. She hoped the Regent was still listening.

She found Tanysha sitting cross-legged beside Lady Novashi, who still had an arrow sticking out of her. Astrin was either dead or unconscious. Tanysha shot her a look. Myla wasn't sure what it meant. Guarded, was about the best she could make of it.

"Well, Wraith-killer. What was *that* about?"

"I don't like being used." She flicked a nod to the Red Witch. "Will they live?"

Tanysha shrugged.

"Did you know?"

"Know what?"

"Why we came here."

Tanysha gave a tiny nod. Then the Regent came to squat beside Lady Novashi, and so Myla walked away, although not before she saw the Regent reach under Astrin's robe and emerge clutching a Moonsteel belt; a belt whose metal flowed and transformed into a twin of the Sunsteel circlet she wore – the same Moonsteel crown, thought Myla ruefully, as she'd handed over six months ago.

"Hey!" Tanysha looked at her with steady curiosity. Myla couldn't think of anything to say; but for some reason, her feet had stopped moving.

The Regent put the Moonsteel crown on Lady Novashi's brow,

touched the arrow and vanished it into dust. "Live, my friend." She turned to look at Myla. "You have stopped a war. Remember that."

Myla left and set to walking along the river, staring at her feet, her head in a spin. She was tired and everything hurt. She was starting to remember that one arm didn't work. It was, she thought, very possibly broken.

I don't belong here. She missed Orien. He could have helped her get drunk. Not that she needed help, except no one had brought any wine.

Or... had they...?

The soldiers with their big shields and their Sunsteel swords were looking at her. *They* might have wine, she supposed, so went and sat with them; and they did, too, even if not very much. She took it, gulped gratefully, listened to their names, and then immediately forgot them. A couple agreed that one of the bones between her wrist and her elbow was probably fractured in her left arm. She let them splint it, because splinting an arm was a bugger to do by yourself. Turned out they were real Torpreahn princes. They'd been ready for a fight and had expected treachery. The half-gods, though, had shaken them.

And then, despite herself, she ended up going along with what she knew the Regent wanted. She made up a story about who she was, the dutiful and honourable monk. She showed them her swords and the mark Tasahre had put on the blades after the two of them had fought the Wraith of Deephaven. She told them what she'd seen; and when they asked whether the Regent could be trusted, she gave them as honest an answer as she could: no more or less than any other king or queen. And that, as far as she knew, the Regent had never lied to her.

When the wine was gone, she walked away along the river, putting a good piece of distance between her and everyone else. She found herself somewhere dry, curled up to rest and maybe sleep, and then there was the Regent, walking out of the darkness. Myla rolled her eyes.

"*Please* fuck off."

The Regent sat down, careful to keep a little distance.

"So that's it, is it? I kill a half-god, you take a prince of Torpreah to bed, one who'll no doubt sod off and take a nice southern girl as his second wife just as soon as he's finished writing *property of House Ar* all over the Sapphire Throne, and everyone's happy?"

"Something like that." The Regent gave a wan smile.

Myla gave her level look in return. "I told those men that you've never lied to me. I think that's true. But I also think that I spent six months with a gang of thieves, robbers and forgers, most of whom treated me with more honesty that you have."

Yeah. Most. Maybe not Blackhand.

"The Wraiths came for me last year in the fading of summer. This was after they murdered my mother and my uncle but before they murdered my father." The Regent's eyes managed to be hard and unforgiving and yet soft and misty and full of sorrow all at once. "Have you heard of men who live in the north beyond the Dragon's Teeth? Mountain Men, they call them, up in those parts. The pictures in my mind were of misshapen trolls clutching spears, spindly little arms and legs poking from a mass of black fur. They were nothing like that. They were proud and noble, wrapped in thick fur cloaks yes, but white, not black, and carrying long silver swords. Hardly savage at all. Elegant. Almost beautiful. And then I saw the Silver Kings, and the Mountain Men were nothing."

Myla carefully settled to sit, cross-legged, her good hand resting on her swords. They could stay in their sheathes for now.

"I speak my words aloud so you can know the truth of them," said the Regent, "but for some parts, it's easier if I show you."

An image formed in Myla's thoughts of a round table hewn from granite and of a vast swathe of ice on the wall behind. Ten Silver Kings in a semicircle, shadow figures, another standing by the door. Except these weren't the Silver Kings Myla had seen in Deephaven. These Silver Kings wore white, not silver, and their weapons were far worse than mere swords. A voice spoke in her head: *What are you?*

Myla jerked.

"The same question." The Regent's face was ashen.

"And? What *are* you?"

"I saw my own face stare at me from the earth with dead, empty eyes. They had a skin-shifter with whom they meant to replace me. I killed it and escaped them. But if one doppelganger, why not another? I don't ask your forgiveness that I peer into the minds of those I meet. I am, by almost any reckoning, an empress, so I don't need forgiveness. But I'd be grateful for some understanding."

Memories that weren't Myla's own swept through her. She was a soldier, trapped in a forest of ghosts as fog and smoke wrapped her comrades, sucking their life. She was summoning living fire, terrifying yet glorious, racing and burning through a hundred upon a hundred upon a hundred Dead Men. She felt herself shrivel in anger and hate as a Silver King stood not ten feet away, palm outstretched towards her, a pressure in her head, crushing her skull, snapping her mind, paralysed in terror...

"They took you?"

The Regent looked her in the eye, letting Myla feel the cold fire of her resolve. "They tried."

"How did you escape?"

The Regent shrugged. "I am what I am, but you're asking the wrong question. Ask instead why try to *take* me at all? I wasn't as I am now, not back then. Had they been sufficiently ruthless, they could have buried me deep and replaced me with their skin-shifter. And they would have done all that, I think, but only if there really was no other way..."

Silence hung between them. "All right," said Myla after a bit. "No *other* way?"

And now, finally, the Regent couldn't meet Myla's eye, and under all that power and fury, *there*, at last, was a scared young woman. When the Regent looked back, her eyes were damp. "They were... They murdered everyone else without a second thought, but for me they hesitated and... it was as if something inside woke from a long, deep sleep." She let out a long angry sigh. "You feel yourself poorly used. I understand." She held out a narrow wooden tablet. "Take this."

Myla took the tablet, read what it said, and then gave it back. "I can't."

"It won't help you much South of The Fracture. But I gave you a mission, sword-monk. I will know what mage helped my grandfather take the throne, and what price they asked."

"And why would I bother with any of *that*, after what you just did?"

"Because you'll answer your own question. What I am."

"You want *me* to find that out?"

"Yes."

"Why? For Kelm's sake, of all people, why are you asking *me*?"

"Well, you *are* one of the heroes of Deephaven. You *did* just kill a Wraith. Your name will fly south ahead of you for that."

"And the real answer?"

"I've seen your soul. I know you'll do what's right. I'm not sure I can say the same of myself." The Regent hesitated. "It's... possible we may become enemies. It's possible I may regret this choice. But... here and now, this is right."

"What the fuck is it *you* think you are?"

The Regent groaned, soft but bone-weary. "Isn't it obvious? I think I'm one of them."

She left, and Myla, feeling like a tree-trunk of bruised meat, tried to sleep. When that didn't work, she headed back to camp. Staring at the stars and listening to the snores of the mages, she found herself squatting beside the sleeping Regent. No soldiers, no crown, no throne. She might, in that moment, have been an ordinary girl, one whose heart beat fast and slow like any other.

But not so ordinary. More like a fabulous Moonsteel blade. Beautiful but dark. Elegant but deadly. Delicate yet unbreaking.

"Any of us could slide a knife through you, yet you sleep soundly," she said, knowing without looking that Tanysha was close. "She knows she's safe because she's looked into *all* our souls."

"She needs love, Myla. Do you not see that?"

"Mostly I see drool." Myla put a hand on Tanysha's shoulder. "Orien gets like that when he sleeps too. Yes, yes, I see it. I also see that grief nurtures the ice in her heart, loss the hatred in her eye. It seems I have an errand, so it falls to you to remind her that she's not a god."

Tanysha raised an eyebrow, then offered Myla what turned out to be the same narrow wooden tablet the Regent had given her. "She said to give you this." She frowned. "Actually, what she *really* said was to make sure that the impossible sword-monk doesn't leave without it, even if you have to tie it round her neck and throttle her with it."

Myla sighed and took it. "Be mindful she doesn't destroy you without even knowing you were there. That would piss me off."

"Do you even know where you're going?"

Myla nodded. "Valladrune," she said.

"Will you be coming back?"

"I don't know."

30
Master of Nothing

Seth crashed into the back room where the seamstress girls were all sitting in their chairs, stock still, not stitching at all as they listened to the ruckus from upstairs. He signed a sigil in the air and threw at them. "Stop the monk," he said. "Don't let her leave." So, this was how it was, was it? When the Path had thrown him out, they'd told him the Sun no longer heard his voice. They'd lied. The Sun heard him fine. The Sun hated him. An actual God, looking down from the sky, taking the time and effort to pay attention just so it could fuck him up.

He ran into the front room where Lucius stared at him in wide-eyed surprise. Seth threw a sigil at him, too. "Stop the monk. Don't let her leave."

My God hates me. He crashed out onto the street. People stopped to look at him. He signed a sigil at the first to catch his eye. "Stop the monk," he said. One, then another, then another. All three frowned, then looked up and down the street in puzzlement.

He ran a bit further and then stopped. What was the point? His strength had never recovered after the plague and hadn't been much to begin with. Where was he going to go? A few dozen yards, maybe, before he collapsed in a wheezing heap? How, exactly, was that going to help?

Fings. Fings was almost certainly dead. Idiot. Idiot!

My fault. I did this.

What had he done in Deephaven? He didn't know.

What the fuck was I thinking? I should have stayed. Let her have me. Then he'd be alive.

And there she was. The monk. Bursting out of the shop a dozen yards behind him, and he felt such a rage inside him, the same rage he'd felt for as long as he could remember, magnified, amplified, boiled into roaring fury. He turned and faced her because what else was there to do? Watched as Lucius bowled out of the shop, grabbed her, tried to pull her back, took two quick punches, fell to the ground in a curled-up ball of agony.

Seth clenched his fist at the sun. *Not my God. Not my God!* "NOT MY GOD!"

Never was, though, was it?

He signed a sigil and threw at the Earth. "Stop the monk! Kill the fucking monk who murdered my brother!"

As if that would do anything. As if the Earth would split open at his command and swallow her whole.

He blinked. Everyone around him had stopped. They were all staring, but not at him. They were staring at Tasahre. For an instant of pure stillness, Seth gawped in surprise, and then dozens of men and women dropped whatever they were carrying and ran at the sword-monk, and everything was chaos.

What have you done?

Whatever it was, probably best not wait to see how it ended. An unarmed sword-monk against an angry mob? Most times his money would be on the monk.

He couldn't move. Fings was inside. His brother. He couldn't leave Fings behind, not even with a Sunsteel sword stuck through him.

"He was my brother." Whispered words lost under shouts and roars and screams and howls. "He was my brother and you killed him."

No, whispered the voice in his head. *You killed him.*

One by one he'd betrayed them all. That was how it was.

"I'm sorry."

The mob were putting up a good fight. Sure, maybe half were

flat on the ground, writhing around in agony, but the other half had swarmed the sword-mistress, punching and kicking and stamping at her, and yes, she managed to avoid most of the blows, but only most, not all, and they simply weren't giving her space, because no matter what she did, they wouldn't stop, because Seth had told them what to do.

The shutters over the shop opened. A figure climbed out, jumped to the ground, looked wildly about, caught sight of Seth, and came running, clutching at his chest.

Fings! Seth closed his eyes. Felt them damp with relief.

"Er... I don't know what any of *that* nonsense is about." Fings caught his arm. "But I do think we should probably get out of here." He groaned. "Also, I think she broke all my ribs."

The sword-mistress was on the ground now. It was tempting to stay and watch.

Watch her die. She deserves it.

Seth shivered. *No.*

He made the sign again and threw it at the mob. "Stop. Go back to your lives."

The mob stopped. They backed away, bewildered at what they'd done. Someone screamed. A couple tried to help the sword-monk to her feet. She didn't move. A part of Seth was tempted to go and take a good long look. Maybe say something clever. Maybe even finish her off. Do it himself. She *was* still alive, after all. He could tell that much. He could sense her spirit. He could sense her pain.

Good!

You know she's going to keep coming after you.

She didn't kill Fings, and I'm not a murderer.

Tell that to Lightbringer Suaresh!

He let Fings lead him away. Fings had his satchel, which was just as well because Seth had nothing. Didn't even have Saffran Kuy's globe. No matter. The memories were all in his head now.

She'll find it.

Let her.

Fings tugged at him. "Er... running away?"

They rounded a corner and almost collided with a carriage trotting down the middle of the street. Seth made sign at the driver.

"Stop."

The carriage stopped. Seth opened the door. A surprised rich-looking man stared at him. Seth threw another sigil. It was starting to cross his mind that he should have done this a long time ago.

"Take us where we want to go," he said. And then, to make Fings feel better, he added: "And give us all your money."

He got in. Fings hesitated and then followed.

"Seth... What's... going on?"

"I have friends." Seth leaned out the door and told the driver where he wanted to go. The carriage started moving. As it did, Seth told the rich young man to hand over all his valuables and then take off all his clothes. He had the carriage stop along the waterfront and told the man to get out and swim to the island. Something to keep him busy a while.

"Where are we going?" Fings asked, as the carriage pulled away.

Seth watched the man wade out into the water and start splashing. He hoped the man could swim. "Valladrune," he said.

INTERLUDE
THE BLOOD MOON AND THE SOLSTICE OF FLAMES

There were no lingering farewells, no salutes, no blasting fanfares as Orien raced west with the mages of the Sapphire Throne. When the three hills of Neja loomed on the horizon, a man on a grey horse rode to greet them. The army of the dead had arrived the night before. The battle had already started. But no Wraiths, not yet.

A pall of smoke hung in the air, the stench of burned flesh, stronger and stronger, until Orien had to ride with a hand clamped over his face. Like Deephaven, Neja had grown beyond its walls. *Un*like Deephaven, everything outside them was gone. Razed. Burned. Destroyed. Bodies lay in heaps, in smouldering piles or scattered out in the open. Boys ran between them; every now and then, one would shout for joy and hold something up. The boys were barely in their teens yet roamed armed. But then this *was* Neja, where the Empire's steel was forged, as well as the bloodline that had birthed Lady Novashi and had birthed other fire-mages too.

Neja. City of Steel and Fire.

Orien steered towards the nearest boy and asked what they were doing. The boy opened his hands. He held three crossbow bolts. Orien saw the golden tinge of the arrowhead. Sunsteel.

The boy bowed and fell to his knees. "Thank you, Master Mage, thank you. Thank you for coming to save us!"

Orien fled through the city gates. The thought of the boy kneeling in the dirt and ash nearly made him sick. *What have I done to deserve thanks? What have I done to deserve anything?*

Neja was old, all narrow streets meandering aimlessly like old men around the city's three hills. They swallowed him up. Soldiers were everywhere. The feeling of nausea grew. The air felt so thick and laden with death that he could barely breath.

You're going to die here.

A whisper in his ear. He looked wildly around, but there was no one.

"The Dead Men will come again tonight," someone was saying. "The fire-mages will watch the walls. The blue robes will keep the dread of the Wraiths at bay. The youngsters are still out working hard. Every hour sees another hundred arrows. Remember: fire and Sunsteel. If you haven't got either, stay out of the way. If you see a Wraith, let it pass. Don't try to stop them. Let the Deephaven sword-monks deal with them."

You're going to die here.

A presence in the air. He could feel it.

"Where's the Red Witch?" called a voice. "Why isn't she here?"

"She will come," Orien found himself saying, because that was what Lady Novashi had told him. "She gives her word. She will be here. This is her home. It will end in Neja." Neja *was* Lady Novashi's home. Same went for most of her new guild.

Yes. You will all end in Neja.

Some guild mage Orien didn't know talked long and earnestly about how they were defending the city. Mages from each guild paired together, distributed along the walls, patrols of soldiers in the streets, always at least one Sunsteel blade. Most of it passed him by. They'd already had knives of ice falling like rain from the sky, and swarms of birds with beaks like skewers and wings of shadow. They'd had voices of despair. They'd weathered all that. Nothing, Orien's partner said, to trouble a *real* mage.

You are ours. You will die tonight.

The sun sank low. As the city braced for the next onslaught of Dead Men, Orien slipped away and hid. He shivered and sweated and clutched himself and threw up. Fear surrounded him like a thick tight blanket, cloying and suffocating.

You will die.

Tonight.

In futile pain...

...and useless agony.

Besieged by memories from the hill outside Deephaven. Death everywhere. Eyes of blood and sorrow. No matter where he turned, they came at him, dragging old resentments in their wake: the Regent for bewitching him; Lady Novashi for failing to make him a better mage; Myla for not being here; Myla again for never being afraid; the popinjay and the gods for giving him a taste of the power he craved and then taking it away.

You are so small. So pathetically tiny.

He held his head in his hands. The sun set. The far horizon lit up under a bloody moon. He felt the half-gods around the city now, drawing closer, calling him. *We are here. The moon will ride full in the sky, stained with the blood of the Earth, and in the killing light, you will come to us. Free yourself, for you will die tonight.*

He shuddered and retched and suddenly his mouth was full of iron. His eyes snapped open. His hands were clutched to his stomach, the hilt of a dagger between them. His own. A rusty brown stain spread over his orange robes. He jumped up and promptly fell onto his back, whimpering. His mouth filled with blood. He coughed, spluttered, tried to call for help and choked. He was drowning. He felt cold. Pain, a deep, dull gut-splitting agony inside. He looked about for help. But in the dark, in the quiet corner he'd found for himself, there was no one.

You see, breathed the wind. *You will be ours.*

Is this... Is this real?

The world blurred. He propped himself against a wall and watched himself bleed. He *was* going to die. The voices had it right. He closed his eyes. He was going to die curled in a dark corner, afraid and alone. He'd never see Myla again. He'd never see their child. No one would remember him.

Far away and a long time later, he thought he heard voices.

"There's another! Here!"

"Oh fuck! Look at him. He's gone."

"No, not yet. Look. He's a mage."

More darkness. New voices. He tried to open his eyes, but they weren't having it. Everything was too difficult. He felt himself lifted, swaying from side to side. Hands on his face. His mouth forced open. Liquid fire on his tongue.

"That's… quite a lot." This voice sounded a lot like the popinjay.

"I need this one to live." Oddly, the second voice sounded like the Regent. But why was the Regent here? And how? And if she was…

"Myla?" Orien croaked.

A hand touched his cheek. "Go and be glorious. You're a god now."

The voices faded. Orien slumped. He counted the seconds. He'd imagined it all, he supposed. The last hopeless visions of a dying–

He was on an endless plain of snow, the moon shining bright as day, motes of ice glittering, coiling around him, bright light welling up, filling him, gushing from his mouth, his eyes, cold fire coursing through him, power unimaginable…

Go and be glorious. You're a god now.

Fire burst from his hands. He forgot about dying. He launched upward, vaguely aware of stone exploding around him. High in the sky, he looked down on a city ringed by fire. Pyres of the dead mounded against the walls. The air thick with the reek of burnt meat. Lashes of flame spitting from the walls. Mages, or men with vats of scalding, burning oil. The dead didn't care about the heat but they cared about the flame, oh yes, they cared about *that*. Burn them. Immerse them in water. Hang them in the air and let the wind flay them. Why these three things would put the dead to rest when a good arrow through the heart did nothing, Orien had no idea. It was enough to know what worked.

And I am Fire.

He dived and swooped through fields of slaughter, skimming battlements, soaring high, exploding incandescent rain on the legions of the dead. Walking, running, climbing corpses piled themselves against the walls and were met by mage-fire, Sunsteel,

Moonsteel, torrents of liquid flame. Men fell, screamed, arms and legs and skulls crushed under stone and metal. The Fire laughed as chaos tore into an ordered world. Laughed as flame fought ice, as the silver ones came, as blades of the Sun and the Moon struck armour of hammered souls, as ice fell from the sky in scything shredding blades and melted in Fire's heat. Laughed and dived low, spreading wings into great curtains of flame, so everything might kiss his plumes and burn to ash.

Little voices of despair whined and wheedled. They wanted to stop. They wanted to leave. They wanted Myla. They wanted to curl up with her in that quiet rickety bed that made the squeaking noises back in Varr... but they were tiny and quickly crushed to silence. All that mattered was what he was, and what he *was* was fire incarnate. Elemental, incandescent, primordial. He was the dragon of the sun, the lord of light, the bringer of life, the destroyer of worlds. Limitless! He *was* a god!

He soared above the highest tower, atop the highest hill, where three women stood with arms locked together. The Regent in Moonsteel. Lady Novashi, haloed in flame and wearing the emperor's crown. A Moon Priestess in silver. The air tasted of salt and sulphur and iron. The Silver Kings came. Moonlight poured from their hands, turning all to dust. The castle walls blew away in the breeze, and the tower; and then the earth and air seemed to shudder as the moon god's sister sang, words Orien couldn't grasp but which felt like the intimate whisper of a lover in his ear. A cataclysm of light split the sky, and all hearts stopped to listen. The dead fell still. The moonbeams of the Silver Kings sputtered and died. Ice shattered, time itself juddered and stopped. He, the fire-god, fell to earth, burning from the inside; he saw, as he fell, the moon in the sky, ruddy and bleeding, saw the Silver Kings falter to their knees. Some drew their swords and sliced the air and were gone while others simply crumbled to ash.

And then...

Darkness. Cast away, flung into the nothingness between the worlds... except he wasn't, and nor was he in the sky, but in a dark corner of a smashed castle, slumped in a litter of shattered stone, the night sky twinkling with stars, an empty phial in his hands. Bewildered, he got to his feet and stumbled across the rubble and looked out across the city. He saw men and women impaled on their own swords and spears. Soldiers who seemed to have been ripped apart. Dazed survivors, standing on the walls and looking out in that euphoric wonder of those who have survived the touch of a god. Out beyond the walls, the dead lay everywhere, like sand on a beach.

"The Wraiths!" he heard. "The Wraiths are gone!"

Had it all been a dream? He'd felt the rapture, the power and the glory. The fear of never having that feeling again hit him like a bolt of ice.

He tried to call the fire. Nothing happened. Not a glimmer.

Distant calls ranged across the city. Disconsolate flames flickered and struggled to burn. He was weak and growing weaker. Everything that he was, draining away. He pushed away from the men on the battlements and sank to his knees, and that was when he saw that his hands were covered in old, dried blood, and so was his robe, right down to the hem.

Oh, he thought. *That.*

Underneath his robe, there was no wound. Behind him, the first rays of the solstice sun struck the city.

Later that same day, in a street in Torpreah, sword-mistress Tasahre, bloody, bruised and broken, pulled herself to her feet and limped back into the innocuous little shop where the warlock she'd hunted all the way from Deephaven had been hiding. She hauled herself up the stairs and was a bit surprised to find her sword laid out and waiting for her on the bed of the thief Fings, beside a pair of ledgers.

The warlock's room was full of books. Scripture, mostly, which was another surprise. She recognised the orb as soon as she saw it, recognised it because she'd been the one to carry it from the House of Cats and Gulls, all those years ago.

She'd so nearly put an end to it, back then. So near and yet she'd failed, and so here they were.

PART FOUR
Valladrune

Look, if you're going to steal shit, then steal shit. Just don't steal shit from Gods, mages or Fat-Eared Abdeen in the Eastern Spice Market
— Fings

31
Unfortunate Choices

Fings lifted his shirt and poked at his ribs. The big dark smudge on his skin, he reckoned, was going to turn into a bruise the size of a hand. A sword-monk's hand, he thought ruefully. He could breathe again, which was something. Whether anything was broken under there, well, he'd have to wait and see about that. What he needed *now* was a bit of a think. Starting with what day it was, because it *felt* a lot like an Abyssday. If bad shit was going to happen, you could usually rely on it happening on an Abyssday.

"We should find a place to lie low," he said. Smacking a sword-monk on the head with a pisspot probably wasn't the smartest thing he'd ever done.

Towerday? Towerdays were good days for hiding.

"Yes," agreed Seth. "And I know where."

Fings had no idea what to make of the madness he'd seen outside Lucius's shop. A mob attacking a sword-monk? Seemed unlikely, but there wasn't anything wrong with his eyes. Stopping because Seth said so? Well, okay, Seth *had* almost been a priest. Some nob showing up in a carriage at exactly the right time, handing over all his clothes and all his money and then taking Seth's suggestion to bugger off for a quick swim in the lake? *That* was just bizarre.

Moonday? Bizarre things liked to happen on Moondays. Known for it, they were.

It's Sunday, you idiot. The Solstice of Flames is always a Sunday.

251

A mob attacking a sword-monk on a Sunday? Fings shivered. That was simply wrong. Then again, some days liked to be difficult, and it *had* been a blood moon last night. If it was going to be one of *those* days, there was a disturbing amount of it still left.

Seth told their driver to head north out of the city, along the lake shore. The driver nodded and did as he was told, as if all of this was perfectly normal, which Fings was reasonably sure it wasn't.

"I know a place we can go," Seth said. "Outside the city."

"Where's that, then?"

"You'll see."

The sword-monk hadn't said anything about missing holy relics. She'd asked about Seth; when Seth had shown up, she'd attacked him and called him a warlock. Fings wasn't entirely sure what a warlock actually *was*, other than an exceptionally bad life-choice if any sword-monks happened by. Some variety of mage? Except... well, he'd known Seth since they were boys, and Seth had spent years working to be a priest, and priests didn't like mages. And everything after they kicked him out? No. Mages didn't try to be priests and mages *certainly* didn't work for people like Blackhand. The notion of Seth having even a sliver of sorcery inside him was clearly nonsense.

And yet...

As the carriage clattered through the streets of Torpreah and then out along the North Road, his thoughts kept putting things together. Little things, mostly. The last night with the Spicers in Tombland, just before Midwinter... Fings had never worked out why Seth had been there or what he'd been up to. Then the whole business of Seth hiding in the Undercity for a month, which had ended up with him being locked in a cell by a pair of sword-monks. *Then* whatever he'd been up to in Deephaven, the Taiytakei popinjay with a penchant for skinning people, a cursed warehouse where a warlock had once lived, that glass ball Seth had been obsessing over in Helhex, the stuff Seth claimed he couldn't remember. Plague, as far as Fings knew, didn't rot people's memories.

All of that, Fings might have shrugged his shoulders and put down to bad luck and Seth's uncanny knack of putting his nose where his nose wasn't wanted; but *then* there was the whole business on the road from Narvel's Pass to Torpreah and the weird signs Seth had made with his hands. The same wiggly-finger bollocks Seth had done when he'd yelled at the mob to stop murdering the sword-monk, and again in the carriage when he'd told his unexpected friend to hand over his money and his clothes and go for an unexpected swim in the lake. Start with the idea that Seth really *was* a mage and a lot of things made sense.

No. Couldn't be right. *Couldn't* be.

Could it?

"I think you and me need to have a bit of a talk," Fings said abruptly.

"About what?"

"Quite a bit to choose from, I reckon."

Seth sighed. "Go on then. Get it over with."

"How about where we're going, for a start."

"The Pillar of Dusk. There are some ruins. We can hide."

"Oh. Great. Some ruins in a place with a slightly ominous name. My favourite! Old ones, are they?"

Seth nodded.

"Goody good. Full of ghosts and shit?"

That earned him an eye-roll.

"Well, thing is, Seth, with old ruins and all that, they tend to either be empty, or else occupied by people who don't much want company, on account of if they *did* want company, they wouldn't be living in old ruins. You know, thieves and bandits and whatnot. An*other* thing about old ruins, I've noticed, is how they don't tend to have shops and taverns and the like. So, what we going to eat, while we're busy hiding? Old stones? Dust? The faded memories of lost civilisations?"

"It won't be for long."

"Alright. A couple of days, we're starving hungry, then what?"

Seth shrugged. "You still want to get back to Varr before the Sulk sets in?"

"Reckon that's right," agreed Fings.

"Show my face in Varr and I'm a dead man the moment any priest or sword-monk hears of it."

"Same in Torpreah too, by the look of things. Deephaven as well, if there's any Deephaven left. Looking like a bit of a pattern, that. Show up, piss off a bunch of sword-monks, leg it to the next place."

Another shrug. Fings resisted the urge to give Seth a slap.

"That sword-monk. You know who she was?"

Seth nodded, then made a *so-what* face which, frankly, wasn't much of an improvement over all the shrugging.

"Well?"

"What do you want me to say?"

"She called you a warlock."

"People call me a lot of things. You too."

"Mostly what people call me is a thief. Harsh, but not entirely unwarranted. What was with all that wiggly-finger shit back there? You know, every time people unaccountably started doing what you said?"

Seth started to shrug, then caught the look on Fings' face. He held up his hands. "Priest tricks," he said.

"Bollocks!"

"What do you want from me, Fings?"

"You wouldn't be here if I hadn't hit that sword-monk with a pisspot. Was me that got you out of Varr. Was me that got you out of Deephaven, too. Reckon that earns me an explanation. So try again, and if you say 'priest tricks', I'll hit *you* with the bloody pisspot next time."

Something flashed in Seth's eyes. Anger, was that? Outrage? "The papers you took from that barge, back when you swiped the emperor's crown. Remember those? I told you about that after we left Varr."

"What you *told* me was how it was all a big misunderstanding."

"And it *was*!" Seth hissed. "Fuck the Gods, Fings! When I tried to give them back to the sword-monks in Varr, they tried to kill me! Ask Myla if you don't believe me! If it wasn't for her, I'd be dead."

"She ain't here, so I'm asking you; and frankly, sword-monks mostly don't go around murdering people for no reason."

"Tell that to the Sad Empress."

Fings glared. Seth sucked air between his teeth and then growled.

"Fine. Those papers were sigils. Sorcery. The sort that warlocks use. Trace them out and shit happens." He pulled a strip of paper marked with a weird symbol from his pocket and shoved it at Fings. Fings recoiled. "Fuck's sake, it not going to bite you. I tried to give them back, okay? Are you happy now? *That's* what I did wrong. This one lets you talk to dead spirits, provided they haven't been dead long enough to be taken by one of the Gods. Pretty useless most of the time." He sighed. Regret, was that? "Thing is… You found those papers with the emperor's crown, right? Which means they were his. Which means he was a warlock – or at least trying to be."

Fings gave Seth a long, hard look. Thing with Seth, he wasn't much of a liar. Had a way of looking you right in the eye when he was hiding something, which he never did most of the rest of the time. "And?"

"And what?"

"No love between the Path and the throne, everyone knows that. Something like what you said, I reckon any sword-monk might want to hear all about it. Good bit of dirt to throw. Might even have said thanks very much and let you go. But they didn't."

Seth stared at his feet. "I made some… unfortunate choices. You remember that night in Locusteater Yard? When you and Myla killed those two Spicers? After I…" He looked away. "You know."

"Oh, right, yeah, the bit where you screwed us all over. *That* the bit you mean?"

"I didn't screw *you* over!" Seth shot back. "At least… Well. And then there they were. Two dead Spicers outside where you lived. I wanted… I needed to know…" He closed his eyes and swallowed hard. "I needed to know if Myla knew it was me. That I was the one who'd done it. So I used a sigil. To see if it would work. And it did."

Fings shrank away. "You… You been doing *mage* shit? Is that what you were up to after Midwinter, too?"

"What else was I supposed to do? I *tried* to give it all back, I *tried* to tell the monks what I'd found. Look what happened!"

"You *got* to be–"

"I was trying to help people!" Seth rushed on. "You know, people who'd lost someone. What was I supposed to do, Fings? Everything I touch turns to ash, then this drops in my lap and I'm supposed to throw it away? I was trying to *be* someone. I was trying to make sure there be some fucking *point* to it all! And yes, make a bit of money too, because it was Varr, in the Sulk, and I was sick of being on the edge of starving or freezing or being randomly kicked to death!" He took a breath and bowed his head. "Of course, *that* turned to shit too. Turned out the people who wanted to talk to corpses – people with actual *money* – were mostly the people responsible for said corpses being dead in the first place. Good coin mind, until they gave me up to the monks."

"You don't mess with sorcery, brother. It fucks you up. Everyone knows that." That crown again. That barge. The Murdering Bastard. Everything *his* fault, as always.

"Tell that to the fucking Guild!"

"What about that glass ball thing then?"

"It's gone now."

"Warlock memories, you said. That why you had a sword-monk come after you all the way from Deephaven, wanting to cut you up?"

Seth closed his eyes. "I don't *know*! I didn't even know I *had* the thing until I woke on the *Speedwell*. Honestly, Fings, I have *no* idea what I did to make that monk come after us all this way."

"And that don't bother you?"

"Of course it fucking bothers me! But not as much as the

memories in that orb. Which, by the way, belonged to that dead warlock from Deephaven Myla was talking about in Varr who, it turns out, was spending his time lurking somewhere hereabouts right before Khrozus helped himself to the Sapphire throne!"

"You *what*?" Fings stared, his mouth hanging open.

Seth snorted. "I *say* dead. Maybe he isn't, for all I know."

This was all getting to be a bit much. Seth mucking about with things he shouldn't was business as usual, the Seth Fings knew, the same Seth who'd gotten himself kicked out of the priesthood for exactly this kind of stupid shit. But the rest? All this stuff about warlocks and dead emperors? "Them people who helped us get away just now. You do that?"

Seth stared into nothing. "She was going to kill us. Both of us."

"Hmm." Fings wasn't so sure about that – the monk could easily have finished him and hadn't. Then again, he was still trying to get his head around the idea of Seth making a weird gesture in the air and causing a couple of dozen people to go completely off their heads and attack a sword-monk.

"You know, I didn't have to call them off," Seth said. "I could have left them to it. I didn't. I let her live, which is more than she would have done for me. I'm not a monster, Fings."

"Takes a bit more than not killing someone to make up for messing with things best left alone, I reckon," Fings muttered, more to himself than Seth. Although a tiny part of him could *sort* of see that maybe Seth had a point, when it came to sword-monks.

"You remember that day you found me on the temple steps?" Seth asked. "You gave me a peach. I'd never had a peach. I thought it was the most amazing thing in the world."

Fings grunted. He *did* remember. He remembered a lot of other things, too. "You got to stop," he said, because that was about all he could manage. The notion of Seth being a mage wouldn't fit inside his head. *Seth*, for Kelm's sake! Seth, who'd always been a bit pathetic, full of ideas too big for himself, getting into scrapes and needing help to get out of them again. Mostly, truth be told, from Fings.

"People keep trying to kill me." Seth wrinkled his nose. "Or you."

"The only time anyone tried to kill *me*, it was mostly because of *you*!"

"Oh, so the Murdering Bastard was *my* fault, was he?"

They rode in silence for a while.

"So, what you going to do?" Fings felt lost.

"I don't know. Get to the bottom of it all, I suppose. Why were those sigils on that barge? What else *can* I do?"

"Leave it be, maybe? Have... nothing at all to do with it?"

"That's what I was trying in Torpreah! Didn't work, did it?" Seth learned forward. "But I know where to go to find the answers."

Here we go again. Same Seth bullshit. "Seth, no–"

"Myla's still alive. The sword-monk told Lucius. She survived Deephaven."

Fings gawped. "Myla? She... What?"

"We find the answers and then go to Varr and find her. We tell her everything. *She'll* know what to do."

Fings gawped some more. "But... She..."

Seth went back to shrugging. Fings was too dazed to thump him. *Myla. Alive...!* He couldn't explain it, but somehow that almost made everything all right again. Almost.

"But... how we even going to *get* to Varr? I mean, we can't go back the way we came on account of Deephaven being full of Dead Men and Faerie-Kings and all that."

"Wraiths. Not Faerie-Kings. Silver Kings, if they have to be any sort of king at all."

"Name makes a difference, does it, when they're busy murdering you?"

"I have no idea how we get back to Varr. *You* were the one who wanted to go. I sort of thought you had it all worked out."

Fings settled into a grumpy silence. The idea of Seth the Sorcerer kept sliding off him. No matter how he tried, it was like trying to grab a greased eel. In the end, he gave up. Sometimes, when things got difficult, the best response was to not think about them, so he thought about Myla being alive instead, which was, frankly, a lot more pleasant. Seth was probably right. If there was one person who could fix all this, it was probably Myla.

Seth shouted at the driver to head for the Pillar of Dusk. A while later, the carriage turned off the road and started bumping down a rutted track.

"So. Old ruins?" Fings gave Seth a glare. Seth at least had the decency to look sheepish. Then he grinned.

"Got to ask a dead half-god some questions." Which Fings assumed was either a euphemism or else a bad attempt at a joke, then remembered that Seth was apparently a sorcerer now, so maybe meant exactly what he'd said.

"Er... I don't think–"

"Look on the bright side, Fings: there's bound to be all sorts of ancient treasures lying about waiting to be pilfered."

"No, there ain't! The only thing you find in *old* ruins is all the useless crap left by all the buggers who came looting before you." Fings shivered, thinking of the last time they'd gone treasure hunting in old ruins, the Undercity in Varr. "That and cursed shit anyone with any sense would leave well alone." Which, of course, meant Seth would be all over it, Seth and sense having parted ways quite some time ago where such things were concerned.

After a lot of bouncing up and down, the driver stopped, mostly on account of the track having petered out to nothing. Seth hopped out and headed off as though he knew exactly where he was going. "We should look for shelter. I'll go this way. You try over there." He pointed away from the lake. "Meet you back here in a few hours, right?"

Fings watched Seth head straight as an arrow towards the distant monolith that could only be the Pillar of Dusk, looking for shelter clearly *not* the first thing on his mind.

Do I really want to know? Mages were bad luck. *Every*one knew that. Fings, of course, knew exactly what to do to keep all that bad luck at bay: turn his back and bow, say good morning to them even in the middle of the night, and mostly get as far away as you possibly could... But how did that work if you *were* a mage? Did you have to say good morning to yourself all the time? Turn your back on your own reflection? Maybe you did? Maybe that was why mages always seemed so bad-tempered?

He sighed and looked around. Not much to see. Mangled bits of white stone, great lumps of it in jumbled overgrown heaps, half swallowed by the forest. *Old* old ruins, the sort that had been lying dead for lifetimes.

Might as well look. People *did* miss things, after all. Maybe there *was* treasure.

An hour of searching later, Fings was bored and disappointed, heading back to the carriage where at least he could snooze somewhere comfortable. That was when he heard the whistle. And it *could* have been some sort of bird; but Fings, who'd done this sort of thing himself enough times to know, reckoned it sounded a lot more like a man trying to sound like a bird and not doing too good a job of it.

Typical, he thought.

32
THE PILLAR OF DUSK

There was a story Seth had once heard, back as a novice in Varr. As was often the case with the most interesting stories, he wasn't supposed to know it; but people got careless with what they said around the Hall of Light after too much mead, and so Seth had made it a habit to eavesdrop on the Dawncallers and Sunbrights when they were in their cups. *This* story was of a sword-monk who'd stayed in Varr after the fall of Emperor Talsin, had spied for the Autarch in Torpreah for a few years, and then disappeared, coincidentally at much the same time as Emperor Khrozus had accidentally stabbed himself in the eye with a poisoned skewer. It had sounded jolly interesting, but the conversation hadn't been about the sword-monk so much as some correspondence between the monk and a senior Dawncaller in Torpreah, correspondence which had mysteriously surfaced again, thirty years after it was written.

Seth had briefly tried finding out more, failed, and forgotten about it. Years later, he'd heard one of Fings' Neckbreaker friends, Red something-or-other, was sitting on some not particularly old or interesting religious books. Stuffed inside one was a sheaf of letters which, best that Seth could glean from what he'd seen, had very possibly come from Torpreah. Seth had given Fings a nudge, Fings had quietly stolen Red something-or-other's books, and there, tucked in with several volumes of tawdry rubbish, were three priceless letters from the Autarch of Torpreah to his sword-monk spy in the court of Emperor Khrozus. Not some Dawncaller, but the Autarch himself.

Back then, Seth had mostly been interested in what he could sell them for. He'd *almost* offered them to Myla. In the end, the Bithwar woman had offered him a decent price, but he'd forged a second set before handing them over. He'd had vague plans of trying to sell them again, all of which had fallen to ash long ago, but he remembered what they said. The prose was florid and verbose, the gist of which was that something terrible had happened in Valladrune, possibly to do with a warlock, definitely to do with Usurper, and the Autarch was imploring his spy to find out more, because twelve sword-monks had turned up dead floating in a pair of boats on the Shroud, apparently murdered at the Pillar of Dusk.

Sword-monks didn't die easy. Not twelve at once. And here Seth was, close to the Pillar of Dusk, on his way to Valladrune, so why not see if he could find out something useful? Never mind shelter – Fings would sort that part. Knowing Fings' luck, the jammy bastard would find a hidden cave full of treasure and a stash of ancient food that was somehow still edible.

He started along a path through the trees, wary that there was a path at all. Judging from the horse dung, it hadn't been *all* that long since someone else had come this way.

The sword-monk?

Hunters, trappers, bandits, army deserters, any of those were more likely – none of whom were likely to take kindly to him and Fings showing up... but any of *those* he could manage.

His first problem was the river Vidra. The forest path spat him out on the western shore. The eastern shore waited across about fifty yards of sprightly flowing water. Fings could have swum it – Fings could probably swim the Arr if someone paid him – but not Seth. Fortunately, the path had brought him to the remains of some recent camp, with a pair of boats drawn out of the water. Pushing them back into the river ought to be easy enough, but Seth wasn't so sure about the crossing. It wasn't *that* far, and he knew how oars were *supposed* to work – he'd been in enough ferries across the Arr – but *using* them did seem like a lot of effort, and he didn't much like things that took effort.

Well, it's that or stay where you are. Unless you can sigil your way across a river.

Cursing and grunting, he pushed one of the boats into the water, fell in the river a couple of times, then hauled himself aboard.

Imagine doing this in Varr in the middle of winter. You'd be dead of cold already.

Yeah, well, this wasn't Varr, it wasn't the middle of winter, the sun was up, the air was warm, so his inner voices could all piss off. He started to row.

This should be interesting.

Get lost!

He discovered quite quickly that he wasn't much good at rowing. There *was* a moment, out in the middle of the water, caught in the current, swearing and panting, when it looked like he might end up swept out into the Shroud. But he managed, pitching up on the far bank of the river just short of the lake edge, exhausted, arms burning from the exertion. He was a lot further downstream than when he'd started, but that only meant he was closer to the Pillar of Dusk and so had saved himself some walking.

Did you want a round of applause or something?

He fell into the river again getting out of the boat, dragged it ashore, tied it up, and tried not to think about how he was going to cross back without ending up adrift on the Shroud. One problem at a time.

Fings would have scaled the Pillar of Dusk in a blink, with all its ledges and handholds and handy dangling creepers, none of which Seth dared attempt; fortunately, there was also a path carved into the rock, spiralling upward; although even *that* was touch and go, old and long forgotten, uneven, parts of it fallen away, a couple of sections spanned by drooping masses of mouldering rope that looked ancient enough to have been put there by the first settlers from Anvor, however long ago *that* was.

It all took a while. At the top, he tried not to think about going back. He went to the edge of the cliff, sat and looked at the ruins below. The same ruins he'd seen in Saffran Kuy's memories.

This had better work.

He'd used the sigil for looking into the past only once, back in Varr, on a dead half-god without really knowing what he was doing. He hadn't much liked the way it had gone; but if Kuy was right, he didn't need the remains of one of the sword-monks who'd died here. *If* Kuy was right, every corner of the world teemed with remnants. They would remember.

He drew the sigil, scratched carefully into stone.

The past. Show me what happened here.

At first, he thought it hadn't worked. Everything looked the same. The same Pillar of Dusk, the same forest with its ruins, rivers to either side, the lake...

A flicker, at the corner of his eye. The ruins suddenly became towers...

He turned to look. They vanished back into ruins. Yet... Not quite, because now he could see the faint ghost of what they'd once been. Great towers of white stone like the City of Spires. Slender bridges hanging like threads of spider silk between them. And now, the forest and the rivers and the lake were gone, covered in a deep white blanket of snow, while in the sky, the sun shone dark, eclipsed by the Black Moon...

Shit. Too far. This was looking back... well, he didn't know how long ago. Centuries? A thousand years?

Yeah, and the last time you dived into the past to look at a half-god, the half-god looked back, and how much fun was what?

Not much. Although it *was* hard not to be curious.

Think about what we might learn! When he squinted, he saw figures moving among the towers...

Alternatively, think about finding yourself possessed by a long-dead Wraith. You do *remember those skulls you ended up carrying about the place?*

Yeah, he remembered. *Fine.*

He shifted away, trying to bring himself forward in time without ever looking too closely. The visions blurred, still ghostly, then came suddenly sharp through some moment of cataclysm. A dark moonlit night. Fire everywhere. Terror and dread as the towers fell and monsters filled the sky. He shot past the city's end and then stopped, looking at the ruins. They were clearer now.

Clearer. Why?

Oh, but he knew the answer. Whatever had brought the half-god city down, a lot of remnants had been made that day.

Had to wonder what that had been, exactly.

You really want to look?

He really did.

You know that's a terrible idea, don't you?

Yeah, but he *really* wanted to know.

He edged back in time until there it was again, the moment of cataclysm; except now he was somewhere else, teetering on the brink of an icy ridge, sheer drops falling away on both sides into murky depths, lightning bursting back and forth across a sky turned dark by churning cloud, errant bolts striking the ice, blasting chunks into an abyss below. Monsters soared around him, dragons as big as warships, as big as castles, and everything was death and fire, tearing at his clothes, almost lifting him off his feet. The Sun hung low on the horizon, a brilliant ring of fire around the Black Moon.

A single red star burned high overhead – the Baleful Eye, the Revealer, the Exposer of Truth, the Unraveller of Mysteries.

Bollocks! He'd seen this before. In Varr, in his visions…

The Earth spasmed. The towers fell. A figure flew beside him. White hair streaming from white skin. Red eyes that matched the star above.

Shit!

The Wraith looked at him. *Welcome, herald!*

Oh. Right. The Destroyer. The Splinterer of Worlds. SHIT! Seth tried to wrench away and found he couldn't. The Wraith held his eye.

In its hand, it held a book. The pages glowed, the sigils offering themselves. Sigils for ending gods.

Fuck, fuck, fuck, fuck!

A second Wraith, carrying a spear, rushed from nowhere and impaled the Destroyer. Seth tumbled upward, helpless in a roaring wind that whispered a name. *Isul Aeiha.* The Black Moon shattered and fell. The Earth tore apart and splintered. The last towers fell. An abyss opened, swallowing the Destroyer as Seth was hurled across continents in a spin and a blur...

...and he was back where he started, sitting on the edge of the Pillar of dusk on a quiet and tranquil evening. A little birdsong, a little whisper of wind. Nothing more.

Well. That was fun. Shall we go again?

He *had* seen this before. Something like it, anyway, although not quite the same. There hadn't been dragons in his visions. And the Wraith hadn't been alone; it had been fighting someone, and not another Wraith with a spear, either. And the book... *Seth* had been holding it...

Sigils for ending gods.

Deep breaths. What he'd seen was the past. Something from long, long ago. The end of the Shining Age. The Splintering, the...

All very fascinating, but unless you can figure a way to use it to not get murdered by sword-monks, maybe do what you actually came here to do?

He took a breath and drew the sigil again; this time, he started at the present and went back more slowly, until he found what he was looking for...

...There! A company of armoured soldiers riding into the edge of the ruins. He watched them find a pair of boats, drawn up on the shore of the Vidra, then head among the trees. He floated among them as they descended into lightless shafts and tunnels with sigils scratched on the walls. The tunnels split and scattered like the tunnels under Varr, the sort of place a man could get lost; but the soldiers knew where to go. They burst into a hemisphere of a room, oddly familiar, to a dozen sword-monks diligently scratching out the sigils on the walls. The monks fought hard as they went down, but down they went.

And then another man, somehow familiar. It took Seth a moment, but he found the memory. He'd seen this one in the flesh. In Varr, in the Circus of Dead Emperors, standing at the shoulder of the Princess-Regent, a generation older than in this vision of the past.

The Levanya.

The soldiers put the bodies of the dead monks into the boats, pushed them into the water, and rode away.

Seth frowned. Unsure, he went back and watched again. The Levanya, with a company of soldiers, had killed a band of sword-monks. That the Levanya and his soldiers had known exactly where to go and what to expect, *that* wasn't a surprise. That the sword-monks had been under the ground, scratching sigils from the walls... yeah, what was *that* about?

Also... sigils. *New* ones...

He watched a few more times. He was still wondering what to make of it when suddenly he was back on the Pillar of Dusk, someone beside him, wrapping a hand around his face and over his mouth, the shock of the surprise enough to paralyse him, all except for one hand, reaching into a pocket for a sigil...

"Shhh!" breathed Fings in his ear, then took his hand away from Seth's mouth.

"Fings?"

"Which bit of *shush* wasn't clear?" Fings shoved Seth down, the two of them crouching side by side. "You remember how I said old ruins might be full of... you know... thieves and whatnot?"

"People like us, you mean."

"Yeah... Except more the sort who settle for bashing you half to death with a big stick before helping themselves to whatever you got. So no, not people like us."

"Oh. So, people like Wil and Dox and Arjay and the rest of the old crew?"

"No! Well, yes, all right, but... But *not* Wil and Dox and Arjay."

Seth's hand was still in his pocket, feeling for his strips of paper. Although... did he really *need* those? He hadn't needed them earlier. He grinned. "A gang of robbers? Like the ones on the road from Helhex?"

"Mysteriously, they didn't fail to notice when some daft bugger's posh carriage rolled up at their front door."

"Do you suppose they have food?" Seth tried to get up. Fings yanked him back down.

"They look like soldiers. Might be deserters."

"And?" With a bit of luck, they'd know the way to Valladrune.

"And? What do you mean *and*?"

"Stay here, Fings. I'm going to talk to them." Yes. Walk right into their midst, write a sigil in the air, then tell them to do whatever he wanted. Make them show him the way to Valladrune and then murder each other. Or give up their feral lives and take holy orders? Maybe become a wandering troupe of dancers and jugglers...

He giggled. Probably wouldn't be very good at dancing and juggling, but that wasn't *his* problem.

Valladrune. Would be nice to have some horses and guides, an armed escort, some food, that sort of thing. Sounded a whole lot easier than making his way on foot, not really knowing where he was going... yeah, he hadn't really thought that bit through as they'd fled Torpreah... but that was what happened when unexpected sword-monks showed up. This? A bunch of outlaws? A godsend.

Yeah, but which God? You might want to think about that.

Fings was staring at him, all scolding and judgemental. Seth glared back. "Well, what do *you* suggest?"

"What *I* suggest," grumbled Fings, "is that we get off this stupid rock and go *that* way." He pointed off into the forest. "Because that's exactly the way them robbers ain't."

"And then? Wander the woods until we're cold and starving because neither of us has the first idea how to survive out here?"

"*I* don't know! This is what you get, isn't it? Mucking about with warlock shit!"

For a moment, Seth thought about what it would be like to sigil Fings. Make him forget everything, maybe. *Sorry Fings. We got into a fight, and someone hit you on the head. Let me tell you about everything that happened since Midwinter.* Skipping a few details, obviously.

He's your brother!

The sound of a shout carried up from below.

"Oh shit!" Fings peered over the edge. "Bollocks! They're here!" He started scurrying around, looking for places to hide. Seth went to the edge and looked down. Sure enough, four figures at the bottom, looking back at him.

Fings pulled him back. "What you *doing*?"

"I'm going to talk to them. They're going to help us."

"Yeah." Fings drew a knife. "Right. Look, reckon I can cut some of them rope bits on the path. Stop them from coming up. Then we wait for dark, climb down and slip away."

Fings could probably do that, too, scale the Pillar of Dusk in the dark. Not Seth. "Fings! Stay here and wait! I'll *deal* with it."

"No, you won't! You ain't doing none of that wiggly-finger shit!"

"You have a better idea?"

"I already told you!"

"I can't climb this in broad daylight. You want me to climb it at night, I might as well jump off right now and spare us both the suspense."

"I'll use some of that rope and lower you down, then."

Seth rolled his eyes. "I want to show you something." *Don't!*

"What?" *Don't you fucking dare!*

Seth fished out a strip of paper from his pocket. "Take a look at this." *He's your brother!*

Fings scrunched up his face and glared at the paper. It had a sigil written on it. "What's that, then?"

Do this and there's no going back. You get that, right? "Take it. It won't bite."

After a bit more frowning and glaring, Fings took the sigil. Then yelped as it stuck to his hand and burned into his skin. "What the–?"

"Quiet!" hissed Seth. "Look, for as long as it stays there, that mark will protect you from mages, okay? And... Wiggly-finger shit. And... And mages won't even know you're there. Like you're invisible to them. Whatever happens, it'll keep you safe, better than any charm you ever had. Sunlight burns it away, mind, so keep it covered. Wear a glove. Now stay here while I talk to them."

This time, when he rose, Fings didn't try to pull him back. *I had to. It's just this once. Just this one thing.*

It's never just one thing.

I'll make sure he burns it off in the morning sun.

No, you won't.

Yes, I will! He'll never know.

Seth picked his way back down from the Pillar of Dusk, slow and careful. At the bottom, he approached the waiting soldiers, waving his hands and making himself as obvious as possible.

"Hello," he said. "I'm Seth. Who are you?"

"I'm Torben," grinned the old soldier who looked like he was in charge. "And who might you be?"

"Well, then. Hello, Torben!" Seth smiled as his fingers danced in the air, twisting the sign of a sigil.

33
The Monasteries of Torpreah

Watching the sun rise over the Thimble Hills was a sight Myla knew she'd carry with her forever. The rugged silhouette of The Fracture lay to the north, the Barrier Peaks to the west. Closer in, the monoliths of the Thimble Hills jutted from the flat plain of the Li and Vidra Valleys. Each pinnacle rose sheer like a colossal finger poking from the fertile earth, spattered with grey where the sides were too steep for even vines to take hold. Between the scattered monoliths, the sinuous Vellan and Li rivers flirted with one another before merging and turning for Torpreah to join with the Vidra. Countless glittering channels spread their waters into lush green fields. Clouds on the eastern horizon lit up in gold and copper and bronze.

It had been a difficult ride. Avoiding the Torpreahn armies and their scouts had forced her into the Cliffshadow Barrens. A week of nothing but sand and rock and dirt, a place without water. The last two days, the parched ascent of the crumbled western edge of the Fracture itself, she'd wondered if she'd survive.

But she had. Then winding down the broken edge of the great cliff, her and Stubborn, and never mind whatever fancy name her horse had had before she'd been given it. She'd found water between these strange round hills that grew taller and steeper with every mile further south, until the Thimble Hills towered around men and women and children working in fields of green. In this paradise, she delighted in the warm air, the ever-present sound of life, the chatter of birds and farmers, the gentle breeze rippling between the hills. And wondered how she was supposed to find this lost city of Valladrune, destroyed on the orders of the Regent's grandfather.

Further, and she spied the first of the mountain-top monasteries. Tasahre had spoken of them in unguarded moments when she talked of her past. A year ago, Myla had thought to seek refuge among them, back when the Hawat brothers were hunting her, but she'd only ever got as far as Varr.

The Hawat brothers were gone but she went looking anyway, searching for the monastery where Tasahre had been trained. She dozed an afternoon at the foot of its peak, leaving Stubborn to roam free. Then in the small hours of the night she climbed a path painstakingly carved by monks long dead to reach the top for sunrise and Dawn Prayer.

And so here she was, gazing out at the rising sun. The monks, curious at having a visitor, offered food and water. They were easy and assured about who they were, unhurried about everything they did, clearly interested but also patient. She watched the sunrise alone. Dawn Prayer wasn't chants and ritual here, but a simple and personal devotion.

Afterwards, a very old monk came and sat beside her. For a long time, he didn't speak, the two of them content to admire the view.

"My sword-mistress was trained here," Myla said eventually. "I can't imagine why she ever wanted to leave."

The old monk shrugged. "What was her name?"

"Tasahre."

"Oh dear. She left because I told her to."

"You were Tasahre's teacher?"

"Tasahre had many teachers, and I have taught many monks. Some turned out quite well." He looked her over. "Tasahre the sword-mistress, eh. I imagine she's very exacting."

"Did she learn that from you?"

The old monk made a noise that could have meant anything, then got up and held out a hand. "May I see?"

Myla offered him the sword Tasahre had marked in Deephaven after they fought the Wraith. He had a good long look, then handed it back.

"Nice blade," he clucked, then cocked his head and put a gentle hand on her belly. "How long?"

"Four months, give or take."

"You won't be able to hide it much longer."

"I know."

"You're Shirish, I think," he said.

"Shirish is dead. She died when Deephaven fell. I'm Myla."

"Tasahre wrote letters. One a month, without fail, always reporting on her various students. She mentioned you. I think she liked you, although I don't suppose she ever let it show. You were a troublemaker."

That drew a wry smile.

"Tasahre always had a soft spot for troublemakers. She liked to think she could save them."

For a long time, Myla didn't answer. She found herself thinking of her fights with Soraya and then Sarwatta. Her flight to Varr. Blackhand, Fings, Seth, the Moonsteel Crown. Then back to Deephaven and Sarwatta and Soraya again, and the coming of the Dead Men and the Wraiths.

"I think perhaps that's exactly what she did," she said at last.

She found herself wanting to talk about Deephaven and Sarwatta, to let it out to some stranger, the worst and the best, no excuses, no false justifications. The old monk listened, quiet and calm and patient. When she finished, he put a hand on her shoulder.

"You will be welcome to return here," he said, "when your work is done."

"Should I not go to the mines? Serve my punishment? Are there any other monks among the prisoners?"

"You'd be our first. But... The laws of men are not our laws. We obey them, by and large, as a matter of convenience, but the path we follow comes from a higher place."

"That sounds perilously close to doing whatever you like and then saying it was fine because God said so." Myla started to pace. Days of riding had left her stiff. "You must remember when Valladrune was a thriving city."

That earned her a sharp look. "No such place ever existed, so I'm told."

"I've been told the same. If I were to find this place that never existed, what would I discover?"

"I have no idea, since it doesn't exist." He tapped the wooden tablet hanging off her belt, the one that said she spoke with the authority of the Sapphire Throne. "Since I'm speaking to the Emperor, I must acknowledge his grandfather's decree, must I not?" He drew closer. "A strange choice to wear that so openly in a place like this. The emperor's inquisitors have a long and proud history of falling to misfortune among the Thimble Hills."

Myla frowned. "Not much use if you don't dare show it, is it?"

"If you want favour in these parts, you need only ask. If those who have answers don't want to help, a fancy lump of wood isn't going to make a difference."

Myla thought about this, then took the talisman off her belt and hurled over the cliff. "I serve the Sun, not the Sapphire Throne. My question, however, remains."

"Come to me this evening for the dusk."

She spent the morning in quiet contemplation, then joined the junior monks as they practiced sword forms. At dusk, she found the old monk, sat high near the top of the monastery, and settled beside him, enjoying the sunset in companionable silence. He looked very happy, she thought.

About three seconds after the last glimmer of sunlight vanished over the horizon, he whipped out a bottle he'd been hiding under his robe, pulled the cork and offered it to Myla.

"God isn't watching now," he said with a wink.

Myla took a slug, screwed up her face and winced. "What *is* that?"

The old monk laughed. "The farmers distil it from rice."

"It tastes like rotting cabbage."

"It *is* quite bad."

"And fierce."

"It's certainly that."

They drank, laughing and talking until the stars shone brightly. The old monk spun stories of Tasahre when she'd been young, stories Myla thought might have a kernel of truth, but sounded like they were mostly embellishment. In turn, she told him of Deephaven's fall, the Dead Men, the collapse of the temple, how she and Tasahre had killed a Wraith. Of Orien, who was her lover and the father of the child she carried and a mage, although not a very good one; of how Orien was quite a long way from being perfect when you stopped to look at it, but that she loved him anyway. She told him of the House of Cats and Gulls, of Tasahre being wounded, of the hilltop outside Deephaven and finally the night at the waterfall in the Raven Hills. They were well into the second bottle by then, and Myla's head was spinning.

"You're getting me drunk to learn why I'm here." She wagged a finger. "Some secrets aren't mine to share."

The old monk nodded happily. "I'm getting you drunk to learn why you're looking for a place that doesn't exist. Also, because I like getting drunk."

"There were mages there. One ended up in Varr." She told him what little she knew about the Mage of Tombland who, according to Fings, had escaped Valladrune and had very possibly been Sulfane's father. Never far from her thoughts, Sulfane, ever since the archer in the Raven Hills, if only for the last words he'd said to her in Tombland: *If she has it, they will come for her. It will be a war like nothing you can imagine. A war of mages.*

He'd meant the Regent and the crown. Turned out he'd been right. Which left her to wonder how he'd known.

She fell quiet, musing on those days in Varr. On the ring Fings had taken from the barge back when they'd stolen the Moonsteel Crown, how it had carried the sign of Valladrune, and what Sulfane had really been after. She should probably have paid more attention; but that was hindsight for you, and she'd had problems of her own.

"A mage, eh," said the old monk. "Perhaps such a man could tell you what really happened there."

"He died years ago." Although that didn't mean his secrets had all died with him.

The monk pointed away through the hills, somewhere northwest. "When I was your age, there used to be a city out that way. I don't seem to remember what it was called. It's gone now. It can't be the place you're looking for, of course, because *that* place never existed."

He contentedly told her how to get to this city he remembered, giving her markers to find her way, the shapes of nearby hills, that sort of thing. He caught her arm as they turned to go inside.

"The city I remember *did* have a cabal of mages. Not like *your* mage, though. More like the one Tasahre is so obsessed with. *She* would have called them warlocks."

"And you?"

The old monk leaned in and grinned. "I will tell a story of a young monk who is now a very old monk. It begins as the young monk returns from a war that has gone badly. To his great dismay, our young monk has been charged with protecting the emperor's priests, a duty he doesn't like, for he is stupid and hungry for bloodletting if he can hang the word 'righteous' on it."

The smile faded. "Fate sees fit to teach a lesson. Our young monk is granted his wish tenfold as the Usurper slips between the emperor's fingers to stab him in the heart. There comes a slaughter of soldiers murdering priests. Many priests, many soldiers, and, yes, a few monks too. Our young monk discharges his duty but is grievously hurt. The priests he saves carry him to safety. The Sun is not ready for his soul and so he lives, but he will never fight again.

The old monk's eyes glazed. He took another swig. "Some say we are allowed one great deed, Myla of Deephaven. That was mine. I have already heard two of yours. It seems avaricious to seek another."

Myla grabbed the bottle and took a swig. "Let my next great deed be to save you a throbbing head in the morning."

The old monk laughed. "With the fight cut out of him, our young monk becomes a travelling collector of stories. One story he hears is of a city with a rot in her heart. It is said to the young monk that within festers a cabal of warlocks, that among them has come another from a faraway land bringing evil words bound into a book of darkness. With him, too, one of the half-gods of ancient times, a Wraith, stripped of much of its power but still a most dire creature. He hears that the usurper emperor has heard of the city's wickedness and sent his keenest sword to cut it out. The young monk finds this hard to believe, for the emperor's keenest sword is well known as a murderer and butcher of children. You know, Myla of Deephaven, of whom I speak."

"The Levanya," said Myla, taking another swallow.

"Our young monk cannot fight. Thus, he does not go with his friends to cut the evil from this city; and because he does not go, he cannot say exactly how it passed, except that all these things are true: that on the day the monks entered this city, everyone died. The people, the mages, the Wraith. Many of the monks, he heard, *did* survive, but died at the Pillar of Dusk, although he does not know how. The only one who was *not* dead when all was said and done was the Levanya." The old monk made a grab for the bottle and drained it. "It seems strange to misplace an entire city, don't you think?"

"One of the mages survived."

"Perhaps he wasn't there. Perhaps it didn't happen as I say. It's only a story."

"And do your stories speak more of these mages? Their purpose?"

"Enough to know that if tears were shed for their passing, it was only for the manner of it."

Myla told him how the City of Spires had vanished, replaced by a lake, how a reflection of the city appeared in the water under the light of the moon.

"That's Moon Priestesses for you." He chuckled. "Awkward for them, this war. They never did like to take sides. They'll be back once it blows over."

"Blows over?" Myla had to laugh.

"It will or it won't."

At some point, she fell asleep. She didn't remember whether the old monk had outlasted her or not, but he was nowhere to be seen when she woke. Bleary and tired, she watched the sunrise and gave it her prayers, spent the day dozing and snoozing and occasionally being sick and cursing whatever had been in the old monk's bottle. She stayed another night and was on her way.

With the monastery far behind her, she came upon a band of men-at-arms, exhilarating colours streaked in gold, velvet cloaks trailing behind them, bright plumes of feathers fluttering from their helms. They rode at the head of a dejected column of what looked to Myla like defeated soldiers, three snaking lines of men bound together. At the rear rode a pair of sword-monks. They looked Myla over, saw her swords and robe, and offered nods of greeting. Myla turned to ride with them a while.

"Sun be with you," she said. "Forgive my curiosity, but are these prisoners from the war?" That was how it looked, although Myla didn't quite see how, unless everything the Regent had said that night at Raven Falls had fallen to ash.

"You're not Torpreahn," said the first sword-monk.

"I'm from Deephaven."

With that, she had their attention. She wondered why, then supposed perhaps she knew the answer.

"My sword-mistress was Tasahre the Scarred. We left Deephaven together. She came south. Do you know her?"

They did, so Myla stayed with them and shared their camp. She heard how Tasahre and some "Shirish" had fought together to slay the Wraith of Deephaven; how Tasahre had reached Torpreah in her hunt for the warlock from the House of Cats and Gulls; how one of the holy teeth of Saint Kelm had gone missing, an omen so terrible it had led some to question the righteousness of the

Torpreahn march against the Sapphire Throne. She heard how on the next day, on the Solstice of Flames, Tasahre had found her warlock; how history had repeated, how the warlock had turned a street full people into a raging mob, how the sword-mistress had almost died while the warlock escaped.

There were no names in these stories. The warlock was running with a thief from Deephaven. The two had been living above a tailor's shop. That was as much as the sword-monks knew. And yes, there were probably hundreds of tailors in Torpreah, and Myla didn't even know for sure what Lucius would have done with himself, but there surely weren't many who happened to be living with a thief from Deephaven.

The prisoners, she discovered, were the household guard of a dead nobleman who'd thought to line his pockets sending mildewed grain to Torpreahn soldiers. Evidence of his crimes had been in ledgers Tasahre had found, left behind by the warlock, with whom he was no doubt in league. Myla had never heard the name Richma Ran Ibsios and had more pressing thoughts on her mind just then, and so she soon forgot it.

34
THE CITY OF THE DEAD

"Can you feel it?" asked Seth, when they'd been following the lost road for nearly three days. He idly flicked a sigil into the air.

"Feel what?" asked Fings, wishing that Seth would stop with the finger-wiggling. The whole business was unsettling; more unsettling, even, than how the deserter soldiers from the Pillar of Dusk had decided that Seth was someone they should listen to. In Fings' experience, no one listened to Seth, not even him... Half the time, even *Seth* didn't listen to Seth... yet this lot had given him horses, food, water, and now days of their time, helping Seth get to wherever it was he wanted to go. Fings had heard of southern hospitality; but *this*, he reckoned, was Seth up to his tricks. It really ought to bother him. Yet somehow, it didn't.

He glanced at his gloved hand. It *did* help knowing he was wearing a sign of protection.

Seth twitched. "We're close."

If he stopped to pay attention, Fings reckoned he *could* feel something in the air. A deep stillness. He gritted his teeth as Seth traced another sigil, as Seth's eyelids fluttered and Seth began to mumble. *Trust that I know what I'm doing* was all very well, but Seth knowing what he was doing and whether it was actually a good idea... Well, in Fings' opinion, Seth and good ideas had largely been living in different villages for as long as Fings could remember.

"What *now*?"

Seth turned a droopy eye on the trail to the horsemen riding ahead. Murderers and thieves, that lot, although Fings grudgingly accepted their story of being deserters. Listening to them talk, it seemed they had designs of heading off after the war to become a troupe of travelling dancers and jugglers. He had no idea what to make of that.

"The walls between this world and Xibaiya are thinning," Seth said.

"Oh. Great. What's a Xibaiya, then? Nothing good, I suppose."

"The Realm of the Dead and the Hungry Goddess."

"Sounds fantastic. Can't wait."

If Seth noticed Fings' sarcasm, he ignored it. "A whole city slaughtered." He pointed. "Look."

Half buried in grass and covered in moss, stood a stone. Fings trotted off and knelt beside it, scraping it clean. "Marker stone. Ten miles to... somewhere." He couldn't read the name, but presumably the place Seth was looking for.

"We'll be there before nightfall."

"Goody good. Can barely contain my excitement – you know, at spending the night in a ruined city where everyone's dead." Being here went against every instinct; but Seth was his brother, and *some*one had stick by him, even if only to protect him from his own stupidity. That and he didn't much fancy trying to make his way north all on his own.

Seth pushed on. The trees gave way to thickets of spiney bushes amid tall yellow grass as high as a man. The sun sank into the western hills and the land lit up like a curtain of liquid gold rippling in the wind.

"Where are all the birds?" asked Fings.

Seth didn't have an answer to that. When Fings looked at the thieves and murderers around him, he saw unease.

See, they *don't like it either! And* they're *a bunch of cutthroats!*

Then, over the next rise, Valladrune. The city looked intact, ringed by a wooden palisade half-swallowed by copses of young trees and lush swathes of thorn bushes. Within, towers and temples and houses of stone stood proud between roads choked with grass. At the heart of it, two great temples of the sun, their golden domes intact.

"It's big!" he said. A vague thought crossed his mind that maybe, if *every*one was dead, might there be treasure left behind?

Seth snorted. "It's nothing next to Varr or Torpreah."

"Still." Fings scanned the ruins. "How we ever find going to whatever it is you're here for?"

"There's an island in the river at the centre. That's where we're going. Where the temples are."

"Oh. Dead temples now, is it." Fings shivered as whispers of wind came and went. Ghosts, probably. "Not like we've had any problems with *those* before."

Trust me! I know what I'm doing. He'd heard those words from Seth more times than he could count, these last few days. Couldn't quite work out why this time should be any different, but for some reason, it was: Fings actually believed him.

"So... if you can make dead people talk, why can't you bring them back?"

Seth gave him a look like he was stupid. "The animating force stays, but... Well, every religion will tell you the higher spirit travels to another place. Dead is dead."

"Yeah... but you said you can only talk to dead people *before* that happens. You know, either you do it quick, or else they have to be buried where the Sun and the Moon and the Stars can't get at them. So... if they're still there to talk, why can't you bring them back?"

"That's what Dead Men are."

"I mean *really* back."

"Maybe you can." Seth shrugged, not interested. "I wouldn't know where to start and I'm not sure I'd want to try. There's a reason the paths of the Sun and the Moon and the Celestial Sisters demand their rites be observed. There's a reason why failure to do so is a crime." He shook his head. "Even if you got to someone before their spirit was taken... Something's wrong. Some of the dead are getting stuck. Or, worse, being caught before they can escape."

"Being caught?" Fings didn't like the sound of that. "By what? The Hungry Goddess?"

"That's what we're taught, but... I'm not so sure. It's been this way for a long time. It has something to do with the Splintering, with the Black Moon and the half-god war and how the Shining Age ended. I think some of the dead are trapped somewhere that was never meant to be. There are other things in that place, Fings. Try and bring someone back, *really* back, I don't know what you'd get."

Fings wished he hadn't asked, if only because now he'd put the idea into Seth's head, a stupid idea, apparently, which made it exactly the sort of idea that would take root, grow into a stupid plan, bloom into a catastrophe, shit unpleasant consequences all over the place, and of course, Fings would be the one cleaning up the mess.

The grass began to swirl and ripple. *Just the wind*, Fings told himself, though he couldn't *feel* any wind...

The valley shimmered before his eyes. He saw it as it was, and at the same time he saw a proud and glorious city in its prime. He saw sword-monks, around two dozen. He saw the gates open to let them enter...

"Er...?"

A touch on his arm and the illusion faded. The valley was as it had been, ruined and wild and empty. The grass was still.

"Er... What was that, exactly...?"

"The dead guard this place."

"Reckon they're welcome to it. You know, we could just leave." Judging from the looks on the faces around him, Fings reckoned he wasn't the only one thinking that way.

Seth touched him on the arm again. "Trust me, brother. Nothing bad will happen here."

"Easy for *you* to say." Odd how Seth's words *were* reassuring, even though Fings couldn't imagine a single reason why that should be.

Seth dismounted and walked on through the grass towards fallen Valladrune. Fings followed. Here and there, he felt the remains of the forgotten beneath his feet. Broken buckets, torn sacks, rusted tools, bones long picked clean and lost to the undergrowth. He saw the blackened skeletons of houses, overgrown with thorns and ivy, giant thickets of leaves and spines. Smaller thickets, he realised with horror, were markers for where people had died, their blood nourishing the soil.

They reached a gatehouse, tangled with brambles and bindweed. Fings followed Seth through the open gate and along what must once have been a broad open avenue, lined with giant ash trees. The trees had grown greedy over the years, devouring the road. Grass grew between old cobbles, tall and yellow and wild.

"Do you see it?" Seth asked.

"See what?"

"The city as it was. Vibrant with life. The trees bursting with green, casting the road into shade." He pointed. "Stalls selling food and trinkets from across the empire. People in bright clothes. Scruffy boys dashing between."

Fings took a step away. "Er… No. Just lots of trees and grass and slightly falling-down bits of building. Oh yeah, and a lot of skeletons." He looked around at the band of cutthroats and bandits still following them. They felt it too, how everything here was wrong.

Seth beelined for the heart of the city, dragging them all behind him like a trail of reluctant children following teacher. They crossed a wide wooden bridge over a river, torpid and brackish, its black water choked in weeds and grasses; when Fings looked over the side, he saw bloated fish and frogs floating dead… And then the water was clear, running between manicured trees and blooming waterside shrubs. He saw men and women in fine clothes, drifting in elegant wooden boats, carved into miniature twins of the great ships that once crossed the oceans and storms to the far-off lands of the Sunking…

"Er…"

Saw it all as though he'd been there; and then the sky darkened and he heard a cry, a shriek that stopped time, and then he was back, standing halfway across the bridge, the world quiet again, the faint perfume of corruption in the air.

"This is a bad idea."

"You're seeing it now, are you?"

"I don't know *what* I'm seeing." Fings shivered. "Shit that ain't here."

"You're perfectly safe. Everything is fine. Be calm. You can trust me."

Somehow, that seemed to help. Fings looked back. The men following had ashen faces. "Reckon this place is cursed," said one.

Seth giggled. "Well yes, it certainly is *that*."

Fings stamped his foot. "If it's *cursed*, why are we–?"

"We're going to lift it, Fings. If we can." Seth looked at the posse of deserters still following along. "Torben! Take your men and check the outer city. If there's anyone alive here, I want to talk to them. That ruin we passed an hour ago. It wasn't like this. You know what I mean. When you're done, go there. Set up camp and wait for me. I'll join you when I'm finished here. We might be several days, so prepare for that."

A dozen grateful men turned and rode away. Fings watched them go in mild horror. *Days?* They were going to be here for *days*?

"Go with them Fings," Seth said. "If that's what you want. We're doing a good thing here. But if you want to leave, I won't hold it against you."

Fings huffed a bit. But… Seth *was* his brother. "Can hardly be worse than Deephaven."

"I wouldn't know." Seth clapped him on the shoulder. "At least you won't have to jump on any sword-monks this time."

"Ain't *them* I'm worried about."

They meandered between abandoned temples and garden plazas. In one moment, Fings saw sickly thorns; in the next, beautiful plants, colours and shapes to dazzle the eye; shrubs with snow white blossoms; Suntrees with orange and yellow blooms the size of a man's head. Butterflies flashed their wings while iridescent dragonflies streaked through the air.

"They once called this place the City of Flowers," said Seth.

They reached a second bridge. Men and women dressed in gold laughed and danced as Fings peered to see them. Seth put his back to the bridge and walked under a wide arch built though a five-storey palace with ornamental windows, an easy climb and clamber onto a tiled roof where Fings might have had a good look around. He wondered, briefly, if he should; but by now, the arch had spat them into a great square, streets and alleys emptying into it from all sides except the south, which was steps and columns and wide-open doors under a huge golden dome, faded by time. A temple to the Sun, as big as the Cathedral of Light in Varr.

The dome of the palace temple lit up for a moment with brilliant ruby flame; when Fings looked again, he saw dull, tarnished yellow.

"Close now." Seth walked towards a sweeping stand of rhododendrons pressed against the eastern wall, fleshy leaves thick with bright flowers, orange and white and lilac. He paced its length. "There should be a door here, somewhere."

"Should there?" Fings puffed his cheeks. "Well... If there is..." He pushed his way into the bushes, pulling branches aside, making openings among the leaves until he found a place where he could duck low and squeeze among them. It was like walking into another world. A twilight place under the canopy, foliage so tight as to block out the sky. He squeezed his way to the wall and then followed it, running his fingers across mossy stone until he found what he was looking for.

"This what you're after?" he called.

He'd seen this trick in Varr: a door hidden behind a shrubbery.

35
Dead Mages

There are other things in that place, Fings. Try and bring someone back, I don't know what you'd get. The words mirrored Saffran Kuy's, which made Seth want to laugh and cry, because how far too late had they come? They hadn't been meant for *him*, of course; they'd been meant for an apprentice who, in the end, had never returned; but none of that mattered. Only Kuy's Book of Endings. So here they were, in the ruins of Valladrune, and Fings had said what he'd said, and Seth had laughed because yes, he reckoned this was *exactly* what he was looking for: a doorway to steps covered in leaf mould, leading down.

He stepped into the dark beyond. Plain walls, steep narrow steps to a rough passage, crude and low so he had to stoop, then a round chamber, walls covered in bricked up arches, the evening sun streaming through a grating in the roof.

Oh look. Sealed archways. Remind you of anything?

These weren't the half-god relics he'd seen in Varr and at the top of the Moonspire. Pale imitations, dull and ugly. But they *were* still archways, inscribed all around by sigils. The same sigils? He wasn't sure. Similar, at least.

Two long-dead bodies lay on the floor, embracing one another. Their flesh had rotted away, but enough remained of their old robes, bright and ornate, covered in arcane symbols. Their fate was clear. Each held a knife in their bony fingers, pressed into the ribs of the other. Two mages, dead by their own hands...

How do I know that?

But he did. *And a third who somehow ended up in Varr…*

Remind you of anything?

The three skeletal corpses he'd found in the Undercity of Varr, that first time he'd gone to look.

Three dead mages. Three dead half-gods. Three days later, they threw you out of the temple. Maybe three isn't your lucky number…

Superstitious bollocks. The Mage of Tombland, if he *was* the third mage of Valladrune, was busy being dead a thousand miles away in Varr. Lucky numbers? Only Fings believed in such nonsense, and Fings was an idiot.

He knelt by the bones and pressed a sigil onto one bleached skull. "You might want to stay outside for this," he said to Fings.

"I've come this far, ain't I? Might as well see for myself why there's sword-monks trying to murder you everywhere we go."

"Fings! Go outside."

"Fine." Fings let off a volley of sighs and left. Seth waited. He was sort of glad Fings had chosen to come this far. Although, in truth, Fings was probably safer well away from all of this, and they both knew it.

Yes. Well. He'd crossed that line a long time ago.

Why are you here? whispered the air. The collective despair of the thousands who died here.

"I want the book the warlock left behind," Seth said.

You are not welcome.

"Perhaps not. But you'll help me anyway."

Why?

"Because my sigils compel you."

So you think.

"Because if you help me, I will open the doors of your prison and set you free."

The wind laughed, raining its disbelief. Seth stilled it with a voice of iron, a voice that wasn't his. "I come with a fire. The stones will crack and melt. I will leave you and there will be nothing. Valladrune and all its memories will be gone." The words didn't feel like they were his. He wasn't sure he liked that.

The half-god's curse holds us fast. The voice of the wind grew soft, almost plaintive.

"I will lift it."

What will become of us?

"You will see. The Book of Endings. Where is it?"

The bones didn't move, but a tiny eddy of dust swirled out of the corner of the room. *Behind the door.*

"And how do I open the door?"

With the key.

"And what is the key?"

In his mind's eye, a sigil formed, rich in subtle detail. It flowed from his fingers as though he'd known it forever. He traced it over the wall where the dust-eddy had swirled. The stones dissolved. A passage opened before him, lit by an eerie moon-glow. A few quick steps and he reached its end and halted in awe. Glittering in front of him, piled from floor to ceiling, was the lost treasure of Valladrune. Gold in abundance.

And...

He scrambled over piles of coins and plates and chalices until he reached it, plain and innocuous. Not the weighty tome he'd imagined. A pocketbook, no bigger than his hand...

The Book of Endings.

We saw him moving among the palace, whispered the ghosts of the dead. *White skin, white hair, white robes, everything white but for his eyes which burned with fire or ran with blood as his mood for revenge blew hot and cold. Here he worked his spells. Here, he nurtured his creatures and his hatred.*

Seth felt a mild squirm of alarm. "Creatures?"

The wind seemed to laugh. *Thick, ugly worms. Angry silver serpents. Blind as though from some deep cave. They glowed like moonlight. We never knew what he did with them, save that he gave one to the usurper and regretted it bitterly. A fine stock, or so we heard, but the usurper took the best from him.*

Seth clucked his tongue. This was all very well and probably quite interesting if you were someone else, but *he* was here for the Book of Endings, which was right in front of him. He reached out to take it, but his fingers slid through nothing. An illusion. He was seeing the vault as it had been long ago; now, he saw it as it was: the piles of gold all gone, the cups and chalices and crowns too. And the book. All gone.

He growled: "Where *is* it?"

The swords of Torpreah come. We gather to turn them away, but our chamber of miracles is gone. In its place, a circle of archways to nothing. The white sorcerer stands in the middle. He screams and all Valladrune hears. None can resist. We pull our knives and stab one another until all are dead. But one of us is not here and thus survives. He comes after the swords of Torpreah are gone. He takes it.

I'm drowning, Seth thought. "*Who* took it? Where did he go?"

To Varr, we hear him say. To build again and make them pay.

"To *Varr*?" Seth closed his eyes. "You've got to be fucking kidding me. The Mage of fucking Tombland had it all along? This whole fucking journey, all one big circle?"

He left the vault, went back outside, and tried to remember how to breathe. When he'd managed that, he screamed, on the off chance it might make him feel better about how shit everything was.

"The Mage of Tombland," he said again, when he was done screaming.

The dead had no answer.

"The Mage of *fucking* Tombland?"

Silence. Seth hissed. His first instinct was to burn this city of ghosts to the ground, burn and grind it to ash and sand, then stomp on it and burn it some more. All this way? All this *fucking* way!

Get a grip! Think!

He'd been there on the night Blackhand had murdered the Mage of Tombland. He'd seen the signet ring on the mage's fingers. A meaningless symbol at the time and for long years after, until Fings had come up with a very different ring, yet with the same symbol hidden inside. The Bithwar woman in Bonecarvers had told him what it was: the sign of the twelfth house of the empire. The sign of Valladrune.

And if Blackhand had had an ounce of kindness to him, he would have given the mage a proper end and sent his body to the pyres, his soul to be set free and returned to the Sun, and that would have been that. But Blackhand *hadn't* had an ounce of kindness in him. Blackhand had been what he'd always been: a vicious, petty vindictive bastard. And so Blackhand had had the Mage of Tombland's corpse dumped in one of the old vaults of the Undercity so the Hungry Goddess could chew on his soul.

Which meant he was still there, all these years later.

Which meant Seth could talk to him.

"Your white sorcerer. He was a Wraith?"

Yes.

"What became of him?" Seth toyed with a fantasy of simply smashing everything until he got what he wanted. Turn north. Head for Varr. Sigil every fighting man he met until he was at the head of an army. Whatever it took to keep the priests and sword-monks at bay. But he'd seen the Wraith of Deephaven, and there was already one army of the dead marching about in the north of the empire, so maybe drawing that sort of attention wasn't clever.

You made a promise, warlock.

"The Wraith. Is his corpse still here?"

Yes.

"Buried somewhere deep and dark?"

Yes.

"Then I'll keep my promise, but it's going to have to wait until I've had a chat with him."

We have waited long. We are patient. But if you betray us, warlock, we will haunt you forever.

"Fine, fine, you do that." For now, he squashed the resentment burning inside him. Yes, he'd talk to the dead here, poking at every corner of what they knew; and when he was done, he'd keep his word and give them what they wanted. Honour his promise and set them free. One great sigil slashed into the heart of a dead city. Valladrune would cease being a city of ghosts and become nothing more than an old ruin. "But the Wraith first."

We already showed you.

Seth went back to the vault. It was dark, now the illusion was gone. He fumbled his way around, feeling the length and breadth of the place until, at the far end where the shadows were darkest, he tripped over broken stone where a part of the ceiling had fallen in, blocking another passageway. He felt himself sinking.

"You're telling me he's through here?"

Yes.

"A chamber of black marble, seamed with gold?" That's what he'd seen in Saffran Kuy's memories.

Yes.

Seth sighed. "Fuck that, then." He frowned. "Wait... If the whole thing is buried, how did Saffran Kuy get out? There must be another way in."

The archways, warlock. The Wraith had doors to everywhere.

His heart finished sinking, coming to rest at the bottom of a deep dark abyss. Archways. Sure. Like the ones in Varr he'd never worked out how to open. The ones Cleaver had used, back when he wasn't being a pin-cushion for Sunsteel swords. So, great, he could go back to Varr, spend years figuring out how they worked, spend some more years working out which one would bring him here, and...

"Wait! A door... to Varr?"

He *did* have a dozen strong and pliant men waiting outside the city, after all. Probably good for a bit of rubble-clearing. And if anyone could tell him how to make those old half-god portals work, it was surely one of the half-gods who'd made them, dead or not.

Would get him back to Varr nice and quick, too.

He grinned. By the time he walked out into the light, to where Fings waited, he was almost laughing.

36
BOΠES

Finding Tasahre in Torpreah was easy enough, a reunion that started with Tasahre drawing steels and all but accusing Myla of consorting with a warlock. A tense moment, but they'd managed not to kill each other and swapped stories instead. Seth, what he'd done in Deephaven and then in Torpreah. How Tasahre had tracked him. How he'd slipped through her fingers. Raven Falls and what the Regent had asked Myla to do, although not the why.

After Tasahre, Myla gave herself a day in Torpreah to see her brother. To see him alive and well and prosperous, *that* was joyous. To know that Soraya was well, even if Soraya hadn't been there to say so. To know that everything she'd done in Deephaven had been worthwhile. Not so joyous to hear Lucius describe the day Tasahre had come and to hear what Seth had done. Yes, Tasahre had already told her; but it carried a different weight, hearing it from her brother, to see the faint mark of a sigil on Lucius's skin.

She and Tasahre set off for Valladrune with the following dawn. Myla wasn't sure whether Tasahre insisting on coming along was simply because Tasahre knew the way, or because, despite never smelling even a hint of a lie, the sword-mistress didn't trust that Myla had told her the truth. A bit of both, most likely.

They stopped for a few hours at the Pillar of Dusk, where Tasahre searched for soldiers she claimed were supposed to be waiting for her there. All they found was a camp, abandoned for maybe a week, maybe more. After that, they rode on, upriver beside the waters of the Vellan.

The days stretched to a week, then a twelvenight. With each one that passed, the land grew wilder. Homes and cultivated fields gave way to shacks and grazing pastures, then wild meadows and hunters' shelters, then nothing except trees and wild water and a road abandoned for thirty years. They passed forgotten villages, almost lost to the wild. No one lived here now. No one to remember what had once been.

Myla paused early one morning, climbed a tree and looked at the road ahead. A majestic morning mist filled the valley, aglow in the sun, the green peaks of the Thimble Hills poking into clear sky above.

"What happened here? What *really* happened here?" she asked after she climbed back down, because it sure as shit wasn't what she'd been told in Varr, that story of the Levanya and an army burning the city, slaughtering its inhabitants, salting the earth, leaving desolation in his wake. Yet the landscape was lush and green, so the salting the earth part was obviously nonsense, and if the rest had been true... Well, three decades later, the stones from sacked buildings would already have been used to build new ones. Cities grew where they grew for reasons: plentiful water and good soil. Farms and villages and fields and crops and animals would all return because they could; in time, they'd need markets; before you knew it, you had a town. Priests would come, and temples, and the town would grow until it looked very much like the city whose destruction had birthed it. That was what happened after a war. It was what had happened in Deephaven, after Talsin's siege destroyed a quarter of the city and drove more than half its people away.

At the very least, there would be people. And since the Levanya couldn't possibly have killed *every*one, some of those people would be old, and would remember Valladrune's fall. Among their stories, she'd thought to find clues. A cabal of mages who'd threatened the throne, perhaps. There was more, she was sure; but if the Levanya was keeping something from a moon-witch who could read minds, he wasn't likely to let it slip to a nosey sword-monk with a bad attitude. She needed the truth, and from someone who'd seen it happen.

No farms, no animals, no people. Nothing.

"I told you that you had to see it for yourself," said Tasahre.

Before long, there wasn't even a recognisable trail. Tasahre led the way, following some tributary of the Vellan into a flat-bottomed valley. The landscape changed again. Tall yellow grass and scattered youthful trees in what had once been irrigated terraces. Myla couldn't tell how long it had been abandoned. Thirty years? Yes, it could be that.

At the valley's heart, straddling the bright gleam of the river, a silent city, its towers still standing.

"Is that it?" she asked.

Tasahre nodded. "Valladrune."

All around, for miles and miles, only the grass and a few trees and dark thickets of... well, from this distance, Myla didn't know.

"And there's no one here? No one at all?"

"No one," said Tasahre.

"And you really don't know what happened?"

"I heard the same story as you."

"You should go and see him, you know. Your old teacher. He thinks highly of you."

Tasahre smiled, face lit by some distant memory. "He said that?"

"Don't be daft, of course not. But he *is* getting old."

Stubborn plodded on, content to walk as Myla guided him, stopping for mouthfuls of grass as the fancy took him. Myla gave him that. After the waterless wasteland of the Fracture, he'd earned it.

"Is it a curse?" It *felt* like a curse, coming all this way and finding nothing. Didn't seem likely she'd get an answer to the Regent's question by wandering an abandoned city, poking through old buildings, praying to get lucky. What she'd needed were survivors.

Or the Levanya needs to spill his secrets.

"It's certainly something. A sense of..."

"Wrongness?"

"Yes."

The feeling was hard to describe. The air was... flat.

Stubborn nickered. *He*, at least, seemed happy.

They stopped for the night a mile short of the wooden palisade walls, cautious, sitting watchful by a small fire, hidden in the remains of what might once have been a customs house before the Levanya came. The insides had been pillaged to bare stone. The floorboards were missing, and the roof tiles too. Taken, rather than allowed to rot or fall, she thought.

"People *did* come back to loot the ruin, then," she said. "And this looks like good land. Yet none stayed?"

Tasahre raised an eyebrow. "*You're* the one who said it was a curse."

A few hours after dark, Myla thought she heard distant singing, rowdy and raucous, fading in and out with the whims of the breeze. She prodded Tasahre.

"Ghosts? Or are we not alone as you thought?"

"Not ghosts."

It started to rain. The singing disappeared. Myla led Stubborn inside. When Tasahre mocked her, Myla pointed out that Stubborn had crossed the wastes north of The Fracture, which was more than Tasahre had ever done; and if she liked the rain so much, why didn't she go out and sleep in it herself? An hour later, Tasahre grumbled something about going soft and brought her own horse inside as well. They sheltered under a tree growing up inside the walls, the four of them together around the embers of their fire. In the morning, they rode to Valladrune, wary and alert. The gates were open, almost inviting them in, their hinges frozen with rust and time but otherwise undamaged.

"If Valladrune was sacked by an army, why are the gates intact and open?"

"Because it wasn't sacked by an army," said Tasahre. "The Levanya's tale is lies."

"Not *all* lies." A cabal of mages? The Regent believed it. The old monk in the monastery had said much the same, so that part was probably true – and that the Levanya had a hand in whatever had happened here, very possibly as its architect. The rest? Untouched walls, gates wide open. No sign of siege or violent assault. Nothing.

The old monk's story had been of a company of sword-monks. But a company of sword-monks couldn't murder an entire city. Not even if they'd wanted to.

The road beyond the gate was choked with waist-high grass. Myla and Tasahre dismounted and walked. A dry old bone snapped under Myla's foot. She picked it up and found herself looking at the fragments of a hand. Before long, she saw bones everywhere. Men, women and children.

"Look how they fell," said Tasahre. "They didn't die where they stood. They were running."

Myla wrinkled her nose. "Trying to escape something?"

"Escape *what*?"

"The Levanya?"

"And a mythical army that no one in the south remembers ever seeing?"

"More believable than a company of sword-monks killing a whole city."

Tasahre clucked her tongue. "If these people were shot by archers, we'd see arrows. If they were cut down by cavalry, we'd see dropped spears and javelins. This is something else. This is... this is like Deephaven."

"The Regent thinks Khrozus made a pact with the mages here."

"*Everyone* thinks Khrozus made a pact with the mages here."

Myla squatted in the grass, trying to think it through. In the old monk's story, there was a warlock from somewhere else and maybe a Wraith, something she would have laughed at as ridiculous a few months ago. "How, so soon after the war, naked hostility raw and bleeding between the Sapphire Throne and the Autarch in his golden cathedral, does someone like the Levanya convince a band of sword-monks to do his work?"

"Because," said Tasahre, "unlike *you*, he knew that some

things, to people like us, are more important than who sits on any throne."

And then everyone, apart from the Levanya, had conveniently died. Under the warm morning sun, Myla shivered. "The Regent said something about the Wraiths... That Deephaven wasn't about who sat on the throne. I got the impression she thought it more personal... Shit! There *was* a Wraith here! Khrozus didn't make a pact with some cabal of mages, he made a pact with a fallen half-god!"

"So... The Usurper bargained with a Wraith, got what he wanted, broke the pact, sent the Levanya to destroy the Wraith and its allies, and then what? The Wraith's friends get angry, inexplicably wait for decades until long after Khrozus is dead, and then come for revenge? Revenge against whom?"

"Not revenge," said Myla.

"Then what?"

"Perhaps they still want whatever Khrozus promised?"

"Which is?"

"I have no idea. That's what the Regent asked me to find out."

"She already knew all this?" Tasahre hissed.

"*Know* is too strong. Suspected? Yes, I think she did."

Usurper. Liberator. Butcher. What bargain did you make? Khrozus had won a throne. But at what cost...?

A tremor through the dirt. Unhurried hoof-beats. Myla and Tasahre slid into the grass, squatting on their haunches, still as stone as a rider trotted by. From his clothes, he might have been a soldier.

"Should we follow?" Myla whispered as the soldier rode out of sight... and then she was suddenly flat on her back, Tasahre straddling her, holding a knife to her throat.

"Did you know the warlock would be here?"

"What the fuck?" Myla glared but the knife didn't move. "What warlock?"

"Shirish!"

"Stop calling me that! *What* fucking warlock?"

"Your friend from Deephaven."

"If you mean Seth, then yes, I suppose I knew he'd likely end up in Torpreah. *If* he escaped Deephaven, that is."

Tasahre's grip tightened. "Not Torpreah! Here in Valladrune. Did. You. Know?"

Myla grabbed Tasahre's wrist and squeezed, hard. "Let. Me. Go!"

"Shirish!"

"The last time I saw Seth was in Varr, a couple of weeks before Midwinter when two of our sisters and brothers tried to kill him for, as best I could tell, no good reason. I haven't seen or spoken to him since, and you *know* I'm not lying. Are you saying he's here? If you are, then no, I had no idea, and how do *you* know?"

Tasahre jumped away, back to her feet, sheathed her knife but drew a sword instead, pointed squarely at Myla. "You're not lying, but that doesn't mean he hasn't turned you."

"Turned me into what?" Myla started up, then stopped as Tasahre hissed.

"Stay down! Show me your feet!"

"What?"

"Your feet! I need to know he hasn't marked you. You may not be lying, Shirish, but I know warlocks. I know their tricks. I need to know, without doubt, you're not carrying his mark."

"You inked my skin yourself on the road from Deephaven! I thought that meant warlocks sigils didn't work on us. Or did you do a bad job of it?"

"I inked you *after* Deephaven."

"What, and you somehow didn't notice a sigil-mark on my skin while I was sitting half-naked for hours and fucking hours while you jabbed needles into me?"

Tasahre growled. "Feet!"

"*Fuck's* sake!" Myla sat up, kicked off her boots, and showed Tasahre her feet. "Happy now?"

"Strip."

"*What*?"

"Any part of you that stays out of the sun."

"Are you serious?"

"Yes, Shirish, I am."

"I'm not going to forget this, *mistress.*"

"Good. You shouldn't. Now lie flat on your belly, and do not move until I say."

It was, Myla supposed, as good a lesson as any in how to search for the marks a warlock might leave. Parts of the skin that rarely saw the sun, so there was little chance of the sigil being burned away.

"I'm sorry," Tasahre said, as Myla dressed.

"You should be. That was fucking humiliating."

"I'm glad to find you unmarked. I would not have wanted to fight you."

"A sentiment I don't currently share."

"Shirish! Please! I've been trying and failing to stop this warlock for almost two decades. Please–"

"Tasahre! Shut up!"

Silence. Myla took a deep breath.

"Look, I understand why you did this, so eventually I'll probably let it go. Until then, there will be some residual bad feelings. While there are, kindly fuck off."

"You should have told me."

"Should have told you what?"

"Is it the fire-mage's child you're carrying?"

"Oh, Kelm's fucking teeth, have you only just noticed?" She had more to say, but Tasahre didn't give her the chance, because now the sword-mistress had grabbed her in a fierce hug.

"I *am* sorry, Myla. I had to be sure. Please."

"*Now* you get my name right?" Myla sighed, feeling her anger slide away. "What makes you think Seth is here, anyway?"

"That rider was one of the deserters I commandeered to bring me here. When your warlock never came, I went to Torpreah. As deserters, they were... less than keen to join me. He was one of the men I left waiting for me at the Pillar of Dusk. That's where the warlock went, after he escaped me." Tasahre closed her eyes and sighed. "Fuck!"

"What?"

"I *asked* him about Valladrune. I *led* him here."

Myla glared. "You want to strip naked in the middle of a city of bones with a few random horsemen wandering about while I search *you* for sigils?"

The rider was long gone, but Tasahre reckoned she knew where to go. Sure enough, as they reached the brackish river running through Valladrune's heart and crossed a wooden bridge to an island covered in overgrown temples, Myla heard sounds of life. She let Tasahre lead, since the sword-mistress knew the way, until they were lying flat on the roof of Valladrune's Cathedral of Light, looking down at maybe a dozen soldiers set up in the temple square. A shrubbery of rhododendrons lined one side, a wall of green with a gaping slash hacked through revealing an open doorway into the stonework beyond. Ropes led inside, slack for now, but ending in a harness for a team of horses. A mound of rubble lay nearby, recent from the looks of it.

"Your men from the Pillar of Dusk?"

Tasahre growled. The soldiers weren't doing much. Sitting around in idle chatter. One, sat on top of the rubble, was smoking a pipe. Gangly and nervous and like he really didn't want to be there...

Myla blinked a few times. *Fings?*

She turned to Tasahre. "Let me guess. We show up, swords drawn. Anyone stupid enough not to stand aside gets stabbed. I stay out in the square while you go looking for Seth and murder him if you find him?"

Tasahre twitched. "Those men know me. That may serve to our advantage, or we may have to fight them. Depends how deeply the warlock has them in his power."

"Then *I* go. No swords unless we must. If Seth's here and I get him to come out, you *listen* to him. Out in the sun. No lies. We understand what they're doing here and why. Then pass what judgement you must. You owe me this, after what you just did."

Tasahre bared her teeth. "And if there's a Wraith in there? Then what?"

"Then I'll probably need some help. But *until* then, no one dies unless they give you no choice. Not even Seth." Myla growled and pointed at Fings. "And you do *not* stab that one. That one's harmless."

"Oh, I remember *that* one." Tasahre touched the back of her head and snorted. "Harmless? I don't think so."

37
The Unrulys

Fings stared in bewilderment at Myla, walking out of nowhere into the square and heading right towards him. He blinked and rubbed his eyes in case he was seeing ghosts again. But no. Myla in the flesh. Not dead. Like Seth said.

He jumped up. For the last two weeks, the soldiers who were following Seth about like he was some sort of prophet had been hauling rubble out of a hole in the ground. Whatever Seth was up to down there, Fings was fairly sure it was something a sword-monk wouldn't like, not even Myla. Something *he* didn't like if he was honest. Had to be done, though. Or so Seth said.

"Myla?"

"Fings!" Myla was smiling, which Fings guardedly supposed was a good thing. Coming towards him with open arms, suspiciously like she was going to hug him. He was less sure about that. "What are you *doing* here?"

Fings took a step away in case he was going to have to run. He didn't *want* to run, mind, because he'd done quite enough of that these last few months. What he *wanted* was to tell Myla everything and then hear some soothing words about how the whole business in Torpreah with Seth and Myla's sword-mistress had been some terrible mistake.

"Seth here too, is he?" Myla asked.

Fings flicked a glance to the open door with ropes leading inside. "Yeah." The admission came out like it was made of lead.

"Who are your... new friends?"

The soldiers were watching, tense and uncomfortable. A few hands strayed towards nearby weaponry. Only a few. Mostly, the soldiers looked like they were readying themselves for a swift exit. Frankly, Fings reckoned they had the right idea.

"Er..." He wasn't sure what to say. Deserters from the Torpreahn armies? Seth's... followers? Although they *did* still seem set on starting fresh as a troupe of combative dancers. He'd seen a few furtively trying to learn to juggle. He had no idea what *that* was about.

It was probably easiest, he reckoned, not to answer. "You're not... *with* anyone, are you?" he asked instead.

"*With* anyone?"

"Just... you, is it? No... other sword-monks kicking about the place?"

Myla's smile faded. "Tasahre is here. I think you know why."

"Oh." Fings bit his lip. "Bollocks."

"Yes."

"That why you're here then, is it? Put a couple of swords through us both?"

"I'd prefer not."

"Right." Fings made a sour face. "Yeah. Thing is... I'm thinking maybe your sword-mistress might not be of the same opinion."

Myla made a what-can-you-do gesture. "She *is* in quite a stabbing frame of mind. Did you really lamp her with a chamber pot?"

Fings bit his lip again. For some reason, Myla was back to smiling, not that Fings could see anything particularly funny about this.

"Nice to see you ain't dead," he said. "But..." Way he saw it, Myla being here ended with either her or Seth on a pyre, maybe both, not much between.

"Yeah. But." Myla sighed and turned and looked up at the roof behind her, the old temple overlooking the square. Fings looked too, and there she was: the sword-mistress. As he did, Mya turned to the soldiers and raised her voice. "If anyone tries to leave, my sword-mistress will stop them. By whatever means it takes. You understand?"

Fings nodded.

"But for now, no one's dead. I'm here to see if things can stay that way. You understand that, too?"

No one moved.

"So, while we're all being civil, everyone stays where they are and keeps their hands away from any weapons. No one need die here today."

Fings shuffled his feet.

"Fings?"

"Fine!" He looked around at the soldiers and gave a little nod, not that he could see any reason they should pay attention to *him*. Most of them did, though, and once the first few sat on their hands, the rest followed with grudging reluctance. He turned back to Myla. "So... you came here looking for Seth, did you?"

"Nope. Something else. Secret mission for the Sapphire Throne, if you must know."

"Right." Fings snorted. Coming from anyone else, he'd *know* they were pulling his leg. Myla... Well, he didn't remember Myla ever having much of a sense of humour, but... really?

Myla looked a bit affronted. "What?"

"Well... No offence, but the last time we clapped eyes, you were off about to burgle and maybe murder some swanky merchant prince. That being after I got you free of a slave-barge, where you were all chained up. Going from wanted criminal to running errands for the emperor's big sister, Sun bless them both, seems... well, a bit of a stretch, to be honest."

"Things changed after Deephaven."

"Yeah, I suppose they did." A part of Fings was back on the *Speedwell*, watching Deephaven fall. "I saw a sword-monk on the docks as we were leaving. On a horse. All alone against an army of Dead Men. That was you, right?"

Myla nodded.

"Why?" Because right there was the thing he'd never understood. Everything Myla had done, everything she'd risked, all to save her family, and then she'd let them leave without her.

"Was the right thing to do." Myla shrugged. "Perhaps *you* should tell *me* why *you're* here. A cursed valley full of restless spirits hardly seems your sort of place."

"Yeah..." Fings winced. "Not keen, if I'm honest."

"The last time I saw Seth, he told me he could speak with the dead."

"Er... maybe?" Fings took another look up to the temple roof. The sword-mistress had disappeared, which was even worse than seeing her glowering down at him. "I don't know much about that. Not sure I know anything anymore. World's gone mad."

"I hear that. Tell me."

Fings sat on a rock and it all came pouring out: the escape from Deephaven; Helhex; the road to Torpreah; how they'd been helping Lucius set up his new shop and largely minding their own business when Tasahre had come crashing in, all set on murdering Seth for no reason; how she's called him a warlock, how Fings had hit her on the head with a pisspot. All pretty much as it happened, except for Seth's wiggly-finger shit and the bit about one of Saint Kelm's teeth accidentally ending up in his pocket. Probably not the sort thing a sword-monk wanted to hear about, he reckoned.

"It's all about them papers from the barge," he finished. "He said you tried to help him give them back, on account of them being cursed sorcery or something. Said it didn't go well."

"It didn't."

"Yeah, and that's hardly fair, right? I mean, it wasn't even Seth that found them. And *you're* the one who gave them to him, and now he's got sword-monks after him, so the only thing he can do is get to the bottom of what all that business was about before he gets murdered." Fings frowned. "Well... that's what *he* says."

"I... think there's a bit more to it than that." Myla sounded like she was picking her words with care. Fings shifted uncomfortably.

"Yeah... Maybe. I don't know. But... I mean... Seth, he's... It's not like he's ever *hurt* anyone."

"Lucius told me how you helped him. However this ends, you have my thanks for that." Myla shivered as if shaking off old dust and cobwebs, then jerked her head at the doorway, at the darkness swallowing the pair of ropes. "So he's down there?"

Fings nodded.

"What's he looking for?"

Lying to Myla wasn't going to work because of the sword-monk nose she had; but that still left options. Seth *had* said he wanted to tell Myla everything, sure; but right now, Seth wasn't here, and it was Seth's story, not his. And the truth was... well, yes, Fings *did* trust Seth when it came down to it. He wasn't sure why, exactly, or why he was so convinced that what Seth was doing was right this time. Simply the way it was between brothers, he supposed. Two of them had known each other more than half a lifetime, after all. Admittedly, Seth *did* have a bit of a knack for bad decisions, but at least he made them for the right reasons.

"He said we'd look for you once he knew. Reckoned you'd find a priest who wouldn't try to murder him on the spot so he could tell them all about how the last emperor was messing with shit people ought to be leaving alone. Said you'd help. Be properly pleased to see you, I reckon." Another glance to the temple roof. "If it was just you, that is."

Myla raised an eyebrow. "What's that about the late emperor?"

"Think about it! Them papers from the barge! You know what was on them, right?"

"I have a fair idea."

"Well... Think about where we found them!"

"Where *you* found them."

"*You're* the one who gave them to Seth!"

"*I* said to leave them buried in the snow!" She took a deep breath. "But I take your point."

"You know we thought you was dead," said Fings, after a long silence. "In Deephaven, when you didn't make the ship."

"I went to Deephaven to make something right. I thought I had to choose. Path or family, so I chose family. Soraya was in danger... But you know what? Fuck that. It was like trying to choose which hand to cut off. I want both my hands, thanks. You're my friends. I don't want to have to choose again. I hope you won't make me." She smiled again, though it didn't quite touch her eyes this time. "I'm glad you got away. I sort of thought you would. Whatever happens next, Tasahre won't hurt you if you don't run. She owes me that much."

"So... what happens now?"

"Either one of us comes out alone or we walk out together. If we come out together, I try to convince Tasahre not to murder us. Which might work or it might not. Either way, save your strength. It's a thousand miles from here to Varr. I hope you like deserts."

"Deserts?" Fings had definite opinions on deserts after the road from Helhex. But Myla had turned away, already walking towards the doorway. Fings could almost see the future hanging in the balance, wobbling in the air. He rubbed the charms in his pockets, then, on impulse, ran after Myla. He caught her on the threshold and pressed an old tooth into her hand.

"Take this," he said.

Myla looked at it, baffled. "What is it?"

He leaned in and whispered. She stared at him, incredulous.

"You've *got* to be kidding!"

"Luck charm," he said. "Best there is."

"Fings, I... I don't know what to say. You really are a menace, aren't you? Whatever you do, for fuck's sake don't tell Tasahre!"

She walked on then, taking that moment with her, still hanging in the balance.

38
The Heresy of Sivingathm

Seth drew a sigil in the air. *Show me again*, he whispered, and reached out.

He watched Fings slink from the high temple of the sun, anxious glee on his face. He saw Orien touch a phial of silver liquid to his lips, saw him burst into flame and streak across a lake, a shaft of fire to set the waters aglow. He saw Myla alone on a horse, riding a narrow path among craggy hills. He saw the Princess-Regent, head bowed in grief at a memorial stone, while in a room of arches deep beneath the earth, she wagged a finger as if to chide him for his peeking and then dissolved into dust. He saw himself, running as though his life depended on it, withering into smoke with every step...

What do you want? asked the dead Wraith.

He was at the top of the Pillar of Light in Torpreah, watching boats on the Shroud. A warm autumn sun, the water still and peaceful, the city tranquil and asleep. Yet under the facade, the Isle of Light and the Sanctuary of the Ever-Radiant Sun were corrupted flesh, boils and warts and pus-filled pores.

"This," he whispered. "This is what I want."

He snapped his fingers and the world burned.

"Wait a minute..."

High in the air, watching the Levanya and a company of soldiers scour a dead city, corpses strewn about as if some cataclysm had struck every living thing where it stood.

Searching but never finding...

This is how it was...

"Stop it!"

The visions stopped. Seth was in a dark vault of marble and gold. He coughed and wiped the sting from his eye, the smoke from his solitary torch in a sconce by the entrance. He felt the voices of the dead welling inside him, singing a strange chorus.

A dead Wraith on a slab in front of him. Charred and burned, yet soul-trapped, like all the other dead of Valladrune.

Lucky for me. "Yeah, enough of that nonsense. How about this: you tell me where to find the book, I'll let you go."

The dead Wraith sighed. *What book, little one?*

"The Book of Endings. Where is it?"

A darkness crossed his vision. Shadows flashing from the corners of the room to rip him into silence...

"Illusions aren't going to work." Seth drew another sigil on withered fire-blackened skin. "Now answer me!"

The dead Wraith hissed. *This is how it will be.*

Seth stood alone in a place deep under the ground, a place he shouldn't be...

"Oh, for fuck's sake! Will you *stop* with that!"

"Scribble it out, slap it down on a fresh corpse and they'll talk to you," said a voice that very definitely *wasn't* the Wraith of Valladrune reluctantly telling him everything he wanted to know. The visions collapsed. "Those were the last words you said to me," said Myla. "Hello, Seth."

Ah. Seth clicked his tongue. *Awkward.* Although, somehow, he wasn't surprised. "How long have you been standing there?"

"Long enough."

She sounded wary.

Can you blame her?

Myla nodded to the half-burned corpse on the slab. "The Wraith of Valladrune?"

"Yeah." Seth licked his teeth. He looked around in case there was another way out, one he somehow hadn't noticed in two weeks of excavations. There wasn't, of course. On the other hand, Myla hadn't drawn her swords. Yet.

"And... you're talking to it."

"Yes." Not much point trying to lie.

"Last *I* heard, dead is dead."

"He wasn't given to the light. No sunlight, no water, no open sky. Oddly, he *does* look like someone set him on fire, which usually does the trick, yet here he still is. That would be the warlock of Deephaven's doing, I reckon."

"And the Hungry Goddess didn't take him?"

"It doesn't work like that. I know it's what we were both taught, but it doesn't. Something's wrong down there. We found that out the hard way in Deephaven."

There was long silence. Myla staring at Seth, Seth wishing he was better at keeping his mouth shut. Her hand moved to her neck. Closer to her swords.

Maybe she has an itch?

"The sigil you gave to the sword-monks in Varr," Myla cocked her head, "you knew what it did because you'd already used it. Yes?"

Well, she's got you there. Seth pursed his lips. Myla's hand hadn't moved. If there *was* an itch, he reckoned it ought to have been scratched by now.

"I went to the House of Cats and Gulls after the Wraiths took Deephaven," Myla said. "With Tasahre. We found the mark of Valladrune, hidden in a box which someone had opened. Tasahre's waiting outside, by the way. She says hello."

"Ah." *Fuck!*

There *was* another way out of the vault, of course. There were the blank archways the half-gods had once used.

Pity you haven't the first clue how to open them.

Yeah, but the Wraith does.

"Was that you, Seth? Did you go to the House of Cats and Gulls on the night the Wraiths came to Deephaven?"

Seth thought about this. It seemed best not to answer. Which, of course, *was* an answer.

"What did you do?"

"I don't know."

Myla's hand moved a fraction closer to her swords. "I'm not sure I see a way out of this for you. I'm willing to try, but you'll have to do a lot better than 'I don't know'."

Seth shrugged. "But I don't. I really don't remember. I'm missing a day and don't know what I did. I was at the Twilight Prayer where the Sunherald called on Deephaven to stand against the Sapphire Throne. I'd gone with Fings so he could tell your sword-mistress about the Wraith he'd seen upriver. I saw them talking and then... The next I remember, I'm coming out of the House of Cats and Gulls, a whole day gone by and there's Dead Men everywhere. That's it. That's all I've got. Have a good sniff. I'm not lying."

"I went to find you on that evening before the Wraiths came. Fings said you were looking for me. You were out, but there was demon blood on the floor. There was a demon in the House of Cats and Gulls. Someone killed it and then brought it back. Was that you?"

Seth's history with sword-monks hadn't been happy. On the other hand, this was Myla, who liked fucking and drinking far more than any other sword-monk he'd ever known...

And how many have you known, eh? Too many. "Just what is it that you and that mad bitch think I did?"

"Are you a warlock, Seth?"

"I suppose that depends on what you think 'warlock' means. Do I speak with the dead? Yes, sometimes I do. Do I make them dead in the first place? Is that what you want to ask?" He turned to face her properly and took a step closer. "Go on then. Use that nose. I can't say for sure I've never been responsible for a death by negligence or accident. Can you? I can't say for sure that none of the Spicers who died that night in Tombland were my fault, but *you* certainly accounted for a few." Another step. "There are men dead because they tried to kill me and discovered the hard way that I could defend myself. You could say the same." Another step and then another and another until he was right in front of her. "But have I *murdered* anyone? Is that what you want to ask? Have I killed in cold blood? For fun or profit? No, Myla. Best I can remember, I've never deliberately murdered anyone. So how, exactly, are you and I any different?"

"A priest in Deephaven set himself on fire. He burned to death right there in the temple yard. I saw the corpse. That wasn't you? Because Tasahre certainly believes otherwise."

"I'd like to think I'd remember something like that. I don't. Now tell me: am I lying?" *Is that what you made yourself forget?*

Myla sniffed the air. Three times. Once above Seth, once to either side of him. She pursed her lips.

Was that why you did it? Not guilt, not a pricked conscience, but so you could lie to a sword-monk and get away with it again? He didn't know. He didn't remember.

"Myla, all I ever wanted was to know the truth."

"I don't even need to sniff the air to know *that's* a lie."

"Yeah, yeah, but it *is* why I experimented with those sigils you gave me. So, either draw those swords or tell me why you haven't already done so."

Myla nodded to the dead Wraith. "That thing really still here, is it?"

"Along with everyone else who died that day, yes."

"Then I want to know what happened. I want it to answer some questions. And *you* can talk to it."

"Oh, I can, can I?" Seth clucked. "And with your sword-mistress waiting outside? Does she know about this?"

"No."

"So, what... I do this thing for you, you don't murder me, we go, she kills me anyway? I'm not sure I like the sound of that."

"Khrozus the Butcher made a bargain with the warlock of Deephaven. Maybe with this Wraith. Understanding that bargain might explain why the Wraiths are slaughtering their way across the empire. That, in my opinion, is bigger than one petty warlock. You get me answers, I will try to placate her."

"Try?" *Petty?*

"I can't promise more."

"No. As the petty warlock who may or may not find himself on the wrong end of an enraged sword-monk, I need better than *try*."

Myla spat. "Let me get this right: you want me to go against my sword-mistress, the woman who taught me almost everything I value, a woman I've fought beside against men, Wraiths and demons, a woman who's saved my life more than once. You want me to go against her when we both know she's probably right? Even if I did, you *do* realise she's better than me. No, Seth. I will try with words. If they fail, they fail. And if that's not good enough for you, that's all I've got."

"I'll have to think about that."

"The armies of the dead ravaging the north may be happy to take a rest while you debate with your conscience, but Tasahre won't. She's outside. She won't wait forever." Myla took a few steps back, propped herself against the entrance and folded her arms across her chest. Seth turned away.

I want to trust her.

Why?

Because if not her, who else?

Good question. Here's another: why trust anyone at all?

We're both looking for the same answers. She stood for me.

Only because she didn't know what you were.

He'd seen the connection between Valladrune and the sigil papers back in Varr because Fings, while he'd been swiping the emperor's crown, had *also* swiped that ring with the sign of Valladrune carved into it; because Seth had seen that same sign on a ring worn by the Mage of Tombland before the mage had been murdered by Blackhand; because Sulfane, while he'd been torturing Fings, had let slip that the Mage of Tombland had once been one of the mages of Valladrune...

And then Myla had leaned hard into her sword-monk side, stabbed Sulfane a couple of times, sliced up any Spicer who got in her way, returned the crown, and that was how it had ended. Except... not quite. Because that still left the sigils. And where they'd come from. And why, *why* had they been on that fucking barge in the first place?

He gave Myla a long look. The last time he'd seen her, she'd been pinned to the ground by a pair of angry sword-monks. They were angry because they'd understood what Seth was, and Myla had stood in their way, and so Seth had escaped. The more he thought about it, the more he didn't understand why she'd done that. He'd betrayed her to Jeffa Hawat barely a week earlier. She hadn't *known* it was him, but still... She'd risked her life, and he simply couldn't see the reason. Why would anyone do that? Why would anyone think he was worth it?

The monks had taken her swords. Seth had stolen them back. Something bad had happened to Lightbringer Suaresh, something Seth had used a sigil to make himself forget. The whole episode still felt like having the last door to something worthwhile slammed in his face, only for Myla to catch it and jam in her foot and hold it open, yelling at him to run, to come, to step into the light while he still could.

And here she is, still holding it ajar. And I have no idea why.

Does it matter?

The feeling had grown in Deephaven. She'd been in his vision from the City of Spires. *Use the sigil. Not on her. On me.*

Still had no idea what *that* was supposed to mean.

Had he really set a priest on fire?

You made yourself forget for a reason. Trust that it was a good one.

If he'd been anyone else, someone outside, looking in, would *he* trust himself, knowing everything he knew? Absolutely not. Yet here she was. Standing for him again.

Fuck's sake!

"Made up your mind?" she asked.

"I always found it odd, growing up, how the people of Tombland hated the Sapphire Throne, yet hated the Path of the Sun with the same passion. I suppose now we know why."

"We do?"

Seth rolled his one good eye. "The Mage came from Valladrune. Do you think he was the only one? When Valladrune died, how many of the people who eventually found their way to Tombland had lost family, or friends, or money, or land, or something else?"

"I wouldn't know."

"Valladrune was murdered by the Levanya, acting with a band of sword-monks. Did you know *that*?"

"I've heard a story that goes that way."

"When it was done, the Levanya murdered all the monks."

"Sounds about right. But why, Seth?"

"I find the answers, you ask your sword-mistress pretty please not to murder me? *That's* your offer?"

"I'll invoke the Sapphire Throne if I have to, but I won't lie to her about what you are. It won't be a pleasant conversation and I can't promise it'll end the way you want."

It won't be pleasant? Seth made a face. "Yeah, but at least she won't try to murder *you*."

"*Probably* not."

"Consorting with a warlock... Aren't you afraid she'll have you cut off from the light?"

"The Sun alone chooses upon whom He will shine. Not Lightbringers or Dawncallers or Sunheralds, or even sword-monks." She gave him a look. "Same goes for you. If you accept it in your heart, the light will always be there." Now a deep breath and a long sigh. "Still. It *would* be nice if it didn't come to that."

"*Nice*?"

"I promise that Tasahre will listen. I promise that if she doesn't, she'll have to go through me to reach you. I cannot promise what happens after that."

"Fine." Seth grimaced. Still that sense of a door to the light standing not quite closed, Myla holding it ajar, beckoning to him to come.

You know you're going to turn tail and run when it comes down to it. Get lost!

Because that's what you always do. Because you're a coward.

Not this time.

Maybe they will *listen. But you know they'll murder you anyway. Probably won't even say thank you.*

Go away!

He went to the dead Wraith. "You know, as best I can make out, half the cities in the Empire are built on ruins of the half-gods, palaces destroyed in the Splintering. Once, long ago, they all had towers like the City of Spires. Most fell, but the half-gods built down as well as up. Their tunnels and vaults and catacombs survive under our feet. Our stories tell us they left after the Splintering. But..."

"But some stayed behind," said Myla. "The Wraiths."

"Ones like this fucker." Seth slapped a sigil on the Wraith to bring him back as a Dead Man, then gave him a stick of charcoal to hold in one skeletal hand and an old book of blank pages for the other. "Ask your questions. It'll write your answers," he said. There *were* other ways to do this. He knew because Saffran Kuy's memories had shown him; but Myla didn't want to know about those. This would do. She'd get what she wanted.

"I want to know what bargain Khrozus made with the mages of Valladrune, with the Warlock Saffran Kuy, and with this Wraith."

"Right then." Myla would have her answers, and he wouldn't have done anything *too* terrible. Talking to the dead because a sword-monk said so? They could hardly burn him for *that*.

And then?

And then they'd set the trapped souls of Valladrune free, a whole city of them, him and Myla and the mad bitch from Deephaven. Them with their swords, him with his sigils. He'd keep that promise.

And then?

Holy work. Ten thousand souls. Surely that was enough to redeem him? Surely...?

And then?

And then he'd face the sword-mistress and take whatever fate gave.

Bullshit.

Yeah. More likely, he *would* run away, because that was what he always did when life got difficult.

39
The Pact of Valladrune

As the Wraith wrote, Myla tapped her foot. A year before Khrozus rose against Talsin the Weak, he'd gone to Valladrune, or so the Regent had told her. This was before the Guild of Mages, sorcerers being regarded by the Torpreahn dynasty as one bad day away from becoming warlocks. For the most part, the mages back then had been hostile, fiercely individualistic, hard to find and, if they had the means and any sense, living somewhere else. She'd heard all *that* from Orien. In Valladrune, however, three mages had put aside their differences and formed a cabal. They might not have been such a bad lot, Myla supposed, but then Kuy had found them. Had the mages known what he was? Hard to imagine they hadn't. The Wraith was another matter. Myla reckoned they hadn't understood what *that* was until far too late.

When the Wraith stopped writing, Seth took the page, looked at it, then handed it to her.

Khrozus had come to Valladrune with a proposition: help him take the Sapphire Throne and he'd make the empire safe for sorcerers. A guild, sanctioned by the palace, with the cabal at its head. The mages of Valladrune had agreed; but Kuy and the Wraith had had no interest in Khrozus's guild. What *they'd* wanted was something else.

She stared at the words, aghast: "The Wraith wanted Khrozus to *build* it a mage?"

"Breed," said Seth. "Corpses have terrible handwriting."

"*Breed?* That sounds even worse."

The most powerful mage the world would ever see. *That* was the Wraith's price. A mage of mages.

"That's just bizarre," said Seth.

"Ask it why."

Seth asked. The charred skin-and-bones-and-silver that had once been the Wraith of Valladrune started to write again. A page and then another and then another. Myla shuffled her feet, trying not to think about the conversation she'd soon be having with Tasahre. *Oh, so instead of killing the warlock, the two of you sat down for a chat and a bit of necromancy?*

Yes, the sword-mistress *really* wasn't going to like that. But Myla waited, nonetheless, because here were the answers she wanted.

The dead Wraith finished. Seth took the page. He read it. Then read it again.

"Fuck," he said.

"What?"

Seth ignored her. He turned back to the dead Wraith. "Why?"

Another page. More reading.

"How?"

Myla stamped her foot. "Seth!"

He held up a hand for her to wait and then read the third page. "Fuck!" he said again.

"Seth! I swear I will slap you!"

"Better than being stabbed." He thrust the scribbled papers at her and shook his head. "I don't know *what* we're supposed to do now. The Wraith wanted the mage as a vessel."

"A vessel? For what?"

Seth nodded at the pages. "It's right there. I don't understand the bit about serpents of moonlight. But that wasn't–"

"Serpents? Silver? As thick as a thumb and a handspan long? Did they glow like the moon?"

"That's... oddly specific."

"Ask!"

Seth asked, but Myla didn't have to wait for the dead Wraith write his answer. It was nodding, its head slightly askew, like it was laughing at her.

"Fuck!"

"Myla… What does that mean?"

"Never mind." The worms were the Wraiths. The Taiytakei popinjay had shown them that. A sliver of essence carved from Fickle Lord Moon. They wore the bodies of men, but…

Vessels? Did that mean the Regent was right? Did she have one inside her? If she did, why wasn't she like the other Wraiths? Why had the other Wraiths come for her…? No, *that* answer was obvious. Because she *wasn't* like the other Wraiths.

She didn't want to believe it, yet there it was. The ugly sense of a truth revealed.

"Myla… maybe read the fucking pages? All of them? Kuy's bone-bag friend here wasn't after a vessel for just *any*thing. They were after a vessel for the Splinterer of Worlds. They were trying to bring him back."

"That's just a story!"

"No, it really isn't. At the Pillar of Dusk, I looked into the past. I *saw* it happen! I *saw* the Splinterer of Worlds. Look around you. Look at this place! At the towers of the city of spires! Relics of the Shining Age…" Seth trailed off. "Your warlock believed it, and this is a *Wraith*, Myla. This wasn't some old legend to him! He'd *lived* it! Imagine them at the height of their powers before their fall! What limits did they know? I *saw* the moment the Splinterer challenged the gods. I *saw* the moment his brother struck him down. I don't know if they really *do* have a way to bring him back, but does it matter? They *think* they do."

Wild-eyed, Seth pointed at the papers clutched in Myla's hand. "It's all there! Your warlock was clever. Four bloodlines. Khrozus never knew until after he'd taken the bargain and won his throne. Look at them! Look at the names! Lord Hendrake of Tarantor and Lady Lorleia of Neja! They were supposed to breed a son. Fuck knows how even Khrozus was supposed to pull *that* one off, things being as they were. But it gets better! Look who was supposed to breed a daughter. Then the son and daughter would breed the Great Mage, who in turn would be a vessel for the Splinterer of Worlds."

"Arianne Lemir? The Sad Empress? You're fucking joking." Myla frowned. "But... she was a child when the war started. Almost a babe."

"I know."

"Really? The Sad Empress?" *The Regent's mother...*

"More to the point, she was the Levanya's fucking niece!" Seth hooted with laughter. "And do you see in whose bed she was supposed to lie? Your warlock! Can you imagine it? The Levanya, hearing the price of Khrozus's nice new throne was for his niece to be given to some geriatric dark sorcerer from fuck-knows-where to be used as a brood mare? He must have shat himself!"

"And the Usurper *knew* all this?"

"Not until after he'd made the pact and got what he wanted. I imagine he got a bit of a shock."

"I imagine he did." Myla blinked, trying to clear her head. "The Levanya," she growled. "Ask about the Levanya. Why did he come to Valladrune? Why did he tell the sword-monks of Torpreah about the Wraith and the mages? He served the Usurper! The Wraith was the Usurper's ally!"

Seth muttered something to the Wraith; but as he did, Myla realised she already knew the answer: the Levanya had come to Valladrune to shatter the Usurper's pact, not to honour it. Scorch the earth. Burn and bury everything, so hard and so deep that no trace could ever be found. Discomforting as it was, she could rather see his point.

Seth cackled. "Old Khrozus sees the truth and doesn't like it. Sends his hatchet-man to clean up?"

"Or the Levanya took matters into his own hands." Tasahre had said something about a falling out between the Levanya and the Usurper right after the war. "Doesn't really matter, does it?"

Seth took the last pages from the dead Wraith. "Got what you came for?"

"Yes." No avoiding what had to happen next. She'd have to question the Levanya. He wasn't going to like that.

"Anything else?"

"Why are the Wraiths here now? What do they want?"

Seth shook his head. "This one died when Valladrune fell so it doesn't know. Well... sort of died. Died enough, anyway. Find me a Wraith that's still alive, kill it, and I'll ask it for you. At a guess, to finish what they started."

Myla gave Seth a look. *I'll ask it for you.* The easy way those words came out of him, like he'd done it a hundred times before. Or at the very least, had thought about it.

She stared at the dead Wraith. *Was* the Regent one of them? But then... who would have done that to her? Not the Levanya, if Valladrune was anything to go by. Not the warlock of Deephaven, because Tasahre had driven him away in the very year the Regent had been born. Not Khrozus either, long dead by then.

Someone who knew about the pact, though. Someone close to the late Emperor. Close enough to have access to his children...

He wanted her to be his heir. He wanted her to sit on the throne.

"Now what?" Seth asked.

What did she know about the imperial family? The late Emperor, Ashahn the First, Khrozus' firstborn, had married Arianne Lemir, the Levanya's niece, the Sad Empress. He'd allowed the Nejan fire-mages to continue their traditions without forcing them into the Guild. Against all sense, he'd brought the Sulking Prince from Tarantor to Varr and feted him like he was family... well, strictly, he *was* family, some manner of cousin or other, but the late Emperor had treated him like a brother...

And kept him close...

A slight movement of the air. A breath of wind, whispering through the passages like a death-rattle.

"Myla?"

Three of the four bloodlines and he'd kept them all close. He'd *known*. No other way to explain it. And the sigils Fings had stolen, the ones from that barge... They'd been his. Had he been dabbling in the sorcery of the warlocks? Was he simply trying to understand...?

"So... Now we go tell your stabby friend what we've learned and ask her very nicely to... not murder me?"

The Levanya. He was the key. He'd been there. Right in the middle of it...

She gathered the dead Wraith's scribbles, took them to Seth's torch and set them alight. "No," she said. "If the Regent's enemies discover this, it will shatter the Empire." Then she drew a sword and drove it into the dead Wraith's remains.

Seth made a weird and complicated gesture with his hands. "Or... there's that." He made another weird gesture. "Shit." Then: "You know... You never actually asked what happened here."

Myla stared at the dead Wraith. Properly dead, now. At least, she hoped so. "The Levanya–"

"No. *Not* the Levanya. It was the Wraith who killed everyone." Seth snapped his fingers. "Just like that. Except... thing is... it didn't *quite* kill them. Well... okay, it did kill them, but then it trapped them here and tied them to its own..."

A distant rumble. Seth clucked his tongue and made another weird gesture with his fingers. Myla's hands were letting her know, quite loudly, that they wanted to be holding her swords.

"Yeah, look, we need to leave. The Wraith killed Valladrune so the city would rise as Dead Men the moment its... its *soul*, for the want of a better word... left its body. You know, so they could slaughter the fuck out of the sword-monks if the sword-monks managed to do what they'd come to do. Which they *thought* they had. But it's... it's soul... didn't actually leave, because Saffron Kuy was hiding right here and trapped it before it could escape. I don't know *why*, but that's what he did, and so the Wraith's curse never triggered, the dead never came back and the sword-monks left, thinking what a fine day's work they'd done–"

"Until they got murdered by the Levanya."

"Yeah, yeah." Seth bared his teeth in a rictus grin. "My point being... Well... you just finished the job, right. So around about now, everything is going to get really fucking interesting."

40
A Bad Day for a Thief

Fings went back to sitting on his pile of rubble. He twiddled his thumbs. He fretted. He twiddled his thumbs some more. In Deephaven, Seth had wanted to talk to Myla. Well, here she was. Had saved them the effort of going all the way back to Varr and looking for her. It was all good, right?

Right?

Didn't *feel* all good. Felt all very... *not* good.

In his mind's eye, he'd imagined how it would be, travelling to Varr with Seth. Weeks on the road together, spending Fings' ill-gotten gains on nice food, nice ale, nice beds. The two of them reminiscing about old times, Fings sharing his escapades in Torpreah. When the journey was mostly done, there'd be an evening when the beer flowed more than usual. Fings would show Seth the tooth he'd stolen from the Sanctuary of the Ever-Radiant Sun. Seth would be shocked and thrilled, and a bit horrified, and a bit awed. And then it would come out, whatever weight Seth had been carrying all these months, and Fings would share it, and they'd be brothers again, the way they used to be, and everything would go back to normal.

Maybe that was still the way it would go, except it would be Myla who got to share Seth's burden first. Fings reckoned he was okay with that. Once Seth had it off his shoulders, he'd spread it about quick enough.

Trouble with sharing burdens, though, was you had to be in the right place in your head. Had to have time to work up to it. Think it through. Let it almost out, then not, then *almost*... That sort of thing. You needed time, and Seth wasn't going to get that, and so Fings had a bad feeling this was all going to go horribly wrong; and never mind the whole business about the *other* monk being somewhere about the place, the sword-mistress from Deephaven. Probably still nursing a grudge about that pisspot.

It was something of a relief, then, when Tasahre walked into the middle of the square, swords drawn and looking all angry. Gave him something nice and immediate to worry about.

"Torben!" she shouted. "Come here!"

Seth's soldiers looked ready to shit themselves. The old one who largely seemed to be in charge rose wearily and crossed to the sword-monk, carrying the sagged shoulders of someone who knew he was deep in the shit. Fings had a good think about running away. He could probably manage it, he reckoned. He was good at running. Good at climbing and clambering and squeezing through tight spaces and all that. They'd been here a couple of weeks, so he knew the island and its abandoned temples. The sword-monk would make a good chase of it, but here and now he reckoned he had her measure.

Torben stood, head bowed. The sword-monk said a few things. Torben said a few things back. After a minute of this, he dropped to his knees and started to strip, which was bit unexpected. The sword-monk kept her distance, eyes flicking between the soldiers, never letting any of them go for long. They landed on Fings now and then. Fings thought he saw them narrow a little, each time that happened.

Yeah, she hadn't forgotten.

Naked, Torben lay flat on his belly. Fings got back to thinking about running away.

Maybe just do it? Get it over with?

He didn't, though, because now the sword-monk was crouched by Torben's feet, taking them in her hands, one after the other, like she was having a good long look for warts or something. Then she started working her way up. Fings winced. Winced a bit more when Torben rolled onto his back and she worked her way over him again, poking in his armpits and... well, yeah, some things just weren't right. Some things weren't meant to be seen.

Whatever she was looking for, Fings reckoned the sword-monk found it. She backed away, shaking her head, irritable and impatient, staring at the door into the vault where Myla had gone while Torben dressed himself, then pointed at two of his men and yelled at them to come over.

It *had* been a bit of a while.

The sword-monk's eyes flicked to Fings. This time, they settled. Didn't move on.

Bugger.

She pointed a sword at him. Beckoned him to come.

Well, Fings my boy, if you're going to run, now's the time...

He didn't move. The sword-monk beckoned again. The two soldiers Torben had called started to strip. They weren't happy but they were doing it. It was all... weird.

Nope. Not having this.

He got up; and he *was* about to run, too, but that was when the ground decided to have a good shake, the rubble vibrating under his feet enough that he almost lost his balance. The whole square rattled. Clouds of dust shook free from the walls all around. He heard a crunch and the tumble of falling masonry from somewhere behind the empty temple. It lasted a few heartbeats, then stopped.

For a bit, everyone stood very still. Tasahre had both swords drawn. She wasn't looking at Fings anymore, which was something. Wasn't looking at the soldiers either. Eyes flickering everywhere.

"Get up," she shouted. "All of you! Get up!" As if they needed telling. Fings heard the scrape of something on stone behind him. When he turned to look, he really wished he hadn't. A skeleton draped in rotting rags looked back at him. It was sitting upright, one of its feet trapped under a piece of stone brought up from the vault. It was trying to pull itself free.

"Er...!" Fings lurched away, pointing, stumbling towards the sword-monk, because however scary sword-monks were, they were a whole lot less scary than some shambling pile of old dead bones that had somehow got it in its head to have a go at being alive again.

Somewhere nearby, a soldier swore. Fings whipped around. "I know, right!" he said, but the soldier wasn't looking at the rubble pile. He was looking at the vault door.

Where there was another skeleton.

Two, in fact.

Click-clacking out into the yard.

Each armed with a knife.

"Oh, *fuck*!"

The sword-mistress moved fast. Two cuts. Sunsteel on bone. The skeletons collapsed and fell to pieces. No one else moved. The yard fell to silence. Except... not *quite* silence. There was a sound that hadn't been there before. A rustle, a crackle of noise almost too quiet to hear.

"What's... happening?"

The sword-mistress didn't answer. She poked at the bones with her swords. Shot looks all around the yard. Fings found himself doing the same.

"Shit!" A soldier pointed to where a wide overgrown path led out of the square towards one of the bridges over the river. Sure enough, Fings saw another skeleton. Heading towards them. This one was missing an arm.

Then another, behind it. No, two... three...

"There!"

Fings whirled. The temple, with its steps and columns, its wide-open doors. Two more skeletons, coming at them. In a blur of motion, the sword-mistress cut them down. It didn't seem to trouble her; but by the time she'd walked back to the centre of the square, the skeletons from the bridge were coming. The soldiers were clustering, ready to fight. Wary, but not yet scared. It didn't look *too* difficult, after all.

Fings thought about this. Thought about all the rag-covered bones he'd seen littering the streets. A whole city of dead people.

A whole city of dead people, and we're right in the middle of it!

"I think... we should leave," he said.

Yeah, but what about Seth? And Myla?

"Yes," agreed the sword-mistress, a wariness in her voice. "I think you're right."

Fings looked at the doorway to the vault. Myla had her swords. Seth had... well, Fings wasn't sure he wanted to know, but he certainly had that sigil the priests learned. Frankly, Myla and Seth could probably look after themselves better than this lot.

Two more coming from the temple. Three from an alley to the southeast. Fings spun around, looking for other ways out. Plenty enough, but now there was a skeleton coming from a door in the west wall, more coming up the street to the east.

"Run!" shouted the sword-mistress. She raced for the north arch, heading for the bridge off the island, cutting a path through shambling bones as she went. The soldiers followed. Fings dithered. Admittedly, there *was* some sense to getting off the island while they still could.... But when there was running away to be done, he really rather preferred to be at the front. He was *good* at running away.

Yeah. Well. Choose fast. Follow the sword-monk you bashed round the head or go for Myla and Seth.

Put like *that*, it was hardly a choice at all. He dashed for the vault. And yes, there *had* been a couple of skeletons there, he'd seen them, but he'd also seen them come out and get cut to pieces, so he reckoned he was good.

Just as long as there's another way out of there!

Yeah. Or maybe the three of them could wait it out for however long it took for a horde of skeletons to get bored and find something else to do. *Did* skeletons get bored? He had no idea.

Myla with her swords. Seth with his priest sigils. It'll be fine. He ran past where the two dead mages had been, to the vault Seth said had once been a treasury.

"Myla! Seth!"

No answer. He squeezed into the passage they'd cleared, scampering over the last bits of rubble littering the floor. Black marble veined with gold, just as Seth had said. Air thick with smoke from a single torch in a sconce by the entrance. A big square slab of stone in the middle, the crumbled remains of a burned body lying on it, dressed in silver. Silver with some rather obviously sword-shaped holes...

Fings shivered. *A Faerie-King? Crap!*

Yeah, well. Wasn't like he hadn't known what Seth was looking for. "Seth! Myla"

No answer. They weren't here! He looked wildly for some other way out but there wasn't one... Except yes, there was! Past the dead Faerie-King, an arch of white stone, carved in sigils, like the ones in the Undercity of Varr, only instead of opening into blank stone, this one opened into a swirling void, wracked by distant lightning, and the sigils around the arch were glowing. Soft, and fading, but hadn't Seth always said they were doorways? Somehow, he'd opened one!

"Myla?"

He ran around the slab, heart in his mouth.

Nothing.

Which meant...

Bollocks!

He looked at the portal. No way was he jumping into *that*.

Yeah. But on the other hand, city full of walking skeletons?

He clenched himself tight. Squeezed his eyes shut, bracing himself. What other choice did he have?

With a slight whump, the swirling void turned back to blank stone as the sigils went dark. Fings stared in horror. He poked the stone with a tentative finger. Found it exactly as solid as it looked. Whatever door Seth had opened, now it had closed.

"Oh... *crap!*"

41
A Door, Ajar

A few minutes before everything went to shit, Seth took the last paper from the dead Wraith. Not words, but a sigil. The sigil to open the half-god gates. Myla wasn't paying attention, which was probably just as well, because Seth really wasn't liking where all this was going. How marvellous for them both, discovering a secret that an entire city had died to keep. A secret Myla would soon realise she couldn't share. Not with anyone. Certainly not with the sword-monk waiting outside to kill him.

And then?

Yes, he knew exactly what *and then* looked like. *And then* looked like a two-foot length of sharpened Sunsteel.

No, no, no. We do not end here.

I need to trust her!

Then Myla put a sword through the Wraith's corpse, sending its soul to the Sun – which probably didn't much want it – and lifting the Wraith's curse. Which Seth *had* promised the trapped dead that he was going to do, true, but *not*, thanks, while he was at the fucking epicentre. Inside, he gave a little sigh. Myla probably had no idea what she'd just done.

Probably done. Admittedly, he wasn't *entirely* sure. He threw a quick sigil at the Wraith, trapping its soul for a second time before it could escape.

Into a stone in his pocket, though. Not back into its own body...

Good enough...?

A slight movement of the air. A breath of wind, whispering through the passages like a death-rattle. He reached out to the dead. There they were. A whole city of them. Suddenly realising their shackles were gone.

Apparently not. Bugger.

"Shit," he said.

They're going to kill you.

No!

The Wraith started to crumble.

"You know... You never actually asked what happened here." *She stood for me.*

"The Levanya–"

"No. *Not* the Levanya." *Do you think she'll believe it, when we go back outside as an entire city rises from the dead, that it was* her *who did it and not you?*

He told her what she'd done. Took a couple of goes before she got it. The ground shivered under his feet. *Even if she believes this wasn't you, do you think the mad bitch from Deephaven will?*

No. No, he didn't.

Why did it always come to this? He looked Myla in the eye, trying to see an answer. Couldn't be sure. *Fuck. Fuck, fuck, fuck!*

Movement at the entrance to the vault. The murdered mages back as Dead Men. Seth threw a sigil and sent them away. Myla reached for her other sword. Probably she'd seen the Dead Men too, but maybe she hadn't? Maybe the swords were for him...?

A two-foot length of sharpened Sunsteel...

No. This *wasn't* how he ended. He ran to the half-god archway, took the Wraith's sigil, slapped it on the stones, squirmed for the half-second it took the portal to open, and jumped through.

He emerged...

Somewhere. What he'd told the Wraith, while Myla hadn't been paying attention, was to write a sigil for opening the gateway to Varr. It occurred to him now that there might be quite a lot of gateways to Varr. Possibly, he should have been a bit more specific.

Why am I doing this?

He had no idea where he was. A hemispherical vault of white stone like the one under the incinerators in Glassmakers. The half-god vaults all looked the same. The same soft comforting glow. No staircase spiralling through its heart, this one, but the usual bunch of tunnels and a bunch more archways like the one behind him. A pile of rags and bones lying on the floor. Not much else. Nothing to tell him where he was.

Is it because you think you deserved better? Is that why? Because you were the best and the cleverest? Because they cast you out? Because you never know when to stop?

He walked to the pile of rags and bones. *All I wanted was the truth.*

You wouldn't know what to do with the truth if it slapped you in the face!

He didn't have an answer to that.

What do you really *want?*

He didn't know.

You want them all to burn.

No.

You want them to know you were right. You want them to weep and beg for forgiveness.

No! No, I don't!

You want to see their faces in that moment when they hear you say no. When they understand there's no hope. When they finally see what they did to you, as you return tenfold their callous disregard for...

"Seth?"

He stopped. Turned. "Oh," he said. Myla, apparently, had followed him through the portal. "Shit." For some reason, he hadn't expected that.

Moron! What else *did you think she'd do?* Although... honestly, he'd thought she'd stay where she was. Go back outside. Find Fings and the homicidal monk from Deephaven. Do something about the vast horde of Dead Men that was about to happen...

"Seth... What have you done?"

He closed his eyes. *Fings! Fuck!* He'd left Fings behind. In a city about be swarmed by Dead Men...

And now she really is *going to kill you. And you know what? You deserve it.*

Although, Myla's swords were on her back again, not in her hands. Not yet. *See! I said* she wouldn't do it! *Any other sword-monk and I'd be in bloody strips by now.*

She can't save you. No one can.

Behind Myla, the portal to Valladrune quietly closed.

"Seth! What have you done?"

"It's not what *I've* done. It's what *you've* done. All *I* did was open a door to get away!"

"Get away from what?"

"Oh, I don't know! Maybe a sword-monk who absolutely wants me dead and an entire city rising as Dead Men all at once? You know, little things..."

Myla held out her hand. "Come back and help me put it right. Show Tasahre you're not what she thinks."

Seth bared his teeth. "But I *am* what she thinks!" Here it was, he knew. That moment he'd been feeling for months, on and off. The door to the light slamming shut, leaving him in darkness. Myla catching it. Holding it open. Reaching for him. Beckoning him back.

"Come closer," he said.

"I don't think so."

"Don't you trust me?"

"I don't trust the power you're calling."

"Necromancy?" He giggled.

"Yes."

"What did you *think* we were going to do? Toss the Wraith's knucklebones and read each other's fortunes?"

She didn't have an answer to that.

"The Path taught us both that it's wrong, but it isn't. What's wrong cuts far, far deeper."

"And what's that, Seth?" And now it was Seth's turn not to have an answer. He started to back away. Myla followed, keeping a constant distance between them.

"Stay away!"

"It was come closer a moment ago." She cocked her head. "Make up your mind."

"Stop!" He threw a sigil at her. It didn't work, though he saw her wince, then glare. He threw another. "Stop! Go back!" Still didn't work. *Fucking* sword-monks!

"Seth! Enough!"

Like she was talking to an unruly child.

"It hurts me," she said. "When you do that."

"Then stop following me!"

"Then come back and make it right."

You know, you could sigil something else. Something that isn't *a sword-monk...*

The pile of rags and bones...

Fine. He threw a sigil in the vague hope it would rise as a Dead Man. It *did* have a bit of a go, the bones shifting and trying to move, but mostly all he achieved was getting Myla to draw her swords.

"Seth!" And she kept walking, and he kept backing away, and she kept coming, and there wasn't anything he could do.

"Stop!" he shouted, throwing sigil after sigil. "Stop! Stop! Stop! Stop!" He could feel himself crumbling, falling apart, tears in his eyes, rolling down his cheeks. He fell to his knees.

"Stop," he whispered when she was right in front of him. "Stop."

"Can we go back now?"

"Just do it," he sighed.

"Do what?"

"Finish it."

"*Finish* it? What do you mean?" She seemed genuinely not to know.

"Thou shall not suffer a warlock to live. Isn't that how it goes?"

42
The Art of Running Away

Fings bit his nails. He fingered his charms. So here he was. Trapped in a mausoleum with a dead Faerie-King, in the middle of a city full of angry skeletons.

Can't stay here, lad!

No. Place was a deathtrap if skeletons started showing up. And yes, there'd be more outside, but at least he could run. He knew about running, and about getting away from Dead Men, too. Wasn't much different from getting away from Longcoats: you ran and hid until they got distracted by something else. In the case of Longcoats, that could be anything, most often a general lack of enthusiasm for their job. In the case of Dead Men... Fings wasn't so sure. In Varr, it had usually been a priest with a sigil.

You saw what was out there. Ain't no priests here...

He'd never had to run from more than one Dead Man at a time, and they hadn't been skeletons dressed in rags either, but he *had* had to run from angry gangs of Longcoats and Spicers. He reckoned the same principle applied: go for the rooftops. Longcoats didn't like being up high, and he'd never seen a Dead Man yet who could climb.

He took a moment to think. Not the temple along the south wall. The sword-monk from Deephaven had been up there, but Fings had no idea where she'd made the climb. The east wall, with the door to the vaults, that was out too, on account of all the shrubbery pressed against it. The north side, though, with its archway leading off to the bridge. Yeah, those nice big ornamental windows... He could scamper up those nice and quick. Would have a good view of what was happening, too, once he was on the roof.

Meant crossing the square, mind. He'd have to run for it. Maybe dodge a few skeletons on the way. He could *probably* do that. Probably.

He took the torch from its sconce by the entrance – Dead Men didn't like fire – then trotted into the upper vault, holding it out in front of him.

No skeletons.

Out to where the two dead mages had been. Still no skeletons.

At the bottom of the stair to the square, he paused. *Right, then. Here goes. Deep breath...*

And then, praying to the Goblin King and all the little gods that he didn't crash into anything coming the other way, he ran out onto the square, and kept on going.

Oh, shit! There were skeletons everywhere, right across the square, all trotting and click-clacking their way with unnerving purpose towards the arch in the north wall. Except... well, that's what they *had* been doing, right until Fings showed up. *Now* a good few were looking at *him* instead.

Bollocks!

Nothing for it. He kept right on going, yelling and waving his torch like a madman. He dodged this way and that, whacking a couple that got too close. He felt something grab his satchel and almost rip it away. He whacked another, changed his mind about where to climb, chucked the torch, and reached the wall. He hurled himself at a window, grabbed the ledge, swung a leg, levered himself up, launched himself at the stone cornice above, hung for a moment by his fingertips while his feet scrabbled for purchase, trying not to think about what would happen if he fell...

His toe gripped on a crack in the stone. He kept climbing, one window to the next. He reached the roof, gingerly pulled himself onto the sloping tiles, then looked back. A cluster of skeletons milled below, pawing the wall and the windows, heads tilted up.

More joined them, click-clacking across the square in ones and twos. Fings levered a tile off the roof and threw it at them. They didn't seem to notice.

Now what?

Back in Varr, when he'd been running from Longcoats and Spicers, *now what* was loping across the rooftops, half of which he knew as well as the streets and alleys below, making his way somewhere safe, climbing down, and buggering off. He scampered across this new and unfamiliar roof and had a look over the other side, out the way the sword-monk and the soldiers had gone. He spotted them halfway across the bridge from the island, surrounded, hundreds of the bony buggers coming at them from each end. He heard shouting. Desperate. He saw a soldier fall, overwhelmed, then another, skeletons piling on top of them in a frenzy. He saw the sword-monk, a dancing whirl of blades, skeletons falling to bits all around, making it look easy, except there was no end to these Dead Men, and the soldiers at her back didn't have Sunsteel, and even sword-monks eventually tired...

A soldier launched himself off the bridge into the water. Another followed, then the rest all at once, diving for the river. Fings watched them struggle under the weight of their leathers, frantically shedding bags and boots and weapons and clothes. They shouted and splashed and flailed, disappeared under the water, came up again, sank again, came up again. Fings couldn't keep track of them all, but it looked like most managed to dump whatever was dragging them down, bobbing and splashing, letting the current take them...

On the bridge, the sword-monk fought alone for a few seconds more, then abruptly sheathed her swords, dived into the water, and started to swim with purpose for the shore. Fings wasn't sure what exactly she was planning to do when she got there, but whatever it was, he was going get a good view. She was heading almost straight towards him.

"Hey!" He stood up and waved. "Up here!"

He had no idea whether she saw but he kept waving anyway.

Skeletons on the waterfront clustered beneath him, scratching at the walls, looking up. He ran along the rooftop, shouting and waving and looking down. The skeletons followed.

Right then. Least he could do. Clear a few of them away.

The sword-monk was treading water, close to the shore. She was looking at him. He waved and she waved back, pointing frantically towards the bridge. He wasn't sure what she was trying to tell him. Probably something bad because it was always...

Oh. Right. The bridge was swarming with the bastards, all heading for the island. Fings ran across the roof to where the arch opened into the square below, then jumped up and down and yelled a lot. The skeletons on the waterfront followed. So did the ones coming off the bridge, until the ground below was a heaving mass of the things, trampling each other trying to reach him.

So... Now what?

He had no idea. All very well, pointing and shouting and taunting because they couldn't climb up and get him, but how long was all this going to last?

The sword-monk pulled herself out of the river. She trotted across the cobbles, hacked down a few straggler skeletons, and started to climb, slow and painstaking, like she wasn't sure what she was doing. Fings waited until she was halfway up, then trotted along the rooftop and lay at the edge, waiting for her to reach him.

"Always tricky, the last bit," he said. "Getting up onto the roof."

She looked up at him, wild and exhausted and soaking wet. She was bleeding. He could see that now. Looked like she was at the end of her rope.

"If I help you, are you going to murder me?" he asked.

"I certainly ought to," she gasped.

Fings offered his hand. "Clean slate?"

She growled. Fings cocked his head. "Fine! Clean slate."

He hauled her up. She rolled onto the roof and lay on her back, breathing hard. Fings watched for a bit, unsure what to say. On the one hand, the two of them had conspired to free Myla from slavery, and the sword-mistress had listened to his story about a

Faerie-King on the river near Deephaven and hadn't treated him like he was an idiot. On the other, she *was* trying to murder Seth, and he *had* lamped her round the head with a... Yeah. That.

"Sorry about the pisspot," he said after a bit.

No response. *Oh well...*

"Looked like most of the others made it," he tried, after a bit more awkward silence. "Let the river carry them off. Clever, that."

That got him something between a grunt and a growl. He bit his lip.

"Look," he said, when he couldn't stand hearing nothing but the clicking of bones from the skeletons below, "I don't know what you think Seth did, but I reckon you might have got the wrong end of all this."

"I don't think so, thief."

"Why? Ain't sword-monks ever been wrong?"

The sword-mistress snorted. "Look around you!"

"Seth? *He* wouldn't have done this. Well, not on purpose. And before you say it, don't bother with the whole 'I'll smell it if you lie' malarkey. Get that from Myla all the time. A right pain in the arse, mostly, but I'll be glad of it here, because I ain't got nothing to hide." He took a breath. "Myla ain't done nothing wrong. Nor Seth neither, as far as I know. He ain't what you think. I don't know what happened in Deephaven, so maybe he *did* do something a bit stupid. But I know my brother. He's a thief and a liar when he needs to be, and so am I. Where we come from, you do what it takes to survive. But what I know for sure is that he ain't ever hurt anyone." He got up and stood in front of Tasahre. "Go on then. Am I lying?"

"So where is he, then?"

"Yeah..." Fings wasn't sure what to say. "About that... There was some weird mystical door thing down under the ground. Reckon they found a way to open it and went through."

"They?"

"Him and Myla."

Tasahre sat up. "She fought at my side," she hissed. "We killed a Wraith together. How could she do this?"

"Do what?"

"Betray us!"

"Who says she did?"

"Thief, I grant you truly believe everything you say, but how do you know *they* haven't lied to *you*. Have you considered *that*?"

"Myla? She don't do that. You know that as well as I do."

Tasahre's face twitched. Fings grinned. *Gotcha!*

"And your warlock? Is he equally honest?"

Fings looked away. When he looked back, Tasahre's expression was easy enough to read. *Gotcha back.*

"No," said Fings. "No, he ain't. But that don't make him someone who don't deserve to live."

Tasahre lay back and closed her eyes, apparently oblivious to the hideous sounds of hundreds of skeletons clicking and scratching at the stonework all around. "Again, he eludes me."

"Look, I've known Seth since he was a boy. I ain't ever seen him do nothing that looked like sorcery until that time in Torpreah when he got that crowd of people to stop kicking the shit out of you."

There was that stuff in the desert...

"To *stop*?" Tasahre laughed.

"Yeah," said Fings. "To stop. That's what *I* saw."

She sat up and sniffed at him, a puzzled look on her face.

"See," said Fings. "Ain't lying."

"In Deephaven, he burned a priest alive."

"What?" *Shit.* "No."

"An old friend who was the temple archivist in Deephaven, responsible for the artefacts retrieved from the House of Cats and Gulls. On the morning before the Wraiths came, my old friend walked into the middle of the temple's First Court and set himself on fire. He burned to death, along with all the warlock's artefacts. Except *not* all. One was missing. A glass orb. I found it in Torpreah, in the house where you were staying."

"No!" Fings jumped to his feet. "He wouldn't! Seth wouldn't... He'd never do *that*!"

She crouched in front of him and took his hand in her own. His gloved hand.

"Thief, you didn't wear this when I saw you in Deephaven."

"So?"

He tried to pull away, but Tasahre wouldn't let go. "Take it off!"

Fings peeled back the glove, careful to keep his hand out of the sun. "It's just a mark," he said. "It's like... well... It's a sign of protection, right? That's all. Not *sorcery*. Nothing *wrong* with it."

"He told you to wear the glove?"

"Have to keep the sun off so it don't burn away."

Tasahre rested a hand on Fings' shoulder. Her touch was gentle. A gesture of pity. Then she rolled up a sleeve, and Fings saw that she, too, was covered in sigils, tattooed into her skin.

"*These*, thief, are signs of protection." She pointed to the sigil on the back of his hand. "*That* is not. *That* is a sigil of compulsion. Of compulsion to obedience."

"No!" Fings jumped up. "No! No! He wouldn't! He'd never do that! He *wouldn't*. He would... He..." The words trailed away. The walls were closing in on him. He felt dizzy.

Tasahre grabbed him, tight and strong. He struggled. He wasn't sure why. Nothing made sense. Didn't matter, though; she was stronger than him, and far more resolute. She held him down and forced his hand into the sun. For a few long minutes, nothing happened. And then it did, and they both watched as the sigil burned away, and Fings felt something lift inside him. A fine veil that had been keeping something hidden; and as it lifted, he knew that what Tasahre said was true.

"No," he breathed. "No!"

She let him go. "The men you were with. They had this mark too, the ones I had a chance to examine. For the little this is worth, thief, I'm sorry it was done to you."

Fings hugged his knees to his chest. "No," he whispered. "No! He wouldn't! He *wouldn't*."

43
A Door, Closed

Seth, on his knees, closed his eyes. "Thou shall not suffer a warlock to live. Isn't that how it goes?" *Go on! Do it! I deserve it.*

He felt her step away. "You think I'm going to *kill* you? Seth! No! Fuck's sake!"

He opened his eyes again. She'd sheathed her swords and was offering her hand. "Come on." She nodded to the archways around them. "Open a one of these... gate-things. Take us back. Help me put this right. It's not too late."

"I have a confession to make," Seth said.

No you fucking don't!

But he did. He needed this out of him. He picked himself up and stood in front of her. "The night the Spicers came to the *Unruly Pig*. Someone let them in, and they came to your door. They knew exactly where to go because someone marked the path for them. That was me."

She stared at him, and Seth couldn't work out whether he was seeing shock, disbelief, or whether she'd somehow known all along. "Why?"

"I tried to get you to leave."

"I remember."

"But you didn't. And I still did it. I want you to know that I wish I hadn't. That I'm sorry."

That I'm pathetic. That I'm a coward.

For a long time, Myla stared back. Then her shoulders sagged.

"He would have found me anyway, sooner or later. Can we go now?"

"That's it?"

"What do you want to hear? That you're forgiven?"

It *was*, oddly enough. Only if she meant it; but this was Myla. She said things because they were true, not because they were convenient.

Not like you.

Shut up.

"Fine," she said. "You're forgiven."

You know *she can't save you.*

Shut! Up! He whirled away. "I was wrong about the Path," he said. "Without Gods, men become monsters. Here I am, living proof. At first, all I wanted was to go back. To be a priest again. Then I wanted the Path to fall. I wanted to watch their temples burn."

"And now?"

"I wasn't wrong, Myla, to look for the truth. At least give me that much. You, of all people."

"Depends on what you do with the truth when you find it."

Seth giggled. "And what are *you* going to do with *your* truth, eh?"

"I'll tell her everything." She winced. "Not much choice there, unfortunately. The Regent is a mage like no other, and there's no hiding secrets. She can reach into your head if she wants to. It's like standing naked. So yes. She'll get it all."

"She can do that?"

"I'm not saying she would, only that she could. Everything you know and everything you are. Everything you've ever done."

"Well," said Seth. "Fuck that, then, eh?"

"Some of us, Seth, don't have anything to hide; and anyway, that's a problem for some other time. Can we *please* go back now?"

"You never stop, do you."

"Not known for it, no."

Seth took another step closer, close enough to reach and touch Myla, though he didn't. "You truly forgive me?"

"I truly do."

"If you see Fings again, tell him I said sorry."

"Tell him yourself. Seth... I'm not a Dawncaller or a Sunherald or a Sunbright or even a Lightbringer. Just a servant of the Path. Nevertheless, for what it's worth, it's not too late to come back."

She reached out to him again.

"Thanks," he said. "But no. It *is* too late. It's been too late for a long time."

He turned and ran away. And when, this time, Myla didn't follow, he knew the door to the light had quietly, finally, closed.

44
Faith and Hope

Myla watched Seth run off into the gloom and disappear down one of the tunnels. A part of her wanted to chase after him. End this, one way or the other. But what was the point? Either she let him go, or she ran him through, and she couldn't do that. Whatever Tasahre thought, whatever had really happened in Deephaven, setting fire to a priest *was* the sort of thing you tended to remember, and Seth hadn't been lying when he said he didn't.

No. He'd made his choice. And Fings was right: it was at least a little her own fault that he'd become what he was. The sigils she'd stupidly given him without looking to see what they were. Would she have recognised them, back then, if she *had* looked? Probably not. But she hadn't. Not even a glance.

Lazy and foolish.

Tasahre's voice in her head. Myla shook it away. She'd follow her own path, not one laid out for her by someone else. Seth, she supposed, would say much the same.

Still ought to go after him. Try again to bring him round. Warlock or not, he was flirting with the same devils.

No. She sighed heavily. What she *ought* to do was go back through the portal Seth had opened, make her peace with Tasahre, settle things in Valladrune, and *then* maybe worry about Seth. Truth was, she felt sorry for him. He was a fuck-up, and *she'd* been a fuck-up, once, and being a fuck-up didn't make you a bad person. In Varr, she'd been with him when he'd tried to do the right thing, when two sword-monks had tried to kill him for it. For all she believed in truth and honesty, she also believed in forgiveness and compassion and second chances.

As Tasahre gave me *a second chance.*

She turned back to the portal, and that was when she saw that it had closed behind her.

"Oh," she said. "Fuck."

It was hard to see her next conversation with Tasahre ending well. How to explain herself? *Seth asked a dead Wraith about its bargain with the godless Usurper because the equally godless Moon-Witch who now pretends to sit on the Sapphire Throne asked me to find the truth because she thinks that she might also be a Wraith, which she probably is, and then he ran away through a half-god gate, and I went after him, but he left and I didn't stop him, and the gate closed while I was shouting at him and I couldn't get back...?*

She winced. Put it all like that... Maybe not.

She ran into the tunnels, chasing after Seth, but the place was a maze, some passages glowing with their own light, others dark except for the light of her swords. She called Seth's name but he didn't answer, and she couldn't see anything to tell her which way he'd gone. After a few minutes of running this way and that, looking for any sign of him, she stopped, made her way back to the vault where she'd first followed Seth, and stood there, hands on hips, generally pissed off at the world. Seth was gone, she had no idea where she was, no way to get back to Valladrune and Fings and Tasahre, possibly no way out at all...

She went to the archway. The door Seth had opened. She smacked the blank stone encased within the arch in case it felt like opening again, but it didn't.

Vaults all over the city, Fings had told her. Vaults like this one, domed, wide and deep enough to swallow a castle, white stone with a pale inner light like moonlight. The same silvery glow from all directions at once, which made judging size and distance almost impossible. It reminded her of the towers in the City of Spires that glowed at night, the same white stone, gentle and soothing. What had Seth said? A ruin of the Shining Age? A place of the half-gods?

The Wraiths, before they fell from grace. Before Fickle Lord Moon turned his back on them.

She swore. Loudly. Getting to the truth of Valladrune still seemed the right thing to have done, although Myla knew exactly what Tasahre would have said. *Let Wraiths and warlocks and the Moon-Witch fight. I'll be here to finish whichever side comes out on top.*

If it was Wraiths or warlocks, Myla would fight beside her without hesitation.

What if it's the Moon-Witch?

And there was the rub. Myla served the Path of the Sun. The Regent didn't. Myla didn't even *like* her, not really. But the Regent had shown courage and mercy. And she'd been, at least as far as Myla could know, honest.

She's been inside my head. How sure can I be that my opinions are even my own?

Faith, she supposed. Faith and hope.

First things first, though. She sighed and started looking for a way out.

INTERLUDE
THE MEMORIES OF SAFFRAN KUY

The Book of Endings? You have learned and understand that the world is governed by four divine powers, the Sun, the Moon, the Earth, and the Stars. Each has a divine focus. They are not myths. The Armour of the Sun, the Twin Crowns of the Moon, the Twin Knives of the Stars, the Spear of the Earth, all are founded in truth. Distorted by legend and age, but real and infused with a touch of the divine. Some say they were forged during the War of Splinters, distilled of the raw power that blistered the earth when the Splinterer fell. Others say they are far more ancient, created at the beginnings of time. Perhaps they existed before creation itself. Perhaps they are the true powers, the Sun and the Moon and the Stars and the Earth merely their reflections. It is for priests to understand the divine, or at least to seek such understanding. Our dealings are more mundane.

That they exist is enough. The armour of the Sunking, the circlets of the Arian Emperors, the Spear of the Speaker of Dragons. This knife, here in my hand. Perhaps their true powers are lost. Perhaps they are in hiding, awaiting their time. Perhaps they never had them. We will never know, and nor does it matter.

But a Book of Endings? A power that can end gods and creation itself? If such a thing exists, surely it must imply a fifth divinity, the most potent of all. A fifth power and a fifth path. Does that seem strange to you? It should not, for that is our path. It is a dangerous path. The Silver Kings followed it, and it all but destroyed them.

PART FIVE
The Book of Endings

It's surprising, when you try it, how much of your life you can throw away and never miss. How little of it really matters.
– Seth

45
Sunrise

Fings lay beside the sword-mistress, the two of them on a rooftop under a bright midnight moon, surrounded by a sea of homicidal walking skeletons scratching at the walls below. Wasn't like either of them had anything better to do, so he'd been talking. Talking quite a lot, actually, because talking took his mind off... well, off the sea of homicidal walking skeletons scratching at the walls. He told her about Sulfane, the barge, the theft of the Moonsteel Crown, and saw she already knew. He told her about the papers he'd stolen, how he'd persuaded Myla not to throw them away, and how she'd given them to Seth. He told her about the Spicers and Blackhand, Seth's story of trying to return the sigils from the barge and how Myla had told the same story, word for word. He told her about Orien's letter, and how he and Seth had gone to Deephaven because Myla was in trouble. All of that, and the sword-mistress didn't seem remotely interested. Her thoughts were far away. Or maybe she wasn't having any thoughts at all. Sitting, legs crossed, hand on her knees, staring out at the horizon. Like she was waiting for something.

"Myla already told you all that, did she?"

Tasahre nodded.

He tried being silent for a bit; but the constant scratching of bone on stone was the sort of noise that got under his skin, like an itch he couldn't scratch.

"You should conserve your energy," said Tasahre.

Fings made another circuit of the rooftops, something he must have done a dozen times by now, so it didn't tell him anything he didn't already know. He came back and plonked himself down. "I don't know what he did in Deephaven except catch the plague." He understood what Seth's sigil had done to him, now that he was free of it. He remembered the Pillar of Dusk. Remembered everything after, too. All the things Seth had said, the things Fings had believed, even while a part of him had wondered why.

Believe what I say, brother. As if there had been some veil in his mind. And, well yes, turned out that's exactly what it was. Just hadn't noticed.

Why, Seth? Why'd you have to do that? He was noticing it a lot, now that it was gone.

"It's your fault," he said.

Tasahre grunted.

"Best I can make out, once we got to Torpreah, all he wanted was a quiet life. He started going to the temple again. And then you showed up."

"My fault he set a man on fire?"

"Yeah, but you don't know he did that."

"Did *you* take that orb, then? You *are* a thief, after all."

He didn't have an answer to that.

Why?

Seth. His brother who'd betrayed him. And he didn't doubt Tasahre was telling the truth about a priest setting himself on fire. That was the thing about sword-monks: you knew what you were getting. When a sword-monk said how something was, most likely they were right, however much you didn't want to hear it. Myla was the same. Straight as arrows, sword-monks.

Not like brothers.

Trust me. How many times had he heard that quiet whisper? *Trust me.*

Levvi in Deephaven, not wanting to come back home to his family, that had been bad. But this? Worst part was that he *had* trusted Seth. Had trusted him for years, in Varr, in Deephaven, even in Torpreah. Had trusted him to do some stupid shit, now and then, sure, but still... they were brothers! If Seth had needed something, really *needed*, all he had to do was ask and Fings would sort it out. That was how it was, how it had always been. How could Seth not see that?

But Seth *hadn't* asked, and all Fings' charms hadn't helped one little bit.

Trust me.

He sighed and tried telling himself that what Seth had done wasn't really Seth. That Seth was possessed, or under some enchantment or something. Trouble was... Well, Seth was Seth. The same Seth he'd always been. The same Seth who could never trust, not completely. The sigil on Fings' hand? Well, if Fings was honest with himself, that was always Seth's way, right from the day they'd met.

"I don't know about that priest," he said. "But this whole business of him making people do stuff, that started after." He told her what he'd seen on the road to Helhex. What he thought Seth had done. What he'd seen in Torpreah and at The Pillar of Dusk; and later, in Valladrune, when Seth hadn't even bothered to hide it.

He had to stop for a bit after that. If he didn't, he'd most likely burst into tears. Bawling his eyes out in front of a sword-monk? No thanks.

"What happens now?" he asked eventually.

"We wait," said Tasahre.

"Wait for what? You got some friends coming to rescue us, then?"

She smiled. "In a manner of speaking."

"And then what?"

"We leave. You go your way, I go mine."

"And your way is what? Going after him again?"

"Yes."

"What, so you can try and murder him?"

Tasahre closed her eyes. "If he comes peacefully, he will be tried. If he resists, then yes, I will kill him. He *is* a warlock. I smell it on him. Get some rest, thief."

"How you going to find him?"

"I have no idea."

"You'll probably want to start with Myla, I reckon."

"Yes."

"Probably easier, eh? Not like she makes herself difficult to find."

"Indeed."

"Probably want to start in Varr, I'd say."

Tasahre sighed.

"Actually, I reckon I know exactly where Seth's going next. The Mage of Tombland. Reckon Seth's got some questions he wants to ask."

"I have no idea who that is."

"No? Well, I do. I know where, too." He told her about the mage, about Blackhand's betrayal, how the mage's corpse had been dumped in an old vault, never to see the light of the Sun. "If I've got it right, that means Seth can still talk to the vicious bugger. He's after that book, you see."

"Book?"

"Yeah. Some book your Deephaven warlock used to have."

Tasahre grunted.

"As for me?" Fings sniffed. "Reckon I'll be going to Varr, too. That's home, that is. So, yeah. Reckon we might as well go together, eh? Probably a lot less trouble for both of us, the way I see it. You can make sure no one gives us any gyp, I'll tell you everything there is to know about the Mage of Tombland and what happened to him."

The sword-mistress sighed. "Thief?"

"Yeah?"

"Do you *ever* stop talking?"

Fings grumbled something and lay on the tiles, staring up at the stars. Not that he much *wanted* to travel with a bad-tempered judgemental sword-monk, but it *would* be quicker and less... difficult.

And he wouldn't be alone.

He must have drifted off at some point. One moment, he

was lying on his back feeling all sorry for himself, half aware of Tasahre sitting cross-legged beside him on the rooftop, and the next moment, she was prodding him.

"Sunrise," she said.

She climbed to the roof ridge and started to pray. Fings shivered, then sighed and went and sat beside her. Still didn't know *how* to pray, exactly, but he thought he might as well give it a go, what with being surrounded by a sea of skeletal Dead Men.

As the first blaze of the sun tipped the horizon, Tasahre got to her feet. "Watch, thief," she said.

Fiery orange light seared the ground. The seething mass of skeletons quivered and quaked. They stopped clawing each other, the walls, stopped their clamour and scratching. They turned their heads from Tasahre and Fings and stared, motionless, at the coming of the light.

A small, distant pop. A clatter of bones as a single skeleton fell to pieces. The sun rose higher. Another pop and jangle of bones; and then, as the full fire of the sun blazed a new day across Valladrune, the skeletons tumbled and broke as though a giant scythe sliced through them, a wave and a roar of old bones clattering to the ground, while Tasahre stood, head tilted skyward, arms aloft. The wave rushed through and passed on across the island and beyond, and then...

In the silence that followed, Fings crept to the edge of the roof and looked down. The skeletons looked like ordinary piles of bones now, fallen and still.

Yeah. Like piles of bones are ever ordinary.

At least they'd stopped moving. And yes, a field of corpses was a sucking swamp of bad luck waiting to happen, but it wasn't like he was planning to linger. Reckoned he could manage picking his way through some old bones. As long as they didn't start getting ideas again.

Tasahre came to stand beside him. "I told you I had friends coming."

"What, daylight?"

"Yes, thief. Sunrise. The daily thunder of a waking God."

"So... That's it, is it?"

"That's it."

"They ain't about to get all uppity again?"

"No, thief. They're not about to get all... uppity. Thief... I have to ask. The ledgers you left behind in Torpreah. I was meant to find them, yes?"

Fings nodded.

"Because you knew what they said?"

"Well..." Fings wasn't sure how to answer, not keen on admitting to having stolen them on a whim. "Not exactly, no. I mean... Not my thing. Couldn't make head or tail of it. But... Well, I'd heard stuff." Heard stuff *after* he'd stolen them, but he saw no need to mention that.

Tasahre nodded gravely.

"Well," said Fings after a bit. "So, you good to climb down from here, or do I need to go get some rope?"

46
THE SCENT GARDENS OF VARR

"I don't know what to do." Myla walked with Orien through the Obra Scent Gardens. It was an odd corner of the city, a maze of narrow paths between dense walls of exotic plants and shrubberies close to the Cathedral of Light, buried behind a labyrinth of alleys and walls. She'd never have known it existed if the stairway she'd eventually found spiralling from the Undercity hadn't brought her into the middle of it. Created a century ago by the Torpreahn Emperor Obra the Second, planted with a menagerie of greenery from across the many worlds, then largely forgotten, though meticulously maintained.

"Tell me again," Orien said.

Myla told him again. The fight with the Wraiths. The Regent's bizarre mission. Valladrune. The unexpected reunion with Seth and Fings. Tasahre. The dead Wraith and the Usurper and their broken pact. What the Wraith had wanted, and why, her voice light, as though it was a piece of old history that no longer mattered; then back to Torpreah, her brother and sister. How she regretted not staying longer, the joy of knowing they both thrived.

"Thank you again for getting Soraya to the *Speedwell*. I don't think I understood how much that meant to me until I was there in Torpreah, standing with Lucius, sharing a cup of wine, knowing she was alive."

The stairway from the Undercity had ended abruptly, as though sheared long ago by an unimaginable force. The way onward had been blocked by a tiny door, stiff with neglect. She'd forced it open and found herself at the bottom of a second shaft, like a simple stone well, with a ladder leading on up.

"Fings stole *what?*"

"One of the teeth of Saint Kelm." She showed it to him, then turned to sniff at a cluster of white blooms, buried in fleshy dark foliage. Sweet and sharp, both at once. Sugar and citrus. She remembered smelling the same scent as she'd searched for a way out of the garden. Hadn't even know for sure what city she was in. What world, even.

Orien flicked fire into his fingers. He held the tooth up to the light, gazing at it, his expression a mixture of wonder and bewilderment.

"*That's* one of Saint Kelm's teeth?"

"Apparently."

"And Fings stole it. From the cathedral of the Sun in Torpreah. From right under the Autarch's nose?" He was trying not to smirk and largely failing.

"He didn't say how he came by it. But yes, probably."

Orien gave a look of bewilderment. "Why?"

"Because... he's Fings."

"And that's why your sword-mistress was after them?"

"No." Myla sighed. "Although I suppose I'd better return it."

"What, you're just going walk up to some distraught Dawncaller, say 'I hear you're missing a tooth', hand it over and walk away again?"

"That's one of the nice things about being a sword-monk: never having to explain yourself."

The ladder had ended in a grating. Myla had pushed it aside and emerged into a shrine to the Mistress of Many Faces, the Infinite Goddess, the Lady of the Stars. Empty but not neglected.

"Does Lady Novashi know any of this?" asked Orien.

Myla took the tooth from Orien and put it away. She crouched beside a cluster of bright yellow flowers and sniffed. Their scent reminded her of the spice market. "I don't think so. Why would she?"

"Lady Lorleia of Neja was her mother."

"Was?"

"She died. A long time ago." He frowned and hummed to himself. "You know, I *think* the story is that she died with the Sad Empress. The Nejans don't really talk about it."

"Wait..." Myla stopped. "So... she was killed at the same time as the Sad Empress? Lady Arianne Lemir? Both killed by sword-monks? Or at least, by people *pretending* to be sword-monks. Two of the Wraith's bloodlines?"

Coincidence? She stooped to pluck a bright crimson leaf and crush it between her fingers. A rich, earthy musky smell.

"What happened to Hendrake Borolan?" A Lord of Tarantor. She ought to know but she didn't.

Orien put on his thinking face, all scrunched up. "Murdered not long after the war, I think. He declared for Talsin but never gave Talsin his armies or access to his lands. If he *had*, I suppose much of the war would have been fought there and ruined him. Either way, he made himself quite unpopular with both sides. There were plenty enough in his own house who thought him a traitor."

Myla kept on walking. "How do you know all these things?"

"I listen."

She'd left the shrine and found herself in this tiny garden, meandering paths twisting among strange plants. Twilight had swallowed their colours but not their scents. She'd wandered, often finding herself back where she'd started until she let the scents guide her. Eventually, she'd found herself at a locked gate in a high stone wall. After a bit of fruitless shouting, she'd scaled the gate and found herself in a warren of alleys; but another perk of being a sword-monk was that you could bang on doors and ask questions like "where am I?" and get answers, however surly.

"Do you think it's possible the Levanya had the late Emperor murdered?" she asked.

Orien stopped and glared at her like she was mad. "*Kyra* Levanya?"

"Yes."

"We *are* talking about the same Overlord of Varr."

"The Butcher of Deephaven. Khrozus' favourite general. The man everyone thought would become regent after the late Emperor died, Sun bless him. *That* Levanya."

"And... you think he murdered Emperor Ashahn the First?"

Myla shrugged. "*Some*one did."

"Maybe one of his many, many enemies? Maybe *not* the man who loyally served both him and his father across four decades?"

They passed a stand of flowers, orange, the size of a man's head, on thick stalks as tall as a horse. The shrine was close now.

"The emperor would have been well guarded against his enemies. Perhaps not against his most loyal friends. And the Levanya was Khrozus' ally, not Ashahn's." They rounded a tight corner. Another scent she remembered. Like woodsmoke. "Nearly there."

"Myla... Ashahn married the Levanya's niece!"

"And then she died."

"I believe we covered this already. Murdered on the road by a gang of sword-monks."

"That's what they say. Doesn't make it true."

Orien paused to admire a bush swathed in vibrant pink blooms. He bent, sniffed, then wrinkled his nose and stepped away. "Ugh. Sour milk." He shook himself. "People say a lot of things about the Levanya. Doesn't make *them* true either."

"Is Her Highness back in Varr?"

"Last *I* heard was she'd set up an impromptu court in the Raven Hills." He wandered to a cluster of lilac flowers shaped like tiny trumpets. "Oh! Hot iron! Reminds me of Khrozir." He raised an eyebrow. "Still negotiating terms with the Torpreahns, I think. Look, one thing I've *never* heard anyone say about the Levanya – and I've heard a lot of things – is that he murdered Emperor Ashahn."

"I'm not suggesting he did it himself."

"Why would you think he had anything to do with it at all?"

Myla crushed a dark variegated leaf between her fingers. The scent was metallic. Yes, she remembered that. The same scent she'd smelled as she'd left the shrine. Almost there.

She didn't answer Orien's question. Not because she didn't trust him – she did – but because some confidences weren't hers to share. If her suspicions were true and the world found out, she reckoned it might just plunge the empire into a chaos from which it wouldn't recover.

They walked in silence around another corner and there it was: the shrine to the Infinite Mistress. Myla went inside, calling out, but the shrine remained deserted. She stopped at the grate in the floor. When Orien joined her, she pointed.

"That's where I came out. There's a shaft that goes down to vaults under the city. Seth says they run everywhere. Empty vaults and empty tunnels. There was a half-god palace here, once."

"Why would the Levanya murder Emperor Ashahn?" asked Orien. "I mean, I suppose I could see it if he wanted the throne for himself, but the thing is, he had the chance to take it, and he didn't."

Could he have taken it? If the Regent objected, Myla thought probably not. Could he and the Regent have been in it together...? But *that* didn't feel right, either. The Regent didn't talk much about her father, at least not to Myla, but when she did, her grief was real.

She went outside and sat on the steps. In daylight, this hidden garden was a wonder. Tranquil and beautiful.

"Tell me about Neja again," she said.

He'd already told the story once – of course, because how could he not? – last night when Myla had found him at the House of Fire, as they'd held each other, lost in the delight of finding they were both alive. She'd heard of the battle between the Regent's sorcerers and the Wraiths, how Orien had witnessed their defeat and even been a part of it. His story had been boastful, the exaggerated bravado she'd come to expect. Yet with an undercurrent of something dark that had left him scarred. She hadn't pressed him then, not wanting to break the happiness of seeing him unhurt; long after sunrise, she'd dragged him away from their tangle of sheets, their nest of silks and furs and sweaty skin, and brought him here. Now, sitting on the steps of this forgotten shrine, she wasn't quite sure why.

"Orien?"

He told her again: the same dashing and heroic defence of a great city against an endless horde of Dead Men; mages and soldiers; hails of arrows tipped with Sunsteel, and the children who braved the battlefield each day to retrieve as many as they could find before the next sunset. Of knives of ice from the sky, same as she'd seen in Deephaven, of swarms of murderous birds made of shadow, with lances for beaks. The coming of the Wraiths. Orien on the battlements with the other mages, pouring fire from his hands. He didn't remember much after it started, he said. Like it was a dream.

Right there. Right there, he was hiding something.

She wrapped an arm around his shoulder. "It's just you and me."

"I felt them," he shivered. "That night. The Wraiths came into me. All of us. Like they did outside Deephaven. I felt their despair. The futility. The inevitable ruin and failure. I... I can't. I..." He bowed his head and clung to her. "You were there. Or... I *thought* it was you. I couldn't move. I couldn't face them... I couldn't..."

"It's okay." Myla squeezed him close.

He told her how the Moon had sung, red and bleeding, called forth by the Regent, her circlet ablaze with a light that destroyed Dead Men across the city, how the Wraiths crumbled and fell at her feet.

"They were really there? In Neja? On the night of the blood moon? The Regent and the Red Witch?" The battle for Neja had been a day after the fight at Raven Falls, the distance between them impossible even if you had an enchanted horse that never tired, which the Regent very possibly did.

"Yes. Afterwards... I remember a darkness after the Wraiths fell. A brilliant and blinding black. It called to me, distant yet persistent. I wanted to go to it. But I heard a voice calling me back. I remember the darkness turning to light, and the light was the sky, and I was lying on the ground, and someone was talking, and the last thing I could remember was seeing myself, crumpled against the ramparts of Neja, blood everywhere from..."

He sank into her. "That night when the Wraiths came. I couldn't stand it. The despair…"

"Orien?"

He grunted something.

"The Wraiths, Orien. It's what they do."

"I know." He shuddered and snuggled closer. "Afterwards was a dream of warm sunlight and a cool breeze, of drifting between fields of honey-wheat and scented grass. Of conversations with crows and arguments with ravens, of singing with nightingales and martins. I remember lying on a bed of light while luminous men swathed in white chanted songs of creation in circles around me. Crowds and shouts and distant cheers and the musky scent of night. And then waking. Slumped against a wall, legs akimbo, burning silver inside me. Cold light. Cruel laughter and endless fire. For a few hours, it seemed I'd had one of the elemental dragons inside me, speaking with the voice of a god of fire. I suppose it must have been a dream or a nightmare. I hope so. Anything else would make me sound like a madman, wouldn't it?"

"We won," said Myla. "That's all that matters. They're gone."

"The dead piled themselves against the walls and burned. They say the fist of the moon struck the earth, that the sun climbed into the night sky and threw down beams of light. I don't know what she did. Some act of sorcery beyond my understanding that stilled the dead and did no good whatsoever to the Wraiths, nor to any mage unfortunate enough to be nearby. Afterwards, the Dead lost their purpose. Many are husks, but it seems many others are not. Did we win? I suppose we did." His voice turned momentarily thoughtful. "I hear they've gathered in bands. The Dead Men, I mean, not the Wraiths. They seem to be making their way back to Deephaven. We left them to the Nejans. The Regent took her soldiers and her mages and headed south."

"But not you?" There was something off about Orien's story. He wasn't quite *lying* to her. More… It was as though the story he was telling wasn't his own, but a story as he'd been told by someone else. Or, perhaps, his story as he thought it should have been.

"I came back to Varr with Vanamere."

Myla rolled her eyes. She'd quietly hoped the Taiytakei popinjay might have disappeared.

"There were dead Wraiths, you see. I didn't have anything else to do, so I worked with him. We stripped their armour of souls and beaten silver. Vanamere cut them open, all examined in minute detail. Deep under the Kaveneth, shelves filled with their pickled remains." He shook his head, clearly troubled. "Strip their armour, remove the serpent that sleeps inside, the Wraiths are just like you or me."

"They *are* us," Myla said, because that was what the Wraith of Valladrune had told her.

A vessel...

"Were you there," she asked, "when the Regent fought them?"

"No. At least... I don't think so." He shook his head. Myla sniffed. And there it was. The faint stink of a lie. She wasn't sure what to do about that.

"Who *was* with her?"

"Lady Novashi. A Moon Priestess too, I think."

Truth, this time, and not a surprising one. The Regent and the Red Witch were practically joined at the hip.

"What about the Levanya?"

"The Levanya?" Orien laughed and wriggled away from her. "No! He rode south with the army and then returned to Varr. Why, under the Sun, do you think he had anything to do with Emperor Ashahn's death?"

"Valladrune. You know the story?"

"Well, there isn't one, is there? Valladrune never existed. But if it *did* exist... If there's a story at all, it's that the Levanya sacked it after the war."

"Yes, except that's not what happened. There was a Wraith. It was killed by sword-monks. *That* was when the city died. The Levanya wasn't even there, although he did make sure the sword-monks knew of the Wraith's existence, and that they all died after it was done. What *I* saw... Orien, I have to wonder whether everything that's happened these few months might all go back to what the Levanya did." She reached out and touched his hair. "There's something you're not telling me about Neja. Something important."

He didn't try to pull away. Didn't say anything either. But there it was, in his face. That... fear, was it? No... No, she understood it now. Shame.

She cupped his face in her hands and kissed him. "One of the perils of having a sword-monk for a lover. Don't answer if you don't want to. We're all allowed secrets. But... I do need to ask this: is it anything to do with the Regent, with the Levanya, or with the Wraiths?"

"The Wraiths." The word came out as a hoarse whisper. "There are fates worse than death. That is what they have suffered and what they bring. Eternal resentment. Eternal regret."

Myla pulled him tight again. "When the Wraith of Deephaven first looked at me, it was as though it tore a hole in my spirit. I felt everything rush out to leave a hollow and empty husk. But it was an illusion, Orien. Nothing more. It passed, and then sword-mistress Tasahre chopped off its head." She almost laughed. "Set it free, maybe? Perhaps that's even what it wanted." She kissed him again. "You've been wounded, like many others. And like those others, you will heal. This feeling will fade, and I will be with you, always, to see that it does."

He was shaking in her arms now, almost sobbing.

"They tried to kill us. Both of us. They failed. We're stronger."

"No," he whispered. "We're not."

"Yes, Orien, we are." She tangled her fingers in his hair and forced him to look at her. "I'm carrying your child, fire-mage, and no Wraith or spectre or Dead Man is going to deprive him of a father." She pulled him to his feet. "You know what always make things better when you're feeling small and brittle?"

Orien shook his head. "What?"

"Vigorous sex with someone you're not entirely sure you deserve."

"Oh?" he said. And then. "Worth a try, I suppose."

She grinned. "*There* you are. And Orien?"

"Yes?"

"If you didn't deserve me, I wouldn't be here. I'm a sword-monk. We don't do pity."

47
THE MAGE OF TOMBLAND

"Yes," said Seth. "But which one *is* he?" He was standing beside a pile of old corpses, long dead and desiccated, in what had once been the Mage of Tombland's oubliette. The place where he got rid of anyone who annoyed him, half-murdering them first, then dropping them from a shaft in the roof of the vault to smash their bones on the floor below. It was fitting, Seth supposed, that Blackhand had given the mage a taste of the same, and quite helpful, since it meant the dead mage's spirit was likely still trapped here.

What *wasn't* helpful was the way Blackhand had stripped the dead mage naked before tossing him down the hole. Same as the mage had done to everyone else, admittedly, because why waste perfectly decent clothes when you could patch them up and sell them; but as it was, all Seth had to work with was a lot of scattered skeletons wrapped in dry leathery skin with wisps of old hair stuck to their scalps. Kill a few people and leave them long enough and it got quite difficult to know which was which.

Xibaiya, the Wraith hissed. *The underworld. The God-father Seturakah, Splinterer of Worlds, reached into the spaces between the gods and found something of unimaginable strength. When the earth goddess opened her mouth to consume him, two powers touched that should never have met and the worlds shattered into shards. Goddess and God-father were destroyed; yet such was Seturakah's will that rather than succumb to annihilation, he created the realms of Xibaiya even as his being unravelled. There he lingers, clinging to existence, and the Earth-Goddess too, and so it is that the dead who once belonged to the Earth now wait, to rise again and restore the Shining World.*

"Did I ask for a lesson in theo-cosmology? No, I asked which corpse is the fucking mage. Wait... Are you telling me the Path of the Sun has been right all along?" The Wraith was being difficult. Probably not desperately happy about being snatched from its journey to the afterlife and being bound into a stone in Seth's pocket. Then again, given that Myla impaling its corpse with Sunsteel had been at least the third time someone or something had tried killing the Wraith of Valladrune and it still hadn't ended up properly dead, maybe a bit of tetchiness was understandable?

Right? What is right, *little one? All paths lead to the same end. Some are short and some are long. When the time comes, this is how it will be.*

Seth felt the familiar sensation of being both in and out of his body at the same time, a bit like back at the Pillar of Dusk when he'd peered into the past; except this, he knew, was the future. A future already mapped by destiny, if the Wraith was to be believed, the weft and warp of its threads already set. He saw a Wraith – probably not the *same* Wraith – in glorious silver at the mouth of a tunnel. He saw himself, too, and then a third figure joined them, in black mail that glittered with moonlight. He knew who she was from his vision in the Moonspire.

The moon-witch is the key. Open the door. Undo what was done. End this place. Let through That Which Came Before. Restore the God-father and you will have what you want.

"Well... I *could* do that." Although it didn't strike Seth as terribly clever, all things considered. Admittedly, yes, it *would* mean an end of the Path of the Sun, no doubt about it, what with their whole reason for existence being to prevent exactly what the Wraith was suggesting he do. Trouble was, he rather suspected it would mean the end of a lot of other things, too, some of which he quite liked. Being alive, for example.

He sighed. "Dead mage? Book of Endings? Can we get on with it?" Although... It *did* give him the beginnings of an idea... "Actually no. Go on then, tell me about your moon-witch."

She comes as you have seen her, filled with flame and with a purpose that will not be swayed. She would unravel the world if it would bring her vengeance. You, who are beneath her notice, can be her undoing.

A part of him, he had to admit, was enjoying the irony of finding himself down here. He and Fings had been in Tombland when the mage fell because Fings had been trying to find a secret vault. And Seth *had* found it, days later, although not in the way he'd expected. He'd never found a way down until now, but looking for one had led him to the vault under the incinerators in Glassmakers.

She is the key and the vessel. If she opens the door, the God-father will take her. Make her open the door, herald.

"Herald?" That word again. The same word the dead warlock Saffran Kuy had used. "I don't think so," Seth grunted. "I mean... how? She's, what, some key or other, which will open some door or other, none of which I know anything about. And if she does that, she ends up possessed by the Wraithiest of Wraiths – not much room for a fulfilling and independent life of her own after that, I'm guessing – and all the other stuff you said will happen... happens. Have I got that right? And you want me to do what, exactly? Wander up, politely explain the situation, ask nicely? You *do* see why I don't think that's going to work? Actually no, don't bother, because I'm not interested. Just tell me which of these corpses is the one I'm looking for."

Although... It *did* raise the interesting question of what happened if someone did all the things the Wraith said, and then slapped a sigil on this God-father, whoever he was, and ended him as soon as he showed for his big moment. What happened *then*?

The *Heresies of Sivingathm*, the book he'd once had Fings steal from the Sunherald's library in Varr, claimed the sigils of the warlocks belonged to the Hungry Goddess, the Earth Mother, as did the sign that novice priests learned to dispatch the Dead Men. Saying stuff like that hadn't ended well for Dawncaller Sivingathm, buried as an apostate in a crypt under the temple in

Varr's Spice Market for his troubles. Sivingathm had been wrong, as it turned out. Close, but wrong. The sigils didn't belong to the Hungry Goddess. They belonged to That Which Came Before, whatever *that* was. They were a way to tap its power.

Seth felt his skin tingle. What if there *was* a way to undo it all? Not only his own life and the last few months, but *every*thing? A way to reverse the Splintering and return the many worlds to one? A way to set destiny as it should have been. They could hardly murder him as a heretic for doing *that*.

The Wraith hissed inside its stone prison.

"Yeah, yeah, be petulant all you like. You might have been a half-god when you were alive but you're dead at least twice over now, which means you do what I tell you. So, fuck all your end-of-the-world bollocks and tell me which of these corpses is your mage. I'll find my own path once I have his book, thanks."

The Wraith told him. It wasn't happy, but Seth didn't give a shit about that. He slapped a sigil on the Mage of Tombland's bones and turned him into a Dead Man, then another sigil to make him pliant, then gave his new skeleton friend a stick of charcoal and a piece of paper.

"Where's the Book of Endings?" Might as well start with what really mattered.

It took a while, and quite lot of questions, to figure it all out. When he did, Seth stood in silence a while.

"You're fucking kidding me," he said at last.

Sulfane's book. The one written in a cypher he'd never managed to crack. The one he'd taken from Tombland last Midwinter. The one he'd had lying around for more than a month, all without the first idea what it was. And then largely forgotten because he hadn't been able to get it to make sense.

All that time, and it had been right there?

He took a deep breath. "Right," he said. "And how the fuck do I read it, then?" It *was* tempting to pick up an old thigh bone and start smashing things. Or at least scream for a bit. Maybe both.

With a sigil.

"*What* fucking sigil?"

The dead mage started to write an answer.

"No. Don't *tell* me. Draw it out, you dead tit!"

The dead mage drew a sigil. Seth looked at it.

"Right. So... What do I do with it?"

He had to try the question a few times before he got the answer he wanted.

"And then what?"

Meditate on what will end. Open the book. The sigil will be there.

"What? *Any*thing?"

Yes.

Seth sighed. "The *Heresies of Sivingathm* says the sigils can end Gods. Even creation itself. You do know that's quite hard to believe."

Didn't have to do *that* to make everything right, though. Didn't have to end *every*thing. Just make everyone forget some things. Ideally, turn back time? Maybe send a message to his old self, back when he'd been a novice. Tell himself not to go to that place in the Undercity. To listen to Fings. To not use that sigil he didn't even understand on that stupid dead rat. To be more careful. Perhaps, even, to not be anything at all except the priest he'd always carried in his heart...

Provided something ends, there is a sigil for anything you desire.

Well, *that* was easy enough. An end to the guilt and the pain and the shame and the envy.

He put another sigil on the dead mage, severing the tether that kept him tied to this place, releasing his soul to the Lord of Light, or the Fickle Lord, or the Infinite Mistress, or the Hungry Goddess; Seth didn't much care which one got him. With the book, he could put everything right. He could make the whole world different and better. Make everything he'd done be okay, because it would all have been in the cause of a greater good.

I had it in my fucking hand?

48
BROTHERHOOD

Travelling from Valladrune to Varr with a sword-monk was, it turned out, a bit of a mixed blessing. On the one hand, Tasahre was extremely good at making sure their journey was full of horses and boats and shelter and food and not getting lost, and entirely free of inconveniences such as bandits and muggings and starving and unexpected rivers or deserts. On the other hand, it was... well... boring. If he ever got back, Fings reckoned the story of his journey around the empire would all be jolly exciting right up to Valladrune, after which it would be *and then I came home.*

Admittedly, ending up trapped on a rooftop with a sword-monk surrounded by an entire city of angry skeletons *did* make for a good climax. He doubted anything would top that. Rather hoped it wouldn't, actually. He really *did* just want to go home.

Outside Valladrune, Tasahre had managed to catch a couple of the straying horses. They'd also found the Torpreahn soldiers. Turned out most of them had survived, albeit a bit bedraggled. To Fings' surprise, Tasahre had let them go. They still seemed all set on heading west and setting up as a troupe of travelling entertainers; a part of Fings had even been tempted to join them. But no. Varr. Family.

A week of difficult terrain and bickering later, he and Tasahre had reached the Tarantor Road. The sword-mistress had set a hard pace, leaving Fings to either keep up or find his own way. When he *had* kept up, there'd been food and warmth and shelter in shrines and temples and waystations. Which had been nice, but would have been a lot *more* nice if Fings hadn't been so exhausted from all the riding that all he could do was eat, sleep, get up, complain bitterly, and then do it all again.

Tarantor might have been interesting if they'd stayed more than a single night. At least it was boats after that, which were equally boring but didn't leave him stiff and crippled every day. They reached the Arr and headed upriver. They stopped for a night where the City of Spires should have been, and Fings gawped at its moonlight reflection in the waters.

A twelvenight later and they were in Varr. Tasahre made him stay for a night in the temple in Leatherworkers, forced him out of bed at the crack of dawn, dragged him to the Circus of Dead Emperors, to Glassmakers and the shrine and the incinerators, and made him show her the entrance to the Undercity vault where Seth had gone, all those months ago.

"There's places like this all over," Fings told her. "The one you want is where the Mage of Tombland used to dump bodies. That's where he'll be. I don't know how to get there." She knew all this by now, along with most of his life story. Not that she seemed particularly interested in that.

To Fings' surprise, she took his hand before he left, the one with the faint scar where Seth's sigil had been. "I once knew another young man who fell foul of a warlock. Younger than you. They're terrible creatures. Now be on your way, thief, and stay clear of the Longcoats." Then she asked him to promise that if he ever saw Seth again, ever even heard anything, she'd be the first to know. Fings nodded, didn't say anything, on account of the whole business of sword-monks knowing when you lied, and left. Outside, he wandered aimlessly, not knowing what he was doing or where to go until he found himself in the Circus of Dead Emperors.

Varr.

Home.

He stood for a bit, glad to be lost in a crowd. He'd managed not to think too much about what Seth had done, what with all the travelling, but it hit him now.

Not good enough for you, was I? Seth had always thought he was better. Better than Fings, better than Levvi, better than Blackhand, better than everyone. Was what always ended up getting him trouble, that idea that he was somehow special. Somehow meant for greatness.

He was *smart, give him that.*

Yeah. Sort of. Knew his letters and his numbers. Knew his histories and heraldries. A right sponge for knowledge. But he'd always wanted more, had always ended up doing something stupid and losing everything. Time and again, always with Fings to snatch his smouldering arse from the fire at the last minute.

Couldn't save him when the priests kicked him out, though, could you?

Always had a sick sense of guilt about that. He'd been there when Seth had slipped into the crypt under the temple in Spice Market Square. He'd stolen that book from the Sunherald's library. He'd gone with Seth to the Undercity, that first time. Was hard not to wonder, now, what might have happened if he'd said no. If he'd grabbed Seth and given him a good shake, pointed out how he had a good thing going and not to be so stupid.

Probably wouldn't have made a difference. A part of him knew that; but even so, Fings *hadn't* said any of those things until it was too late, and even then, hadn't said them loud enough.

Saved your skin in Varr. Saved it again in Deephaven and again in Torpreah. Still wasn't enough, eh?

He headed west through what had once been Spicer territory until he got to Threadneedle Street and the *Unruly Pig.* Didn't even think about how long he'd been gone as he walked in. Simply sauntered through the door and plonked himself on a seat by the bar. If he was going to flounce about feeling sorry for himself, he reckoned he might as well do it somewhere comfortably familiar.

"Fings!" Arjay was the bar.

"Arjay." Hadn't thought this through. He was hardly going to be left alone when he'd been gone for half a year, travelled the

Empire and been right there at the start when a war had broken out.

Bollocks.

"I need a drink," he said. "And not the watery piss Blackhand used to give us."

"We save that for the people we don't like," said Arjay. She went to a barrel and poured a foaming mug of ale. As she did, she called over her shoulder. "Dox! Brick! Fings is back!"

Dox sauntered out from the kitchens and gave Fings a hearty slap on the back. Fings winced. "Ow!"

"Rescue Myla, then, did you?" Dox asked.

"What?"

"Your Ma said you were off to save some sword-monk who'd been kidnapped."

Fings frowned. Had he told anyone that? He didn't think so; but Seth probably had, while Fings was busy coming up with reasons why they had to leave in such a huge hurry that weren't the real reason, the *real* reason being that Seth was in the shit again.

"So, rescue her then, did you?" asked Arjay. She slid Fings' beer across the counter in front of him.

"Yeah," said Fings. "Sort of." Because he had. He really *had* done that. You never knew with Myla, how much rescuing she needed. Usually not much, but she *had* been chained to a rowing bench on a slave-barge at the time.

"What she do?"

Fings frowned. "Some sort of family shit."

"She back too?"

"Not sure," Fings shrugged. "Maybe."

"We going to see her? What about Seth?"

Fings shrugged again.

"Fings! You can't just piss off without telling anyone for six months and then show up again and not say anything!"

Fings was about to ask why not, since that was exactly what he'd been hoping to do. But they were clustered around him now, and there was Topher, coming down the stairs, and Sara and Lula waltzing out from kitchens, and half a dozen other familiar faces, all stopping what they'd been doing to come and welcome him home. He didn't want it, not now, but he reckoned he'd probably be glad of it soon enough, this family of misfits he called friends, so maybe now wasn't the time to be all mopey about how Seth was a dick.

"Your Ma said you were looking for Levvi, too," said Arjay. "Don't supposed you found *him*?"

"Yeah. I actually did." Much to his own surprise.

"Right. So, you rescued Myla, found your missing brother after what, five years?" Arjay raised an eyebrow. "Slay any dragons, while you were at it?"

"No, but I did see one."

"Piss off," said Dox.

"Yeah, pull the other one." Brick was chuckling. "Let's have the real truth, eh? You nicked something, right? And whoever you burgled, they got proper pissy about it, so all this time, you've been hiding. Right?"

"I did everything I said," said Fings, a bit defensive, because the whole not believing him thing was getting up his nose, even if *he* wouldn't have believed him. "And that ain't the half of it. You really want to know? Best you gather round and pour a few drinks then. Going to take a while to tell it all."

It *did* take a while, and they were all quite merry by the end. Fings told them about travelling the river to the sea, the sights and sounds of Deephaven. About the plague, and the charms he wore to keep it at bay. How he'd broken into Deephaven's Solar Cathedral and found the wrong sword-monk. How he'd rescued Myla and seen a Faerie-King. He was quite tipsy by the time he got to the bit where he found Levvi, and so Levvi wasn't a slave-sailor on a Black Ship, but an officer, second in command, destined to be an admiral of a whole fleet, most likely. He told them of Deephaven's fall, as much as he knew, what'd he'd seen with his own eyes and what he'd heard later. Told them how Myla had killed a Wraith all on her own. For the most part he kept Seth out of it.

Around him, as he spun his story, the business of the *Pig* went on. People drifted away to do whatever needed to be done, then came back and made him tell the same bits of story again, enough that he ended up telling most of it at least twice over. Hours passed. The sky outside turned dark. A happy warm buzz filled the air. People talking, drinking, eating. The *Pig* at its best, the way it used to be when Blackhand was in charge, busy and vibrant with possibility. Hadn't realised how much he missed this.

He became distantly aware of a kerfuffle outside. This being the *Pig*, he didn't pay any attention, not until he saw Arjay looking past him, eyes like dinner plates.

"Fings!"

Myla?

She came bursting in, marching right through the crowd. He barely had time to recognise her, all dressed up in sword-monk robes, before she pulled him off his stool and wrapped him in an enormous hug that seemed to go on for days. And for once, he didn't mind. Never knew what to do with Myla's hugs, mostly, but right now...? Right here, yes, it was what he needed, and so he hugged her back for all he was worth, and then burst into tears.

"Fings?" She let go. "What's the matter?"

He laughed, trying to shake it off. "It ain't that," he said. "It's just... I don't know. Well... Wasn't sure..." He grabbed her again and held on to her. "I'm just... Happy, you know? To be back. And that you're back too. Happy we're all alive."

She pulled away, eyes all quizzical. "Why wouldn't we be?"

Arjay slid a cup of wine Myla's way. Fings noted how she sipped it, didn't simply knock it back and immediately ask for another. When she caught his eye, she patted her belly. Which was, now he thought about it, a bit rounder than he remembered.

"Oh," said Fings, as it sunk in. "Right."

"The Moon Priestesses tell me I have to be a good little monk for the next few months," she sighed. She didn't seem too unhappy about it though.

"Er..." he had no idea what to say.

"I saw Tasahre earlier. She told me about Valladrune."

"Uh huh. Interesting conversation, I'm guessing?" Fings reckoned the sword-mistress might have had a few things she wanted off her chest.

"It was a bit... tense. I'm sorry we left you there. I had no idea. I would have come back if I could. I..." She gave him a look of pity. "Tasahre told me what Seth did. You should know... I tried to get him to come back. Face it all, but..." She shook her head. "If I'd known... We parted ways without bloodshed but... I don't think he's coming back. I'm sorry. I really don't know what to say."

Fings shrugged. "Then don't."

"It *is* good to see you. It makes me happy." She slid on a stool beside him, bought another cup of wine for each of them and talked and talked, her escape from Deephaven, fighting Wraiths, Orien, her journey to Valladrune. Fings had a notion there was a lot more, stuff she wasn't saying, but he didn't press, happy enough with what he had, happy to see her again, her and Dox and Arjay and all the other idiots of the *Unruly Pig*. She listened as he told her how he'd saved the sword-mistress from an army of skeletons, how the two of them had watched the rising Sun together, the trip back to Varr, until the night was almost done, the *Pig* all but empty, and all that was left was him and Myla, deep in their cups, and Dox and Brick and Arjay, yawning and clearing up.

"I need a piss," he said, after Topher made him tell the story of how he'd rescued Myla's sister – over the course of several retellings and quite a lot of beer, that was what his infiltration of House Hawat had become – for about the fifth time, all the while with Myla, who knew the truth of it, sitting quietly and smiling and nodding, as if the way Fings told it was the way it had really happened. Made him feel all weird, that did. All soft and squishy inside.

Best big sister ever.

Which made him think of Seth again.

Topher slid off his stool and staggered off. Fings stared into space. Didn't know what to say. Myla took his hand and squeezed.

"I'll be keeping an eye on you," she said. "Now that you're back."

"You know, I reckon you're the best thing that ever happened here."

She laughed, and then suddenly she was hugging him again. "Stay safe, Fings."

Probably time for bed, he reckoned. But he *did* need a piss, so he stumbled through the kitchens and to the alley that slunk into the backstreets of Haberdashers. Once upon a time, Blackhand had made a point of kicking the shit out of anyone who took a piss outside his back door – *that's what we have neighbours for*. Old habits died hard, so Fings staggered on around the corner to the stables, which always stank of piss at the best of times. He braced himself and let out a long, satisfied sigh as he emptied his bladder.

"Fings?"

He jumped, spraying everywhere. *Seth?*

"Sorry."

Fings finished up, sorted himself out, then turned to find Seth at the stable door, half in, half out. Fings took a good long look at him.

"How many times have I told you not to go creeping up on a fellow when he's taking a piss! Anything I can do for you?"

"You got back alright, then."

"Like *you* care!"

He saw Seth's puzzlement. *Yeah, well.*

"You remember the Midwinter Festival? The Murdering Bastard trying to win that archery contest? The old man with his chicken feet? You remember how you said it was all bollocks, was just the foot of a dead chicken, nothing else." Fings sniffed. "Turned out it *was* bollocks. You were right."

"I remember you gave him a full silver moon for it."

"Yeah, well. I'm a fool, ain't I. That's what you think, right?"

"What? No. Course not." Seth frowned and shook his head. Fings felt a vague urge to punch him in the face.

"Yeah, you do. You always thought that. We both know it, if we're honest."

"Fings!" Seth took a step into the stable. Instinct made Fings take a step back, keeping the distance between them. Seth stopped. "Fings? What the fuck?"

Fings shook his head. "How about you just piss off."

"Fings!" Seth's voice took an edge. "I think you'd better tell me what this is about."

"Oh, you do, do you?"

"Fings!" A sharper edge. "Tell me what this is about!"

And there it was. That little sting of expectation. Like Seth knew Fings would answer because Fings didn't have a choice. Except... well, now he *did* have a choice.

"All right," Fings said. "I will. Do you know what happened in Valladrune, while you and Myla were pissing about with the Forces of Darkness?"

"I can guess."

"You can, can you?"

"I would have come back, if there was anything I could have done."

"You would, would you? Funny, that. Myla said much the same." Fings sneered. "Difference being, when *she* said it, I believed her. She's right here, by the way. In the *Pig* at the bar. A bit wined-up, but I reckon she'd be happy to see you. You know, if you wanted to say hello."

Seth didn't move.

"Yeah. That's what I thought. So there I am, sitting on a rooftop in a city full of Dead Men, with that sword-monk from Deephaven. You know, the one I lamped with a pisspot on account of her wanting to murder you. Sharp as her own swords that one. Sees I'm wearing a glove. What's that for, she asks. To hide that mark my brother put on me, I say. The one you said was for protection, remember? Keep it from the sun so it don't burn off?"

He stopped then and looked Seth in the eye and saw it happen. The shock. The understanding. The realisation of what was about to come.

"Yeah. Wasn't for *protection*, though, was it."

"Yes, it was," said Seth.

"No, it was because despite everything I ever done for you, you didn't trust me. Or maybe you did, maybe it was because you knew all the time that I was right!" Fings pursed his lips. "You know what I can't stop thinking about is this: I lamped that sword-monk with a pisspot. Drew blood and everything. Sort of business where you might expect someone to hold a grudge." He shook his head. "She don't like me one little bit. Don't even try to hide it. Yet she's honest. Almost kind, once she sees what you done. Got no reason to be either of those things, yet she is. And then there's you."

"Whatever she told you about me, it isn't true."

"Ain't it?" Fings held out his hand, the one that had carried Seth's mark. Which it still did, if you looked closely. "You still going to tell me that was for my protection?"

"Fings! It was!"

"Fuck off, Seth. Just fuck off. I can feel the difference."

They stood and stared at each other in silence. Finally, Seth bowed his head. "I'm sorry, Fings."

"Yeah. Me too."

"But it *was* to protect you. So you wouldn't ask about—"

Fings punched him in the face. Seth staggered a couple of steps and then fell on his arse.

"It *was* to keep you safe!" He glowered from the floor, wiping his bloody nose. "You kept asking fucking questions. And I know you, Fings, you don't let go. The less you knew, the better! Not for me, because they were always going to kill me if they got their hands on me. But you? If they caught you and you didn't know anything, they'd have no reason to hurt you. So yes, it *was* for your own good! And you know what? It fucking worked, too. Didn't it!"

Fings spat on the ground beside Seth. "You decided all that for me, did you? All on your own?"

Seth didn't have an answer to that.

"What about that priest you burned in Deephaven? Was that for *his* own good?"

"What?"

Fings walked away. Behind him, Seth struggled to his feet.

"Fings!"

Fings ignored him. He walked back to the *Pig* and the kitchen door. As he reached it, Seth caught up and landed a hand on his shoulder to stop him. Fings let himself be turned, then punched Seth in the face a second time.

"Lies. That's all you are." He shook his head. "You want to come inside? Like I said, Myla's here. Come say hello?"

Seth didn't move.

"We're done, brother." Fings took one last look. Seth lay in the dirt, face bloody, clothes covered in filth. Then he slammed the door in Seth's face.

49
THE LIGHT AND THE DARK

Seth tried to remember the last time Fings had hit him and found he couldn't. Couldn't remember it because it hadn't happened.

He picked himself up. *You deserve this.*

I was trying to protect him!

You were trying to protect yourself. Selfish coward. Pathetic little worm.

He stumbled into the dark alleys of Haberdashers. *What have I done?*

You want to know? I've got a list, and that's not even starting on all those holes in your memories. Fuck knows how bad those are.

Go away! Go away!

The voice inside him fell quiet, but he could feel it lurking in its corner, tittering to itself. *Brought this all on yourself, you did.*

No. No, no, no. There *had* to be a way to make this right!

Too late. You can't undo this.

He could confess and plead for forgiveness? But forgiveness had to be earned. There had to be a *reason* for what he'd done, a reason that made it worthwhile, that would make Fings understand. So that when you added it all up, it balanced. So Fings could give a little nod and say yes, Seth *had* done some pretty shitty stuff, but it had all been the means to a bigger end. That it all came to something worthwhile.

Why does it have to come to anything at all?

Because it does!

You know that that's been your problem right from the start? This idea that you have to mean something.

Everyone had to mean something, didn't they?

Why?

Because otherwise... what was the point?

If it's the meaning of life you're after, maybe you shouldn't have got yourself thrown out of the priesthood.

Except... that was precisely why he *had* been thrown out. He'd kept looking for meaning. Deeper and deeper and ever deeper.

Maybe the meaning is as simple as having some friends and not fucking them over?

No. There had to be more. *Had* to be. No point wishing he'd done things differently. And yes, he *had* made mistakes, he knew that, but he was still right! Get on and fix it, that was the thing. And he knew where to start...

You know you're going to fuck this up. Like you always do.

He headed north through Haberdashers and then east through Bonecarvers, past Tombland to the Circus of Dead Emperors and Glassmakers. When the sword-monks had caught him and taken him to the temple in Spice Market Square for questioning – to be followed, Seth had presumed, by a good old-fashioned warlock-burning – he'd told them about his lair in the Undercity. A desperate attempt to buy some time and, maybe, if he made his fawning sufficiently pathetic, a little leniency. He'd told them about Cleaver and about the skeletons of what he thought were long-dead half-gods, about the sigil-ringed archways that became sorcerous portals for anyone who knew how to open them, which *he* didn't. As far as he could remember, he'd never mentioned Sulfane's book. He hadn't hidden it, simply left it where he'd been skulking, under the incinerators, in a corner under an old piece of sacking. Hadn't known what else to do. In Deephaven, he'd mostly assumed the sword-monks and priests would have found it and hadn't much cared. He went back, now, on the chance they hadn't.

They had. It was gone.

He sighed. Fings had seen priests and sword-monks here, the day before the two of them fled Varr. In the end, it amounted to the same. If they'd found the book, they would have taken it to the Cathedral of Light. It would have gone to the Sunherald-Martial, along with anything else. What *he'd* done with it was anyone's guess. There was really only one way to find out.

Find the book. Find the sigils. Change it all. Once Fings saw what Seth could do, he'd understand. Probably give Seth a proper apology for being so untrusting. When it came, Seth would be magnanimous. *You see, now?*

Of course, I do, said imaginary Fings. *I'm sorry I didn't believe you. It was very hurtful.*

I should have known you'd never do something like that without a good reason. I'm sorry, brother.

And I'm sorry too. And Fings would understand, and they'd be brothers again.

You really think?

He crossed the city, slipped into the Paupers' Chapel to listen to the Twilight Prayer one last time, then slipped out again. He settled in a tavern, used a sigil to make friends with the owner, helped himself to a nice room for a few days, a nice meal, had a couple of cups of expensive wine, and quietly settled to down to thinking, long and hard, about how to summon the Destroyer of Worlds from his abyssal prison so he could end an ancient half-god once and for all and make everything right.

50
THE LEVANYA

There were, Myla thought, several ways she could go about confronting the Levanya. The easiest was to present what she knew to the Princess-Regent, ask her to summon the Levanya for a private audience, then question him under the Regent's gaze. *Yes, I do think you're a Wraith, your Highness. I can't prove it; but if you are, this one knows all about it, so you'd best crash into his head and rip out all his secrets…*

She wasn't sure how the Regent would react if Myla had it right. Badly, probably. And if Myla had it wrong, the Levanya would have her killed. More to the point, the Regent was still in the south, negotiating a peace, or possibly a surrender, or possibly something in between, with the Torpreahns. Or else she was crushing them with her sorceries, or simply wandering into their heads and changing their opinions on things. From what Myla had seen and felt, from the accounts of what had happened in Neja, she understood why, unlike everyone around her, the Regent seemed to have considered war with the south as nothing more than an irritatingly timed nuisance.

She wondered what she should do about *that*, too. The Regent was, once you understood what she could do, utterly terrifying. But what someone *could* do and what they actually *did*, those were two different things. Plenty of people thought sword-monks were utterly terrifying. And they were meant to be, but only if you were on the wrong side of them.

When you were her age, you ran off after an Anvorian elementalist.

And had won. Not quite the same as fighting a Wraith, but still...

What's she done that's wrong?

There *was* the whole climbing into other people's heads and harvesting their thoughts and memories without consent.

The measure of a woman isn't what she knows or the power she holds. It's what she chooses to do with them. The Path itself had taught her that. With the Wraiths defeated, how the Regent treated the Torpreahns would say more about who she was than anything Myla had learned in Valladrune. She deserved that chance, at least, didn't she?

Which left her with the Levanya himself, who wasn't going to be easy. While the Regent and Emperor were away, he ruled as Overlord of Deephaven. She could ask for an audience, but everyone knew the Levanya despised sword-monks and so she'd be declined. She *could* try and slip into his rooms in the palace, catch him alone and off-guard... But given how long he'd lasted, the Levanya surely had a cornucopia of tricks up his sleeve for would-be assassins. Which she wasn't, but she doubted he'd see the difference.

In the end, she settled for doing it the sword-monk way. She dressed in robes of sun-yellow and made of Taiytakei silk, edged at the collar in white and gold and red, the colours of the imperial house, spent a few days watching the Levanya and his movements, then barred his path as he walked the palace gardens. When she didn't move aside and kow-tow like everyone else, his Moonguard tried to shove her out of the way. Myla danced out of reach, drew her swords, and settled into guard.

"I have words for the Levanya," she said.

Six Moonguard, armoured and skilled, probably thought they could take her. They were probably right, but she wasn't about to back down. Sword-monks never did. The Levanya looked on. Furrowed brow, thick eyebrows like knives, eyes that bored into whatever caught his attention. He might be ancient, but he still had fire in him. She met those eyes and waited to see what would happen. She thought she saw him swear quietly under his breath.

"Hold!" he sighed. "Sheathe your swords. All of you." He sounded more bored than alarmed. Not even interested. Myla waited for the Moonguard to go first, then slid her own swords into the sheaths across her back.

"I don't like sword-monks," said the Levanya.

Myla gave him a nod, the closest she could bring herself to bow or kow-tow to the Butcher of Deephaven. "I've been to Valladrune," she said. "I know the truth. I'll be at the peak of Talsin's spire at sunset, if you have anything to say before the Regent hears it."

She wasn't sure what reaction she'd expected. Alarm? Anger? Fear? Rage and bluster? But there was none of that. No reaction at all.

"I told my grandniece about Valladrune years ago," he said. "By all means, bore her with old stories."

"*My* story continues into the years after she was born. It is a story of why the Wraiths came for her."

She thought she saw him flinch. "*Your* story?"

"One I will share with only one other. You or her. The choice is yours."

"Should I come alone? Bearing a bag of jewels, perhaps?"

He thought she was blackmailing him? Of course he did, because it's what *he* would have done. The Butcher of Deephaven. It was a wonder he didn't threaten to kill her, here and now, or simply order it done.

"Bring whatever makes you feel safe," she said. "I have no secrets to hide. Ponder, though, before you decide. I don't think you can say the same."

She turned her back and walked away before he could answer. If he came, it would probably be best if he *did* bring a few Moonguard. Enough to quell the temptation she'd feel to throw him off the top of the tower. Anyone who'd grown up in Deephaven knew the stories. The things he'd done.

Talsin's spire stood to the rear of the palace. Jealous of Khrozus, Talsin had wanted a tower to rival the City of Spires. What he'd got, when it was finished, barely reached a tenth the height of the white spires left by the half-gods. Even so, the Folly had used more stone than the great Southern Gatehouse and taken twice as long to build. It *was* a marvel, in its way. In the magnitude of its folly, in the ingenuity of its construction, in its height, visible throughout the city... but also in how insignificant it remained beside the spires of the half-gods.

Talsin had considered it a failure and exiled the architect. A year later, he was dead.

Myla climbed it early in the afternoon. The inside dripped faded opulence, largely untouched since Khrozus had paraded Talsin's head around the streets of Varr. There were exactly five rooms, evenly spaced up the tower shaft, where anyone making the climb might stop and rest and take refreshment. Myla was surprised to find each occupied by a handful of servants and a pair of Moonguard, as if waiting for her. They offered her water, which she accepted, and food, which she refused. So many people idly waiting with nothing to do struck her as more folly, until she understood: they were here because the Levanya was coming.

For all Talsin's disappointment, it *was* quite a view from the balcony at the top. The sky was clear, the air warm, the city spread below, out to the walls and beyond. She traced the line of the river, glinting in the sun until she lost track of it. She imagined she might see all the way to the waystation on the road to Deephaven where all this had started, had she known where to look. The place where Sulfane had sent Fings to steal a crown.

To the west, the land rose towards the Nejan hills. Further south, she fancied she could see the sun glinting from the City of Spires, then remembered that the City of Spires had gone. More hills to the northeast where the Levanya had called home, once upon a time. The Imperial Forest beyond the Torpreahn Gates. She thought she could maybe see the outline of the Raven Hills; although, obscured by the haze, perhaps she only imagined it.

When the sun reached a hand above the horizon, the Levanya emerged from the stair. Given he was old enough to be her grandfather, he looked remarkably untroubled by the climb. He gave her a nasty grin and sat carefully out of sword reach. She saw it then, as he lowered himself, the creak of the years he carried.

"Why this place, sword-monk? Did you think my age would humiliate me?"

"I fancied a place where I needn't concern myself over the possibility of hidden archers," Myla said.

"If I want you dead, you'll be dead. There's only one way out of here unless you have wings."

She stared at him. "Do *you* have wings, Levanya?"

"You can call me Lord Kyra."

"I might call you Butcher."

He snorted. "Deephaven! Yes, I heard that's where you're from. War is war, sword-monk. Lest you forget, Khrozus and I were *inside* the city. *We* were the ones besieged."

"I thought you'd bring some men with you. I confess, I wasn't prepared for how tempted I am to simply throw you over the edge."

"Then do it. I dare say I can't stop you."

Myla shook her head. "You doubtless think me young and foolish, but I have hopes that my generation will do better than yours." Tasahre's words from Deephaven echoed in her ears. *It is not your actions, Shirish, it is your lack of thought for their consequences.*

I have learned, Mistress.

The Levanya was laughing. "Kelm's Teeth, monk, do you think that makes you special? Do you think we weren't the same? I wasn't much older than you are now when Khrozus took us to war. Do you know, I even hear his voice in your words. *We'll be better than them.* And yet here we are. *Were* we better?" He got up and turned his back, leaning over the balcony, looking out across the palace and the river and the city beyond. "Do you know what comes with age? It's not *wisdom*, sword-monk. It's erosion."

He stayed with his back to her, as though inviting her to give him a good hard shove and watch him fall. After a minute, when Myla didn't move, he went back to his seat.

"My grandniece likes you. I don't. Say your piece. What do you want?"

Myla looked him in the eye. "What is she?"

There. A flicker. The Levanya was good, give him that. Decades of never letting anything show, but they failed him here. Myla sniffed the air as he answered.

"I don't know what you mean."

A lie. He knew *exactly* what she meant. Which all but answered the question she'd brought him here to ask. "Yes, you do."

He held her gaze. Said nothing.

"Who did this to her?"

"I have no idea what you're talking about." The words came through gritted teeth. Another lie, reeking of anger.

"So, you *do* know. I don't think it was you. Was it her father? Is that why you had him killed?" Everything, in that moment, seemed to slot into place.

"How dare you!"

"Do you deny it?" She sniffed the air, pointedly.

"I don't need to."

"Perhaps not. Not to *me*, anyway. Your grandniece though... Well, perhaps that's best left between the two of you. Here are the things I know, Butcher. There was a Wraith in Valladrune. Khrozus bargained with it. After the war, you betrayed it to the monks of Torpreah. It was the Wraith who destroyed Valladrune, not you and some army, though you seem content for people to believe otherwise."

"A healthy dose of being known as a vicious bastard never hurts when you lead men to war."

"With the Wraith gone, you murdered the monks. To bury the Usurper's pact forever, but you didn't dig deep enough. I know what Khrozus bought, and the price the Wraith demanded, so I know why you did what you did. You did it to protect your niece."

The Levanya had gone very still. She met his eye once more and again sniffed the air.

"Truth or not?"

He shifted to face the setting sun. "It *is* beautiful up here, sword-monk. I've never made the climb until now. I'll remember this sunset after you're dead."

"Is that why I passed so many Moonguard on the way up? It's to be swords, then? I'm quite good with those."

"You don't know anything."

"I know your grandniece has it within her to rule the Empire well."

Silence. He hadn't expected that. Good.

"I hear you killed a Wraith," he said, after a bit.

"Yes. I did."

"Do you really think she doesn't know what happened in Valladrune? What *really* happened there? I told her, long ago."

"What about the Nejans? Did you tell them? Lady Novashi? Does *she* know? Lady Lorleia of Neja was her mother, after all."

"Do you know why I despise sword-monks?"

"Because sword-monks murdered the Sad Empress. Your niece. The one you betrayed the Wraith to protect. I know the story. If it's true, it was a shameful act. That's not what we are for."

The Levanya grunted. "What *are* you for, sword-monk?"

"Here's another thing I know: the Taiytakei sorcerer from Deephaven has been dissecting dead Wraiths. I think, from the path he follows, he will find a sword-monk in his future, perhaps not long from now, although that I will leave for another. Inside each Wraith exists a parasite. A serpent. A handspan long, white and glowing like moonlight. The Taiytakei claims they are the source of the Wraiths' powers. Fragments of Fickle Lord Moon. That's *his* story, not mine. Although from what I've seen, there is truth in it."

She waited in case the Levanya had something he wanted to say, but he seemed content to watch the sunset.

"Your grandniece sent me to Valladrune because she suspects that she, too, has one inside her. She thought I'd find the answer there. She was wrong about that, but I've found it here instead. I think it was her father who did it to her. I think you found out. A little more than a year ago, perhaps? I think you're the one who had him killed, and I think that's why."

The Levanya turned slowly to face her. "Ashahn wasn't her father."

"Really?" Oddly, he seemed to be telling the truth. "Then who?"

The Levanya shook his head.

"The Sulking Prince? Don't tell me that rumour is actually *true*?"

"Do you know how Khrozus's war started?" He leaned towards her, his eyes narrowing with an old bitterness. "It begins with three ill-mannered neighbours: Khrozus, Hendrake Borolan, and Vispar of Neja, squabbling over Deephaven. Talsin encouraged it as a way of keeping them in check." He sighed. "Talsin's favourite mistress was Ygalla. If you come from Deephaven, you might know the name. She liked to bathe every morning in water perfumed with a scent shipped from Brons or Caladir or some such. One day, a careless servant broke the last urn in the Sapphire Palace. Rather than be punished for denying the emperor's lover her bath, he reported that supplies had run dry because of a dispute in Deephaven. By the next day, another urn had appeared, but not before Ygalla had bent Talsin's ears to her woe. Talsin summoned Vispar, Hendrake and Khrozus to Varr. The Borolans were in favour at the time, so Talsin ordered Khrozus surrender his claims and Vispar to give his sister to Hendrake in marriage. It was no secret Hendrake desired her, never mind that the mother of his first two sons was still warm in her grave. When Vispar protested, Talsin sent men to Neja and took her by force."

The Levanya smiled, wan and distant. "History plays strange tricks. Hendrake Borolan was a decent man. Past the brutality in the way it was done, he treated his new wife well enough. Perhaps she was even happy. A year after the wedding, Hendrake returned a portion of Deephaven's trade to Khrozus as a peace offering; and that, perhaps, should have been the end of it. But Khrozus and Vispar had their pride. Talsin had done both a grievous wrong, and all for a drop of perfume. The rest you know. The feud grew from words to war. When Khrozus took the throne, Vispar summoned his sister back to Neja and Khrozus had every record of her marriage to Hendrake destroyed. He had a bit of a fondness for that. For pretending things had never happened."

The Levanya let out another long sigh. "And the point of this tedious tale, sword-monk? By the time the war started, Lady Lorleia of Neja had already given Hendrake of Tarantor a son. When she left, the son stayed behind. The Sulking Prince. Lady Novashi's half-brother. My niece's secret lover."

Myla took a sharp breath. "Lady Lorleia and Lord Hendrake had a son? That's two of the warlock's bloodlines! And that son was Arianne Lemir's...? The Regent is their daughter? But that makes three! Three of the warlock's bloodlines! They came together despite you."

The Levanya nodded. "I wonder, sometimes, if the Wraith of Valladrune already knew the future. Whether it had a hand in Talsin's decision. So now you know it all, sword-monk. My grandniece. Our Princess-Regent. The Wraith of Valladrune got what it wanted. Well, almost. Just as well it's dead." He bared his teeth. "And yes. It *was* Ashahn who made her what she is."

"And for that, you had him killed?"

"He did it a very long time ago. I'll never understand his reasons." He gave her a look that was almost sad. "You know I can't let you leave here."

Myla shook her head. "It doesn't matter. The Wraiths already know everything."

"Yes. They almost certainly do."

"Butcher, you miss the point. Even if you silence me, she *will* find the truth. She's almost there already. I say again: the Wraiths know. That's why they're here. They want their fucking vessel! If you don't tell her what she is, *they* will. Are you ready for that?" Myla walked slowly to stand in front of the Levanya, then crouched so their eyes were at the same level. "Look at me, Butcher."

He met her eye, and what she saw was defiance, and also pain and grief and defeat.

"Would you sacrifice your life for her? For Katleina? For your niece's daughter?"

"Without question, if I saw purpose to it."

Myla sniffed. Truth. Good. She stepped away. "She is a sorceress without peer. She's a half-god whose life has been sculpted by grief. She scares me. I suspect she scares you, too. It would be so very easy for her to become terrible. Many would say that was enough to put her down. But I disagree. If you see no other way but blood between us, then by all means bring on your swords, but I brought you here to reach an understanding, you and I. We cannot hide from her what she is, and thus what she will become. She will discover it for herself soon enough. If she crashes into your head with fangs and fury and tugs apart everything you know, what then?"

"Or yours, sword-monk." The Levanya chuckled, although without humour. "Should I throw myself from this tower and take my secrets with me? Will you be joining me?"

Myla gave an exasperated growl. "It wouldn't matter even if we did! No. We walk away from here, both of us. I will give her the truth of her nature as kindly as I can. The rest of your secrets I will keep. For now, let her believe the Torpreahns killed her father, or maybe the Wraiths. One day, when she's ready, you will tell her the truth of what you did and why. She may forgive you, she may not, but that's the burden you bear." Myla understood all too well how difficult that could be. "Until then, you see she that doesn't become a monster. And I will do the same."

"That's it?"

"No small task, Butcher, to heal the wounds that you and Khrozus made. But if you can guide her to magnificent compassion over ruinous vengeance, maybe you were worth something after all."

"And you?"

Myla stood. "I will watch from afar." She smiled and patted her belly. "I *do* have other matters to attend to."

51
The Book of Endings

The Cathedral of Light. The place where Seth's world had gone wrong. The obvious entrances had Sunguard on watch, even at night. The less obvious were mostly locked. But a place this size never went fully to sleep, and Seth knew all about the night-duties assigned to shamed novices who'd attracted the ire of some petty Lightbringer.

Example: the run to the bakeries. Two novices sent out in the small hours every morning so the Lightbringers and the Sunbrights could eat fresh bread before Dawn Prayer. Sure enough, long before the first glimmer of daylight, a pair of novices emerged from the kitchen gate: a young man and a young woman pushing an empty handcart, more interested in each other than in anything around them. They didn't notice Seth until he stepped in front them.

"I got a letter," he said. "For the Dawncaller from Torpreah."

They looked at him like he was mad. He meandered closer, swaying like he was drunk. "Take it! Take it!" He sidestepped the man, grabbed the woman, and pressed the sigil against her hand. As she yelped and jumped away, he slapped a second into the other novice's face.

"Be still, be quiet, take no action to raise any alarm!" he snapped.

They both froze.

"Follow me." He led them into the darkness of an alley. "The keys to the kitchen door," he said. "Give them to me."

The woman handed over the keys hanging from a rope knotted at her waist.

"Do you like him?" Seth asked, jerking his head at the other novice. "Tell me!"

"Yes," she said.

"And you." To the other novice now. "Do you like her?"

"Yes. I do."

Seth handed the woman a couple of coins. Silver half-moons, which would be more than enough. "The *Rose*. You know it?"

The woman nodded.

"Go there. Both of you. One coin will get you a room for the day. Do that. Stay in it all day. Do what you like. Eat, drink, fuck, sleep, I don't care, but you don't leave that room until after sunset. When it's dark, go to the Imperial Docks and take a barge towards Tzeroth. Once you're out of the city, enjoy the next sunrise together."

A day and a night for his sigils to hold them. The sunrise they shared would set them free. By then, he'd be long gone.

I'm not a monster.

He pointed to the man. "Give me your robe. Wear my clothes."

The man disrobed. Seth undressed. They swapped clothes and Seth sent them on their way. He hoped they'd be happy together. Thought, from the way they'd been looking at each other, they probably would. Whatever happened after tomorrow's sunrise would be in their own hands.

Not a monster.

He left the handcart, made his way to the kitchen gate, and let himself in. He avoided the kitchens themselves, leery of going back to the exact place they'd caught him, close to a year ago and at almost the same time of day. The morning he'd brought a dead rat back to life.

Getting superstitious, are we?

He shook the thought away. Too much of Fings in an idea like that.

He scurried down a side passage, one the novices would use in a couple of hours, bringing breakfast to the Sunbrights and Dawncallers in the High Refectory. Halfway along, he darted into a cramped spiral stair that took him up and out into the kitchen gardens.

None of the other novices even knew this was here...

He hurried past the shed where the garden tools were kept, his favourite spot for a bit of malingering back in the day. Checked the sky, the position of the Moon and stars. He had a good hour before the cathedral came to life, preparing itself for Dawn Prayer.

The Chapel Gate, which led into the garden, would be closed but not locked. From there, a quick run up the stairs would get him to the Hall of Penitence where the Sunherald and the Sunherald-Martial and the Dawncallers had their rooms. There would be Sunguard on watch, who'd forget they ever saw him. He was fucked if he ran into any sword-monks, but sword-monks weren't usually up at night unless they were hunting.

The Chapel Gate swung open. Seth darted into the tool shack as two men emerged into the night. He waited, sigils ready, but they hadn't seen him. They stopped outside. One lit a pipe. The Commander of the Sunguard. The other... Seth had no idea. Some Dawncaller? Their talk was politics, the progress of the war, or lack of it. They'd been looking forward to a new Regent for the Empire: one who worshipped the Sun, wasn't a mage, was a bit older and, well, not to put too fine a point on it, a bit more male. All very well, except the Torpreahns had apparently run into difficulty in the Raven Hills. With the Regent's victory at Neja, it was beginning to look like their revolution wasn't going to happen.

In the memories of more senior priests, Seth supposed, Khrozus' massacre of the Sun-priests after he'd seized Varr probably loomed rather large right now.

The two men went their separate ways. Seth wrote more sigils. Yes, he could sign them in the air, but slapping a bit of paper on someone felt more certain. He slipped out. The Chapel Gate, and then two narrow flights of stairs spat him into the Hall of Penitence, long and wide, lit by glowing strips of Sunsteel set into the walls. Two bored Sunguard eyed him. Seth tried to look humble as he approached. They couldn't be expected to remember *every* novice, but a novice with a ruined face and one blind eye? He didn't fancy taking any chances, so he held out a strip of paper, waving it about, and tried to sound a bit slow and stupid.

"I have an urgent message for the Sunherald-Martial."

As the first Sunguard snatched it and the sigil on the paper flared, Seth signed another in the air and threw it at the second. "Be still! Be quiet! Protect me! Both of you."

He waited for a tense second, but no. No cries of alarm or fear. No warning shout of *warlock! Warlock!* No noises from the rooms around him, no puffy-eyed Dawncallers coming to the door, fresh from sleep, asking what all the fuss was about.

They're going to remember you when that sigil burns off.

"Show me the Sunherald-Martial's room!" Seth tried to recall where everything was up here and found he couldn't. Novices rarely penetrated the Hall of Penitence.

Hard face to forget, yours.

The Sunguard pointed to a door.

How long, do you think, before that sword-monk from Deephaven gets to hear?

Didn't matter. He was going change the world. "Stay here. You never saw me."

The Sunherald-Martial's door wasn't locked. Why would it be, in a place like this, with soldiers keeping watch in the hall outside? Seth marched into the Sunherald's bedroom, shook him awake, gave the old man a moment to focus, to grasp what was happening, then slapped a sigil on his thinning hair.

"Be quiet, be still, do as you're told!" A pause. "Do you remember me? It might be hard. Look through the scars. I didn't have them before."

The old Sunherald stared. His eyes went wide.

"Ah. You *do* remember? Nod if you wish to say yes."

A nod.

"Whisper my name."

"Novice Seth."

"Warlock Seth, now, and none of what I've done would

have happened if you'd simply told us the truth. A month after Midwinter, your sword-monks caught me. Probably made a few waves. You remember it?"

Another nod.

"Bet it upset a few people when I didn't *stay* caught, eh?" Seth cocked his head and bared his teeth. "Your monks found where I was hiding in the Undercity. There were things there that belonged to me. They would have brought them to you. I'm looking for a book." He described Sulfane's book as best he could remember. "It was written in a cypher. Do you know the one I mean?"

A nod.

"Where is it?"

A shake of the head. Seth frowned. Refusing to answer? That wasn't supposed to be how this worked.

"Listen, you spiteful old man. I need it to make everything right. For there to have been some point to all of this. Where it is? Speak!"

"Torpreah."

"*What?*"

"We sent it to Torpreah," said the Sunherald again.

"*Where* in Torpreah?" Someone was taking the piss. From Varr to Deephaven looking for a warlock who wasn't there. Deephaven to Valladrune looking for the book only to find it had been in Varr all along, in his fucking hands. And now it was back in Torpreah, the place he'd just left?

"The Forbidden Archives."

All these years since he'd read Sivingathm's *Heresies*. All the years of never quite believing that the Book of Endings existed at all, only to discover he'd had it in his hands and let it go?

"Torpreah," he murmured. *Fine. Back the way I came, then.* At least it would be easier this time.

Two forgetful Sunguard. Two novices on their way to Tzeroth. A Sunherald bent to your will. All with sigil marks.

He looked at the Sunherald.

This one knows you. Let him live and they'll have a name for their warlock.

The Sunherald who'd kicked him down the temple steps. Physically, literally, kicked him down the steps while two Sunguard made sure Seth didn't resist.

Right. Like that sword-monk from Deephaven couldn't put two and two together on her own?

This one knows what you're looking for. And where you're going.

In his hand, Seth saw he was already holding the sigil he needed. He pressed it against the old Sunherald's skin.

"Die," he said, and the Sunherald died.

I had to do that.

Except... well, he *could* have simply made the old Sunherald forget.

Petty revenge, was it?

Because you are *a monster.*

The Sunherald-Martial had cut him off from the Light.

You could have made him forget. But you didn't.

Go away! He stood over the dead Sunherald. The Sunguard outside had seen his face but that didn't matter. On his way out, he'd make them forget he was ever there. The two novices pushing the handcart might not come back to Varr at all.

There are sword-monks here.

At the first sign of a sigil mark, the hunt would begin. The next time he saw Myla, she'd be swords-drawn the moment they locked eyes. Fings? Fings was never going to forgive him, not after this...

Prophet of the Destroyer. Herald of the Black Moon.

One tiny mistake, that was all it had taken...

One?

If he could prove everything that happened in Valladrune...

One of the many times you disobeyed your teachers?

If he could prove that old Khrozus had made a pact with a Wraith...

The time you betrayed Myla and Brick and Topher because it was worth getting them killed if Blackhand died as well?

...that all of this, the destruction of Deephaven, that everything that had happened lay at the door of the Sapphire Throne?

The time you murdered Lightbringer Suaresh and brought him back as a Dead Man, which we both know is probably what you did?

Wouldn't the Path of the Sun forgive him if he gave them that? *The priest they say you set on fire in Deephaven? Something else?*

No. Not after this. After this, the sword-monks would never *ever* let him go.

Which one, Seth, which one, tiny, little mistake?

Shut up! Shut up! Shut up!

He could still make it right. With the book, he could undo it all. The Forbidden Archives? Yes, he'd heard of them, but that was about as far as it went. Torpreah? Well, he knew how to get to Torpreah...

With a sigh, he brought the dead Sunherald back as a Dead Man. "I need you to write two letters. I need you to sign and seal them." He went out to the Hall of Penitence, instructed the Sunguard that the Sunherald-Martial was not to be disturbed, then made them forget they'd ever seen him. He told the Sunherald what to write. When it was done, he told the Sunherald-Martial to dress, that he had an errand to run, of the utmost urgency, across the river. Coincidentally, an errand that required aid from the two Sunguard from the hall outside and a novice, which was how Seth got out of the Cathedral. While the Sunherald and his two Sunguard hurried south, Seth slipped away. He didn't really want to be there when the Sunherald-Martial of Varr inexplicably jumped into the water halfway across and drowned, along with his Sunguard escort.

No bodies. No sigil-marks. It wasn't the best plan, but no one was pointing and shouting and waving swords at him come mid-morning as he reached the Circus of Dead Emperors. He was exhausted, dressed as a novice, had no money, carried nothing except a few strips of paper and a stick of charcoal.

Right back where he started, before he fell from grace.

INTERLUDE
The Princess and the Monk

"What am I?" The Regent stared into a mirror. She'd been doing that a lot, these last few days. "Who am I?"

What the answer *ought* to have been was "a success." A respected and admired ruler of a vast empire who'd simultaneously faced down both an invasion of sorcerers and Dead Men *and* an uprising by the entire cohort of southern provinces. A peerless sorceress who'd fought Wraiths and beaten them. A skilled diplomat who'd exploited the weaknesses of her southern enemies to reach a peace without bloodshed, on terms to her advantage. She'd done it fairly, too. No climbing into their thoughts. Well... maybe a little.

That's what it *ought* to have been.

Who am I? Katleina Nevisha Falandawn. Empress in all but name.

What am I? A trophy.

Well... She'd done that to herself, hadn't she? The cost of not having bloody war streak across the south. The Torpreahn prince she'd agreed to marry wasn't as awful as she'd feared. Given time and the right circumstances, might she even get to like him? In a world where a mage and a sword-monk could be lovers, perhaps a Princess of the north and a Prince of the south *could* find a way to get along that didn't involve her having to climb into his head and tell him what to think. Could they even become friends? If they could, wouldn't *that* be a surprise for everyone.

Which was why, to universal horror, she'd decided to winter

in Torpreah. It was the practical choice. The Levanya would watch the northern half of the empire as he always did. Novi would soothe ruffled Nejan feathers while investing them in the reconstruction of Deephaven. *Her* duty, like it or not, was here in Torpreah. To either heal the wounds her grandfather had dealt a generation before she was born, or else finish the job and crush them into the ground, which in many ways would have been the easier path.

The wedding negotiations were dragging. The Torpreahns wanted a double betrothal. Her to one of their princes, a child princess to her little brother, Ashahn the Second. The Torpreahns seemed to think that whoever she chose for herself would become the new Regent of the Empire. It was an illusion she was happy for them to keep, at least for a while, but an illusion was all it would ever be. She'd probably let her new consort be Overlord of Varr, although on a very short leash and with the Levanya holding the other end. She had no idea which Torpreahn princess to give to her little brother. Their pale faces all looked the same.

News filtered southward. In Deephaven, the Dead Men left by the Wraiths weren't behaving the way Dead Men were supposed to. Unexpectedly resilient to the Sun, many seemed to be trying to return to their former lives. They remembered who they'd been and kept acting as though they were still alive. She read Novi's reports and sent word back, telling the Red Witch to stop hunting and burning and let the Dead Men build instead. See what happened. Stop them if they were trouble, but otherwise step back and observe.

Other things. The Taiytakei sorcerer from Deephaven wanted to create an institute of learning to study the Wraiths. She thought she might allow it, if only to see what happened, but not in Varr. That was too near, and the Taiytakei mage was too... unsettling. Khrozir, she decided. Out of sight but close enough to be in easy reach. A place where she could keep an eye on him.

A footnote in one of the reports from the Levanya: the sword-monks of Varr were hunting a warlock who'd killed the Sunherald-Martial. The Levanya's opinion was that the priests deserved everything they got. Katleina Nevisha Falandawn, sorceress, half-god, trophy-Empress, whatever she was, was inclined to agree. Despite that, she told him to lend the Sapphire Throne to their hunt. She'd grown up believing sword-monks had murdered her mother, Novi's mother too. She had no reason to believe the story false; but she'd also seen them fight Wraiths. They'd earned her respect, however grudgingly given. She'd let them have that.

"What am I?"

Lonely, that's what. She cherished the feeling, though, because it was the sort of feeling that belonged to a young woman, not much more than a girl, who'd lost many of those closest to her. It wasn't a feeling that belonged to a thousand year-old half-god, even if that *was* a part of what she was.

She was sure by now.

The sword-monk arrived in Torpreah as winter settled on the north. They met in the Cathedral of Light, sitting together beside the bones of old Saint Kelm. The Regent chose it because she thought the monk would be pleased and because she knew it would annoy the Torpreahn priests to host her Moonguard. Little more than a month in Torpreah and three people had already tried to murder her. She'd had a good long look at the memories of the last, before he'd died. His paymaster was a Dawncaller, like the one the Levanya had rooted out in Varr, the one behind the theft of her father's crown and very possibly his murder.

She let the monk come wearing her swords. The Moonguard howled at that but there was no danger. She flicked a glance at the monk's swollen belly. "Are you close?"

"Another few weeks."

"I'm told that one of Saint Kelm's teeth went missing," the Regent said, patting the bones beside her. "It was considered quite a bad omen for the armies marching against me."

The monk bit her lip and looked somewhere between abashed and annoyed and not in the least surprised. She leaned close to whisper; as she did, she pressed something small and hard into the Regent's hand. Something about the size and shape of a tooth.

"I'm sure you can find a way to return this before you leave. Let your unwelcome visit become an even more unwelcome miracle."

The two shared a secret smile. "I hear some priests were murdered in their Forbidden Archives last week," said the Regent. "I suppose they could do with a good omen."

They exchanged pleasantries a while longer, but the monk obviously had something on her mind.

"Well. You came here for a reason."

She listened to the story of Valladrune, of her grandfather's bargain with the Wraith and of what the Levanya had done after the war, all of which she knew because the Levanya had already told her, although it was nice to hear the story from different lips.

"All before I was born. Am I a Wraith?"

The monk nodded.

"Who made me this way?"

"It wasn't your great-uncle, that much I know. Dislike him as I do, his loyalty to you is beyond question." A sigh and a shake of the head. "I think it happened long ago. Most who might have had the opportunity are beyond my reach."

"Perhaps not mine?"

"I wouldn't know. Of the people who surround you now, none are guilty. But... though you may consider it misguided, foolish, even dangerous... I wonder if it was meant as a gift, not a curse. It can be either, I think." The monk shrugged. "Depends on what you do with it."

A gift? She'd never considered that. Yet with that thought, others slotted into place. Her father's murder. The stories of warlock papers among his possessions. Although... her father had never been one for gifts without purpose. Say one thing of Emperor Ashahn the First, say he always thought into the future. If it *was* a gift, he'd meant for her to do something with it.

She cast a glance at the monk's swollen belly. "May I?" When the monk nodded, the Regent put her hand on the monk's silk robe. She felt the taught skin underneath. And movement. Something quite special. "Do you have a name for her?"

"Her?"

"Or him."

"I want to see him first." The monk smiled. "Or her."

The Regent's hand stayed where it was. "So, I am a Wraith. Doesn't that mean you should be trying to put an end to me?"

"As if I could!" The monk laughed and put her hand over the Regent's own. Touching her skin. Anyone else, the Moonguard would have put an arrow through her for that. "Rule with courage, with compassion and with honesty, and I will stand for you, always. Rule otherwise and I will not. That's all there is to say. Although if you start raising armies of Dead Men, you and I *will* have a fucking problem."

The Regent didn't know what to say. No one spoke to her like that. No one. Never.

"Our deeds define us, Highness. Nothing more and nothing less. Something my sword-mistress used to say." The monk squeezed the Regent's hand, then let it go.

"Not everyone will agree with you there."

"Jealous arseholes will be jealous arseholes. Fuck 'em, I say."

The monk rose and left. She didn't bother waiting to be dismissed. The Regent watched her go, one thought lingering louder than all the others.

If it was a gift, he meant for me to do something with it.

Quietly, without fuss, she stopped time while she replaced Kelm's missing tooth. She wouldn't say anything, she decided. Let the priests discover the miracle for themselves.

PART SIX
The Splinterer of Worlds

Truth wins few friends but loses none. Deceit wins many but loses all.
– Myla

52
SETH

It was a long way to Torpreah, with the small matter of at least one large army and possibly an entire war in the way. Fortunately, Seth didn't need to worry about that. The Wraith trapped in its stone opened a half-god gate and took him straight to Torpreah. This turned out to be a mistake: Seth emerged into a familiar-looking half-god vault with all the usual accoutrements, but with a few *un*usual ones, too. The most obvious was the metal cage wrapped around the exit arch, wedged in place by several blocks of stone far too large for Seth to ever shift. There was no way he was getting through the bars. Even if he did...

"Oh," he said, staring at the two sword-monks looking back at him. "Shit."

The sword-monks shouted and ran at him; fortunately, big metal cages held in place by heavy rocks cut both ways. One monk reached to throw something. Seth dived back through the gate to Varr.

"Close the door, close the fucking door!"

A knife sailed through the portal as it closed, missing him by an inch. Seth picked it up and pocketed it.

"Right, then," he said. "Have to admit, I didn't see that one coming."

For once, none of his inner voices nor the trapped Wraith had anything to say. Seth supposed they were quietly sniggering to each other behind his back.

"Right then," he said again. "The Pillar of Dusk it is."

It was long hard walk from the Pillar of Dusk to Torpreah but at least there weren't any lurking sword-monks. He wondered, as his feet complained, what had happened to his deserters. They probably hadn't escaped Valladrune, he supposed, but he rather hoped they somehow had and were on their way to Tzeroth, off to pursue the wild fantasy he'd given them of becoming a troupe of roving entertainers.

A few miles short of Torpreah, a group of Torpreahn soldiers caught up with him. Outriders of the returning army. Seth expressed his gratitude, threw a few covert sigils, and soon had them all convinced they'd found a novice priest on a pilgrimage. He entered the city, belly full, pockets jingling with money the Torpreahn soldiers mysteriously chose to share. He wondered vaguely whether he should worry about sword-monks again. Probably not. Torpreah was big enough for him to hide.

I am not a monster.

He went to Lucius's shop. Watched for a bit and then moved on. Nothing for him here, not now. He was, for the first time since he'd crossed the river Arr as a boy and washed up in the Spice Market, truly alone.

He found a rich man's house, knocked on the door, sigilled the servant who opened it, sigilled everyone else, and set about what needed to be done. A small wagon. Food for what he hoped would be a few months. He could get water from the lake. When he had all that, he crossed the Shroud of the Sun to the Isle of Light, just another pilgrim, and went looking for the Forbidden Archives. He carried his letter from the Sunherald-Martial of Varr, permission to enter the archives to study the history of the heretic Sivingathm. By now, he was dressed as a Dawncaller.

The letter got him far enough. Sigils did the rest. He walked away with the Book of Endings and returned to his rich man's house, took his gathered supplies, then set the house on fire. They'd seen his face on the Isle of Light. The sword-monk from Deephaven would know him if she ever came back this way. He needed his trail to end, and so it did.

Under the ruins by the Pillar of Dusk, down deep, he spoke to the Wraith trapped in its stone.

"Teach me," he said.

He stayed through the winter. By spring, he knew how to turn the world back the way it was meant to be. The Wraith had done the hard part: the vessel was ready. Not perfect, but adequate. All Seth had to do was wander off with the vessel to the edge of the Abyss at the heart of the world and then write two sigils. The first to release the Splinterer of Worlds from his prison. The second to kill a half-god. The Destroyer of Worlds would be ended, the world restored, the Splintering undone, and *he* would have made it happen. He'd be a hero. The Path of the Sun might fall, devoid of purpose, or it might make him a saint. He wasn't sure he cared anymore.

A sigil to free the half-god from its prison.

A vessel to hold him.

A sigil to destroy a half-god.

The book could give him the sigils. The Wraith could take him to the Abyss. It didn't particularly want to, given what Seth had in mind, but Seth wasn't planning on giving it a choice.

It all sounded almost... easy.

Well... *Sort* of easy. There *was* the small matter of stealing the Imperial Regent and taking her to said Abyss. The Wraith was all for using sigils, murdering people left and right and doing it by force; but Seth had paid attention to Myla's words in the Undercity and didn't think the Wraith's plan was going to work. Attempting to sigil someone like that into compliance would, he rather suspected, be a quick path to an unpleasant end.

"What we need," he mused to the Wraith, "is for her to think it's all *her* idea. Let her think *she's* going to destroy him."

He gave this some more thought. Around Midwinter, he reckoned he knew how. He had the Wraith show him how to make a container for his memories, like Saffran Kuy's orb. Seth put all his own memories inside it, nice and safe, then used a sigil to get himself a servant in Torpreah. He made a charm, carved with a sigil of protection. Wrote a letter and handed it to his tame servant along with the Book of Endings, the charm, and the stone of his memories. Told the servant to return them to him at the Pillar of Dusk in a twelvenight. That done, he made himself forget the servant, the package, and everything he'd said.

A sigil to free the half-god from its prison.

A sigil to restore his memories.

A sigil to destroy a half-god.

When the servant had gone, he started cutting at memories inside his head, and never mind how he'd sworn he'd never do this to himself again. By the time he was done, what he remembered was almost, but not quite, the truth. Everything he'd done in Varr and in Torpreah. How he'd uncovered the truth of Valladrune. How he'd sought out the Wraith in a desperate attempt to put everything right. How he'd forced it to teach him sigils not only to free the Splinterer of Worlds from his prison and tether it, but also how to destroy it. The only difference would be which sigil was which.

A sigil to free The Splinterer of Worlds from its prison.

A sigil to tether him.

A sigil to destroy him.

When he was ready, he told the Wraith to look inside his head and roam his memories. The Regent, if Myla was right, would do the same. What she saw had to convince her. When the Wraith was satisfied, Seth made himself forget *that*, too. There *was* a moment when Seth found himself suspicious of the Wraith's cooperation, what with the end *he* had in mind being exactly opposed to the one the Wraith had died to protect. But the Wraith was bound to him and subject to his will. It had helped, and Seth soon forgot his doubts.

He was a bit surprised when some strange fellow he'd never seen before turned up at the Pillar of Dusk with a letter and a package for him. The letter – written by his own hand, apparently – told him what to do. It was full of surprises, not least of which was how clever he'd turned out to be.

After reading it, he burned it, as it told him to.

The Wraith opened a gate. Seth returned to Varr, taking the

package. He wasn't sure what the package *was*, but the letter's instructions had been precise. He settled somewhere quiet, paid handsomely to be left alone, and delivered his package to the *Unruly Pig* with a message asking Fings to take care of it; that in a month or so, all being well, Seth would claim them, that he was sorry for everything he'd done.

He *was* sorry. He hoped, once everything was settled, Fings would understand.

Then he made himself forget all that, too.

Myla next. He'd tell her everything. Convince her to take him to the Regent with what he knew. Which she would, however reluctantly, because what he was offering was the chance to destroy the greatest Wraith of all. With the Splinterer of Worlds forever lost, the other Wraiths would have no use for their Vessel. They might leave her alone.

A sigil to free the half-god from its prison.

A sigil to bind The Splinterer of Worlds to himself.

A sigil for the Regent to use, to destroy the half-god trapped inside him.

There *was* a niggling voice. Something he'd heard once. Something about a Herald of the Black Moon. The Splinterer of Worlds had been given many names. Black Moon was one. Seth wasn't sure why it bothered him. He couldn't place it. Something to do with something he couldn't remember.

Myla wasn't in Varr. He tried looking for Orien, but the fire-mage wasn't in Varr either. For a while, Seth wasn't sure what to do about that; but a few weeks of poking around dug up the Taiytakei popinjay, off in Khrozir, away from any priests and sword-monks, happily dissecting Wraiths killed at the battle of Neja.

The popinjay didn't recognise him at first; when he did, he seemed surprised to find Seth still alive.

"A lot of people want you dead," he said.

"I think they probably want *you* dead too," said Seth. "Anyway, long story short: the Wraiths want to free the Splinterer of Worlds.

Failing this time just means they'll try again a few generations from now. I'll be dead, but I'm thinking *you* won't. If they succeed, we'll have another war. Since the first literally shattered creation, I'm thinking you might find this quite inconvenient. So, help me out here. Get me to the Regent. Tell her I have a way to end this once and for all."

Then he sigilled the popinjay. Possibly it wasn't necessary, but he *did* rather enjoy it. Payback for their visit to the House of Cats and Gulls.

Sometimes, in the small hours of the darkness, he doubted. He knew the sigil to end the Black Moon's imprisonment. He knew the sigil to bind the Black Moon to himself. He knew the sigil to destroy the Black Moon forever. In doing these things, he'd likely die before he even knew if he'd managed to save the world. And it struck him as odd, in those moments, that he was willing to make such a sacrifice. And why, in those moments, did he call the half-god Black Moon?

Each time those moments came, Seth made himself forget. Then he went back to sleep.

Eventually, the Regent came to Khrozir. Seth told his story. She didn't believe it. Seth wasn't surprised – *he* wouldn't have believed it either. He *was* surprised – and horrified – when she crashed into his head, froze him to the spot, and riffled through his memories from start to finish.

Didn't matter. He was telling the truth. He *did* know a way to destroy the Black Moon forever, one that would cost her nothing, him everything. He had much to repent. He wanted to make things right. This, for him, was redemption.

A sigil to free the half-god from its prison.

A sigil to bind The Splinterer of Worlds.

A sigil to destroy the half-god trapped inside.

As the Regent tore through his memories over and over, Seth caught a whiff of an errant escaping thought. *This is why he did it. This is what I'm for.*

He had no idea what to make of that.

53
Myla

After telling the Princess-Regent what she was and why, Myla retreated to the monastery she'd visited on her way to Valladrune. The monks welcomed her. They even tolerated Orien. When she gave birth to their baby girl, Orien was holding her hand and trying not to throw up. Lucius looked equally ill. To Myla's surprise, he'd come with their mother, now a Holy Celebrant. Of the three, her mother was the useful one. Orien and her brother, it turned out, weren't very good around so much blood.

They argued over names. Orien wanted to call their daughter Katleina. Myla toyed with Tasahre. Orien countered with Novashi. Myla told him not to be a fucking idiot.

They settled on Shirisoraya. For Myla, it was a way to let her sister know that she was still sorry for what had happened in Deephaven.

"She'll come around," Lucius said. Myla supposed yes, she probably would, although it might take a couple of decades, stubbornness being something of a family trait.

A few days after Shirisoraya was born, the Princess-Regent came. No one saw her enter the monastery, there was no warning, no announcement, no grand entrance. She appeared alone and suddenly, as if out of thin air. It took a lot of shouting from Orien and pointing at the Regent's Sunsteel circlet before anyone else even understood who she was. When they did, the monks offered a collective shrug. If a Princess-Regent wanted to be treated like a

Princess-Regent, she could arrive like one. If she didn't, she'd be treated like any other guest. Fed and watered and made welcome, nothing much more.

The Regent stayed long enough to sit with Myla and watch the sun set over the Thimble Hills.

"Come back to Varr," she said. "In the spring, I'll be marrying a Torpreahn prince. I'd like you to be there. And then I'd like you to stay."

"We both know you don't need a bodyguard."

"Not for that."

"Then why?" asked Myla, who'd imagined spending most of the rest of her life quietly being a mother and, maybe one day, a teacher – and definitely *not* getting involved in anything to do with Wraiths or the politics of the Imperial Court. Her agreement with the Levanya was to stay away and watch from afar.

"I was going to go back to Deephaven," she said, when the Regent didn't reply. "It feels right. The city was my home." Orien's mistress was there, organising the rebuilding of the city with its new Necropolis full of Dead Men who weren't behaving the way Dead Men were supposed to. It seemed a fitting place for the three of them to make their home.

"Deephaven will do," the Regent said, after a long silence of staring at the horizon. "But Varr first. I'd like you to meet my new prince."

"Why?" asked Myla again.

"I was hoping you might tell me what to do with him."

Myla snorted. "As if *I'd* know."

"My mother died when I was very young. Lady Novashi has enough to deal with in Neja and Deephaven. I am surrounded by men. There are certain matters in which I do not think I wish to seek their advice."

It took Myla a moment to understand. When she did, she snorted. "Yes. Well. I'm not the most... experienced."

The Regent raised an eyebrow. "Really? *I* remember being inside your head in the Kaveneth. Quite eye-opening. Effective, too, at the time, but it bites you now. Besides, can you imagine me asking advice from my uncle for my wedding night?"

Myla smirked, trying to imagine the Levanya's face. "*That* I'd like to see."

When the Regent didn't reply, Myla took her hand. She'd seen this woman face down Wraiths, knew the power she held, arch-sorceress and ruler of an Empire, at least for another decade until her brother came of age. In her time, she would be either terrible or magnificent. One or the other. Which often made it hard to see through to what lay beneath: a girl, too young for the weight she carried, lonely and a little scared.

"I'll come," Myla said. "And I'll stay as long as you need. But... when it comes to your prince, I really think you'd do better to take advice from a priestess of the Moon." She tried not to think about the conversation she'd have with Orien, later, who'd doubtless be desperate to know everything the Regent had said. *Well, she basically came all this way for sex tips.* She could see his face perfectly. Bright crimson as his thoughts ran in all directions at once, some of which they probably shouldn't.

Probably best not mention it.

"Thank you," said the Regent.

She left after sunset, as quietly as she'd come.

Tasahre, too, came without warning, although at least she had the decency not to appear out of thin air. Their words were strained. The sword-mistress told Myla how Seth had entered the Cathedral of Light in Varr and murdered the Sunherald-Martial. Myla didn't want to believe it was true; but by the time Tasahre was done, she didn't have much choice. Tasahre was certain that Seth had returned to Torpreah and stolen a book from the Forbidden Archives. She wanted to know whether Myla knew what book, and why, and where Seth might be, and what he'd said to her in Valladrune that had been worth keeping him alive. Myla told her about the dead Wraith and its intent to release the Splinterer of Worlds to forge the world anew. She didn't say how.

"There is more," Tasahre said, when Myla was done.

"There is. But they are not my secrets to share."

Tasahre didn't like that. "I will find him. When I do, I will get the truth. Then I will end him."

"I thought he could be saved."

"You were wrong."

Myla bowed her head. "I don't like to give up on people."

Tasahre reached a finger to Shirisoraya, who reached back to tug on it, which earned a rare smile from the sword-mistress. "Mothers make poor sword-monks," she said.

"Really? Why?"

"You will discover fears and doubts for which I could never prepare you. The fear of losing something more valuable than everything in which you believe." She looked Myla in the eye. "Is the secret you guard really worth the lives he's taken since you let him go?"

"That remains to be seen." Which was as honest an answer as she could give.

Tasahre left without saying goodbye. Her words lingered. They worked on Myla in the months that followed, all through the journey back to Varr. They reminded her that the burden she'd placed on the Levanya was also her own. She'd placed her trust in the ideal that there was decency in everyone. She'd given that trust to Seth and, apparently, she'd been wrong. She'd given it to the Regent, too. Well, then, she would learn from her mistake and see it through. Deephaven would have to wait.

The Imperial wedding was as tedious as expected. She found herself decked again in silk sword-monk robes, pale yellow with a red and white and gold-edged collar that left her with the uncomfortable sense of being on a leash. She understood she was being used. A sword-monk at the Regent's side was a powerful symbol, a visible declaration that the Path of the Sun stood with the Sapphire Throne. There were no other sword-monks, but there *were* priests, guests for the wedding, who made no secret of their disapproval. A Moon-Witch sorceress as Regent to the throne, granddaughter of the man who'd once butchered half the priests in Varr? They didn't like it.

When the new Sunherald-Martial as good as ordered her to leave, Myla politely refused. He could demand the return of her swords, could strip her of her privileges as a sword-monk, but she'd walk where she wished. It seemed he didn't know that the warlock who'd killed his predecessor had been someone she'd once called a friend. At a guess, she had Tasahre to thank for that.

She settled in a corner to watch Orien, in his element. He'd told her the truth of Neja, eventually. A long, painful confession whose words hadn't come easily. The despair he'd felt, the worthlessness the Wraith had put inside him. How it was still there, never as strong but never gone. She'd felt that same despair in Deephaven, if only for a second before Soraya had somehow broken the Wraith's spell.

"What do you think of him?" the Regent asked, sidling up beside her and nodding at the Torpreahn Prince who would, after tomorrow, sit to the left of the Sapphire Throne, while the Regent sat in Khrozus' chair. The Regent had – and for this Myla gave thanks to every god she knew – taken Myla's advice and spoken to a Moon Priestess about her wedding night.

"I don't." Myla had barely spoken to the man.

"Oh, do better!"

She knew his name, but it didn't mean anything. Watching him, she saw what she expected. He was a southern prince. A dashing flair to him, a bit of charm, the inevitable arrogance and conceit, but weren't they all like that? "You'll have to teach him to be honest with you, and yourself to be honest with him. Then, perhaps, one day, you'll have a partner you can trust." It didn't seem a likely lesson for either of them to learn.

"That will be a touch easier when the Torpreahns stop trying to murder me. Four attempts now, since they killed my father. Five if you count marching an army to seize my throne. Should I count that?"

"It *does* seem a little rude." The Regent still didn't know that the late Emperor wasn't her real father, then. Probably for the best.

"What?" The Regent must have seen how her thoughts had wandered.

"Well, you *could* start with that, I suppose. A quiet word, ask him to ask his friends to stop trying to poison and stab you, something like that? Slide into his head and find out his secret desires. Just don't let him know you're doing it. Or failing that, threaten to make his cock wither and fall off if it happens again and make sure he believes it. *That* would probably work."

"Oh, *that's* allowed, is it?"

"In this case, you get a free pass."

"Just armies of the dead I'm not allowed, is it?"

Myla smirked. "You'll need to teach him more than he thinks he needs to learn. Men are like that. The trick is to make him want it. And to remember that respect is better than fear, albeit harder. It's like breaking in a horse, really."

The Regent stifled a snort. "After we're done with this distraction, you and I need to talk about the future."

She moved away before Myla could ask what she meant.

54
Fiпgs

Fings spent the winter in Varr generally quite happy. Which was odd and unexpected, given how everything since he'd left for Deephaven had been a bit shit, the whole business with Levvi and then Seth being... well, Seth. In his heart of hearts, he knew Seth had always been that way. Couldn't have said when the boy he'd once met and given a peach on the temple steps had turned bad. When he thought about it, had it always been there, right from the start?

Not turned *bad*, exactly... Something else. Broken? Fings wasn't sure.

Seth was gone. Fings tried looking, in a quiet sort of way, before the winter Sulk settled in. A part of him was sad when he turned up nothing. Another part wasn't. Maybe it was better this way. Wherever Seth was, whatever he was doing, it was probably best not to know.

He spent his days in the *Unruly Pig*. A bit of cleaning, a bit of tidying, a bit of serving drinks, running errands, that sort of thing. Like it had been in the days of Blackhand, except without the organised violence and occasional murdering. No one was quite sure exactly who *owned* the *Pig* these days, but no one seemed inclined to argue with Dox and Arjay, who in turn were happy to share the running of the place with Brick and Topher and what remained of the old crowd who still called themselves The Unrulys. With Fings, too, now that he was back.

It helped that Myla dropped by now and then. The world saw how the *Pig* still had a sword-monk in its corner, and no one messed with sword-monks unless they had a death-wish. Especially not a sword-monk who'd single-handedly killed a Wraith, which Myla hadn't actually done, but Fings was happy to help the story grow wings and fly its way into legend.

The last time she came, shortly before the Sulk set in, she asked about Seth. Fings told her how Seth had come that first night she'd visited. It made her sad, which sort of made him wish he hadn't said anything. Then again, it made *him* sad too. *If* he thought about it, which mostly he tried to avoid. They drank wine and then she left, saying she probably wasn't coming back, which was worse.

The other sword-monk came. Tasahre, full of the same questions. And then she, too, was gone, and the whole sorry year was behind him, and he found himself content, sitting around the *Pig*, running errands for Arjay, spending time with a family that had grown bigger in his absence. Somehow, not one but two of his sisters had managed find idiots willing to marry them, idiots who weren't complete jerks. He was going to be an uncle soon. He wasn't sure how he felt about that. Good, mostly. Happy to see them prosper.

The Sulk came and went. Truth was, he was happy to let it all fade into the past, as if it had never happened.

He *was* getting a bit of a paunch, mind.

The letter from Seth arrived a week before the Equinox of Rebirth, when the Empire's new Regent was supposedly going to marry some Torpreahn Prince, make the Empire whole again, make sure there wouldn't ever be more wars and all the other stupid nonsense people spouted about these sorts of things. Varr was in a festive mood. Wood carvings and straw effigies hung around the walls of the *Pig*, celebrations of spring. Arjay, it turned out, knew a lot about that sort of thing. Mind you, Arjay *had* gone a bit soft in the head ever since *she'd* turned out to be pregnant, too. It was quite terrifying, really, the idea of Dox and Arjay settling down and living like ordinary civilised folk. Something like that could happen to *them*... well, could happen to anyone.

The letter came with a package. Fings shuddered as he opened it. He knew it was from Seth because he recognised the writing. Wasn't sure what to make of Seth sending a letter, mind, since they both knew Fings couldn't read; but it turned out Seth had considered this. He'd kept the letter short and simple. With a bit of guarded help from Arjay and a couple of the kitchen girls, Fings managed to work it out. Mostly.

Fings. I am very sorry. I have to something something something to make it right. Keep these. They are for me. They are what I am. If you see me again, give them something something and I will tell you something something. The charm is for you. This one is real.

Seth having to *make things right* didn't bode well. As far as Fings could tell, Seth had spent half his life trying make things right and had usually only made things worse. The letter also left him with the idea that maybe Seth was back in Varr.

So... go look for him, right?

Yeah. Probably should. Find him and smack him round the head a few times, drag him off somewhere until the idiot remembered what common sense looked like, and how what it *didn't* look like was mucking around with dead half-gods, and *particularly* didn't look like using dark sorceries on the only friend you had just to make him shut up about what an idiot you were being when you clearly *were* being an idiot!

"It don't mean making things right, it means not making them wrong in the first place! Bloody idiot!"

"Bloody what?" Dox was looking at him. Fings bit his lip, not quite sure how much of that last bit of thinking had accidentally turned into words. He *did* miss Seth, even after what Seth had done. Had had plenty of time to ponder whether he could forgive. Didn't seem like it ought to be possible, and yet it was. Wasn't that what family did, after all?

He had no idea what *they are what I am* was supposed to mean but didn't much like the sound of it. Didn't much like *if you see me again*, either. Especially the *if* bit. Until now, he'd mostly reckoned on Seth showing up again one day, maybe after the Sulk, penniless and starving, asking if he could maybe stay a few days. Had mostly reckoned he'd say yes to that, albeit after a good long rant about what a twat Seth had been.

If you see me again...

No. Didn't like that at all. Was the sort of thing Seth would say right before doing something monumentally stupid.

He opened the package in case it gave him some idea where Seth was hiding. Looking inside, he wished he hadn't. A funny-looking bit of rock that didn't seem to have anything special about it all. A charm of some sort, which frankly he wanted nothing to do with. A book, although one look told him he wasn't going to be asking anyone to read what Seth had written *there*. Weird squiggles and funny-looking shapes... but the sort of weird squiggles and funny-looking shapes he'd seen Seth use now and then, when Seth hadn't thought Fings was looking, the same weird squiggles and funny-looking shapes he'd seen down in the Undercity, those few times he'd convinced himself to go.

If you see me again... What you done this *time?*

Except... the way Seth had chosen his words didn't feel like a thing he'd *done*, more like a thing he was *going* to do.

There wasn't anything he could do about it, of course.

Probably.

Well...

He gave a long, weary sigh.

Bollocks.

Thing was, Fings knew of at least half a dozen entrances to the Undercity scattered around the southern quarters of Varr. There were probably a whole lot more. He didn't like going down there, on account of it being full of bad luck – look at Seth – and so he generally didn't unless he absolutely had to. Still, just because *he* didn't go down there, didn't mean he didn't know people who did. Friends of friends of friends. Well... not friends, exactly. The old network of Blackhand's connections.

He had a good think. Then a word with Dox and Arjay. Took a few days, but by the end of a week they had watchers on every entrance. Any sign of Seth – and it didn't seem likely anyone was going to miss someone with a half-ruined face and one blind eye trying very hard to look like they weren't doing something shifty – and word would come running to the *Pig*.

What he'd do if someone *did* spot Seth... he had no idea.

Just as well he knew someone who would.

55
The Prisoner

Myla woke to a tapping on the shutters. She yawned and rubbed her eyes, wished it wasn't the middle of the night, wished she hadn't had quite as much to drink, and tried to go back to sleep. The tapping came again. She sighed, climbed out of bed, and threw the shutters open. There was a squawk as they banged against something. Hanging from the window ledge, Fings looked back at her.

"I *was* trying to be polite, you know?" he said. "No need for that."

She offered him a hand and pulled him inside. "You know, you could just come through the door during the day like a normal person."

"Oh, right, because someone like me can walk up to the Sapphire Palace, have a word with one of them black-armoured types lurking about the place nowadays, and they'd be all happy to let me in and take messages and the like?"

He had a point, but still... "So you thought a better idea was to sneak into one of the most heavily guarded places in the city, with literally hundreds of soldiers who'd skewer you on sight, not to mention probably a dozen mages who'd cook you from the inside? I'm barely back from Torpreah, Fings! I would have come to the *Pig* in a few days."

"Yeah. Well. Was important, right?"

"How did you know where to find me?"

Fings tapped his nose. "The Unrulys are back in business. Got eyes everywhere."

428

"Come to that, how *did* you get in? I'm sort of the Regent's on-and-off bodyguard. I think that means I'm supposed to care about this sort of thing."

"Yeah. Well." Fings whistled. "We all got our secrets, right?"

Myla glared. "Right. So–"

"Seth. He's back in Varr."

After Fings' visit, Myla started asking questions, because yes, something *was* a little off with the Regent, and it *could* be the whole getting married malarkey and everything that came with that, or the whole ruling an empire thing; but it *could* be something else, and Seth was the only other person who knew what had *really* happened at Valladrune.

The answer eventually came from Orien. Seth was in a cell under the Kaveneth, which Orien only knew because he'd accidentally gotten lost, found himself in the prison block, seen Seth and completely not recognised him. A man with one blind eye and a face half ruined by scars, though? Yes, he remembered that.

No one else had thought to mention this to Myla. Maybe that was nothing – even if they knew Seth's name, who apart from Orien and Tasahre knew he'd once been Myla's friend? If they *did* know his name, well... Seth was being hunted by sword-monks. And *she* was a sword-monk, so maybe they decided it was better she didn't know?

Whoever *they* were...

In the Kaveneth's chapel, she spent time with the old Lightbringer who lived there. She told him Seth's story. Parts of it, anyway: how he'd been a novice, how he'd been expelled for dabbling with forbidden knowledge, how it was her fault, in part, that he'd become what he was. When she was done, she asked the Lightbringer to let her know if anything happened to the prisoner with the scarred face. If, for example, he was moved. Then she went to see him. Afterwards, she supposed she'd let Fings know what she'd found. Although... maybe not *exactly* where Seth was being held, given Fings' penchant to getting into places he shouldn't.

Seth had always imagined the cells under the Kaveneth to be damp and cold; instead, the air was warm and stuffy and humid. He kept sweating, which was annoying because he couldn't do anything about the resulting itching on account of his hands being wrapped in leather mittens and tied behind his back, presumably so he couldn't be drawing sigils in the air, not that anyone had come out and said so.

In hindsight, getting the personal attention of the Princess-Regent had been too easy. If he came out of this with all his bits attached – which he knew for sure he wouldn't, but never mind – he wondered about offering his services to make sure it would be at least a *little* bit difficult for the next warlock who came along. Wander up to someone, sigil them to do what you wanted, get them to lead you to the next person in the chain, so on and so forth, right up to the top. Could have popped one off on the Regent herself, probably. He was, he had to admit, curious to know whether that would work.

Maybe it wouldn't be as easy once Myla was back in town. He didn't doubt she'd find him here, eventually, if he lived long enough. He had a notion their next conversation wasn't going to be as forgiving as the last. She likely knew what he'd done, by now. He wasn't sure how he'd fucked it up, covering his tracks after the Citadel of Light, but he had. Maybe the two novices with their handcart...?

That, at least, he could remember. Along with everything he'd done in Deephaven until that last day, everything he'd done in Varr before he'd fled. Torpreah too. *Those* memories were pristine and perfect, unlike the shitshow of holes that were the last few months.

You took the book. You used the Wraith. You forced it to give up its secrets. You're going to give your life to destroy the Black Moon and make the world whole again. You're doing something good. Cling to that.

A sigil to free the half-god from its prison.

A sigil to bind The Splinterer of Worlds.

A sigil for the Regent, to destroy the half-god trapped inside him. And himself as well, most likely, although he reckoned that having a half-god inside him would do the trick all on its own.

It kept taking him by surprise that all this *did* seem to be what he was planning to do. Noble? Yes. And yes, he deserved to be the sacrifice, after everything he'd done. And yet, the whole idea didn't seem very... *him.*

Trust yourself!

He'd written everything down and then made himself forget and then had the words delivered back to him. He'd tricked the Wraith of Valladrune and then destroyed it, smashing the stone that held its soul, the one new trick he *had* learned from the memories of Saffran Kuy. He really did know how to end the threat of the Wraiths once and for all. He was doing what he was doing to put right all the terrible things he'd done before, most of which he couldn't remember.

He remembered the Sunherald-Martial. He remembered Torpreah. That was enough, wasn't it?

The Regent had seen what he was. She'd almost disintegrated him on the spot. It was frightening, the realisation she could do that. In Kuy's memories, he'd seen a Wraith do the same, but the Regent was only a sorceress.

Wasn't she?

He spat a bitter laugh. *Only* a sorceress?

She'd crashed into his mind and ransacked his memories, ripping into who he was and why he was here and what he wanted. She made him remember things he thought he'd forgotten. Things buried. Memories of Fings, mostly. He tried not think about those. The look on Fings' face, that last time at the *Pig*. The hurt and the betrayal. Fings simply hadn't understood why Seth would do such a thing. Seth wasn't sure that *he* did, either.

But I do.

She was in and out of him constantly. He was a spectator in his own head, watching her go over everything again and again, poking and prodding at the holes where he – or maybe someone else – had made himself forget. He assumed he'd done it to himself, but the Regent wasn't so trusting.

He felt the occasional slip of a thought come back the other way. Or... not *thoughts*, exactly. Feelings.

Mostly she worried that Seth was some sort of trap, but that wasn't the only thing that leaked through.

This is why he did it. This is what I'm for...

She was tempted. He had no idea why. Couldn't imagine for a moment. Mostly, what he expected was for the Regent to take what he knew and then hand him over to the sword-monks for a quick bit of warlock-burning.

The cell door opened. Myla stepped in.

Oh. Right.

"I should kill you where you stand," she said.

Seth gave a bitter smile. "I thought I was so clever, finding a way to lie to sword-monks. Even to you. I did things and then made myself forget them." He raised an eyebrow. "Did I murder Lightbringer Suaresh? Probably. Did I make a Lightbringer in Deephaven set himself on fire? I don't know. I have no memory of it, but I *do* have a hole where a memory should be, so maybe I did. The ones after you let me go..." He shrugged and watched her bow her head as she saw the inevitable truth of him.

"I trusted you."

"I remember betraying you to the Spicers. I remember that you stood for me, nonetheless. I suppose you won't be making that mistake again."

"No."

"Nor will Fings."

"Why, Seth? Why all this?"

Now *there* was a question. Although Myla presumably meant why all the murdering and the meddling with sigils, rather than why had he given himself up. "Because I could. Because the world is harsh and uncaring and cruel, and I wanted to punish it." He shook his head. "All the things I did, I did for power. Never thought what I'd do with it if I got it. Become a dark and terrible warlock like the one from Deephaven, I suppose, but to what end, Myla? What's the fucking point? Skulk around and terrify people until some sword-monk shows up?" He started to chuckle. "Punish the world? That just makes me the same as all the people I despise.

No. You showed me a different way. I can make it better instead. What you did in Deephaven. Sacrificing yourself to right your own wrongs."

"That's not really how it went, Seth."

"Doesn't matter. You showed me the way."

"And what way is that?"

"The Wraith of Valladrune's grand plan? We're going to turn it on its head. Call the Splinterer out from the Abyss. I'll use a sigil to draw it into me, not her, and then she'll use another to kill it. No more Wraiths. My last act of redemption. Drawing the splinter from creation's wound, so it might finally heal."

"Are you quite mad?"

"You know your history. The Path of the Sun exists to defend us from the Splinterer of Worlds, or another like him. Sword-monks... Well, I suppose you know your real purpose by now. Not to kill warlocks and put down Dead Men. You're Wraith-killers."

"Yes."

"Imagine if you didn't have to be. Though, you might have one more left to deal with, after I'm done. Spend enough time communing with Wraiths, you know when one comes rooting around in your head."

That stopped her. One little thing the Regent hadn't been able to hide. Although... As he looked at Myla, he saw she already knew. He hadn't expected that. Which, in hindsight, was stupid. The Regent knew everything he knew. She must know he'd guessed her secret. Probably knew he'd share it.

He smiled. "I always liked you, Myla. Envied you, too."

"I liked you too, Seth, until you started killing people."

"I'm going to be the architect of an end for the half-god who shattered the world into pieces. *You're* a Wraith-killer, but *I'll* be the one who brings them down. I'll be the saviour of everything. Not that I'll be alive to enjoy the adulation."

"You're not going to be the architect of anything," Myla said. "She won't do it."

Seth closed his eyes. He kept them closed until Myla left, swearing under her breath. He wasn't sure whether Myla had that right. All he could do was hope and pray. Although maybe not *pray*, given the circumstances. Honestly, if it came down to it, who was it for, this need to make everything right? For himself? If it ended with him dead, what *was* the point?

The answer was a mystery as he drifted into sleep, still a mystery the next morning, except not as important a mystery as why he was suddenly in the Undercity, in the lower and smaller of the two vaults beneath the incinerators of the Glass Market chapel, with no idea how he was there, or why he was standing in front of one of the blank archways ringed in sigils, one of the enchanted portals he'd never been able to open, and so had relied on Cleaver to do it for him, and then the Wraith of Valladrune.

There's a reason for that, whispered a voice in his head.

There she was, riding along inside him, watching over his every thought. He tried to lift his hands and found he couldn't. Couldn't even move his eyes. He was a passenger in his own body.

You don't imagine for a moment that I'd give you any choices in something like this, even if I hadn't seen everything you've done?

He supposed not. *He* didn't trust him, so why should anyone else?

Fings had trusted him. Even Myla had trusted him for a time.

He really was the lowest of the low.

A sigil to free the half-god from its prison. A sigil to bind the half-god into him. A sigil to destroy the half-god trapped inside. He repeated the words in his head like a mantra, over and over.

I know you think of binding the Splinterer to me instead.

How could he not, even when it was obviously never going to work?

You're afraid.

You'd be insane not to be.

You will have your redemption. Though no one will ever know.

Yes, yes, redemption. All very good but... well, now it was right here in front of him, he *really* didn't want to die.

The Regent stood at the portal. Seth understood, then, that it had never been about understanding the sigils carved around each archway.

No. It never was.

You had to be a half-god. A Wraith. Like Cleaver had been. His first fucked-up experiments, a sigil he didn't understand used on the skeletal remains of something ancient.

Yes.

The archway opened in an instant, the white stone fading to a blackness and then something else. A passageway unlike the other tunnels of the Undercity. A long, wide maw of black and red marble, spiralling down. If he'd been able, Seth would have rolled his eyes. What were the chances of that? The door to the Abyss had been right here all along?

The doors lead wherever you ask.

He wondered how she knew that. How long she'd known what she was. How much she understood of what it meant for her. Or anyone else, for that matter.

Not as long as you might suppose, warlock. How much might have gone differently had it been otherwise...

He was walking, leading the way. Each step brought it home a little harder. He was about to die. And he didn't want to. What the fuck had he been thinking?

Would Deephaven have been spared?

He had no idea. Didn't much care. Mostly, all he could think about was how his heart was trying to escape out of his chest. On the whole, he could see its point.

Would my father have been spared? My uncles?

The tunnel curved in a sweeping downward semicircle. Dark, not lit by its own substance like the tunnels of the Undercity. He could see where he was going because the Regent, walking behind him, had made light.

My mother?

He managed to look down, the Regent distracted enough by her own thoughts to give him a vestigial glimmer of self-will.

The war. My grandfather. The siege of Deephaven. The butchering of the priests. The death of Valladrune. A whole city. Talsin's son nailed to Pelean's Gate. All of it. A litany of suffering. For what?

A failed vision of resurrecting a dead half-god so he can go back to reforging creation in his own image?

Not that *this* version of creation was so great. At least, not from where Seth stood, staring death in the face. Why couldn't it at least be quick? Why the *fuck* had he done this to himself? There really wasn't any way out. None. A perfect trap he'd made for himself. Why? So Fings wouldn't hate him? What fucking use was that if he was dead and no one ever knew?

He was holding something. Three pieces of paper. Sigils. All three extraordinarily complex. He couldn't make them out but he knew what they were. She'd had him draw them out already, had she? He didn't remember doing it.

There are a lot of things you don't remember.

True enough.

One to open the prison. One to bind the Splinterer of Worlds into you. One to end him.

Doing this? Sacrificing himself? It simply wasn't who he was. And yes, it might be *right*, putting an end to the half-god that broke the world, the creature the Wraiths kept trying to call back. And yes, being the *right* thing, it *was* what he would have *wanted* to do. But... the thing was... he'd never been all that good at doing the *right* thing, not when there was a much safer *wrong* thing that could be done instead.

Could he really trust himself? The choices he'd made? The memories he'd chosen to forget? He wasn't sure.

That makes two of us.

He looked at the sigils in his hands. If he *was* going to pick a moment to finally find some courage, he'd picked well, he supposed.

The tunnel widened into a cavern and then stopped, a tiny hole in the side of a titanic shaft at least a mile across and endless in depth and height. A column of gold and silver light skewered the heart of it, flickering slightly. It seemed to Seth, when he squinted, that it was moving. That the light was rushing downward.

What do you make of that, warlock?

He didn't know. Except... maybe he did. The column was a river of souls, streaming down to feed whatever waited at the bottom. What that was, exactly, he didn't know. The priest in him wanted to say it was the Hungry Goddess lurking there. The warlock of Deephaven would have said it was the Splinterer of Worlds, feeding on them, the Black Moon. The Wraith would have said it was That Which Came Before. Did it matter? A river of souls to feed some monster. Well, that was about to end. Which was good, wasn't it?

Yes.

How could she be so sure?

Doubts, warlock? Are you afraid to die?

Yes, he *was* afraid to die. He was *more* afraid, somehow, that all of this was a trick.

I don't think we should do this, he tried.

His legs ignored him, walking him to the edge of the precipice. Then his arms, as he tossed the first of his sigils out into the void.

Right then. I guess we are *doing this.*

He watched it flutter down. He wasn't sure what was supposed to happen next. Something monstrous flying up the shaft, he supposed. Not the pathetic leftovers the Wraiths had become, terrible as they were, but a true half-god. And then he'd sigil himself and draw it in, and the Regent would end it.

A sigil to end a half-god. It was simply going to stand there, was it, trapped inside him, and let her destroy it?

I will hold it.

A half-god? A real half-god in all its power?

You mistake me for a Wraith. I am not. This is what I am for.

Seth giggled. If he *was* going to die, this *was* about as spectacular a way to go as any, wasn't it? Murdering a god?

He'd lost sight of the sigil he'd dropped, wafting ever downward. He wondered how long they'd have to wait.

56
The Abyss at the Heart of the World

When a messenger from the Kaveneth came knocking on Myla's door in the middle of the night, breathlessly informing her that Seth had disappeared, she wasn't surprised. The sensible thing was for the Regent to hand Seth to the new Sunherald-Martial for trial and execution. She surely *hadn't* gone galivanting down to the Undercity attempting to summon and then slay a dark god on the say-so of a wannabe warlock with a history of treachery and deception, because no one, surely, would ever be that fucking stupid.

Half-god, she reminded herself. *Dark* half-*god*. Although the difference was hardly comforting.

Surely...

Oh, for fuck's sake...

She tossed Orien out of bed, told him to get dressed, threw on her robe and swords, and went out. The Moonguard outside the Regent's suite refused to let her in. No one got to disturb the Regent in her private quarters at the best of times, definitely not at night without an invitation, and *very* definitely not carrying steels...

She left them sprawled on the floor, gasping for air, kicked in the door, and entered regardless. If the Regent *was* here, there was a fair chance Myla was about to have a very unpleasant night.

The suite was empty.

"Fuck."

Orien was waiting outside, slack-jawed and wide-eyed, gawping at the two prone Moonguard. "Did you just–?"

She grabbed his arm, dragged him after her, left the palace at a run, straight to the Imperial Docks, commandeered a boat across the Thort, raced up the winding cliff steps to the back entrance of the Kaveneth...

The message had been true. Seth wasn't in his cell.

"Fuck!"

"What are we–?"

"Wake everyone! Find someone, *any*one, who saw something!"

No one had seen Seth leave. Of course not, because the Regent had quietly slipped into their heads as she passed and made them look the other way. But she couldn't do that to everyone, all the time...

Can't she?

A watchman who'd noticed two hooded figures heading towards the Military Docks. At the docks, yes, someone had commandeered a boat. No memories of who or why but they'd headed down the Thort, then upriver towards Boatbuilders.

Well. Myla knew exactly two ways into the Undercity. The shrine to the Mistress of Many Faces in the Scent Gardens, up near the cathedral, and the one Fings had told her about, near the Circus of Dead Emperors; and if you were heading for the cathedral, you didn't cross the river to Boatbuilders. She told Orien to go and wake every sword-monk he could find and tell them that Seth had escaped, then headed south across the river, as fast she could.

Seth couldn't stop looking out across the shaft. At the column of light shrieking down into the depths. All those souls. He'd lost track of time. How long since he'd dropped the first sigil? Sometimes it felt like minutes. Sometimes like hours.

He was past scared now. Had almost made peace with knowing he was about to die. He'd tricked the Wraith of Valladrune! He'd used its sigil to break the Black Moon's prison. He'd brought the Vessel down to the Abyss at the heart of the Earth. All he had to do was wait for the Black Moon to come.

A sigil to free the half-god from its prison.

A sigil to bind The Splinterer of Worlds to himself.

A sigil to destroy the half-god trapped inside him.

The Black Moon would take him, mind and body; and in that moment when the Splinterer of Worlds thought he was free, the Regent would slap the god-killer symbol on the mad fucker's face. *His* face, what was left of it. The Splinterer of Worlds would die. The world would be free.

And he, too, would die.

At least it would *mean* something.

The sigil to kill a half-god.

Wait a minute...

Shit!

The *Regent* was a half-god! He hadn't known when he'd first sought her out and shown her what to do. Or... Or *had* he known, then made himself forget?

The holes in his memory. There was something else...

Abruptly, the column of falling souls flickered out to darkness.

Across the river, Myla whispered a quiet prayer of thanks for the way people tended not to argue with sword-monks, even when they were stealing your horse right in front of you. She charged through Riverside and Tanners beside the Stinkwater, ignoring outraged shouts. South into the familiar streets of Seamstresses and the Bonewater. Tombland, the Circus of Dead Emperors, the chapel in Glassmakers. She barged through to the incinerators, to the walled-off old garden. She climbed the wall and fought through the overgrown gardens to the abandoned hut with its hidden stairway. Seth's old lair...

She was a bit surprised to see someone already there. More surprised when she saw who it was.

"Fings?"

* * *

Fings stood at the top of the stair, looking down. Not that he wanted to go down into the vault. Bad shit always happened in the Undercity, on account of good luck and bad luck being like oil and water, with the good luck rising to the top, which was why folk who lived in tall towers tended to be rich, because that was where all the best luck got trapped. Down was bad. But this was Seth, and Seth was his brother, so what else could he do?

"Fings?"

He almost jumped out of his skin. "Myla?"

She was at the doorway right behind him, all dressed up in her monk robes and with her swords.

"What you doing here?" he asked.

"What are *you* doing here?"

"Someone reckoned they saw Seth."

If anything, Myla looked relieved. She started for the stairway. "I don't know how much time we have."

"You what?"

She sighed. "Fings... He's been locked up under the Kaveneth, going on about how he knows how to end the Wraiths for good. I think the Regent brought him here. Perhaps with the best intentions, but I don't trust him. I don't trust *either* of them. I think they're about to do something monumentally stupid. Now move!"

"No! Well... yes, but... No." Fings barged in front of her, making her stop. Monumentally stupid? Sounded about right...

"Fings!" She put her hands on his shoulders. A gesture of solidarity, but also of get-out-the-fucking-way. "Look, I know what he did to you, and–"

"Yeah." Fings looked away but didn't move aside. "Well. Got to expect that sort of thing, I suppose. But... before you go down there... you need to see this." He pulled a rock from the old satchel slung over his shoulder and thrust it at her.

Myla eyed it suspiciously. He could sort of see her point. It *looked* like... well, like an old rock.

"Take it! Look into it!"

Myla took it, looked at it, shook her head. "Get out of my way!"

"No!" The word came out as a wail. "Not look *at* it! Look *in* it!"

"Fings! It's a fucking rock!"

"No! No it isn't!"

Myla closed her eyes. Fings wondered if she was thinking maybe she might simply throw him down the steps ahead of her; and then he saw it hit her. Something from inside the rock, rushing into her head, same as it had done to him back in the *Pig*. A vision of being in another place, at another time. Standing in somewhere dark and underground, talking to a skull.

Not a vision, though. A memory.

Seth giggled. He couldn't remember the last time he'd been this scared, this helpless. *It* was coming. The half-god destroyer. And they were going to end it. *He* was going to end it.

A sigil to free the half-god from its prison.

A sigil to bind The Splinterer of Worlds to himself.

A sigil to destroy the half-god trapped inside him.

He had the last two ready in his hands. The first to use as soon as the Black Moon came, opening the door to his mind, dragging the half-god inside him. The second... Well, all he had to do was hold it. The sigil to end a half-god. Merely having it in his hand would do. The moment the Splinterer of Worlds came into him, the moment he died and was reborn as a god, the sigil would do its work.

"I'm afraid," he said.

Myla heard herself asking a question. Something to do with the history of the Shining Age. Only... it wasn't *her* voice doing the asking, it was...

Seth?

She dropped the rock. Stared at Fings. Fings, wringing his hands.

"After Deephaven, he had this... thing. Some glass ball nonsense. Full of old memories, he said. From that warlock your sword-mistress tried to kill. Said he couldn't remember how he got it, but always kept it close like it was precious. He lost it when she caught up with us. But this... it's... It's sort of like, the same."

Myla had no idea what she was supposed to do with this. "These are... Seth's *memories*? Why would he put them into a rock...?"

Oh.

Oh, *shit*!

After Valladrune, when she'd followed him through the half-good door. What had she said? *It's like standing naked. There's nowhere to hide.*

"Fings... How do you fool someone who can look inside your head and know everything?" She didn't wait for an answer. She already knew. *By fooling yourself.*

Fuck! He'd put his *real* memories where the Regent wouldn't see them.

"You got to look at the last ones." Fings was shaking his head. "That's where it is."

"Where *what* is?"

"What he's going to do!"

"And what *is* he going to do?"

"Something really, really bad." Fings was back to wringing his hands.

"Fings! Just tell me!"

"No! You got to *look*!"

"It's coming." Seth held out the final sigil. "You might want to take this. I have no idea what happens next."

No answer. When he tried to move, he discovered he couldn't. He was a puppet now. An extension of the Regent's will. In one quiet little corner of his head, he was free to consider the choices that had brought him here. The rest of him would do exactly what she wanted, when she wanted, how she wanted.

But you knew it would be like this.

He had. It was always going to end this way. He supposed he must have known. Holes all through his own memories, but etched around the last crater he'd smashed into his existence he'd left a message for himself.

Trust that you know what you're doing.

Yeah. About that…

It took Myla a moment to get herself used to the idea that she was seeing through Seth's eyes. He was looking into a mirror and talking to his reflection. "Gods can read minds," he said. "The trick to betraying them is never having the first inkling you're about to do it…"

She almost dropped the stone. Forced herself to hold it tight. If she concentrated, she could see two realities superimposed. The stairway leading down. Seth talking to himself in a mirror.

His words were brief. When he finished, she pocketed the stone, pushed Fings out of the way, and ran.

"What you going to do?" Fings shouted after her.

"Stop him."

"What if it's too late?"

"Then we're all very, very fucked."

Seth felt a presence roaring up the shaft towards them. So fast, so vast. Not that he could do anything about it, paralysed as he was.

The Regent must feel it too. He wasn't sure. The roaring in his head was loud. The half-god. It would come, it would possess him, and then he'd kill it as he died. He wouldn't be remembered, but at least no one would burn him as a heretic. Maybe, one day, the story would surface and the Path would see him for what he truly was: a visionary, the saviour who'd ended their need for constant vigilance.

He felt the beginnings of its presence brush through him. The half-god destroyer: Black Moon; Silver King; Splinterer of Worlds! He felt a sliver of its consciousness, riffling through him.

Now? he asked.

* * *

Fings ran down the steps, chasing after Myla. He *really* didn't want this. Would have refused good money to avoid it. On the other hand...

"What was he looking for in Valladrune? *Really* looking for?" Myla was taking the steps two at a time. Given how the staircase spiralled down through the middle of a yawning void of empty space, this struck Fings as alarming.

"Well," he took a deep breath. "Can't tell you *exactly*. Something to do with that warlock of yours."

Myla slowed briefly, apparently registering the fact that she was running down a staircase through the middle of huge underground vault made of white stone that glowed like moonlight and was held up by nothing more than stubborn indifference to the laws of gravity.

"He went poking around that place. The–"

"The House of Cats and Gulls."

"Yeah." Yeah, him and the Taiytakei popinjay, though maybe right now wasn't the time to go off on one about how Fings had seen the popinjay talking to a dead sword-monk with all his skin peeled off. "He was after some old book." Myla was back to running, taking the stair at such reckless speed that Fings wouldn't have been surprised to see her simply jump off and dare the ground to do anything about it.

"Khrozus," Myla growled. "Khrozus made a bargain with the Wraith of Valladrune. The Wraith won the war for him."

"The freezing of the rivers thing?" *Why am I doing this? Leave it to Myla! Go home!* Bloody steps! Place like this, would be just his luck to slip and fall! Couldn't even risk a hand into a pocket for his charms...

"Yes. Then, when the Butcher of Deephaven discovered–"

"What is it with you Deephaven lot? You call *every*one you don't like 'Butcher', is it?" Talking. Talking helped. He always talked when he was anxious. Kept his mind off... other things.

"The Levanya nailed a twelve year-old boy alive to the city gates to protect them from a battering ram!"

"Did it work?"

"Did it... *Fings*!"

Shouldn't be here! "Fine, so the Butcher shows up and gets a bunch of other butchers to butcher the Butcher who–"

"Fings! The Wraith wanted a vessel to resurrect their fallen king. Seturakah. The Black Moon. The Splinterer of Worlds. *That's* what's Seth's doing. *That's* why we're all fucked if we don't stop him."

"You what?"

Myla reached the bottom of the vault and looked wildly this way and that, trying to work out where to go. Fings pointed to the hole in the floor, in the centre of the spiral of steps. They peered over the edge together.

"The Regent! *She's* the vessel. And *Seth*, of all people, has lured her into a trap."

Fings tried to let that sink in. "He's done *what*?"

Maybe there would be a moment, he thought, long after all of this was over, after it all turned out all right in the end because it always did when Myla was around, when he might get his head around all this. *Maybe...*

In the moonlight glow of the white stone walls, he saw the floor below. The old mosaic he remembered, faded with age. The bones of two skeletons, both with missing skulls. He shuddered. Skeletons...

They didn't have a rope or a ladder. No way to get...

Myla slid into the hole, clung by her fingertips a moment, then let go. He heard the crash as she landed.

Oh. Right. He wondered, idly, how she planned on getting back out again.

"They opened one of the half-god doors."

Well... *That* didn't sound good. *Best thing now would be to go home! Curl up in bed and wait for it to be over. You don't belong here.*

"Wait there!"

"Wait... what?" But Myla was gone.

Now!

Seth pressed the sigil against his skin. The sigil to bind the Splinterer of Worlds to his own soul. Not that he wanted to, but his hands had no choice. They did as the Regent demanded. He closed his eyes. Here it was. A glorious end. He had no idea what to expect. A rush of something overwhelming? A near-instant oblivion? Or would some part of him linger long enough to feel the second sigil, ready and waiting and pressed against his skin, as it burned into him and slew the half-god Destroyer of Worlds?

Something *did* rush into him, but it wasn't a half-god. It was... Memories?

Wait here? In this *place?* Fings wasn't sure about that. Better to wait up top, surely? Better yet, go find some priests or sword-monks, that sort of thing. Leave the problem to people who knew what they were doing.

Yeah. You know that's right.

Yeah. He did. A lot of being a good burglar boiled down to common sense. If something *looked* difficult or dangerous, most likely it *was* difficult or dangerous. And if it was difficult or dangerous, a burglar with any sense wanted nothing to do with it. Getting Seth out of whatever mess he was making this time? Difficult and dangerous, Fings reckoned, was hardly the start of it.

Seth, you bloody idiot!

How many times had he found himself thinking that?

Priests or sword-monks... Except... well, any sword-monk who wasn't Myla would absolutely murder Seth on sight. Wouldn't think twice.

Voices from above. Two or three. They were in a hurry.

Bollocks!

He lowered himself into the hole and jumped.

Gods can read minds. The trick to betraying them is never having the first inkling you're about to do it.

Seth staggered as memories crashed into him. The overpowering hunger to make everything right, to undo all the things he'd done.

He *had* truly believed everything he'd said, these last months, but none of that was what he'd *really* come to Varr to do. He'd remembered Myla's words after Valladrune, and then done the only thing he could: he'd fooled the Regent by fooling himself.

There is no sigil of binding. The Splinterer of Worlds will take whomever he chooses. The sigil was to free you from the half-god in your head and make you remember why you're here. You can thank me later.

The lies he'd told himself, the memories of what he'd done and what he was going to do, all in the stone before he'd made himself forget them. Before he'd made himself into someone who truly believed he was going to end a dark god, not bring it back and set it free.

But that is *what you're going to do.*

Everything that had happened at Valladrune. What the Wraith had planned. The Levanya's betrayal. All of that. He'd known because of the questions Myla had asked. He'd seen the Wraith's answers.

The Regent is a half-god.

The Wraith of Valladrune had known. Had told him. And Seth had listened and then made himself forget that yes, his sigil would indeed kill a half-god, but it wouldn't be the Splinterer of Worlds he'd be murdering.

Now use it. Sigil her!

The tunnel curved in a downward arc. Only one way to go. Seth's memories in the bag slung over her shoulder. In her head, too. *Gods can read minds. The trick to betraying them is never having the first inkling you're about to do it.*

Seth and the Wraith of Valladrune. The bargain they'd struck.

The Regent is a half-god.

She'd never told him. Not her secret to share; besides, she hadn't known for sure herself, not back then.

The Splinterer of Worlds can't take her while another half-god lives inside her.

The Wraith of Valladrune had known.

Light billowed ahead. Brighter; and then she saw them. Silhouetted against a gaping void by a column of silver-gold light. Seth standing at the edge. The Regent sitting cross-legged and patient, a few feet behind.

Bring him back, Herald, and everything will be yours.

"Seth!" she called.

Without warning, the light died.

Fings trotted along a dim tunnel in the middle of some place he really didn't want to think about. He tried telling himself he'd settled for jogging rather than an all-out dash because he was already knacked from running across the half the city. Truth, though, was that he didn't want to be here, plain and simple. Wherever *here* was.

Half-gods? Vessels? He'd hardly understood a word. He was what he was: a petty thief and a burglar who didn't know shit about anything. So, yeah, maybe, if he was a bit slow, Myla would have done whatever needed doing and it would all be over?

He was bit surprised at hearing running feet coming up behind him. He had a vague look for a place to hide; when there wasn't anywhere, he pressed himself against a wall, put a feather between his teeth and sucked on it. He wasn't terribly hopeful that it was going to work in a place like this.

The feet turned out to be Myla's sword-mistress in a flat sprint, swords drawn, one in each hand, jabbing the air as she ran like a pair of stabbing machines. She shot him a glance as she passed, a mixture of surprise and puzzlement and a healthy dose of what-the-fuck-are-*you*-doing-here.

What *was* he doing here? What did he think he could possibly achieve?

He gave a little sigh as she passed. Then ran on after.

"Seth?" Seth watched Myla draw her swords. Their glow wasn't much; but down here, in the pitch black, it was enough.

"Myla!" he laughed. "I'm going to be a god!"

He thought he heard the Regent say something too, something like stay out of this, sword-monk.

NO, HERALD, YOU ARE NOT.

What the fuck?

Having the Regent in his head was like a hand in a cold velvet glove, caressing his thoughts. Irresistible, yes, but soft and almost soothing. This? *This* was like having a horde of angry fucking dragons let loose inside his skull.

Oi!

NOW, HERALD!

The Splinterer of Worlds. Seth staggered from the edge of the abyss, the sigil in his hand, heading for the Regent. Which *was* what he'd apparently been planning all along, now that he had his memories again, except… He suddenly didn't have any choices again, and hadn't that been the whole fucking point? To be *free*?

Fuck you! I decide!

Had the Wraith seen this coming? Had it had known all along? That the moment he freed himself from the Regent, the moment he gave himself the freedom to choose, the Destroyer would say thanks very much, march right in, and take it away again?

He felt the Regent's anger, her fury at how he'd tricked her. The half-god was inside *her*, too, or maybe it wasn't, maybe they were both inside *him*, smashing against one another. She was fighting better than Seth ever could, but never enough, because nothing, no man or even half-god, could ever match the Black Moon.

NOW, HERALD!

It *was* what he'd come here to do. To free the Black Moon. To let it loose on the world once more. And yet…

This was supposed to be my *choice! You don't get to take that from me! Either of you!*

But they had. Both of them. He was nothing but a puppet. All that mattered was who could tug hardest on his strings.

"Seth!"

No! I decide who lives! Not you! Either of you!

The half-gods raged inside him. The sigil in his hand. Nowhere else for it to go. He *had* to do it. Had to do it right now...

My choice! Mine! He fought it.

"Seth! Don't!"

He was laughing, a laughter that wasn't his, the sigil in his outstretched hand, the Regent right in front of him...

"Seth! Don't!" Myla sprinted the last yards between them. The air was thick. She felt a presence batter at her, trying to get inside, the sigils across her skin burning as they held it back. She felt them begin to fail. Seth lurched but didn't stop. His hand reached out, holding a sheet of parchment. He was at the Regent, and the Regent wasn't moving. Lost in the fight against whatever it was, and Seth was about to touch the sigil to her skin, and there was nothing else Myla could do.

"I'm sorry." She leapt, sword raised. At the last, Seth finally seemed to see her. He tried to make words. Failed. But she saw it in his eyes. *Why?*

The sword came down, severing his hand at the wrist. The sigil slipped loose and fluttered free. Seth's eyes followed its drift to the floor, oblivious to the blood pouring out of him. He watched it to the ground, then screamed, fell, and Myla too staggered, the presence of the half-god fierce like a giant fist around her, its fingers clenching, crushing, trying to force its way inside.

Out of nowhere, the mistress of swords. Joy, desperate relief, turning to horror as Tasahre hurled herself at the Regent, blades aloft, swinging them down.

"No!" Myla threw herself in the way, caught Tasahre's swords on her own, reeled from the force of them, staggered as Tasahre bared her teeth.

"Move aside! Both must die!"

"No!"

"*Stupid* girl!"

Tasahre struck, no pause or hesitation, nothing held back.

* * *

Fings heard Seth scream. He raced on. All he could see were the glowing swords of two sword-monks, hammering at each other like it was the end of the world, which he was beginning to think it probably was.

Turn around! Leave! You've no business here. But he was still running, wasn't even sure why, except he *was* sure, because he could see now that one of the sword-monks was Myla.

"The Splinterer of Worlds!" Tasahre's swords sliced and cut. Sparks flew, steel on steel. Myla pressed ever back. Seth lying on the floor. Moaning. Clutching at himself.

"You don't understand!" Myla dodging, desperate, always between Tasahre and the woman sitting cross-legged on the floor, whoever she was.

Seth. Seth was family. Myla was a friend. Close enough to count as family too, really, if you thought about it.

"Stand aside, Shirish, or I *will* kill you."

Myla didn't budge. And it was all wrong, wrong! Fings shouted, yelled at them to stop, but they didn't hear, or if they did, paid no attention. Now the sword-monk from Deephaven, driving Myla back while Myla tried furiously to stand her ground. A sword slipping through her guard. Blood. Fings saw her stagger, a killing thrust barely deflected, the next ready to come... Did the only thing he could think to do; bellowed and roared and hurled himself before it was too late. Had worked the last time, after all...

In his head, he was going crash into the sword-monk from Deephaven, knock her down, they'd both go sprawling; and then they'd all stop fighting, shout at each other a bit, realise they were all on the same side and sort out whatever this was. In his head...

The monk danced aside. Flicked her wrist as he lurched past, slicing Sunsteel across his path. Fings felt it bite, and then his legs went from under him, and he was crashing to the ground, and something was very, very wrong.

He lay still for a moment.

Oh.

He didn't want to die. Not yet and certainly not here. But apparently, that was the way it was going to be.

Seth howled and clutched the stump of his ruined hand. *No, no, no!* He was *not* going to end here! He drew a sigil, written in his own blood. A sigil to end bleeding. He hadn't understood until far too late how wrong the sword-monks had it, how sigils weren't *dark* sorcery, any more than any other magery. The darkness was in the heart of whoever *used* the power, not the power itself.

Still time. Still time.

Out of nowhere, the sword-monk from Torpreah came. Seth cringed and curled into a ball; but no, it wasn't *him* she was coming for with her swords.

You know you'll be next.

Now Myla was fighting her, neither paying him the slightest attention.

Sword-monks killing sword-monks. He grinned, half mad with delirium. *Truly the time of chaos is come!*

Yes, yes! Chaos!

Fucking sword-monk! All this way to kill you! But you can stop her. He *can stop her!*

He could do that now. Two sword-monks at each other right at her back and the Regent hadn't moved. Hadn't moved for hours.

Yes, yes, yes! Use it. End the half-god! Let the Black Moon rise! Let him take that fucking monk in his armoured fist and crushed her to dust!

He crawled to the sigil and picked it up, then eased back towards the Regent.

END HER!

The sword-monk from Torpreah sliced Myla open.

You know you're next.

No!

YES.

My choice. My choice!

Another figure came out of nowhere, hurled himself at the sword-monk from Torpreah, got slashed up for his trouble, and crashed to the floor to bleed out...

Seth froze.

Fings?

Fings. And in that moment, nothing else mattered. Fings being here made no sense, yet here he was. Fings. His brother. Dying...

My fault! All my fault!

...And hadn't *that* been the whole point of all this? Not some abstract notion of freedom, but to make things right, somehow? At the end of everything, wasn't that all there was?

The Splinterer of Worlds, the Black Moon, rose from the abyss. A Wraith, spectral, made of moonlight. It towered, looking down at the Regent, still cross-legged, the eye of the storm all around her.

Myla stared at Fings. At Seth. At Tasahre. At the Regent. At the Wraith ascending from the Abyss, silver moonlight washing out of it in waves and waves. She felt its rising power bite, the sigils on her skin burning bright as it battered at her and found no way through. She tensed, ready, knowing she wouldn't be able to stop Tasahre for a second time.

The circlet on the Regent's brow flared, suddenly bright as the midday sun. The moonlight around her recoiled and flared and withered, flared again, then dissolved back into the shape of the towering Wraith. The Regent rose, reached up, grabbed the Wraith by the throat with one hand, tapped the blazing circlet with a finger of the other.

"Time to end, old friend," she said.

Old friend? Words from the half-god the Regent held inside her. Dormant, she'd said. Asleep. But no more.

Figures climbing over the lip of the shaft. Spectres of the dead, some naked, some in clothes, some armoured, fashions Myla didn't recognise, or maybe had seen once or twice on the Sea-

Docks of Deephaven. They shambled and staggered and stumbled, converging on the Regent.

"Tasahre!"

Ghosts. She knew ghosts. She slashed them, and at the touch of Sunsteel, they shivered and lost their shape, dissolved into clouds of golden light, soared into the heights above and disappeared.

Be free!

She whirled and danced between them, shreds of golden light in her wake, driving them back. It was almost too easy, until she reached the lip of the shaft and saw what was coming, clinging to the sheer walls, climbing upward. Thousands. Millions. More. Every soul sent to the Hungry Goddess, across every world, for centuries.

Oh, fuck!

"Tasahre!"

Tasahre didn't move. Bewitched by the Regent with her hand at the Wraith's throat, the air between them a rage of silver light.

Fings felt Seth beside him, scrabbling at his clothes, pulling up his shirt. There was a lot of blood. *His* blood. Fings had a nasty suspicion that if he looked, he was going to see parts of him that were supposed to be on the inside making a bid for freedom. Then he'd probably pass out.

"Seth," he croaked. "Brother."

"You're going to be fine," grunted Seth.

"I forgive you," Fings murmured.

"What? No. You're not going to die. I can make this right." Fings had the odd sensation of Seth's fingertips on his skin, tracing out some weird pattern. He sighed. He couldn't move. Didn't have the strength.

He closed his eyes.

"I'm, sorry! I'm sorry!" Seth drew a sigil on Fings' skin. In blood. One handed, fingers shaking. He fucked it up, smeared it out, started anew. *You're not going to die. I won't let that happen!*

Myla by the lip of the cavern, a tornado of steel and golden light and murdered ghosts. The Regent with the Splinterer of Worlds by the throat. The sword-monk from Torpreah, looking at him. At Fings. At the Regent. At Seth again. Murder in her eyes.

Seth stared back.

You did this to him!

The sigil, right there, right in front of him. Pick it up, stumble a few steps, slap it on the Regent, all this would be done.

Do it.

Let the Splinterer of Worlds take his vessel. The sword-monk would die. Fings would live.

Do it!

Staring at him. Weighing him up.

"Tasahre!"

Do! It!

Let the Wraiths be reborn. Let the Path fall. Let the Shining Age return!

Do it, do it, do it!

Fings. Fings, his brother, bleeding and dying, and for once there really *was* something Seth could do.

DO IT!

Fuck off!

The sword-monk from Torpreah leapt towards him. Seth squeezed his eyes shut. Opened them again; but she'd raced past him. Towards Myla.

A spectre caught Myla by the ankle. She felt it, like a foot trapped in treacle. A slash, a flare of golden light and she was free...

Another had her, then another, their sheer number about to overwhelm her... but now Tasahre was with her, two more swords flashing left and right, sword-monks fighting back-to-back as they had once before, slicing through the spectres as they swarmed out of the shaft.

"I hope you know what you're doing," hissed Tasahre.

"We fight until we can't."

Four slivers of silver light split away from the Wraith. She didn't see until the first wrapped itself around her.

Fings opened his eyes. Seth crouched over him. When Fings looked the other way, a small woman with a fiercely bright circle of light banded around her head held a very angry-looking Faerie-King by the throat. The cave was full of golden ghosts, climbing all over Myla and her sword-mistress, both wrapped in serpents of moonlight, squeezing and crushing and biting.

Am I dead? He'd never been dead before, and so he wasn't entirely sure. On the other hand, none of this could possibly be real.

The small woman threw out her other hand. Dazzling sunlight filled everything. Fings blinked. When his vision cleared, the spectres had gone... Well, except for a whole load more climbing out of the shaft. Then two figures of silvery light slid out of the darkness. Two of the Faerie-King things Fings had seen in Deephaven. Wraiths, Seth called them. Only like ghosts.

Ghost-Wraiths now, is it? Oh, goody... He *really* wanted to be somewhere else, but he didn't seem able to move. One climbed onto Seth's back. Seth screamed and tried to claw it off, but the Wraith wasn't having it. Seth grabbed Fings' hand. He was weeping as the Wraith enveloped him.

"I love you, brother," he said, as it slid inside him.

The other crouched at Fings' side. It looked at him. Fings sighed and lay back.

Seth felt the half-god rush into him. A tiny sliver of its true self. Small enough that he could put up at least a token resistance.

Fuck off! Fuck! Off!

Use the sigil!

Another sliver slipped into Fings. He saw Fings' face change. He'd been smiling there, for a moment. Might even have said something. Now his face twisted. He started to rise. Seth pushed him back down. *No. You can't have him!*

He heard Myla call his name. Heard her call for the sigil he'd dropped.

Let him go!

The sigil! Himself or Fings. He could save only one. But that was fine. He knew who it had to be.

Fings lurched to his feet, throwing Seth off.

Get the sigil. Use it on Fings. Get him out of here! He made himself think it over and over and over while he started to draw a new sigil on his own skin, in what precious seconds he had left before the Wraith made him its puppet.

Get the sigil. Use it on Fings. Get him out of here!

A sigil to make himself forget. Since the Wraith was in his head, it would make the Wraith forget as well, or at least, this piece of it. How much to lose? He didn't know. Would the last few minutes be enough? The last hours? Days? How far to go?

STOP!

Get the sigil. Use it on Fings. Get him out of here! No time to think. How far? Well, there was an easy answer, wasn't there...

STOP!

Get the sigil. Use it on Fings... He drew the last line of the sigil. And forgot...

Everything.

A burst of light and the spectral Dead Men fell away. Myla, a piece of the Wraith wrapped around her. The Splinterer of Worlds fighting through the sigils that warded her skin. Tasahre, swords flailing, wrapped in silver light. Fings stumbling to his feet. Seth as he crawled for the sigil loose on the floor. Her sigil wards failing. Wasn't sure how long she could hold.

"Seth! Sigil me!" *Come on then, come in and take me!*

Fings with a knife. Didn't seem like he had much idea where he was. He took a faltering step towards the Regent.

Shit!

"Seth!"

She ran at Fings. Ploughed into him. Knocked him down. Saw as Seth picked up the sigil.

"Seth! Use the sigil on me! On *me*!" *Come on then, half-god! Come on in!*

One by one, the wards on her skin fell. She felt the Wraith squeeze between the gaps. Felt it climb inside her. Felt its glee. Felt her hand reach for a sword as her eyes moved from Fings to the Regent. *Kill her!*

No, no, no, not yet you don't!

Fings pushed Myla away. Seth grabbed him by the ankle, tripping him. He held the sigil but didn't seem to know what to do. Fings kicked him in the face and broke free. The Wraith was right inside her now...

Myla let herself fall, crumpling sideways. As she did, she grabbed Seth's wrist, shoved his hand, sigil and all, pushed it inside her robe, and pressed it against her skin.

Die!

A scream. Her scream, but also the scream of the Wraith-fragment inside her as Seth's sigil unravelled it.

The Ghost-Wraith around Tasahre shook itself free and shot away, screeching into the shaft of the abyss, vanishing upward. Fings collapsed, a second streamer of silver light tearing free as he fell. Myla watched it go, following the first, vanishing into the void of the Abyss.

"Seth!"

Seth had Fings in his arms. Struggling to his feet. Myla picked up her swords. The Regent held the Splinterer of Worlds fast, her hand round its throat. Her Sunsteel circlet filled the cavern with light.

"This is why I was made," she hissed. "This is what I am for."

Twice the Regent's bulk, yet helpless, pinned by her hand at its throat. Myla walked up to it.

"Any idea how to kill the ghost of a half-god?"

Tasahre shrugged. "Not really. But this usually works." She drove her Sunsteel swords through its heart. Myla took its head. Seemed like a good place to start. She would have split its skull, too, looking for the worm inside, but the Wraith shrieked and shattered and then dissolved and evaporated into nothing. Myla stared at the emptiness where it had been. When she looked down the shaft of the abyss, the spectral dead were dissipating into clouds of light, wafting slowly upward.

"Right," she said, a little hoarse. "That's that, then."

The Regent lowered her hand. A nod. "It's finished."

Tasahre shook her head. "No." She pointed a blade at the Regent. "Do you know what you've done? *Do* you?"

"What are you–" Myla started, then stopped, because Tasahre's sword had suddenly become nothing more than glittering light. A gesture from the Regent and it was sparks in the air and then gone.

"My father understood," the Regent said. "One way or another, the Wraiths would find a way. He made me what I am so I might destroy them when we had the chance."

Tasahre was shaking. "But you *didn't* destroy it! Two echoes of that... *creature* escaped. Where did they go, half-god? You haven't destroyed it at all! You've set it free!"

"Diminished. Scattered. Weak. A pale shadow of what it was, stretched so thin it barely exists."

"But free!"

"I will hunt them down."

"No, you will not."

The Regent cocked her head. "You think you're going to stop me, sword-monk? I'm no warlock."

Thirty seconds, Myla reckoned, from slaying the Splinterer of Worlds to this. She moved between them. "Fuck's sake!"

Tasahre hissed. "She is a Wraith!"

The Regent bared her teeth. "I am much more than that!"

Myla stamped her foot. "Both of you! You cannot judge

someone for what they are. Only for what they do. *Your* words, sword-mistress."

"I am doing exactly that!"

"And *you*!" Myla rounded on the Regent. "Are we strutting cocks measuring dicks now? Because if we are then maybe yours should wilt a little when you consider how you were tricked by the first warlock to come along, and that he was an idiot, thank the Sun. *We're* the Wraith hunters, not you."

"Oh? And where will you hunt? The Splinterer is crippled beyond recovery. But if you give him *enough* centuries, he might just come back."

"The Path is everywhere, Highness. Every sword-monk in every temple. Every Lightbringer and Sunbright and Dawncaller. Every woman and man of faith. We are the swords, they are our eyes and our ears. We are meant for this. All of us. *You* are not. Go back and sit on your throne. This is what *we* are for."

"She's still a Wraith," hissed Tasahre. "She cannot be–"

Myla rounded on the sword-mistress. "And how exactly are you going to stop her? Because I'm not."

The Regent considered this for a long time. "And if I *do* decide to raise armies of the dead?"

"Then I will stand against you, and you will have to kill me."

The Regent fixed her eye on Tasahre and cocked her head at Myla. When you find him, I will end him. While you hunt, this one stays at my side. The voice of my conscience, if you like."

Tasahre pursed her lips. Didn't seem she much liked the idea, which Myla supposed she ought to find insulting.

"Sixteen years ago in Deephaven," said Myla, "you tried to stop a warlock. You failed. But in the end, it turned out you'd done enough. Maybe this is the same?"

Tasahre's face wrinkled in disgust. She glared at the Regent. "We will be watching, half-god. There will be consequences from this, and in more worlds than one. Ones that even *you* fail to foresee." She looked at Myla. "Be vigilant, Myla. Be pure and be brave, but most of all, be vigilant."

With that, she turned and left, leaving Myla and the Regent alone, Seth and Fings having apparently slipped away already.

"Your conscience?" Myla asked.

The Regent shrugged. "Let's both hope you're not needed."

57
The Spice Market

Dying was weird, Fings thought. He remembered seeing Seth. He remembered a Faerie-King had come, then turned into five Faerie-Kings, all of which was probably his imagination getting the better of him, understandable in the circumstances. He'd had the strange sense of something rushing into him. Soothing. Like it was the light of the Constant Sun, come to take him to have his soul forged anew. Although... odd images had flashed through his mind in those last moments. Images that weren't his. Visions that belonged in ancient tales of the Shining World.

His imagination again, he supposed.

He remembered Myla's bag lying on the floor, discarded as she fought. A stone rolling out. His fingers, reaching for it... A vague memory of wobbling up and down, like when he'd been on the *Speedwell*, only with too much lurching-about. Someone carrying him.

Seth. Seth, carrying him to the great forge in the Sun. A nice feeling.

A tunnel, then a room of glowing white stone. Moonlight. Sword-monks. He had no idea why, but they'd been cross about something. Had to be, because the first thing they did was hiss and draw their swords.

Some weeks later, Myla walked into the *Unruly Pig*. She found Fings propping up the bar, slightly drunk. Being slightly drunk seemed a good idea, so she joined him, bought a cup of wine, then thought fuck it, and bought the bottle.

"Business good?" she asked.

"Got another sister getting married soon," Fings said.

"That's nice."

"Yeah. It is."

They drank in silence for a while.

"They're going to take him away tomorrow," said Myla at last.

Fings gave a vague nod.

"Somewhere out of the way. Once he leaves, you won't see him again."

"Yeah."

Some more silence. Some more wine.

"Was he really going to do it? End the world or something?"

"You showed me his memories." She wasn't sure, by the end, whether even Seth had known what he was going to do.

Fings nodded slowly.

"Where *is* that stone, by the way?"

Fings shrugged. "I gave it to you, remember?"

"I lost it in the fighting."

Fings snorted. "You want to go back and look for it, I ain't going to stop you. *I* ain't going back if that's what you're suggesting."

"I wasn't."

More silence. More wine. Eventually, Myla got to her feet. "You good?"

"Reckon I am." Fings looked around the *Unruly Pig*. "Family. That's what matters."

Myla squeezed his shoulder. "Always."

"Thanks," said Fings.

"For what?"

"For still coming by."

"You need anything, you know where to find me. Better if you come through the door, though, not the windows?"

Fings chuckled. "Maybe."

* * *

The next morning, Fings went to the temple on Spice Market Square to be there when they took Seth away. He watched sword-monks come out of the temple, Seth in chains between them. Myla was with them, and the sword-mistress from Deephaven. He didn't recognise the others. Was quite something, he thought, that they reckoned there needed to be six of them.

For whatever reason, they were loitering on the temple steps, the monks all talking to each other, Seth seemingly forgotten. Fings sidled closer, swiping a peach from a fruit-seller's stall. As he reached the steps, Myla caught his eye. Took a moment to hold it, then gave a little nod. Fings scampered up, sat beside Seth, and gave him the peach.

"Got this for you," he said.

Seth took the peach. He looked at it, confused. Then at Fings. "Do I know you?"

Fings had to leave when he heard that, so he didn't see how Seth stared and stared at the peach, how a tear maybe formed in the corner of his eye as he did.

After a bit of time to clear his head, Fings settled back to watching. He knew Myla was keeping an eye on him, but if she was keeping an eye on *him*, that meant she wasn't keeping an eye on Dox and Arjay and Brick and Topher.

It *was* true. He *had* given the memory stone to Myla. Wasn't *lying*, exactly, not mentioning how he'd snaffled it back when the old King of the Faerie-Kings had shown up to make his trouble. Or how he'd hidden it in his satchel and then dropped it on the way out, then gone back later, when the sword-monks had finally decided he didn't have a sliver of a dark god inside him and so they didn't need to burn him.

He patted his satchel. There it was. Nice and safe.

A wagon pulled up outside the temple, with a metal cage on the back. The monks bundled Seth into the cage and then got up to ride beside him. Still all six of them. He watched the wagon pull away. Somewhere else in the Square, depending which way it went, one of the Unrulys would quietly follow. They'd take it in turns, all the way to whichever gate, to whichever road from the city it took.

After that, it was down to the men he'd hired from the Bithwar Woman in Bonecarvers. Cost a bit, that had. Once he knew where Seth was being taken...

Well, he *was* a burglar.

After Seth was gone, Myla returned to the House of Fire. She slipped out of her sword-monk robes and stood in front of the mirror she'd had Orien bring and ran a finger over the marks written across the skin of her thigh. Faint, but there. Copying them had taken longer than it should. Orien had kept getting... distracted.

Seth's sigil. Etched into her. The sigil to kill a half-god.

Well. Fine. Maybe I got distracted too, sometimes.

But it was done. Three copies. One to Tasahre in Deephaven. The second... well, she'd never know. That was sort of the point.

Happy hunting, sword-mistress.

And the last always close to hand. Just in case. Maybe she was naïve. Tasahre would have said so. But naïve didn't have to mean stupid.

POSTSCRIPT
The Bloody Judge

There will be consequences from this, and in more worlds than one. Ones even you fail to foresee.
– Tasahre

58

Men pressed from all sides, crushed together. Soldiers pushed against his back and to either side. He met the enemy, forced before him by their own numbers, slashing and stabbing for any inch of unguarded flesh. The black Moonsteel edge of his sword glittered in the sunlight. Dark as night and sharp as broken glass, it slew with a hunger of its own. Spears and swords broke. Armour ripped like skin beneath a tiger's claw. Bones splintered; entrails spilled across the ground to join the bloody mess of severed heads and limbs. His feet slipped and slid beneath him. Sweat stung his eyes. The air stank of iron and death. A part of him forgot his name, forgot why he was there, forgot everything, gave itself to the savage inside, letting it fill every pore, every hair, every thought.

There was a peace to killing. He'd always found it so.

He was the Bloody Judge. The Crowntaker.

The enemy broke and ran. He watched them scatter into the long grass, racing for the line of trees. The savage wanted their blood, but the savage was on a leash, always.

A last knot of soldiers ran at him, a mad suicidal charge. He drove his Moonsteel blade through the first man's mail and into his heart. Blood sprayed as he snapped the sword away. Then suddenly a warlock was in front of him.

A warlock! The Crowntaker grinned, gleeful as he drove his sword through heavy robes, flesh and blood and bone, until the point emerged from the dark sorcerer's spine. The easiest thing in the world...

Pinned by Moonsteel, the warlock pressed paper to the Crowntaker's chest, clawed a handful of blood and threw it at his face. Then crumpled and fell, lips drawn back across his teeth, grinning blankly at the clear blue sky.

"For Saffran," he breathed.

The world blurred; and as it did, a name slipped inside the Crowntaker's head. He felt himself falling, while something vast streamed the other way.

The twin remnants of the great Wraith, Black Moon, Splinterer of Worlds, slid through the void, searching through the endless rain of souls fleeing Xibaiya and the tear opened in its heart. Searching until there it was. A light. A call and a touch of That Which Came Before. Two souls adrift. An exchange, of sorts. One soul into another body, and back the other way. The remnants met them as they crossed. They slid inside. Two quietly monstrous passengers.

In the light of the battlefield, surrounded by the faces of strangers, the Bloody Judge opened his eyes. He looked about at a world fresh and full of gawping faces. He tore the half-ripped sigil from his breast and got to his feet. Alive as never before. A flare of sliver moonlight flashed across his eyes.

This one will do.

ACKNOWLEDGEMENTS

Thanks to Eleanor and Gemma and Desola and Robin and Travis and everyone else at Angry Robot. Thanks to all of you who read and poured love onto *The Moonsteel Crown* and so made this possible. Thanks again to Nigel, Matt, Michaela, Sam, Ali and Pete, and forgive me, again, for the liberties taken. A lot has changed from the adventures we had together, but I like to think the spirit is still there.

The story of how Tasahre got her scar is in *The Warlock's Shadow*. If you want to know what really happened to the warlock of Deephaven, *The King's Assassin* will tell you. For now, the stories of Myla, Fings, Seth and Orien end here. I'd like to think there will be more. I miss them already.

As for Tasahre's consequences? They begin in *Dragon Queen*.

ANGRY ROBOT

We are Angry Robot

angryrobotbooks.com

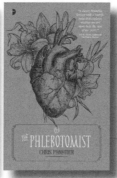

We are Angry Robot

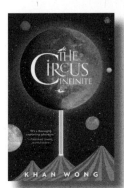

angryrobotbooks.com

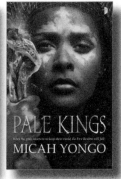